"ABSORBING."

—Pittsburgh Press

THEY LOVE, LAUGH, AND CRY TOGETHER THROUGH THE BEST YEARS OF THEIR LIVES.

They arrive with new husbands and fresh dreams, carving a frontier in suburbia after World War II. In the years to come, they grow up and grow older together, have babies and discover surprising new sex roles, as each pursues her own brand of happiness in the midst of a violently changing world.

The Ladies of Levittown

You may already have met them.
Now get to know them.

"THIS MAY BE VERY WELL THE WAY IT WAS."

—Times-News

ABOUT THE AUTHOR

GENE HOROWITZ, author of *The Velvet Jungle*, as well as *Home Is Where You Start From* and *A Catch in the Breath*, taught high school in Levittown before moving to Manhattan.

THE LADIES
of
LEVITTOWN

Gene Horowitz

FAWCETT CREST • NEW YORK

*Grateful acknowledgment is made for permission to use
the following copyright material:*

Lines from "An Ordinary Evening in New Haven" by Wallace
Stevens, copyright © 1954 by Wallace Stevens, reprinted by permission of Alfred A. Knopf, Inc.

Excerpts from *Ulysses* by James Joyce, copyright © 1914, 1918 by
Margaret Caroline Anderson; copyright © 1934 by Modern Library,
Inc.; copyright © 1942, 1946 by Nora Joseph Joyce, reprinted by
permission of Random House, Inc.

Lines from "You Made Me Love You" by Jimmy Monaco, © MCMXII
by Broadway Music Corp., © renewed MCMXL by Broadway Music
Corp., © 1973 by Broadway Music Corp., all rights reserved, reprinted by permission of Broadway Music Corp., 221 West 57th
Street, New York, NY.

Lines from "Let the Rest of the World Go By," lyrics by J. Keirn
Brennan, music by Ernest R. Ball, © 1919 Warner Bros. Inc., co-
pyright renewed, all rights reserved, reprinted by permission of
Warner Bros. Music.

Lines from Canto LXXIV of *The Cantos* of Ezra Pound, copyright
1948 by Ezra Pound, reprinted by permission of New Directions Pub-
lishing Corp.

THE LADIES OF LEVITTOWN

for the Siegels—
    Ben, Esther, Allan, Mark, Evan—
    with love

... we seek
Nothing beyond reality. Within it
Everything.

—WALLACE STEVENS,
An Ordinary Evening in New Haven

PART ONE

1944—1949

Evelyn Selden née Howard
Loretta Massi née Kovalic
Melissa Geiger née Riordan
Corinne Feuerstein née Grossman
Cynthia Klein née Berk (née Berkowitz)

Evelyn Selden née Howard

[1] It was early October when they drove out there from
Brooklyn to see the model homes. Early October 1947, because Morty was only a few months old then. Danny was
three. Both boys were in the back of the car with her mother
and father. Harold was driving, the first car they had ever
owned, a black two-door Chevrolet, a coupé. Soon, within a
half-year the agent had told Evelyn on the telephone, maybe
a little less, maybe a little more, they would also own their
first house. Levittown was about to be ready. Be patient
awhile longer, the agent had said.

Most of the farmland was gone by then. Some patches of
cabbage and cauliflower and broccoli she could see from the
parkway. Some leftover rows of cornstalks, some potato
fields, but whatever was left was turning brown and brittle
in the brilliant October sunlight, the sun so clear it brought
tears to her eyes. Or was she just so excited she felt like
crying? For joy, crying! To own a house! On Long Island!
Where there were trees that changed color in autumn!

The models were on Hempstead Turnpike, which didn't
have any trees on it. There were four model houses and outside each was a lineup of young couples and their children
waiting patiently to look inside.

Four Cape Cods. Pretty much the same, as far as Evelyn
could tell. Only the colors were different.

A milky yellow with white trim.

Barn red with white trim.

Semi-demi-royal blue with white trim.

Grass green with white trim.

The barn red and the grass green had a pathetic two-post
piece of fence that was supposed to hide the side entrance.
The milky yellow and the semi-demi-royal blue had no fence:
you just saw the door. Frankly, she preferred that. At least
it was honest. She also wouldn't mind if they got the grass
green one because it had a plus. It had a picture window,

even if it was divided into little squares. Hard to clean—but she'd prefer it. It showed some touch of originality. It was a little different.

Inside, each model had four rooms. Just behind the front entrance, facing you when you entered, was a central staircase leading up to nothing but an unfinished attic, which was easily expandable, the agent told the group. "Add a room each time you add a kid."

Each model had identical fixtures. Identical toilet bowls, identical tubs, identical sinks, and in the kitchen identical stoves, identical refrigerators, identical stainless steel sinks, even identical light switches. There would, however, be four interior colors to choose from. Evelyn chose white. Out loud. For her mother to hear. For Harold to hear. She also shifted Morty to Harold so she could inspect the cabinets more closely. Harold wanted to leave. It was too crowded, "...and your father is getting impatient to drive over to Jones Beach. While there's still some sun left. Danny has to go to the bathroom...."

South of Hempstead Turnpike the potato fields were totally gone. Macadam had been steamrolled into streets that crisscrossed, into a maze of lanes curving around and around and seeming to lead them nowhere but around. The lanes were dotted with homes in various stages of completion.

Some were no more than rectangular slabs with identical cutouts and recesses into which the pipes would be set, the electric lines led in. Harold stopped the car. He wanted to show Danny where the water main would go and where the oil burner would be set, and then Danny had to trace out the pattern of little trenches running the entire length and width of the slab. "For heating coils," Harold told him. Harold had read about that, radiant heating. "It's a new thing, so the floors will be warm all winter." The floors would also be covered with a speckled vinyl tile, black-and-white speckled, so the dirt wouldn't show so easily. Evelyn had read about that in the brochure.

They stood around the slab studying the cutouts, the recesses, the indentations, the crossing rows of trenches for the heating coils. Evelyn looked up to the sun again to hide her tears. It was the excitement. It was imagining the future together. It was being in their own house together, Harold's, hers, Danny and Morty's, not cooped up in her mother and father's two-family upstairs apartment, her parents, her brothers, them, all crowded together. For three years. Enough

9

was enough. The best intentions in the world couldn't make that good. The most love in the world couldn't. She held on to Harold's hand. She squeezed it so he had to turn, had to smile his best Hollywood-star kind of smile. "A few more months. After so long, a few more months won't matter," she said, leaning against him. Morty slept on in her arms.

Across from them there were her mother and father, thinking their own thoughts, she supposed, about the house they had never owned. Her mother had wanted to buy instead of always renting. For as long as Evelyn could remember her parents' arguments, the recurrent theme of them had been about owning something, "—anything, before they died," her mother would say. Not her father. He didn't care. "I'll let my children do it for me." And now Evelyn was. She and Harold were. They started back toward the Chevrolet. The sun was brilliant overhead, very hot for October. Indian summer. "A beautiful day," her father said, to Harold most of all, "You've got to hand it to the Levitts. They put a new dot down on the map of Long Island, and it's Levittown. In Pennsylvania they'll do the same. It'll be everywhere soon. Like Horn and Hardart's. Americans are something. They win wars. They build houses. What next?"

They passed other slabs. Some had their sides attached. Some had their sides, walls with window cutouts, attached. Some had sides, walls with windows preset in them, parts of roofs, attached. Some even had doors in place.

Some looked like finished homes. Like the models.

Milky yellow with white trim.

Barn red with white trim.

Semi-demi-royal blue with white trim.

Grass green with white trim—that was the model with the picture window filled with small square panes.

In front of those homes close to completion, the rich earth that had been farmland, potato farmland, was, even then as they slowed to watch, being turned by machine, which was being followed by a team of workmen who planted saplings, three to a plot, Danny counted, four if the house was on a corner plot.

"A maple, an oak, a willow," Harold told them. Harold knew trees. Her country boy, she used to call him—before the war, when his mother still owned the farm in the Cats-kills. Gone. His mother. The farm. The boy. Now he was a man buying his family a home, a veteran of the air war over Europe, and not quite thirty years old. Almost, but not quite.

Around some of the houses they passed, seed was being sown.

Some even had lawns beginning. A long way from mowing, true, but a fuzz at least. A beginning, a new dot on the map: Levittown.

Not yet, that beginning, for them. Patience for a while longer, for them....

[2] When Harold finished his fifty bombing missions in Europe, he was eligible for an early discharge from the Air Force. That was in 1944, before the war in the Pacific was over. He wrote to Evelyn, telling her about how the whole crew would be rotated back to the States, to Texas first, and from there to home.

But home, then, was Evelyn's bedroom in the upstairs part of the brick two-family in Brooklyn. It was that or it was out in the streets, literally, because no one was building anything new yet. Harold would have to come home to the same old bedroom Evelyn had grown up in, that she and Harold had been married into, that she had brought Danny home from the hospital to; so small a room that with Danny's crib in it and the double bed, the chest of drawers, that was that as far as space was concerned. To say nothing of the fact that at the back of the floorthrough her mother and father had their room, and off the kitchen her brothers shared another bedroom. "From the wide blue yonder to a rented upstairs in a Brooklyn two-family? That's progress, Harold? That's why you gave up four years of your life?" Evelyn wondered it out with him when they lay awake late at night, whispering, because Danny was such a light sleeper. "It just isn't fair."

"Fair or not, at least I'm alive. I'm here. Nothing'll ever be as important as that. Nothing, Ev. I got back. I got through it. And as soon as I can find some kind of decent job we'll get started out on our own. We'll get our own house. There's time. You'll see. Soon. Be patient." And then he held her tighter and kissed her, quietly, very quietly, so Danny and the others asleep in the apartment wouldn't wake up, wouldn't hear them moving closer together.

[3] Evelyn's mother thought Harold should go to college, "...instead of looking for a job you'll take without liking. What'll be the good of that? Taking a job just for the sake of taking it? Better if you go to school, if you take a chance, so

11

someday you'll give yourself an opportunity to choose from this, that, and the other. Not just one thing...you're listening, Harold? And you, Evelyn?"

Evelyn wasn't. Evelyn had heard it all before. She watched her mother rock Danny, up and down, on her lap. They had just finished dinner and Danny had cried out from his crib for Grandma to come get him, so she had, because no matter how many times Evelyn said, "Please, Ma, don't," her mother would answer, "A first grandchild is a first grandchild, so let me spoil him a little." She hugged Danny—but she also wanted to talk some more. "Listen to me, just once more, Harold. I realize it's cramped here. It's not...private. But we manage. We've managed so long, we'll manage a little longer, because if you don't go to school now, it'll be never. Some things I know—even though my husband will be quick to tell you I don't know much about anything."

"Don't start in, Ellie. Don't start in with that *my husband* crap." At the head of the dining-room table, her father turned away, as if he were preparing his nightly departure from the table to the living room, to his paper, to his radio, right next to his easy chair.

"Stay, Morrie. Tonight, stay for a minute extra." It was the closest Evelyn ever heard her mother come to a command. She even put Danny into his high chair. She gave him a crust of bread. "Chew, sweetheart. Chew. For your teeth. Chew it good."

She stared over at Harold. She stared at Evelyn. She had that look in her eyes. Evelyn had seen it a few times only. Something pleading in them, like the time she had tried to persuade Evelyn to wait to marry Harold, to wait until *after* the army, *after* the war, because maybe Evelyn should give some thought to school for herself. Had she thought about that at all? Yes. She had thought about it. She had...but she loved Harold more. He came first. She just wanted to marry him. That's all. Because Harold was the kindest, most generous, most thoughtful and considerate and handsome man there was ever going to be in her life. She knew it—and that was that. "Who's denying that?" her mother had said on that occasion. "To everyone he looks like a movie star. He does, and that part won't change in a few years, but maybe you will. Would it hurt if you went to college instead of an army base to live?" In response, then, Evelyn had cried and not given in. She wasn't going to cry now. She wouldn't give in either, no matter what her mother said.

12

"My husband put off doing things too, Harold. He could have invested in businesses. He didn't. He could have bought this house we're living in. He wouldn't. But my husband's chances didn't come to him early. He didn't have a habit to take chances. When he was young there was no one there to do for him. When his mother brought him from Russia it was a different kind of time altogether."

"Don't compare, Ellie. There's no point in comparing." Her father studied the crumbs he smoothed back and forth across the tablecloth. But he wasn't going to leave for his easy chair. He was pleased by her praise. His usual edge of annoyance gave in to remembering. He sighed. He smoothed. "Then was then."

"And now is now. But when it counted that if you didn't work no one in your family would have food to eat, you worked, Morrie. You couldn't choose, so you did. Right through the Depression you worked and you still managed to find time to read and to teach yourself what was what and to find out more things than most so-called educated people. You had to do it that way, so you did it." She stood up, she gestured for her sons to hand her their plates. They obeyed mutely, listening, following the exchange as if it were a game, an event. She began to scrape them. "But now it's different, Morrie. David and Irving, for example." They looked up at her then, waiting to hear their fate. "You'll want to send them to college, won't you? And why? Because why else did you work so hard all your life? Wasn't it to make it different for them from the way you had it? And you, Harold?" She paused in her scraping to bend toward Danny, to kiss him. "Before the war you wanted an education. You were planning for it. I remember how you said you were saving money for it. Wasn't that why you worked all those summers at the hotel? And now, all of a sudden, you don't care anymore about that? Now? After you've seen so much dying? If you don't give yourself the chance to choose one thing over another, what's the use of so much dying? It's a sin if you don't take the chance now. It won't come again...this time."

"Please, Ma. Don't say that." Evelyn had to stand up or explode. "It will. I'll make sure it will. Both of us will." She took Danny from his high chair. She wanted Harold to say something. Why didn't he? It was his life. Their life! To do with it as they pleased. For the first time! Her mother and father had had their turn. Now it was Harold's turn. And

13

hers. They'd decide what was best for themselves. "You just don't want to understand us, Ma."

"Of course not. Of course I don't want to understand. I just want to be stubborn like you." Her mother lifted the pile of scraped plates. She would be off to the kitchen. She would wash up. She would put things back where they belonged. She would put the kettle up for tea. She would portion out the apple cake she had baked for their dessert. She would keep on doing one thing after another, day after day after day. Her mother! Her thin slice of a mother so filled with all the checked energy of all the things she'd wanted for herself and her family and had never gotten and knew now she'd never get.

Harold stopped her before she moved away from the table. "I promise you, Ellie, that as soon as I can get us started out on our own, as soon as that happens and I've gotten a decent job, I'll go to night school. I promise it."

Her mother nodded, silent, lifted her pile of plates higher, trying to hide what Evelyn saw on her face: something angry and resigned, something settling into the corners of her mouth, closing her lips. Closed for the duration. Sealed.

Evelyn took Danny back to his crib. Even if he started to cry, he would stay there. Her mother was not going to come to rescue him. Evelyn knew what she was doing. So did Harold.

[4] If the Air Force trained you to be a navigator, what kind of job do you look for when you're discharged? If you grew up on a Catskill Mountain farm that wasn't even any longer in existence, if you waited tables in nearby resort hotels during the summer months, what do you do, afterwards, when before you realize it, you have a wife and a son and you're living with your in-laws and you can't even talk openly to your wife even when you're sitting next to her, even when what you have to ask her is so important? What do you do?

Well, Harold had tried two lousy selling jobs before a neighbor, who wanted to retire, told him all about custom peddling. About how you fill up the trunk of your car with *tchochkees,* pretty nothings you buy from wholesale jobbers, little semi-inexpensive extras you figure people will want, things they'll want for special times, like jewelry, silverware, watches, rings, all kinds—and then you go out to a territory and sell right to the people, right there on the street from the back of your car. Mr. Rappoport had been doing it for twenty years. An independent in America. In the old country too. From door to door. On foot, selling. In America too, at first. So now he had a car. He'd picked out his territory and he treated his customers like people. They bought—but twenty years was enough, and so if Harold wanted, Mr. Rappoport was willing to turn it all over to him. "A veteran deserves something from us, and I'll tell you, Harold, there are worse things a man could be...."

It wasn't exactly what Harold had come through the war planning to do with the rest of his life—not that it had to be the rest of his life. He could do it for a while. He could be his own boss, manage his own time, make time to go to school at night, maybe. And, yes, it was true, there are worse things a man could be, especially when there wasn't going to be time to wait. If the Levitt house didn't come through right away, there wasn't going to be room for another crib in Evelyn's bedroom. He reached for her hand, resting between them on the sofa. He wanted to ask her about the doctor. No, she whispered, not yet.

So he went back to his *Life,* or tried to. She left her hand on his. She went back to *The Fountainhead.* She was midway through it.

"Lux Presents Hollywood," Cecil B. De Mille announced. Her father turned the volume of the Philco higher. The Philco was next to his club chair on a dark oak end table. His: all his to control. "Tonight we are proud to present Van Johnson and Phyllis Thaxter recreating their memorable performances from the film *Thirty Seconds Over Tokyo....*"

Evelyn let *The Fountainhead* slip from her hand. She wouldn't be able to concentrate, and now it would have to be another hour before she would get the chance to talk to all of them. Her father had closed the book he had been reading, *The Unvanquished.* He loved reading about George Washington. From George Washington to the bombing of Tokyo. Some progress! She made a sound that sounded like a groan. Or was she crying? How she would have loved to get up, to leave the room, to leave the apartment with Harold and go somewhere else, anywhere else but where she was. The two of them could just stand up and go.... And Danny? What about Danny? What about what was going on inside her at that moment?

"It's really coming down, Ma." Her younger brother, David, was standing at the front window watching the snow fall. "It's sticking, Ma." Her mother nodded. She was in the wing chair right behind him. She was darning socks. David couldn't see her nod. "Hey, Ev, come and see."

"What's all this talking, David?" her father yelled out. "I'm listening, dammit."

"Couldn't you change to another program, Dad?" Evelyn knew better. He ignored the request. He had listened to *Lux Presents Hollywood* every Monday night. Week after week. Year after year. And she was twenty-five years old now and still listening to *Lux* with her mother and father. She was really going to cry. She grabbed Harold's hand. She squeezed it. She wondered if she was showing yet. It was January. She was beginning the fourth month. So they had until May. If the Levitt house didn't come through by May, what then?

May 1947? Another year lived in the past. She was crying. She couldn't help it.

"Evelyn?" Her mother stopped sewing. "Are you all right?" She stared over at the two of them. She knew. Her mother could see through her every time. All her life, her mother could look at her and know something. "Are you, Evelyn? Because you look very flushed to me."

"Fine, Ma. I'm fine."

"Only what?"

"Only nothing. Nothing's wrong, Ma. Stop worrying."

"I'm not worrying, I'm asking." Suddenly her mother's face turned red, her breathing became labored. David turned around to look at her. She wiped her forehead with a tiny cotton handkerchief she had had rolled in her palm.

"What about you, Ma? What's wrong with you?"

"Nothing. Nothing's wrong."

"Aren't you people ever going to shut up tonight?" Her father raised the volume of the radio.

"Why is that program so important, Dad? Why is it more important than talking? I was trying to talk to Mom." Evelyn felt out of control. She didn't want to have an argument with her father. She didn't want to have an argument with anyone. All she wanted to do was love them all, particularly that night.

Her mother's face turned suddenly pale—and then just as suddenly red again. She wiped her forehead again with that silly tiny handkerchief. "What is it, Ma?"

"It's starting."

"What is, Ma?"

"The changes."

Evelyn got up, went across the room to her, leaned down

16

over her to whisper. "And what's wrong with me, Ma, is that I'm pregnant." Evelyn knelt in front of her. Her mother began to cry, but she was also hugging Evelyn, happily hugging her. "Morrie, did you hear that?"

"Hear what? How can I hear anything with all of you talking so much? The only one not talking is Irving, and that's because he's in the bathroom. What the hell is he doing in the bathroom so long?"

"Never mind that. Did you at least hear that Evelyn's pregnant?"

"So why are you crying?" But he turned the radio off. *Lux* was finished for the night. He got up. He went to Harold, shook his hand, patted his shoulder, and then it was Evelyn's turn. He helped her up. He kissed her. "My little daughter. My grown-up little daughter ... who's not so little anymore."

Her father held her close, and over his shoulder she saw her mother's face go pale again. Suddenly pale—and then another flush. She was crying quietly, and smiling too, smiling up at them. A tiny slice of a woman, her mother, and then she was saying, "It happens faster than you think, Evelyn. When you reach my age, you'll see how fast it happens, living. Very fast...."

By the end of May, Danny's crib was moved out into the dining room to make way for Morty's crib inside the bedroom.

[5]   And then it was the next year, more than a year after the day they had all driven out to see the Levitt models on Hempstead Turnpike that they were able to take possession of their house in Levittown: October 1948. Morty was over a year old by then. Danny was four.

Their house was in the S section. On Spring Lane, if they could find it.

In the beginning, everyone got lost in Levittown. Inside each square grid was a maze of hidden lanes that seemed to circle smaller and smaller, leading them nowhere but around. And Danny had to, "...go, Ma. Bad."

"Hold it in, Danny. A few more minutes hold it in and Daddy will find our house." Morty, asleep on her lap, had already "gone." The car smelled of it. Fortunately, her mother had reminded her to put rubber pants on him. At the last minute, as they were pulling away from in front of the two-family, her mother had reminded her—and from now on there would be no more daily reminders.

"Harold? If we're lost, can't we stop and ask someone?"

"Who, Ev?" He turned the car south onto Gardiner's Avenue. There was no other car on it. There were no people. "I navigated bombers back and forth all over Europe, and I never got lost like this."

In the beginning, the only place to go to for help was a village green. Each section was supposed to have one, eventually. A touch of New England on the Island, the brochure had said of them, where stores would be, and a restaurant, a bar, a bowling alley, a movie house maybe, a library maybe, eventually—but not that day. Not even a map that day, and the grocery store that was supposed to service the S-section green was closed, so there was no bathroom for Danny, and it had started to rain.

Mercifully, it was a gentle rain.

Mercifully, leaving the green in the opposite direction— "What can we lose, Ev?"—making a wrong turn, turned out to be right.

Spring Lane.

Their house was milky yellow with white trim.

The bathroom had a tub-shower combination with a sliding glass door. The tub, the basin, the commode, whatever tiles there were, were pale milky yellow. The walls were white.

"Done, Ma. Wipe me." Wiped, flushed, the first flush in their new house.

All the walls in the house were white. Her choice. Maybe she should have chosen an accent color, something with more life in it.

Next time they paint.

When they finish off the attic, they can retouch. Danny wanted to explore the stairs leading up to nowhere, but the floor up there was unfinished too, none of the black-and-gray-speckled tiles that covered the downstairs floors, the soon-to-be radiantly heated floors.

Harold had arranged it so that the moving van would arrive before they did. Whatever they owned was there, inside, piled up, ready to be sorted out.

Not much. Beds. Cribs. A playpen. A kitchen set her mother had insisted she buy for them. A new set to start using in the new house.

Her mother had also insisted they fill the trunk of the car with food so when they arrived they would have something to eat. If they had nothing else, they would have food and beds and a roof over their heads. A challah was stuffed among
18

the jars and bags, a box of kosher salt alongside it—for good luck, for a long, healthy life. And there were bottles of pickled herring and bags of fresh vegetables and borscht and eggs and onions, chopped liver, everything homemade, and her mother had made Danny his favorite pinwheel cookies and some baby honeybuns for Morty, for Harold his favorite apple cake, the apples runny, the crust thin and rich and crisp.... Evelyn set all of it out on the kitchen counter, between the electric stove and the gleaming white refrigerator—she turned that on, filled the trays with water for ice, abracadabra, begin. Run water into the stainless-steel sink, hear the oil burner start up for the hot water. Even the clothes washer was magic. New magic—and theirs. Well, not quite. Not until the mortgage was paid off. Like the car. Not really theirs until the payments were paid. But theirs enough to call it theirs.

She would set the table. She would make it look pretty. Their round wooden kitchen table, which was really theirs because her parents had bought it for them, that she would set with their best silverware and plates and glasses. She would make it a little circle of order inside all the mess of the rest of the house.

From the main bedroom she heard Harold telling Danny about how to set up the beds so they wouldn't collapse.

She looked up and through the kitchen window facing Spring Lane. Rain fell harder. Mud oozing on what would one day be green lawn.

The afternoon light had darkened. Maybe a thunderstorm. Well, let it. They were safe. They were protected now.

She was ready to call them to come eat.

As if on cue, Morty began to cry out from his playpen in the living room. Harold went to get him.

When she turned from the sink, they were there, Harold holding Morty, Danny alongside him, looking at her, her family.

In their own house. On their own. Their life together really beginning, now, after what seemed like another whole lifetime of treading water, floating, waiting, for the war to be over, for a house to be built, for both of them to take charge of their lives.

Harold kissed her, Danny getting pressed between the two of them. Morty seemed to think it was all funny enough to laugh at.

2

[1] Picking through personal things, private possessions, a ring, a pin, earrings, a necklace with charms on, each charm given to her by Harold, and a slave bracelet that Harold had given her and which she never wore anymore—they went out of style in a hurry—but she wouldn't throw it away, ever: she was unpacking the past, sorting things out, putting things into drawers, into cabinets, into closets, preparing for the shape of things to come.... She hadn't read that H. G. Wells book in such a long time. She used to love it: *The Shape of Things to Come*. Personally, she always tried to shape things, expect things to happen that she wanted to have happen. She had always expected to meet someone tall, dark, and handsome and to fall in love.

And she had.

And before that, when she read *Little Women*, she expected to be like Jo Marsh. She would fall in love and life would be a struggle, but love would win out in the end.

And before that she had wanted to shape her life into a life like Amelia Earhart's—without disappearing, of course.

And there was a time when she was sure she would become an actress or a teacher or a lawyer or... But when she lifted her personal photograph album out of its packing, the first picture she opened to was the one of her in her first Lastex bathing suit, a one-piece shiny brown, which had been taken of her by the first boy who ever had a crush on her. Seymour his name had been. Sy. He was always annoying her that summer. That first summer—that was the summer Harold first came to work at her grandmother's hotel in the Catskills. Firsts...her first Lastex. The first crush. The first summer Harold was at the hotel...1937. She was fifteen. 1937. July 1937, printed on the back of the picture. Her handwriting. Even now she was careful to date pictures. August 1937. Of Harold. Taken in front of the entrance to the dining room. He was nineteen. In his waiter's uniform. Everyone at the hotel used to say he looked like Gary Cooper. So handsome. And she...in her brown Lastex. How she loved that bathing suit. She'd never forget it. How she had to fight with her mother to be allowed to wear it. Too tight, too revealing, her mother had said. It was. She'd always been big-busted...but her legs were always good legs. Shapely. Never too heavy, like the rest of her. She tended toward heaviness. Her face too. Too round, so she'd worn her hair in a high pompadour, upswept in the back, to make her face seem thinner. She was smiling, her one dimple showing. Her teeth too, showing too much. Slightly buck. She was not exactly beautiful. Not nearly as beautiful as Harold was handsome. So why, why had he fallen in love with her too?...Maybe not that first summer. But by 1939. By then, certainly, even though, "Every woman guest loved him a little bit too"—her Aunt Lila liked to shock Evelyn's mother by saying teasing things in front of Evelyn that way—"but Harold seems to have picked out our little Evelyn over the others—not that I know why. I only know because he told me. He also told me he thinks he's going to be leaving his mother's farm because he can't run it by himself. His brothers have all left it, and he and his mother can't make ends meet. He wants to go to college. He's saving up for it...."

Not that any of his plans and hopes ever got to matter much. All that did matter from that summer on was that, yes, he did love her. As her Aunt Lila said, he had picked her. He told Evelyn he wanted to marry her.

January 1940, a picture of Harold in his army uniform, just after he'd been drafted, one of the first from Ellenville to be drafted—another first—and after his mother died and the farm was sold....Harold in uniform, 1941, when he was stationed in Panama. He was seated beneath a palm tree, his hair pomaded close to his scalp, parted in the middle, "A Latin from Ellenville," he had written on the back of the picture. Also, "My love, always...."

Why?

"Because," he would say, "I just do."

When she was twenty-one and he was twenty-five they were married, just before he was shipped overseas. He navigated his crew in their Flying Fortress overseas to Italy. In 1943—that picture was serious, none of his I-just-do kind of smile. But on their wedding picture, both of them smiling: her dimple, his cleft, their cheeks pressed together. Her pompadour was lustrous, higher than usual, dangerously high,

21

she remembered feeling that day. She lifted the picture close to her lips. She cried; she laughed out loud.... She listened to hear if she had awakened Morty from his nap. No stirrings—and Danny, she could see through the window, was playing quietly, absorbed by the mound of dirt outside the side-door entrance. And she was really wasting too much time with her photograph album when there was so much yet to do.

She put the wedding picture back inside the tab corners of the album page. Such a perfect wedding. At the Jewish Community Center a few blocks from the two-family in Brooklyn. Her mother and grandmother had made all the food. Everyone there was family or a close friend, a loving neighbor. Harold wore his second lieutenant's uniform and her best friend sang *their* song, "Moonlight Becomes You." And then it was over and in a few days he was gone, until 1944.... January 1944. Of Harold. Looking thinner than he'd ever been before. And so tired and with fear in his eyes. From Italy, nearing the end of his fifty missions, including the first shuttle raid over Romania to Russia and back again to Italy, and all during the period of those raids he wasn't able to write to her, for two weeks no letters from him, and the feeling growing inside her that he was dead, that he was never coming back to her and to their...child—because by then she was pregnant with Danny....

Who was coming into the house just then with, "A lady, Ma."

A lady with two sons. Arlene Zweig, "From the house on your right." Marvin was Morty's age and asleep in his carriage. Joel was Danny's age.

Joel and Danny eyed each other. So did Evelyn and Arlene. Evelyn would have preferred to go on with her unpacking.

Joel had a bicycle, and would Danny like to ride it for a while?

Danny would. But Joel didn't want him to. "'S mine."

"Let him ride it for a while, Joel. Do you hear me? I don't like it when you're selfish." Arlene pulled Joel away from the bicycle.

Danny pedaled from the side door down to the curb. The ground was still too wet from the rain. There were no sidewalks yet. It was rough going. Danny gave the bicycle back to Joel. He didn't thank Joel. Joel didn't care. Danny didn't care either. He sat down to play with his car in the mound of dirt.

"I don't know what's gotten into Joel. It's not having friends, I suppose. I'm so glad you've finally moved in. He was starved for a friend. So was I, to tell the truth. Your other neighbors are the Massis, Loretta and Joe. They have daughters. As soon as Loretta realizes I'm here, she'll be over. You can be sure of that, if you know what I mean. Loretta has Angela, about Danny's age, and Maria. Maria's a year younger than Angela. They're Catholics. . . ."

Evelyn turned to a box of glasses and dishes and Arlene was content to watch, never stopping to ask questions, just telling what she was sure Evelyn would need to know, like how long it took to push a carriage up to the village green grocery store and then back again, fully loaded; how many Jewish families there were as compared to Catholic and Protestant. "We are way outnumbered. The high holidays, I had to go for miles to find a synagogue for my mother and father. It's a far cry out here from the Grand Concourse. You're not from the Concourse. I can tell that. Don't ask me how. I can just tell those things. I've got a sixth sense. Max always tells me that. Max is my husband. He's a lawyer. From Chicago originally. His family moved to the Bronx from Chicago. Is your husband a professional?"

"Harold . . . sells. Custom peddling they call it."

"Oh. . . . I notice you don't have a telephone yet. We do. Loretta doesn't. So if you need to call someone, don't hesitate to come over. Anyway, you'll come over to see our house. I'm so glad a Jewish family moved in here. It would have been so hard for the children otherwise. I hope we're going to be friendly. I hope we can organize a club or something, because you'll find there isn't very much to do. Once you get your things unpacked and set up, you might just as well be living on the Great Plains instead of next to New York City."

Arlene stopped, out of breath. Her stopping was such a surprise, it stopped Evelyn too. Evelyn was in the middle of entrée plates, a wedding present she had kept wrapped up for when they moved. A pretty pattern. Plain. A simple small green leaf in the center. A ring of the same green all around the circumference—just the opposite of Arlene. She had too much on. Rings and pins and necklaces and bracelets and a black sweater and a heavy sack of a tweed skirt, a jersey blouse, printed with big flowers. She wore a flower in her hair, a fake rose. Carmen from the Grand Concourse, with brown hair yet—and out of steam, lonely, ". . . starved for someone to talk to. The sidewalks close up, Evelyn. I'm not

23

kidding. Do you knit? There's someone over on Spoon Lane gives knitting classes. Missy Geiger. You'll like her, I think. A mixed marriage. He's Jewish. She was born Catholic.... There's no stopping me for long. I'm sorry, and you've got so much to do. Maybe I can help."

"How about later, Arlene? This afternoon? Come for coffee and cake?"

Arlene didn't drink coffee.

Neither did Evelyn.

Arlene didn't smoke either.

Neither did Evelyn. "... and maybe when you come back later you can bring some of your friends from Spoon Lane."

[2] Evelyn went to ask Loretta Massi from next door to come over in the afternoon. Loretta brought Rita Moskowitz with her. They both smoked; they both drank coffee, black. They were both built the same way, low to the ground, chunky, chubby. Rita bordered on fat and had the blackest, straightest hair Evelyn could remember seeing on a human Jewish woman. Loretta's was curly, tight black curls close to her scalp, and when she smoked, she smoked hard and long and palmed her cigarette, until she realized she was. She talked a lot with her cigarette dangling from the corner of her mouth. She was immediately interrupting Arlene to tell everyone about Rita's plan to organize an action group.

"To do what?" Since Evelyn was the newest and since it was her house, she felt obliged to ask the questions everyone else knew the answers to.

"About the clause."

"What clause, Rita?"

"You see!" Rita slapped the kitchen table. "No one catches the clause." They were three just then, except for the children playing in the empty living room. The sun had been going hide-and-seek, so they had brought all the children back inside to Mort's playpen: Danny; and Loretta's Maria and Angela; Rita's Mark. Danny and Mark were the same age. Danny gave Mark his car. Mark gave Danny his truck. "That's friends. That's the way it should be. Not like the clause. You read your contract with the Levitts, you'll see. Read it carefully, Evelyn. The small print where it says you can't sell to non-Caucasian. Non-Caucasian. Negroes, it means. The same ones who were in the army and good enough to die aren't good enough for Levittown. That's the clause, and no one sees it.... So I'm organizing an action group, and
24

I hope you'll be part of it because..." Rita stopped, because there came Arlene Zweig and Gladys Ginsburg, who had a Nathaniel and a Myrna, and Melissa Geiger, "the knitting lady," Arlene reminded Evelyn. Melissa had Donald and Adam and carried Teresa, exactly Morty's age and therefore eligible for the playpen, where all of the children by then wanted to go. "No" for Joel and Marvin from Arlene, and for Nathaniel and Myrna from Martha, who would have coffee, light, with a little sugar. Evelyn would make tea for Arlene and herself. "For Cynthia Klein, too, Ev. I asked her too to come and to bring Corinne. You'll like Corinne. Won't she like Corinne, Rita?"

"As a matter of fact, she will. And you want to know why, Arlene? But even if you don't want to know why, I'll tell you. Because when you meet some people you know immediately if they've got a conscience or if they haven't. Corinne's got. I can tell those things about people. I can tell it about you, Evelyn. Right or wrong? I'll tell you another fact, too. If I hadn't married Abe soon after Pearl Harbor, I'd have gone to City College. Into psychology I would have gone, because I can tell things about people from how they behave. I knew right away about you, Arlene. That you wouldn't join us. And that neither would you, Gladys. About you, Melissa? Well, you're another question altogether."

Melissa Geiger was. Evelyn could look at her too and see that. Without psychology. Melissa—Missy, she preferred being called Missy—Missy was pale and blond and delicate. Not fragile delicate. She was a determined kind of person. She knew how she felt. She kept smiling all throughout Rita's longer speeches, humoring her, turning one cheek and then the other, composed, revealing next to nothing.

And then Cynthia Klein arrived with her Melanie. Corinne would be coming separately. She was bringing another newcomer to meet everyone.

Cynthia was no joiner, but she turned no cheeks. She said exactly what she wanted to say whenever she felt like saying it, "...and what I want to say to you, Ree-tah"—Cynthia was originally from Charleston, South Carolina, and she liked to make more of her accent than was absolutely necessary—"Ree-tah, do you mind please to keep quiet for one little minute? You're always spouting forth about ten things at once and forgetting the chief reason we're all he-ah. Which is to welcome Evelyn. Frankly, what I wish you'd organize instead of your action committee is some kind of more formal

hospitality group. I hate this hit-and-miss kind of thing."
Cynthia wore a navy-blue rayon blouse, and whenever she
was done saying exactly what she wanted to say, she folded
her arms across her breasts, crushing in on them. She was
full-breasted too, about the same as Evelyn. But Cynthia was
taller, bigger-boned, and thin. Long and thin and . . . handsome.
Stylish, Evelyn would have said, if asked. Dark-hued. Still
waters and all that, she thought.

Not Corinne Feuerstein. She was a wind, whirling right
into the center of the crowd, plopping her Gregory onto the
kitchen table while she got a Kleenex out for his nose. "I
don't know where the hell he gets his colds from, but he
manages." With her was Sally Plotkin. Sally had moved in
the day before too. Sally had a daughter, Penny. "I hope you
don't mind that I brought Sally, because when Arlene called
Cynthia and Cynthia called me, I thought I might as well
bring Sally too. Kill two birds with one slingshot. What the
hell. Right?"

"Right"—and what would Corinne like? And Sally? Both
coffees. Sugars. Creams.

". . . or whatever. I don't care, Ev. Go, Gregory. Go crawl
in with the others. Sally? You want to put Penny into the
playpen?"

Unfortunately, the playpen was just about full up. Morty
and Teresa were in it crying because the older ones kept
climbing in and out, kicking and flailing. Evelyn cleared
them out, to the surrounding floor, ". . . not inside. Now, here's
Penny, Morty. Penny Plotkin, Morty, like Penny in your hand
when Grandma gives you one." Penny was coppery. So was
Sally. So was Corinne, but Corinne's copper was reddish,
from a rinse red, an intense red rinse that dazzled, like Rita
Hayworth's. Her hair was long and wavy and was forever
wisping into the corners of her mouth. She seemed to enjoy
pulling it out and pushing it back from one shoulder and
then from the other, like all the great stars did. Corinne
didn't sit still—in this case stand still, because there was no
room for everyone to sit around the kitchen table. And the
children were in and out and underfoot.

Melissa tried to get them organized, tried to get the older
ones to lead the others outside, just outside the side entrance,
where ". . . we can see you all. There you are. I see you."
Melissa spread her delicate fingers and peekabooed. "I see
you all."

Cynthia would not let Melanie go. "She'll sit on my lap

26

and be content, won't you, sweet lambkins?" Others might stand around, not Cynthia. Sally stood and Arlene did, but not Loretta, not Rita. Melissa was up and down, and so was Evelyn, getting more coffee, more tea, whatever was left of her mother's cookies and honeybuns and apple cake—Melissa had to have the recipe for the apple cake because it was about the best she'd ever had. Cynthia thought it was the best she'd ever had since she'd left home, but, no, she didn't want the recipe, because baking was not something she took to.

"Enough with the cake and coffee." Rita wanted to know who was with her and Loretta on the clause issue.

Evelyn would join. Evelyn would work "...in a few days. I have to get settled in a little, but I certainly am on your side." Sally was too. Of course Corinne. Not Arlene. Not Gladys. "Well, maybe." But definitely not Cynthia. Not Melissa, on this one thing, although she understood the principle, all right. "...but Carl and I have just been through enough as it is without more right now. Levittown seems like a paradise to us right now...."

"Some paradise!" Corinne lit up, and therefore so did Loretta and Rita. "Which way is it for us Jews back to the Garden of Eden? All I see is sidewalks and asphalt and mud."

"Before you know it, it'll all grow up." Melissa's certainty directed her fine hand to a fine little gold cross she wore around her neck. Until then it had been hidden under her beige cashmere cardigan. She played with it, fingered it, smiling blondly.

Loretta speared the air in front of Missy with her cigarette. "Before you know it, we'll all be dead."

"You'll be, Loretta." Corinne unwisped hair ends from her mouth. "Not me. I've got too much to do yet....Gregory? What the hell is that taking-your-pants-down business?" She raced to the side door, felt his backside. "You didn't, Greg, did you?...You did...See you, ladies. Thanks, Ev, and welcome. You too, Sally....*Arriverderci.*"

[3] Harold didn't want her to get involved so fast. "Can't we wait to see what's what? According to law, the Levitts have a right to do what they want with their own property."

"You sound like Cynthia Klein."

"Bet I don't feel like her—and I'm saying that without seeing her." He turned her to him, made her move inside his arms. "Come on, Ev. Don't be like that." He whispered into her ear, smoothed her hair back from in front of it.

27

Clear darkness outside their bedroom window. A quiet. A country quiet, and then the wind gusted, went still. The oil burner started up. She could hear the boys breathing peacefully. "It's important, and you make fun of it. You make fun of what Rita said. You don't even know her, but because *she* said it, what could it mean. Sometimes you do that to me too. You do, Harold. Admit it."

"I'm not making fun. It just so happens I've got something else on my mind. You I've got on my mind. Didn't I come home early so I could help you with the boys and the unpacking and dinner? Didn't I?"

"You did—and I love you for that and for everything." She did: *1937*—since 1937 when she had raced into the dining room of the hotel looking for her Aunt Lila and Grandmother and there was Harold Selden smiling. Her Aunt Lila had introduced him to her. So handsome, and his loving her, her loving him, had changed everything in her life since then: 1937...1948. In the blink of an eye. In a kiss. He kissed her. He held her tighter. "I do, Harold. You know that, don't you?" Whispering into his ear.

"I do too."

"Levittown is *our* chance, Harold. We're going to have to push it along, nurse it, like we do our trees. That's all I'm talking about."

"Okay. Only, no more talking for a while." He wanted to move inside her. She let him. She closed her eyes. She held on to his neck. He squeezed her closer to him—and she remembered: she had taken the diaphragm out because of a pain down there, and because of the ladies that afternoon, she'd forgotten to put it back. "Harold, you're going to have to stop—or just be careful. I'm sorry. I . . ."

He fell back off her. He was exasperated—but he understood. "Tomorrow. It can wait until tomorrow. I understand, Ev."

[4] Rita's husband, Abe, had a Negro friend from the Marine Corps, from their days in the Pacific when they were on Guadalcanal together. They had been close friends then. Since discharge they'd hardly seen each other, although they spoke on the telephone a lot. Calvin Rogers and his wife, Maryellen, lived near City College uptown, on 145th Street in a walkup. Fifth floor. They had two daughters and one bedroom. They were at Rita and Abe's for a Saturday after-

noon meeting about the clause, about testing it. Cal had decided he'd be willing to be the guinea pig.

Only five of them showed up: Loretta, Evelyn, Corinne, Sally, Marcia. Marcia's "maybe" had turned into a "yes." Rita was sure there'd be more as soon as they got things organized better. They would now, now that Cal and Maryellen were willing. Rita thought they should hire a lawyer, plan everything carefully with him so that when the time came for the actual moving in, the Levitts wouldn't have a legal leg to stand on. Rita and Abe were going to rent a house in their own name and then sublet it to Cal.

Evelyn suggested that maybe they should also call a group like the NAACP to help, in case of an emergency.

Corinne thought that might bring in too much early publicity.

Loretta suggested it would be a better idea if Evelyn organized a committee to get more help from right in the neighborhood where Rita and Abe would rent the house. "As soon as they knew what section, we can start canvassing around in there."

Evelyn agreed. No hesitation. It was instinct. For a principle? Always. She'd always work hard for a principle, for a right....

And there would be a little time, because Cal wasn't exactly ready yet. He was finishing up at City, but at night. He'd need a higher-paying job first to pay for a Levitt house, but he was ready to be a guinea pig all right. Just as long as he could keep his girls safe, he'd try almost anything to get more for them than he'd ever had or his wife ever had. He held her hand as he spoke, but he didn't look at her. He didn't look across at any of them either. Evelyn imagined he was talking to someone inside himself, someone distant, or maybe someone dead he kept alive inside his memory. He wanted...he deserved... "I've earned my chance, and I've earned it for my girls and for my wife." Calvin Rogers was a tall, lean, quiet-spoken man, quiet and fierce and very dark, so dark the afternoon sunlight, reflecting on his dark skin, seemed to turn it white. "But I'll also tell you right here and now there's going to be limits. They start in on Maryellen and the girls, and I'll be setting limits. If your husbands were here, they'd understand. I'm sorry they're not, tell you the truth, because we might just need them eventually."

"We won't." Evelyn felt certain of that. "All of us who

moved out here have all been through hard times. We all know enough about suffering. It's going to be easier than you expect, Mr. Rogers."

"It's going to be harder, Mrs. Selden. Just because of that."

Standing next to Cal's chair, Abe Moskowitz was nodding, agreeing. Abe was a stocky stub of a man, angry about things, just like Rita was, and like Rita, ready to do something about what angered him. "On the other hand, Cal, don't forget they gave us Israel for 1948. Maybe they'll give all of us Levittown for 1949."

The Moskowitz house was green with white trim, the one with the big picture window divided into all those small panes. It was on Shelter Lane, one of the short curvy lanes that ended at Spring. Evelyn's walk home wasn't long enough for her to get too depressed about all the injustice Cal Rogers must have suffered growing up. And, anyway, Loretta never stopped talking about how she and Evelyn were going to get people up off their asses, get them working for the right causes, human causes. "You're the kind of person that can do that to people, Ev. Get them active. I can tell that about you. It's how you are instinctively."

And Evelyn could tell Loretta had the same kinds of instincts, only she didn't let that show too often. . . . Anyway, injustices didn't have time to overwhelm her on that short walk. Besides, Harold and the boys were at home, waiting for her.

[5] Even on a short walk Loretta could cram a lot in, ". . . if you let me, Ev. Which you do. Even if you don't hear it all, you let me keep talking. But I can tell the difference when you're listening and when you're not. I'm not like Arlene. I try to say things'll keep your interest. Nothing trivial, you understand. Like what I started to say about Joe and me the other day. It's the truth, so I say it. We got a few more minutes' walking, so I have to hurry to say it. Still, fast or not, it's the truth. Joe and me never should have gotten married. If it wasn't he was going into the Navy then, we wouldn't have. We both had such lousy starts we felt sorry for each other then. I don't anymore. He still does. Whatever happens to him, it's okay. He takes it. No whimpers, even."

But they had reached the semi-demi-royal blue Massi house with the white trim. Joe was sitting on the side entrance step, sitting there watching the girls pull their pull toys back and forth.

30

Evelyn waved. Joe waved back. The girls saw Loretta and ran toward her.

Out in front of the Zweig house, Max was digging something. A path. A slate path, she remembered. Arlene had told her Max wanted a slate path leading down to the sidewalk. The Zweig house was barn red with white trim. It was set the farthest back from the sidewalk. That feature was part of the famous Levitt touch: staggering the distances in from the street so that when you looked out of the windows of any house you would see more than just the next house. You would also see the trees growing, the lawns being sown and eventually mowed, the flowers flowering. What flowers would the Seldens plant?

Daffodils, certainly. Azaleas, probably. Rhododendrons, maybe. Depended on what their neighbors put in. For harmony's sake. They weren't ready to plant, yet, anyway. She wanted Harold to make bookshelves for the living room and for the boys' room. She wanted the house to be filled with books and plants and Early American. If they could afford Early American antiques, she'd start collecting right away—but that was a long way away from December 1948.\ . . . Why wasn't Harold outside with the boys? Something must have happened, although every car was where it belonged.

She hurried in. Morty was in his high chair. Danny was setting the table for lunch. Harold was chopping up some hard-boiled eggs and onion. The kitchen radio played Patti Page singing "Tennessee Waltz." All seemed right inside their little house. Peaceful progress. She kissed Morty, then Danny.

Harold stopped chopping. "Almost ready, hon." They kissed. They always kissed each other whenever they returned from wherever they had been.

"Maybe after lunch, Harold, we can drive down to Jones? Just to see the ocean? Winter ocean is beautiful."

"Max Zweig was going to take me to play golf, but I can cancel that. I can go another time."

"No. You go with him. We can always drive to the ocean. The ocean will be there."

"You sure, Ev?"

"Sure."

"One of these days I'm going to start teaching you how to drive."

"Soon, Harold. Soon. First things first."

3

[1] It wasn't easy for the couples to get together on weekends, and almost never during the week.

All of them had little children, which meant baby-sitters. And there weren't any. Except for grandparents, and getting them meant planning in advance and a special event, like the New Year's Eve party Evelyn and Harold decided they would give. "...so the husbands can get to know each other better, Harold. The wives are always getting together."

Missy Geiger had organized the welcoming committee Cynthia had suggested. Cynthia didn't exactly join, but she always helped. Evelyn couldn't get her to join the Levittown Ladies Against Discrimination, either. So, whatever Cynthia was, she was at least consistent: she was no joiner.

This would have absolutely nothing to do with whom Evelyn invited to the party. Whether they joined or not was beside the point, because they all had one thing to celebrate together, at least one thing this particular December 31, 1948: a Levitt house. So she made out the list impartially, not excluding nonjoiners in the fight against discrimination.

From Spring Lane, the Massis and the Zweigs. They'll come.

From Shelter Lane, Rita and Abe Moskowitz. Yes.

From Slip Lane, Sally and Ken Plotkin will come, and so will Audrey and Murray Halpern, Esther and Martin Aronowitz.

From Spiral Lane, Cynthia and Sandy Klein were yes. So were Missy and Carl Geiger, Corinne and Lionel Feuerstein.

So were, from Swan Lane, Ina and Burt Silverstein yes Ruby and Roy Rabinowitz, Gladys and Gordon Ginsburg ...what was the word for sounds like that? She'd read it Or a teacher, in high-school English, had taught them about sounds in a row repeating, at the beginnings of successive words in a row, repeating...she'd absolutely forgotten... Gladys and Gordon...Ruby and Roy. Old before her time...

Anyway, from Spoon Lane, Edna and Bud Leventhal had said yes. So had Rose and George Newman, Toby and Jack Margolies.

For a grand total, including themselves, of thirty-two.

Too many for their house.

Too many for their budget, but her mother was going to help with the food, her father was going to help Harold get the liquor as close to wholesale as he could, and the boys were going to stay in Brooklyn for the party night and the next day, which it just so happened was a Saturday, thank God. It would be the first big party Evelyn and Harold had ever given. They would have plenty to drink and plenty to eat, and nothing could go wrong. The guests were all...acquaintances. At least that. Some were already more.

Some were already friends. Loretta was, and Corinne Feuerstein. Missy might become one. And Cynthia might. Rita too, if she could learn how to relax once in a while.

Some never would be. Arlene never would be, not even if they were to remain living next door to each other for the rest of their lives—but, on the other hand, Harold liked Max. He didn't dislike Joe Massi. It was just that Joe Massi was a painful case. Some of the other husbands and wives Harold hadn't met yet, which was the best reason to have the party. Everyone could get to know everyone else....Well, not everyone else. Not when she went over the guest list.

When she went over the guest list, she got the feeling that everyone in Levittown was Jewish. That, of course, was not true. But the only non-Jews on the list were Loretta and Joe and Missy. Catholics. Not one Protestant. Three out of thirty-two...and not one Negro, either. Strange how Jews found each other, no matter where they were, even in a place like Levittown, where they were certainly outnumbered. Plenty of churches around. Catholic churches, mostly. A few Protestant ones. Not a single synagogue. Outnumbered, the Jews, and so always sticking together, for protection, as if their blood told them to, even after the gas chambers, even in a Levittown in 1948-almost-49....And not one Protestant on her list. Well, she hadn't met everyone in Levittown. Not yet. She was only just starting out...she and Harold were. Their first big party.

[2] Fortunately, for party-giving, not for living, there was so little furniture to move back against the walls, Harold was able to wait until almost the very last minute to do that.

Nor was there any rug to roll back from over the radiantly heated floor. The half-dozen throw pillows Evelyn had so far sewn she threw...wherever. That was that: the arrangements—although no matter how she arranged or rearranged, there would never be enough room for a comfortable edge. Thirty-two people drinking and eating in their living room was a crowd.

In the kitchen, Harold prepared the bar. He would cut the turkey later when it cooled. The roast beef was ready. He had made cole slaw and potato salad and there were pickles and mustard and greens for another salad ready to be tossed. Her mother had made a mound of chunky chopped liver, the kind Harold liked, and she had also given him, for the party, some new pickled herring and four apple cakes. She called from Brooklyn to let Morty gurgle and Danny wish Evelyn and Harold a Happy New Year before the party started. Danny said he was going to stay up until midnight, to see what happens, "...and will I change, Ma, really?"

"Into what, Danny?"

"Uncle David said I would change into a man at midnight. Will I, Ma? Like Daddy?"

"Not yet.... Not so fast.... But if Grandma lets you stay up to see, you can...."

Then, all there was to do was to wait and be nervous and lift one and another throw pillow and throw it into yet another position, or for the fifteenth time check her hair in the bathroom mirror, make sure there was no lipstick on her teeth, button and then unbutton the top button of the embroidered silk overblouse Harold had brought back for her from Europe. It was the richest thing she owned. Ivory silk ground and the embroidery in vivid-colored silk threads, magenta, deep forest green, an orange-red, all done into a Chinese motif, with black embroidered frog closings. Harold had bought it in Paris. It had come from Saigon. It had that name on its label: Saigon, French Indochina, somewhere she'd never go or ever hear of.... She had done her hair in an upsweep. It was shiny and healthy and for that night as straight as she always dreamed it would be. Dark and shiny and straight. Not herself. Not beautiful! too round, too full, the mirror said, but not plain, and not every face had one perfectly placed dimple. She could live with it.

So could Harold. He nodded, behind her, holding her, kissing the back of her neck, approving. His white shirt, his red silk tie, both new for the occasion. She had bought them for him.

"Remember that first New Year's, Harold, after we were married? When you got the word about going overseas? Remember how we decided and undecided and decided all night long about having a baby? I'm glad we finally did. I'm glad it was Danny. I'm glad about everything in my life so far—but you, most of all. You I'm glad of."

"So am I.... Maybe this is a good time to open the champagne your father sent out for us. We can have it now, before anyone else gets here."

"Let's save it for later. It's almost time anyway. And that way it'll be just for us. Some things in our life have to be just for the two of us, no matter what happens, no matter even how many children we have. Just the two of us. Promise?"

"Promise." He didn't want to let go of her, but then the bell rang.

[3]   Arlene warned Evelyn about Corinne Feuerstein. "She can drink," behind her hand, into Evelyn's ear, "She loves it."

But when Corinne came through the kitchen for her food, she seemed steady enough, except Lionel, next in line, grabbed at her behind, "A husband's got a right, for Christ's sake," then she lost her control—and rightfully, Evelyn felt. Lionel was the drunk one; he could hardly hold his plate still enough for Harold to fill. "My wife's some babe. You ever hear her sing yet, Evelyn? You ever hear her play the piano? Talented broad, my wife. Talented in all kinds of ways...." What Corinne did to shut him up was to half-turn and knee him. He shut up, all right. He doubled over, Harold grabbing for, reaching in time, his plate, though even doubled over he was a big man for a Corinne Feuerstein to be fooling with. She had to know just how far to go. When he stood up, he was quieter. Corinne fluffed her free-falling red waves, unbuttoned one more rhinestone button on her long-sleeved black crepe shirt dress. That button opened into her cleavage, her considerable cleavage. Another notch down and she would be out in the open. Evelyn could see no visible signs of a brassiere strap. "You're a real innocent, aren't you, Ev?"

Evelyn felt her dimple blushing, but she went right on smiling. Corinne was drunk; she just knew how to drink without showing it. Evelyn had more people to feed. Burt and Ina Silverstein were next. They were the only couple in

35

the group with no children, so Burt was back in school. He was going to get a college degree if it was the last thing he did in this world. After his second gin on the rocks, he had gone from person to person to tell them why, and with him Ina had to go. Burt was a big brown bear of a man, and Ina, "...she's my little Dresden doll. She doesn't look like a Dresden doll. But to me she does." He kept her stuffed and wrapped inside his arm. "My sweet little Ina. She works for me so I can go to school and get my degree. Ina understands my mind, how it works." Burt was European-born, but from where in Europe, Evelyn didn't know. He'd been in the U.S. Army, in Europe, on V-E Day. She knew that, and that he'd been in the infantry, on D Day, too. "Ina knows what happened in my life. Ina appreciates." Ina nodded. Ina said nothing. Inside his arm Ina seemed to be holding him up. "My Ina knows there's a time...there's only one time...when you take a chance...or you lose everything. My whole family lost. Ina knows...in the gas chamber...because they wouldn't take a chance and leave...when I begged them to...." He had to let go of her then to take his plate. He had no choice, but he followed Ina back out into the living room.

The Philco was on out there. Ben Grauer from Times Square. Fifteen minutes until midnight—and by then almost everyone had been fed. Ben Grauer drowned out whatever conversation remained. Borrowed silverware clanged against borrowed plates: all the ladies had made some kind of donation.

"...and as I look down at the crowd, I sense exhilaration... and relief. Nineteen-forty-eight has been a good year in many ways for many people all over the world. The crowd down below me is a big one, perhaps one of the biggest ever..."

"Last chance to eat, for now," Harold called out from the kitchen, loud and clear. His hotel training. She leaned against him, thinking of him at the hotel. The Hotel Washington, situated on beautiful manmade Lake Linden. She, in her one-piece brown Lastex, 1937, and there was Harold Selden being introduced to her by her Aunt Lila....Sometimes you're lucky. Sometimes chance happens to you. Sometimes you blink your eyes—or you keep them open, it doesn't matter which—and your life is never the same for the rest of it because of that chance. Harold Selden in the hotel dining room because her grandmother had sent him out there to get something for her, her glasses. Her grandmother was the boss. But it was Uncle Max who showed Harold everything.

36

Uncle Max taught Harold everything there was to know about running a hotel. Uncle Max had taught Harold...how to make a good turkey, a good roast, a good steak, and how to make salads, and how to carve.... "You make a woman a good husband, Harold." She kissed him, but he was otherwise occupied. He was watching Loretta approach. She was being forced to approach. By Joe. Who was angry. And embarrassed.

"I apologize for her. She's drunk. She's really stinko. Maybe I better just take her home." He was leaning down over her—he was easily a head and a half taller than she was—and at the same time supporting her by the elbow. "Goddammit, Loretta, pull yourself together, will you? Straighten the hell up...or else."

"Or else what?" She pushed him back. "I'm not afraid of anything you can *or else* me with, you know."

Evelyn went to her. Evelyn moved her toward Harold and a plate of food. Loretta, when Evelyn urged it, went without resistance.

"Whatever you say, Ev. You're okay in my book. I'll be good."

So there was peace in the kitchen—and also, according to Ben Grauer, in Times Square, where it was only, "...five more minutes to go. The crowd is of course, as you can hear, getting noisier. A sea of noisemakers and hats and confetti. The weather couldn't be better....Just under five minutes to go..."

And just Cynthia and Sanford Klein left to feed, before they could feed themselves. "We'd've been out he-ah before, Evelyn, but I just couldn't get Rita away from Sandy. Rita has to try proselytizin' with everyone. That's such a New Yorkese way—not that Sandy can't take care of himself with the likes of Ree-tah...."

"Rita is perfectly fine." Sanford Klein's accent was pure Boston proper. "You're the one who could use some mind-twisting." He was more Sanford than Klein; almost more beautiful than handsome, Evelyn kept thinking. Lithe and graceful and yet muscular, just a blond hair shorter than Cynthia, as fair as she was dark-hued, and, yes, she thought, he could take care of himself. A strange pair, the Kleins. Cynthia had been drinking ginger ale all evening; Sandy drank Scotch without ice, in little sips, never a gulp. The only person he had talked with at all, all evening, had been Harold. He had insisted earlier on helping Harold with the bar, serving, mixing, getting more ice. He felt comfortable being out of the way, doing things, instead of standing around, he had told Harold. He was an electrical engineer, a graduate of MIT.

"...three minutes and forty-eight seconds until 1949..." Time for them to fill their own plates—but wouldn't you know it, the only other professional in the group, Max Zweig, the Lawyer Zweig, was back for seconds, "Fast seconds, fast eater," followed by Gordon Ginsburg, horse-faced, big sad-eyed, semidrunk, and always outspoken Gordon Ginsburg, whispering how Max Zweig was a bastard, "thinks he's better than all of us put together. Most lawyers do, you know. Fat little pudgy bastard. Eats too much. So do I. So does Gladys—but Gladys's built to take it, if you know what I mean."

When Ben Grauer began his countdown to midnight, Evelyn and Harold were still out in the kitchen—where they would stay, Evelyn decided, until afterwards.

"...5...4...3...2...1...Happy New Year. Happy 1949," the voice lost in the roar, and then the sound of Guy Lombardo's orchestra, the shouts, the screams, the "Auld Lang Syne" chorus coming from their living room.

Harold held her. He leaned his head down gently on top of her upswept. He just wanted to tell her one thing, and she knew what that one thing was, always would be—he couldn't be happier, "...to love you and be here, after the last few years, to be here, in our house. It's going to be a great life for us. I know it, Ev." He kissed her eyes because she was crying, for joy, crying. "You are an innocent, like she said, that Corinne lady, but I love you exactly that way." And then he kissed her, a long kiss, which he only broke off because there was Missy Geiger bringing in a stack of plates.

She looked away—but she really did have to do something with the stack of dishes. "I'm terribly sorry. I really am." Before she could set them down anywhere, Carl Geiger appeared with a second load. "So that's where the two of you are. What the hell is this? The two of you doing it standing up?" Carl had seemed a quiet man.

Missy was mortified. "Excuse him. Too many drinks." When blonds blush, they are defenseless. Before she had a chance to pale, it seemed like everyone from the living room was crowding around in the kitchen, Happy New Yearing each other, wanting to see what the hell Carl was laughing about.

38

[4]   The cold snap of wind rattling the bedroom windows made her suddenly rise up out of wherever she had been in her sleep, listening for the boys. But they weren't there. They were in Brooklyn—and then she didn't remember any of the places she had been to in her dream.

She lifted up a little to read the clock: 4:30, and then higher, sitting up, so she could lean up over Harold and watch him sleeping. They were both naked. They had gotten into bed when everyone finally left, ready to have sex, and then he couldn't, and she didn't want to then; they were both exhausted anyway. Later. In the morning. They could sleep late, she reminded him. They didn't have to go for the boys until the afternoon—but she wished he would wake up now.

She wanted to wake him up. She wanted to show him how uninnocent she was. He had been so quick to agree with Corinne, so quick to say that's one of the things he really loved about her, that she was innocent, that he hoped she'd always stay that way. Why?

What was so good about being innocent?

Which she wasn't, anyway. And which he certainly knew, since he had been the first...but before they were married, before he left for the army, they did it. When she was eighteen. Before that she was innocent. She certainly was. He could have done anything he wanted to do to her then, she loved him so much...and still did, of course. Even more....

More now than then. In a bigger way now. In a way that she was sure could only get bigger and bigger because their life would get bigger and bigger, include more and more, more than the few seconds it had taken to fall in love with him. That was just the beginning, the center of it. The center of their lives...falling in love: an eyeblink, in the space of a second, and all the rest of her life spinning around that center, spinning in bigger and bigger circles away from it, that center, that fact, a whole life starting up around it. A husband. Children. A house. Levittown.

"Happy New Year," she whispered to his sleeping figure.

4

Loretta Massi née Kovalic

[1]   "Do you have to yell, Loretta? I'm right here. I'm holding you up."

"That's why I'm yelling. Let go of me. I'm not drunk anymore." She wasn't—but she was yelling. Thank God the girls were in Ozone Park at her mother's, so if she got out of hand . . . but Joe wouldn't get her going that way. Joe wouldn't yell back. He'd turn quiet; he was turning quiet already. He was letting go of her. In a minute he'd go into their bedroom or into the bathroom and lock her out. Or he'd get into their car and drive off to somewhere. She didn't know where. She didn't care where. "So? So now you've got nothing to say to me?"

"Loretta, do me a favor? Okay? Do me a favor and shut it off for now? Three-thirty in the morning? New Year's? Do we have to begin the new one like we left the old one? Huh? How about it? Could we do it different?"

"How? You changed since midnight happened?"

He left the living room, without so much as a "Fuck you," all thirty-five feet of him. Tall, all right, and skin and bones and a wang to match. The tallest Italian man in captivity. Long in the tooth too. The original sad sack.

Thinking bitchy—so she really had had too much to drink. She took a deep breath. She counted to ten. She sat down on their daybed-sofa. She forced herself to concentrate without letting the spinning take over. The room, their living room . . .

Pale green. Ugly. Why had she chosen that color? The organdy tie-backs. Why did she have to put them up? Just because her mother-in-law gave them? Fuck it! Ugly. And the ugly, itchy secondhand maroon mohair chairs, the dim lamplight. Depressing. All of it. Except for her drawings, pen-and-ink drawings of her friends, of Evelyn and Corinne and Rita—those were the best—and the oils, of flowers, still lifes that looked it, still and dead. Maybe that's what she
40

should do next. Art school. She and Joe could split up when the girls got old enough, and she would go to art school then and maybe college and...and she was not going to start crying. Hell no.

She turned off the lamps.

Joe was in bed, but he wasn't sleeping. He wasn't even making believe he was asleep. "When you get into bed, no fights, Loretta. You hear? No fights. We'll start the new year without a fight so maybe this year we can end it that way too. Okay?"

"Okay. I agree. No fights. I'm too tired to fight. And anyway, I'm impressed. That's your longest speech on record." But she laughed so he would be sure she wasn't making fun. First crying, then laughing. She was probably going crazy. That's what it was—but when her head hit the pillow it wasn't crazy she was going, she was going to be sick. Her head kept spinning around inside. Around and around.

She had to sit up. "I'm going to be sick, Joe."

He sat up too, alongside her. He was naked. All thirty-five feet of him. He tried to hold her, but that only made it worse. Her nightgown was even choking her. It was too tight. He helped her take it off. She was ashamed of how she looked, a little tub, a little tub of shit. She was no bargain—and yet he liked her. He was kind to her. He wasn't bad. There was nothing bad about him. He was just...just...boring. She was crying again and she was going to throw up. She was no bargain either. Spinning inside her. Around and around.

She would not be sick. Hell no.

No and no and no.

She rocked back and forth alongside him.

No...but it wouldn't pass away.

She moved fast. Out of bed.

The bathroom, just in time.

Retching. On her knees in front of the commode.

And then Joe was behind her, kneeling behind her, holding her each time she retched forward. "You'll feel better now, Loretta. You'll see. When you're sick, it's the best thing, to throw up. Get it over with. Then you feel better."

Retching, until there was nothing left inside and on her face a silent scream.

He helped her back to bed, helped her back into her nightgown. She felt cold. She wanted to sleep. "Thank you, Joe. Thank you."

"Never mind that. Just have a good night." He tried to

kiss her, but she rolled away. He fell back against his pillow, pulled the blanket up to his neck.

She heard the cold snap of wind at the window—and then the oil burner started up.

She would sleep late.

She would sleep very late, right up until the time they had to go for the girls. And maybe Joe could go for them. She would just go on sleeping until they came back from her mother's.... Oh, sure, Loretta. Dream on, Loretta....

[2] "Oh, sure, Loretta. Just dream on, Loretta," her best girlfriend, Connie Clark, was always saying to her. "You'll dream on so long, Loretta, you won't know which end's up. Joe wants to marry you. So do it or don't...." They were sitting in the Automat on Times Square after the Paramount. They had cut school to go see Frank Sinatra. It was Loretta's idea that morning to cut school and see Sinatra. Connie had to be coaxed into doing it. Connie had to be coaxed into doing most things Loretta wanted to do.

They were seniors in Jamaica High School and Connie was probably going to be picked Most Beautiful. Connie was also intelligent. She wasn't just a dumb blond like they read in the Dorothy Parker story in English. Connie was everything—and also Loretta's best friend. Loretta loved her; she didn't love Joe. "I only like him, Connie. I feel sorry for him, but I certainly don't love him enough to get married to him and he's saying he wants to get married right after he's inducted. That'll be a week after we graduate. And I thought maybe the two of us, you and me, Connie, we could go away and celebrate after graduation. Maybe we could go down to Atlantic City for a few days."

"Oh, sure, Loretta. Just dream on, Loretta." And then, even though it said all around them "No Smoking," Connie lit up a Pall Mall and handed the pack over to Loretta. "Where am I supposed to get money for that? My mother'd scream holy murder before she'd let my father give me money. She'd send for the priest if I ever said I was going away with you and wanted money for that. I told you before, Loretta—so don't get hurt feelings again like you always do—my mother doesn't like me hanging around with you. She says you get me into trouble. And you can't say she's wrong. You do. Like right now. In the middle of Lent having franks and beans in the Automat." And then Connie laughed and pushed her heavy blond hair back from each shoulder,

42

moved her head back and forth so that her hair would hang free.

Miss Most Beautiful of Jamaica High School, June 1942 Graduating Class: Constance Clark. Loretta would see to it the picture in the yearbook was a big one and prominently placed. Loretta was Art Committee chairman. She'd make sure. Why should she marry Joe when she loved Connie more?—whatever that meant!

What the hell did it mean?

What the hell did it mean when Joe felt her up and she let him do it and got no sensation out of it at all, no matter how hot he seemed to get? What was that all about? And why should she have to marry him just because her mother and Mrs. Massi happened to be close friends? What kind of reason was that to get married?

But still, what did it mean to say to yourself: I love Connie? What did she want to do with Connie? Did she want to feel her up and kiss her passionately on the lips?

Yes.

And then what?

"What're you looking at me so funny, Loretta?"

"Was I? I didn't realize it. I was only just admiring you. You must be the most beautiful person I've ever seen in my life, bar none."

"I hate when you talk that way, Loretta. It makes me squeamish.... I think we should start for the subway, Loretta, if we're going to time it right. If I get home after my father does from work, I'm in trouble."

"Connie?"

"What?"

"Connie, what if... what if I was to tell you..."

"Tell me what?"

"What if I was to tell you that I feel ... that I don't really love Joe enough to get married." Loretta looked away. She couldn't go on staring at Connie that way without saying the truth. And it just seemed so wrong to lie to someone you really loved.

But then Connie went on, as if she knew something too, "That's not what you were going to say, Loretta, and I know it. I know it in my bones you were going to say something else entirely. I'm no fool, Loretta. I've known you too long not to know what you're like and how you're always acting around me. You're my best friend, Loretta. If I don't know you by now, I'll never know you, so I feel as if I should be

43

able to say things to you I wouldn't automatically say to anyone else...and vice versa. You should feel that way too. I hope you do, anyway. And so all I'm trying to say is that there's nothing that you could say would shock me into disliking you."

"I don't know what you're talking about, Connie. I just was thinking how I wish we could go to Atlantic City for graduation. That's all."

"Oh, sure, Loretta, Just dream on, Loretta. You'll dream on so long, Loretta, you won't know which end's up. Joe wants to marry you. And so do it or don't...but do it or don't for yourself, not on account of anything pertaining to me. We're always going to be best friends, no matter what. I swear it, Loretta."

[3] After graduation, Connie left for Pennsylvania. Her father had gotten her a job as a counselor in a children's camp up in the Poconos.

Two days after Connie left, Joe was supposed to be inducted into the Navy. He was going to be sent to Norfolk, Virginia, for boot training. Up until the last minute he was still trying to convince Loretta she should marry him. He had taken her out, to the city, to Radio City Music Hall, and then to a Chinese restaurant, Ruby Foo's, on Fifty-second Street. They sat upstairs on a balcony where it was dark, and Joe ordered Manhattans for them.

He was such a good guy and he knew a lot more about how to do things than most guys she knew. He knew the city and he knew his way around a restaurant—and a Chinese restaurant, too. He ordered all the food and he didn't seem embarrassed about anything. There's always something more you get to know about people when you see them in a different setting. Sometimes it changes things to see them that way.

Not the way Joe looked. That wouldn't change. He was always going to look hangdog. Long face. Long nose. Lots of long teeth—but decent. Kind. He liked her. He had even said, that night, he loved her. Maybe it was the Manhattans—they had two of them. Maybe it was that he was leaving the next morning, or that Connie had left the day before—she didn't know what it was exactly, whether it was Ruby Foo's and the darkness or how he got her to laugh on the subway ride home or how he pressed against her on the porch of her house when he was trying to get her to say yes, after boot camp they'd get married. Maybe. Maybe it was a combination of all those
44

things. And more. Many more things she didn't know how to talk about but that she felt as a knot of things, a clump of things strung together, inside herself too. Not just Joe. She felt sad for herself. Sad, that up until then her life had been mostly about being Connie's best friend and double dating with Connie and every one of Connie's new boyfriends and always Joe and herself along for the ride. All the time. And knowing that if it hadn't been for Joe, no one else would have asked her out and then she wouldn't have even gotten to be Connie's friend at all. Let alone her best friend. Who was going to want a Loretta Kovalic? Who was always getting in trouble in school? Who was always fighting with her mother and her two older sisters, who, thank God, were married, about going to church? Who, unlike her sisters, wasn't interested in clothes and jewelry and makeup? Who wasn't interested in anything else but Connie and drawing and looking at pictures and skipping school to go someplace, anywhere, as long as she didn't have to be cooped up all day long? Who would want that kind of person? Who was ever going to want that? She wasn't any bargain. She wasn't exactly ugly. She wasn't exactly beautiful. But she was too fat, and too short. And could she do anything about that? No. Nothing at all.

Still, Joe didn't seem to care. He liked her the way she was. He said so. And that night she liked it that he was tall and could practically lift her to reach his mouth when he kissed her. She liked it that he would be able to take care of her—if she would just shut up and do what she was expected to do, if she would just stop thinking about what she really felt inside, if she would just feel...aroused the way Joe did when he pressed against her and tried to lift her up to him....So, all things considered, she said, "Okay. Sure, Joe. Yes. When you come home on your first leave, we'll get married, war or no war. It's not going to end so soon, so why wait. You're right. About that you're right, Joe. About me, I hope you're right...."

[4] Joe was assigned to North Atlantic duty. Escort for convoys. To protect the supply ships against U-boat attacks. His particular job was ship's medic, which, in one way, was good, because he had to go to an extra school after boot camp, but which also delayed their getting married until the beginning of 1944.

Joe wasn't much of a letter writer.

Neither was Loretta, but she made up for it by sending him drawings, little pen-and-ink drawings of the neighborhood and his parents and her parents and particular places they used to hang out in, like the corner candy store and the grocery his parents owned but wanted to sell because without Joey home to help out they couldn't manage. "Your mother was never in the best of health anyway," Loretta wrote as a caption under her drawing of Joe's mother sitting out in front of the store, in front of the window, inside which Loretta drew the shapes of spaghetti boxes and noodle boxes so realistically, Joe said, he could practically take one out to cook....

The wedding itself was simple. A church service in the Croatian monstrosity that Loretta had spent her life trying to stay out of, it was so ugly. She wore a lacy gown her mother made. Connie Clark was supposed to be her matron of honor, but she wasn't able to leave her husband, who was in the hospital at Fort Sam Houston in Texas. Connie's husband was one of the first men wounded in the Philippines. Loretta got her cousin to stand in for Connie.

Afterwards, there was a reception at the Kovalics', a brief one because Joe and Loretta had to leave for Boston. Joe was going to be shipping out from there, and as it was, they were going to have only one night up there for a honeymoon. She was going to be gone so short a time she didn't even have to quit her job, which was the one thing she would have loved to do. She worked in the accounts-receivable department of a wine company. She hated the job but had stuck with it because it was located on Fifty-seventh Street right opposite the Art Students League. As long as she could take classes there, she would hold on to her miserable job—at least for the duration.

Her duration turned out to be shorter than it was for servicemen: by the end of 1944 she had her first daughter, Angela.

That was the last time she heard from Connie Riley née Clark. Connie sent the baby a pink nylon baby-carriage cover. Loretta wrote back a thank-you and included a drawing of Angela, but Connie never answered.

Whenever Loretta saw Mr. or Mrs. Clark at the Massi grocery store, she would ask after Connie. They never said much more than that she was doing as well as could be expected under the circumstances, the circumstances being that Connie's husband was going to lose sight in both his eyes. They were going to have to stay at Fort Sam Houston for a long while more. The doctors were still trying, but Connie knew it was hopeless.

All the more reason for Connie to answer Loretta's letters. She never did.

5

[1]   When they finally got down to doing something about where they would live, Loretta's idea won: either they moved to Levittown or they split up.

Because anyplace had to be better than living behind the Massis' grocery with all the smells and the mice running around half the night.

But until Levittown came along, it was either going to be behind the store, where they had been since Joe got home, or with her mother and her mother's yelling every day how if Loretta didn't take those poor girls to church on Sundays they'd be lost, "...lost, Loretta. It's a sin you're doing to them."

As she had done all her own life, she refused to take the girls. Never. Even more than ever before, she didn't believe. A God who lets horrors happen? Like concentration camps? Never. And if it wasn't her mother, it wasn't going to be the Massis telling her what to do with her own children.

Joe was always trying to get her to change her mind. Just to keep some peace around the house or in the store. "You think the girls'll care? In a few years they won't remember any church."

That particular argument stuck with her, because it was the first time she'd ever said out loud, yelling it, either we move or we split. Her in-laws were up front in the store taking care. Angela and Maria were napping. Afternoon nap. Their cribs were behind a chintz drapery that separated them from the kitchen. Past the cribs was another piece of chintz separating the cribs from their bedroom. But their bedroom at least had a door you could open, and you could sit on a stoop and look at the little herb garden Mr. Massi had started planting years before back there. They could sit out and be a little private back there too, if her in-laws were taking care of the store. If the girls were napping.

That afternoon Joe had made some coffee for them. He

just wanted to persuade her to give in on this one little thing. "Just to keep some peace around here, Loretta. Until I can get going on my own."

"Your own? Sure. Just go on dreaming, why don't you? You know what's going to happen us, Joe? You're going to keep on working in that lousy store for the rest of your life. I can see it happening. Your mother's going to tell you over and over again how sick she is—"

"Do you have to yell, Loretta? You'll wake the kids."

"I have to yell because otherwise you don't hear me. You don't pay any attention to me. You just walk away and do what you want to do anyway. And what do you mean when you talk about get going on your own? What's that about? You want to go to medical school? You want to become a doctor? Of course. The Navy really trained you for civilian life, really gave you a profession for peacetime. Sure. Now all they have to do is give you the money to go to school, if you could find a school that would accept you. Of course. Easiest thing in the world. Sure. So you want to hear what's going to happen? According to Loretta is going to happen? I'll tell you what, even if you don't want to hear. You're going to sit here behind this grocery store on your ass forever. And when your parents die, you, their only child, their son, you're going to take it over and live happily ever after, and so, therefore, I'm telling you right now, Joe, I'm not. I won't do it. I won't stick with you. You can call in a priest to tell me otherwise. You and your parents and my parents can call in every goddamn priest in the world to try to get me to change my mind or to send my girls to parochial school and to church, and I swear to you right now, as sure as I'm sitting here on this goddamn stoop next to you, I won't do it. And if you don't get a job soon, if you don't go out and get a job soon so we can move out of here, so we can move out of this goddamn neighborhood, I'll go get a job myself and I'll move myself and the girls out of here and out of your life forever."

Joe didn't answer. Joe wouldn't answer. He just kept staring down at his coffeecup, which he had placed between his big feet inside his big loafers, which were on the concrete step of the stoop he had sat on all his life, had sat out there on that stoop and stared out at his father's basil and parsley and oregano, year after year, until the Navy, taking whatever came his way. He didn't care what. Loretta knew that about him. He had told her that, over and over again. As long as he knew Loretta, he was going to be content enough, no matter what he did with his life.

"I don't mean to threaten you, Joe. I'm not blaming you. I don't even want to raise my voice to yell. Maybe some people would actually be happy living this way. Inheriting a good store like this one—but it's not for me, Joe. I can't be cooped up this way. I can't have everything settled in my life already like that. I got lots of things inside me I want to know about. So have you. You just never want to talk about them. Why you don't, I'll never understand. Unless you talk about them, how can I know?... Oh, what's the use. All I'm going to say now is what I said already. I'm not threatening. I'm just warning you. Get a job, Joe. Any kind of job so we can move the hell out of here....Please?"

[2]   Joe did get a job, selling tickets at the Jamaica Station of the Long Island Rail Road.

He also got a GI mortgage and a GI loan and they bought a Levitt house, sight unseen—except for a picture of one in the rental office they went to on Queens Boulevard.

Their house was barn red with white trim.

They were able to move into it before the end of July in 1948.

The nearest neighbors were the Zweigs, Arlene and Max. The Zweig house was green with white trim. Between Loretta and Arlene was a yellow with white trim. It had been sold, Arlene told Loretta that first day, but there was trouble with the water line and so whoever was going to move in had to postpone. They think September. Joe had left for the Jamaica Station and Arlene came by right after breakfast to introduce herself and her Joel and Marvin, who were exactly the same ages as Angela and Maria. They realized almost at once that they were not going to be very close friends. Loretta knew a few words of Yiddish, among them being the word *yenta,* which she was sure Arlene was, because Arlene wanted to know *this* and she wanted to know *that* and she had to let Loretta know Max was a professional, a corporation lawyer— and Loretta said, "How thoughtful of the Levitts that when you look out of the window, the front window, you can't see a straight line of houses. You get a view of sky. They staggered them. Someone there was an artist."

To which Arlene merely nodded, and once again welcomed Loretta to Spring Lane and repeated how if there was anything, anything at all Loretta needed, not to hesitate, just to
50

come and maybe that afternoon they might walk with the children up to the green, to shop for whatever. "You just get yourself unpacked and I'll see you later. By the way, I have a telephone already, so if you want to use it, come over, don't hesitate...."

Arlene wasn't just a *yenta*. She meant to be helpful. She was starved for people to talk to. There weren't very many people nearby, because only those who had bought their houses had moved in. The renters wouldn't be coming until September-October, after the Levitts had had a chance to sell off as many houses as they could.

Loretta didn't care. The one thing she wasn't going to miss for a while was people. She loved the space and quiet more, and behind their house was a mound of dirt the girls enjoyed playing on top of. She didn't care how dirty they got. There was always hot water, and Joe had a great time giving them baths every evening. The main thing was that even if the girls fell, they fell on dirt, not concrete.

Those first few afternoons were about as enjoyable as any time she could remember from her entire life. Even the walks with Arlene and all the children were enjoyable. Every street they turned down, there was that space, and, for Arlene, there were all those people to meet. Some, even Loretta liked. Rita Moskowitz, on Shelter Lane, Loretta liked instantly. Rita was a dark flash of lightning, a bundle of ideas exploding, "Let's do" and "Did you read that article in the *Times?*" and "One of these days take the time to study your deed and learn something interesting."

And there was Corinne Feuerstein, who lived on Spiral Lane—which was a perfect description for Corinne: a coiled spiral. She was a flamer. Hot. Ready. Cynthia Klein was another matter. Cynthia had a Southern accent. Very refined—still and all, Cynthia had to be a pioneer type too. Loretta kept reminding herself of that, because Cynthia was coping too, with the mud and no vacuum cleaner and a shortage of things up at the green, and Cynthia wanted to be helpful. She was trying to get a Melissa Geiger to form some kind of welcoming group. All of them, Melissa—Loretta had met her for only a second—Corinne, Cynthia, they were all neighbors on Spiral Lane.

When Melissa finally formed the Welcoming Committee, she put Loretta on the cleanup subcommittee.

Loretta agreed. She agreed to almost anything that summer and autumn, she felt so free.

So what if Arlene was a *yenta?* So what if Cynthia was a snob? Or if Melissa was forever telling everyone about the beauty of giving and doing for others and being compassionate? There were always Rita and Corinne to talk the truth to, and then there were also Rose Newman and Audrey Halpern and Edna Leventhal and more, and there was the freedom of just walking around and going up to the green or to the turnpike to shop, or taking the kids to the little parks the Levitts were doing with swings and sliding ponds and all the time keeping her eye on the trees: the saplings turning green, tender green colors everywhere, everything beginning. It was all so fantastic, as if for the first time in her life she felt like she had more, not less, of what she had always wanted. She was even starting what she called a visual diary, of her new friends, her new house, the new trees and plantings, of how everything looked at the beginning, everything, even the girls, even Joe—even he looked...new....She was teaching herself to paint with oils for her visual diary....

Even the fact that they barely had enough money to keep their prewar Buick wreck of a car in gas after mortgage and oil and food and clothes and a hundred other bills, even that couldn't dampen her happiness that summer and autumn.

Even Joe preferred sitting out back, watching the girls climb the mound of dirt, to the back stoop in Ozone Park and his father's herb garden.

And when it got dark, Joe would take the girls in for their baths, leaving her to study the sky until the last bit of light drained from it. Those kinds of nights, if Joe pulled at her in bed, she went, sometimes even willingly. Whatever she did that summer and autumn, she did more willingly; even driving in to Ozone Park to see her parents and his parents seemed easier. They all appreciated each other more, now that they weren't tumbling all over the tiny space behind the store and her mother-in-law stopped sighing and complaining about being left alone to die. She would hug and squeeze Angela and Maria until they cried, and then she would make a big fuss over putting five dollars in each girl's palm, no matter how much Joe said, "No, Mama. Don't, Mama."

The girls always turned the money over to Loretta, never to Joe. Loretta had never told them to do that, they just knew who did the shopping. Angela would hand Loretta the five dollars and say, "Mama, buy me." And Maria, watching, would do whatever her sister did.

52

Loretta always told them to say, thank you. "Thank Grandma, girls."

Loretta saved as much of that money as she could. When she had saved enough for a set of oils, she was going to buy it and a how-to book and maybe a small easel. She could set the easel up in the back, afternoons, when the light was good. She might even set it up behind the house next door, the yellow house with white trim—at least until it was occupied—that way Arlene might not be so quick to find her, to force her into her house to see a new something that Max had just bought for her, a gold or silver or brass ugliness that meant absolutely nothing, nothing at all. Loretta had no desire for anything in her house that had no personal meaning. Her house had plants and her drawings and some photographs of herself and Joe and the girls. Even their furniture was hand-me-down, from Joe's parents, from her parents. She wanted their lives to be theirs, to belong to them, to be no one else's idea of what they should have or buy or be. Levittown had set them all free.... Well, not quite all, Rita would point out, when she and Loretta and the girls and Rita's Mark and Corinne and her Gregory went out walking. "Not quite all of us are free to live in Levittown."

Loretta agreed, of course.

Loretta listened. She wasn't ready to do anything about it yet, she told Rita. "I want to enjoy things here for a few months more and then I'll fight. I swear, Rita. I'll fight in the streets like the guerrillas did in Yugoslavia."

"Ditto for me," Corinne said. "But in Israel. Now that there's finally an Israel."

The three of them were inseparable that summer and on into September. They were inseparable until Evelyn and Harold Selden moved into the yellow house with the white trim between the Massis' and the Zweigs'.

[3]   And then they were four inseparables: Evelyn fit right in. And then eight. Ten. A dozen. But when the number reached that high, it became two all over again: Evelyn and Loretta. Loretta hadn't felt that close to anyone since Connie Clark.

Evelyn and Connie didn't look anything alike. Evelyn had dark hair and a pretty face, round, with one dimple, and her teeth protruded a little, not too much. There was a fullness about her, and a warmth, an openness. She listened and she talked, and she seemed to gather you into her life. When she

53

understood what someone was saying, when she understood how someone felt, only then she would say something. She never butted in like Cynthia was always doing, always impatient. So was Rita sometimes. Not Evelyn. Evelyn was steady. Evelyn could hear the hardest things without blinking. Loretta would find herself talking about how she dreamed of becoming a painter someday, of going to art school in the future, maybe when the girls got a little older she would, she was saving up for it—and Evelyn would sit there in Loretta's kitchen, sipping tea, listening, absorbed, making Loretta feel as if she were talking about the most important things in the world, like a cure for cancer or something. And when Loretta would finish arranging the details of her dream, Evelyn would say something like, "I really envy you that you can draw. That's the kind of talent you can see the results. I always thought maybe someday I'd like to teach school, do something worthwhile, give something back to people. But maybe I don't have any talent for it. Maybe there'll never be time for me to find out . . . or to go to school after the boys are older—but at least you can always be painting. That's a real advantage. . . ."

They weren't exclusive friends. The real truth was that Evelyn Selden was one of those people other people love to be near. Rita did. So did Corinne and Sally. Arlene too. And Cynthia and Missy Geiger. The ladies were always dropping in next door at Evelyn's. Loretta was happy to live so close.

[4] Levittown Ladies Against Discrimination had an active membership of ten by the time Calvin and Maryellen Rogers and their two daughters were ready to move out there.

Most of the ladies volunteered to do something to help the Rogerses, if it came down to welcoming afterwards, but Rita, Evelyn, and Loretta were the only three of the ten who were actually willing to wait with the Rogerses for their moving van to arrive at their house on Division Avenue.

Admittedly—Loretta was persuaded to admit it by Evelyn—Saturday morning was not the easiest time for any of the ladies to drop everything else they had to do and to go and wait, for how long no one knew for sure. Still—and on this point Evelyn couldn't have agreed with Loretta more—exceptional events demand exceptional efforts, even sacrifices, if it came to that. If Loretta could send the girls in to Ozone Park with Joe to the Massis' before he went to work, if Evelyn was able to persuade Harold to take the boys into

54

Brooklyn when all week long Harold had been driving all over the Island, Westchester, New Jersey, if Rita and Abe Moskowitz could put themselves on the line the way they had—Abe was actually there with them, so was little Mark; he was playing with the two Rogers girls on the floor of the empty living room—if they could do all that, then why couldn't Corinne just tell Lionel to entertain his own mother and father for a few hours? And why couldn't Sally Plotkin bring Penny with her that morning instead of taking her to a dancing lesson? And couldn't Audrey Halpern leave her Deborah alone with the chickenpox? And Edna Leventhal? For once maybe Edna had to tell herself that the best intentions in the world couldn't make up for a failure to act now? And Ruby Rabinowitz the same thing? Everyone got afraid, but maybe the time had come for women like themselves to stop wishing for things to get better. They had to do something for themselves about making them better. Evelyn had made that speech at their strategy meeting—and look what had happened. Loretta thought it was an insult. At least Ina Silverstein had an excuse. An official sickness like pneumonia was certainly an excuse in Loretta's book. Not Missy Geiger's excuse. As far as Loretta was concerned, Mahatma Gandhi's passive resistance might be great for India but it wasn't going to work in Levittown. Loretta thought that was just plain bullshit—and she had said so, to Missy's face. Missy had just smiled and stroked her gold cross. At any rate, as Evelyn had also pointed out to Loretta, Missy had offered to come over to the Rogerses', with Carl and the children, after the van had been unloaded, after she was sure there would be no violence, and then to help. Cynthia, who wasn't a member of LLAD, but who was chairman of the Welcoming Committee, was going to be out of town that weekend, very conveniently, Loretta felt. "You're always willing to see good in people," Loretta had said to Evelyn on their way home from the strategy meeting at Rita's. "If I start out only seeing bad, it gets too depressing too fast, Loretta...."

So they waited there, Calvin and Maryellen Rogers, Evelyn, Rita, Loretta—Abe was inside with the two little girls and his Mark—in front of the house. The Rogerses' house, leased in the name of Abe and Rita Moskowitz, had one of those short two-stile fences meant to hide the side entrance. "It might someday," Calvin Rogers said, "if they ever give me the chance to train some ivy to grow through it and around."

It was ten o'clock. A perfect kind of late-March morning, the kind Loretta felt could surprise you. It was windy and cold one minute, sunny and warmer the next, warm enough for you to think it was going to be spring any minute—and then the wind gusted and you were glad you still had on your muffler. Loretta wished she could learn how to paint that kind of idea, to think something and turn it into the look on a face, an expression of one sensation overtaking another—and then receding, not disappearing altogether, never really disappearing altogether, like winter giving in to spring, and spring overtaking summer. For a while. Only for a while. A season. A time. On Calvin Rogers' face there was, just then, something of what she felt, what she meant, being afraid, but also being determined, determination overtaking his fear. He hoped for the best, but he was worried, and the worry wouldn't disappear altogether. Not for long it didn't. Not from his eyes. His eyelids kept quivering as he scanned the people collecting in one group, then another group, across the street. Just the eyelids. The rest of his face was set, hard, a dark brown square-jawed shield of a face that matched his broad-boned body. He was ready to take on anyone who wanted to try.

Loretta felt her fear in a different way, like a flickering, like the one dimple in Evelyn's flickering smile. On. Off. On again. Evelyn was frightened too. They all were. Which was some consolation. And they all stood their ground next to Maryellen Rogers, who might just need some protection. She was a little wisp of a woman, even smaller than Rita, who stood on one side of her; Evelyn was on the other side. They were as ready as they were going to be.

By eleven o'clock the groups across the street had grown larger. Up and down each side of the street twos and threes and fours talked together, pointing at them, wagging fingers at them.

And then the moving van arrived: Home Sweet Home Moving and Storage. Loretta, all the others following, followed Calvin down to the curb. They walked slowly, trying for a naturalness no one felt.

But there was nothing natural in the movement of a man who broke away from the largest group directly across the street. A big man, and for a man so big, he moved fast. The proverbial fat man. Fast on his feet. A dancer. He was talking to the driver of the van, a white man, before Calvin was able to reach them.

They all heard, "...a Mr. Rogers hired us." And then the driver and two workmen, one white, one black, got down from the cab of the truck and Calvin extended a hand to the man from across the street. "I'm Mr. Rogers. Calvin Rogers. We've rented."

But the man from across the street ignored Calvin's hand. He moved just as quickly back, back to where his group waited, to where, when he reached them, the twos and threes and fours began to move together. They were about twenty, Loretta estimated, but their number was sure to grow. As soon as the men from Home Sweet Home began to open the side of the van, ten more appeared from a side street.

And they were only five, not counting the workmen, who, the driver was saying to Cal, "...just want to do our job, mister. Without any trouble. We got nothing to do with what goes on here. We'll start, and we'll see."

By then Abe had joined them. He had left the children inside. "Should I call the police, Cal?"

The question unfroze them. Rita and Evelyn said no.

So did Cal. "Not yet, anyway.... Why don't you bring the kids outside. In front of the house. Maybe if they see the kids playing, they'll calm down."

Maryellen moved to her husband's side. Determined too, and worried. Worried more than determined, now Loretta could see. And with good reason. The girls and Mark were outside now. The sight of them together only angered the crowd across the street more. The fat man was pointing. And if Loretta could hear "Nigger" repeated like a chorus, certainly the Rogerses could. "I think you should call the police," and Loretta also felt it should be sooner, not later. She was hoping Evelyn and Rita would agree.

But they didn't. They had gone to the side of the van to look inside it, to see just how much there was to unload.

Not much. The Rogerses were moving with very little. Like all of them had done when they moved to Levittown. Start out with little and build new. Start out with beds and dishes and pots and maybe a sofa. Just what's essential—and hope for the best.

The man from across the street was on his way back. But he avoided Cal and Maryellen. He headed for Rita and Evelyn. Loretta moved to join them. "You did it, didn't you? And you think you're going to get away with it, don't you?"

"Did what?" Rita asked, under control, but shaky. "What did we do, Mr....? Did you say your name?"

"None of your goddamn business my name. The renting guy's coming down here. We called him. And the police too. So we'll see what's what."

"What's what is"—Rita unfolded a piece of paper she had been holding in her hand "—that I have a lease here signed by the renting agent, myself, and my husband."

"So how come niggers are moving in here?"

"They're our guests. Mr. and Mrs. Rogers and their two daughters. Negroes. Not niggers."

He turned with that, started away. "Goddamn kikes. How come Hitler didn't get you all!"

He was fast on his feet, faster than Cal Rogers' reaction, which, when it came, was to go after him.

But Maryellen, little Maryellen, held him back. Then Abe did.

And by then the police had arrived.

So did a representative from the Levitt office. So did a reporter from the Levittown *Tribune*. Evelyn knew him from an interview he had done of her: Mrs. New Levittowner. Evelyn filled him in on what was what.

The police stayed on the other side of the street.

The Levitt agent began arguing with Rita and Abe. "...illegal. Absolutely illegal. They will not be able to stay here. Are they going to pay rent to someone? Are they going to pay rent to you? The lease says you cannot sublet. It says it in black and white. You're breaking the law."

Meanwhile, the workmen from Home Sweet Home continued to unload the van.

Loretta went to the children. They were frightened. She sat down on the ground with them. She hugged them all close to her. She was probably going to start crying, and she knew she had better not, not if she was going to be of any help to anyone.

Evelyn wasn't crying. Rita wasn't.

And then she saw Corinne getting out of her Kaiser. She had parked it across the street just behind a police car. She was done up in one of her reddest plaid coats with red slacks and a red scarf dangling down from her neck. She just very calmly crossed the street, walked right over to the Rogerses, welcoming them to Levittown. "As a member of the Ladies of Levittown Against Discrimination, I want to welcome you. I'm sorry I couldn't get here sooner." She didn't just say it, she screamed it, like a banner, a challenge flung into a sudden gust of wind.

She took her place next to Evelyn and Rita. She was ready.

And next, who should appear but Missy and Carl Geiger, and with their three kids—Teresa, the youngest, in Missy's arms, Donald and Adam holding on to Carl's hands, skipping along on either side of him. Carl looked like a center pole, tall and straight, but with hair, black, wavy hair, blowing every which way in the wind. A sketch. It was going to turn into some kind of a sketch, because the people from across the street weren't going to attack women and children, were they?

"Very smart, Mr. Moskowitz," the Levitt agent was saying. "But it won't be smart enough when you get to court. Then we'll see."

And from across the street, from behind a police car with its two policemen standing outside it, standing, arms folded, staring across at the Rogers house, came the chorus of "nigger" and "kike," "nigger" and "kike," and something in between, which Loretta didn't strain to hear. She didn't want to. She didn't want the children to hear it either. She tried to smother them with hugs, to smother the shouting beneath their laughter as she rocked them back and forth, the two Rogers girls and Mark Moskowitz and then Donald and Adam Geiger who ran to join them—"London Bridge is falling down," for as long as she could, "...my fair lady...." Rocking and laughing...and crying.

[5]   The pieces of furniture came out of the truck, went past them into the house. A few big pieces. Mostly odds and ends. Some clothes. Some books. Some pictures, photographs, framed, tied in a bundle. It didn't take all that long to unload the truck. A little longer, though, than her load of things, Loretta remembered.

Missy, acting in her capacity as co-chairman of the Welcoming Committee, was putting some kind of lunch together inside, with the newly arrived help of Audrey Halpern and Edna Leventhal. Edna, who had more compassion in one of her pudgy fingers than most people thought about in a lifetime, came in crying, kept on crying during the continuing chant still coming from across the street; even though they had all gone inside by then, the members of the chorus had not disbanded. If anything, it had gotten bigger and louder. Another police car was out there—doing nothing but keeping the peace. Edna was afraid. She was finding it hard to smear a piece of Wonder bread with mayonnaise. "There won't be any violence," Missy reassured her—and herself. "The police will not let that happen."

"Don't count on that." Corinne shot straight from the shoulder. Her shoulder was next to Edna's. She was working with peanut butter and jelly and she kind of bumped Edna affectionately. "Count on me, Edna. If they storm the barricades, I'll watch out for you."

"Please, Corinne, the children." Missy was not amused, even though her Mahatma Gandhi smile never once flickered or otherwise gave the slightest evidence of flickering. Loretta couldn't think of a time when that smile wasn't in evidence— so it didn't mean she wasn't nervous like the rest of them. They all were. Loretta was more than willing to admit she herself was, if anyone should ask.

So was Evelyn, but Evelyn wasn't standing still. She was moving back and forth. She was doing...something, anything. Unpacking. Helping Maryellen. Maryellen was the most nervous. Maryellen was going to have to go on living in this house when the rest of them left it. And for neighbors, look who she had to turn to for comfort and human contact! So Evelyn was trying to keep things moving along, while Abe and Calvin and Carl set up beds and put chairs in some sort of order in the living room, where the children played cards on the floor, underfoot but protected. And out in the kitchen Missy and her committee got lunch together and Missy talked herself into believing there would be no violence, "...absolutely none. The law is the law."

"Just go on dreaming, Missy."

"Loretta, please! Can't you see that kind of talk won't help?"

"Neither will yours."

"Loretta!" from Evelyn, passing through. "Not now. At our next meeting." And, coming from Evelyn, Loretta accepted the request. From Evelyn she took it. She spread the butter smoother on the rye bread. Coming from Missy, a reasonable request became an order. From on high. From Miss Madonna Compassion of Levittown. That was Melissa Geiger. But Evelyn was the genuine article. Evelyn was the real McCoy. Evelyn was a human being acting humanly, reacting humanly to a situation and a principle she felt strongly about. The trouble with Missy was she was too much an actress. Always acting a part. Evelyn never did. Neither did Rita. Corinne did, though. Corinne was always wearing some kind of costume, acting out some kind of part...so, how come from
60

Corinne it was all right and from Missy it wasn't? How come Missy's orders she resented but not Corinne's? Not Evelyn's? She passed the pile of buttered rye bread on to Audrey, who proceeded silently to spread each piece with tuna-fish salad. Audrey Halpern's famous tuna-fish salad! Loretta loved it from before, from when they had first met last July, from before Audrey's Deborah had chickenpox and her husband, Marvin, had had his minor heart attack. "How is Deborah doing, Audrey?"

"A few less pox. I put gloves on her so she wouldn't scratch. Scratch a pox, I told her, and you leave a mark for life."

How come for Audrey she'd do almost anything? And for Edna too? Not that either of them would ever ask for anything. They *did* for others. They were doers. So was she, for that matter. She followed where others led her—but not everyone could lead her. That was true. That was something. Not much, but something.

How much?

How much? and How Come? and What Was She Worth?

If she were to add up all those kinds of questions she had asked herself for all of her twenty-five years, she would have put together the biggest pile of dumbness anywhere on the face of the earth. She didn't know anything. She didn't know anything about herself or about the people closest to her or about how people like the Rogerses, and who knew how many more, millions, could stand to hear "nigger," "kike," over and over again without going crazy or killing someone. She wished the girls were with her. She wished they could be there to remember what some people had to face. They weren't going to have to face anything like this. They were Christians. White Christians. Like herself. Like Missy Geiger. Like Donald and Adam and Teresa...only that wasn't exactly true. If Carl was Jewish and Missy was Catholic, what did it make Donald and Adam and Teresa Geiger? What did it make them to the people across the street who wouldn't go away and wouldn't stop shouting?

Wouldn't they ever go away?

Wouldn't the police ever make them go away?

Because Calvin and Maryellen Rogers and their two daughters, Bethann and Serena, were going to be left alone in their new house on Division Avenue in Levittown, on Long Island, in the state of New York. Soon. Alone. The four of them. And if there was any trouble and if they called the police, what would happen then?

Everyone had a sandwich. Everyone had something to drink. The adults stood around the circle of children seated on the floor. "It's a party, Mommy," little Teresa screamed, clapping her hands for joy, "a party."

Loretta turned to stare out the window.

Across the street the chorus had grown in number.

Won't they ever go away?

Won't they ever leave anyone alone?

6

Melissa Geiger née Riordan

[1] "Especially us, Carl. We have to go over there. The Rogerses have two little girls. Rita will have Mark with her. If
we take ours, not even the worst kind of bigot will do anything violent when there are children involved. Don't you
agree about that, Carl? At least that much."

He didn't, obviously, because he wouldn't let her kiss him.
He sucked on his pipe, turned his head away as she leaned
over his chair—and only then he gave in, after teasing her.
"Okay. Have it your way for a change." He removed his pipe,
set it down carefully in the ashtray on the marble-topped end
table, opened his arms for her to fall inside of. She obeyed.
She always did what he wanted—after she had persuaded
him to want what she wanted. Her big baby! He *was* a big
baby.

And nothing at all was going to happen at the Rogerses.
She had reasoned it out for him all morning. She would never
risk the safety of the children if she thought there was any
possibility of trouble. Would she? But if he was so concerned,
why didn't he come along too? He could protect them then?
He could also act on a principle. Didn't he believe in equality
too? For everyone?

He did. Of course he did. So . . . he had to give in.

He would dress the boys.

She would get Teresa ready. Teresa was about to get up
from her morning nap anyway. It would be good for the children to be a part of what was going on at the Rogerses. It
was important. They may be young now, but they'll remember it years from now—that was the way she dealt with her
husband, telling him things like that. She appealed to his
best instincts. She always had. She always won her point,
too. Right from the beginning. On their first date, telling him
to meet her in front of the movie, not to try to come to pick
her up at her house, to do it her way because it was going

to be important. She knew it was going to be. She just felt it was. She had been right then. She'd be right now too.

She zipped Teresa into her snowsuit. She pulled the strings for the hood tight. It would be windy outside and they should walk to the Rogerses. The walk would do them good. It was such a beautiful day for a walk.

Their house was barn red with white trim. On Spiral Lane.

Carl had the boys outside. The carriage was all prepared, the quilt pulled back. He offered to push it. It would be something of a walk over to Division Avenue.

"No. I'll push. You take care of the boys."

Donald and Adam attached themselves to Carl's hands. They skipped along on either side.

"Almost spring, Carl."

"Beautiful. I hope it stays that way."

Some of the trees had buds and even the lawns looked like they might make it into green by summer. At least patches did. Hard to tell, because how could anyone keep the children from running and playing all over them? Impossible—but eventually, even the lawns would take. And the trees. And the shrubs and flowers people planted all around their houses would grow and bloom. Like the jonquils. Some houses actually had jonquils coming through already. Or did they just set them out there in bloom? "Jonquils are bulbs, aren't they, Carl?"

He thought so. He didn't know for sure. "No one knew one flower from another in Washington Heights. You know that. We were all going to be scientists. Remember?"

She remembered. She certainly, most assuredly, did remember.

Adam was tired. Adam wanted to be carried. He was three. Donald was four. Teresa was almost a year old. "You want to sit in the carriage with Teresa?" He did, but then the carriage was too heavy to push. Carl took over. She took hold of Donald's hand.

Then Donald was tired. ". . . no, I will not carry you. You can walk. We're almost there."

"Listen to what your mother says, Donald. No acting up. Do you hear?"

He heard. He obeyed. When Carl issued an order, it was clear he meant it. Army training. First sergeant. Infantry. She never could understand how such a sensitive, intelligent Jewish man could have become an infantry first sergeant. It was hard for her to imagine him in battle. If it hadn't

64

happened, she wouldn't believe it still. Except there was the scar. On his leg. Maybe they shouldn't have walked. "Is your leg all right, Carl? You're not tired?"

"You want to carry me?" Even his laugh was quiet. More a murmur with the hint of a smile.

"We're almost there. Another block." She joined him at the carriage. Donald was skipping again. Donald was like his father. Tall for his age, with shiny, slippery black hair that fell all over his forehead just like Carl's, especially when the wind gusted. And thin like Carl. For as long as she had known Carl, his look was gaunt. Like Abraham Lincoln with a better nose. Solemn too. Glum a lot, since the war.

When they turned into Division Avenue, they stopped. By then the police cars had arrived. Workmen were emptying the moving van. She could hear the shouting. She could hear the words. Disgusting. Repulsive. "Why do people have to be like that, Carl? Why?"

He said nothing. They crossed the street so that they would be on the side of the Rogerses house when they got closer.

"The police won't let anything happen, Carl. And the children being here..." But suddenly she wasn't so certain. Police or no police. And what she couldn't stand most of all in the world was any kind of violence. Donald kept skipping along, tugging at her hand, humming a song to himself, a numbers song, counting. She squeezed his hand. She bent down to kiss him. So much like his father. He'll be the scientist Carl should have been....

[2] Later that afternoon, after the cleanup committee had cleaned up and some of the children were napping and some of the others were just leaning and lolling against their parents, Missy thought that maybe the time had come for all of them to take the next step.

The crowd across the street had thinned. There was only one police car. Rita, as head of LLAD, had thought out a plan for the entire day. Everyone would leave, except Abe. She would take Mark home for a while, collect food for a dinner and sleeping things, and then she and Abe and Mark would spend the night here.

Evelyn said she could too. She would get Harold to come back to stay too. The boys would be in Brooklyn at her mother's, overnight anyway. She had arranged it that way.

Loretta would do exactly the same thing, although she

65

wasn't sure she could get Joe to come back with her. "He's on our side, I guess, only he's not very active about things."

"You'll persuade him, Loretta, if anyone can." But Missy knew better. And she hated herself for saying things like that that she didn't really mean. She said them to Loretta all the time. Just for the sake of trying to say something nice to Loretta. Loretta saw through it, too. Loretta thought she was a phony. Loretta didn't want to be treated in any special way by Missy just because they were the only two Catholics in their group of friends. No, Loretta wasn't a hypocrite—but neither was she. Hadn't she gotten Carl to come with her? Out of principle?

It was Calvin Rogers who decided what would happen next. It was certainly his right to decide. He thought everyone should leave and get on with what they each had to do, "...because sooner or later we're going to have to be left here by ourselves. If those people rush us, I'll just call the police. I've got the telephone. I can also call you, Abe. It's time to see what's what. And I—we—can't tell you enough how much we appreciate what you've done for us. But enough is enough. We're grown-up people. We can take care... if they'll let us. If they won't, well, then we'll see what comes next."

Maryellen said she and Cal would do everything in their power to see this thing out, "...but the one thing I won't let happen is if our girls are threatened in any way. Ourselves...we're used to it. America raises us that way. But since the war, since Cal came home...I thought maybe something would have changed. Just maybe, I thought...because hating takes a lot out of a person...."

They all left together, Rita insisting she and Abe would come back later with dinner things. "Abe and I got you into this, so we have some kind of responsibility for seeing it through with you."

[3]   Rita and Abe drove Evelyn and Loretta home.

Corinne drove Audrey and Edna.

Missy and Carl wanted to, were glad to, walk back. Adam and Teresa fell asleep in the carriage. Carl carried Donald. Donald fell asleep in his arms.

It was dusk when they reached Spiral Lane. Lights were on in every kitchen. Only parked cars in the streets.

She looked up at the sky before stepping through the side entrance. Still clear. Stars. And an almost full moon. A beautiful evening.

66

After the children were put to bed, she'd make a special dinner for the two of them. She had splurged on some of that beautiful pink veal, and she would make the rice dish he liked so much, the one with the mushrooms. And salad. There was some pie left over for dessert.

He took the boys right into the bathroom, started running the bathwater.

She got to work with Teresa.

Later they could be together quietly, over dinner, and, later, after dinner, in bed together, and in the morning she would let him sleep as long as he wanted to. She would go to early Mass and pray, pray, pray for the Rogerses to be left in peace. It would all be okay. It would all work out. Everything would get better and better.

In their own life too. Better and better. With her mother and father. With his mother and father.

Better and better. Slowly. One step at a time. With love. With understanding. Because she was tired of all that hating too. Just like Maryellen Rogers. Only it wasn't exactly the same thing. No. Not quite. Maryellen was always going to be a Negro. She would always...stand out.

7

[1]   She made it to St. Bernard's in time for the eight o'clock Mass. The children had behaved. Carl was still sleeping when they left. This Sunday had begun well....And on the way home she would stop for the *Times* and the *News*...."Donald, you must sit still. Ssh...."

The priest had turned away from the congregation. He knelt before the altar. A young priest.

In a young town...but with the oldest hope...some peace, she prayed. Some peace for a while. Sweet Jesus, some calm for a while. Some quiet in everyone's life for a long, long while....

Teresa stared up at her, smiling, content on her lap. Teresa of the pale blond hair and blue eyes. Teresa was Riordan through and through. Not a Rachel, which Carl had wanted to name her. After an aunt he had particularly liked, an aunt who had died just before their marriage....Teresa Geiger. Donald Geiger. Adam Geiger. Her choice. Then Carl's. Then hers....

Donald on one side of her. Adam on the other, the dark, the light, they drowsed against her, bored, yet well-behaved. Such good boys.

"*Christe eleison,*" the priest mumbled nervously. "*Kyrie eleison...*"

If she tried to take Communion this morning, how would she manage it? She'd better stir them—or better let them drowse. They're quiet. She'd wait until the following Sunday. She'd go to a later Mass. She'd take only Teresa with her. The following Sunday...It stuck in her head, the following Sunday...something about it? The following Sunday was Palm Sunday. That was it, of course, and she had promised her mother and father to bring Carl and the children to their church in Rockville Centre.

Why did she make promises like that?

She didn't have the right to do that without first asking

Carl. Even though she knew he'd do it, she didn't have the right. What if it was Passover too? What then? Sometimes they came out together. One year, the first year after Donald was born, their seder had been on a Palm Sunday. She remembered.

She'd like to forget that one. Carl's mother and father told her they would never forgive her. They would never stop seeing her—for Carl's sake, for the child's sake—but love her? her father-in-law had said, never! Not with that kind of attitude. With him it wasn't even a religious matter. She knew that. Had he interfered when Carl said he was going to marry a Catholic girl? Never. He didn't care. His wife, maybe. Not him. For him what it was, was a human-being matter. The least she could have done was to pick up the telephone and tell us, I'm sorry, it's also Palm Sunday, we have to go to my folks'. But no. Nothing. "You think Jesus Christ is so important?" he had said to her, in person, the next night at the second seder, with Carl's sister and husband and his brother and his wife and their children, all of them, seated there around the huge dining-room table. "So if he's so important, then at least you could practice a little of what he preached."

And Carl had said nothing in her defense.

He didn't think she had any.

She didn't. She admitted it. She would change. She promised him she would change. Oh, she remembered that evening. She'd like to forget it. But she remembered *that*. She remembered that and more. A lot more. And not all of it did she want to forget. Some she hoped she would remember forever. Some she certainly, most assuredly, hoped she would remember forever, especially how she'd met Carl....

[2] He was getting off his school bus at exactly the same time she was getting off hers. The buses had parked so that the doors were opposite each other. They stepped down. It was fated. It had to be, because they both kind of stumbled, for no reason, and their arms kind of grazed each other's, and he reached out to steady her, to ask if she was all right, standing there over her, opening his eyes wider, staring at her, and all she could do was just stare back—until Sister Margaret nudged her, whispering loudly, "Start moving. Catch up with the others, Melissa."

Her class, juniors at Our Lady of Sorrows High School in Rockville Centre, was visiting the World's Fair.

So was his senior class from Bronx High School of Science. June 1939.

That kind of day she never wanted to forget.

Somehow, no matter what building her class went to visit, his class did too. Every time she turned around, he'd be standing there, staring at her.

In the Steinmetz Hall of Science, with all that manmade lightning flashing across the darkened ceiling of the building, from one end to the other, flashing and sizzling and cracking light, he had somehow managed to sit right behind her. She jumped when the light crashed into sound. He leaned forward, telling her not to be afraid of it—or of him. And then he asked where she lived and was it possible he could maybe phone her and maybe they could have a date.

After her yes he had gone on to say that science, after her, now, interested him most of all. He was hoping to go on to City College, School of Technology. But he hadn't heard yet about being accepted. He'd taken the test, but he hadn't heard. His grades weren't great enough, and if he didn't make it into City, he wasn't sure what would happen to him—and then the manmade lightning was over and the nuns were getting the girls up and moving, and she asked him if he was Catholic.

No; his lips formed the no, but no sound came out of them. He never had time that day to say what he was.

And when his teacher led the class into the Russian exhibit, her class didn't follow.

He caught up with her at the Italian pavilion, but not for a long enough time even to say, "Jewish."

When her class returned to its bus, his had already left.

She prayed he would call. All the way out to Rockville Centre she prayed. She said her rosary and she thought about how beautiful he looked. Not perfect. He wasn't perfectly beautiful, and he was different from any of the boys she had dated from Rockville Centre. He had a somber, dark look. Her opposite. The dark and light. Together.

He had to call. He just had to.

[3] From their very first date, the only thing that worked out well was their being together. She wouldn't let him come to her house. She was afraid. Her father had a terrible temper. She'd never forgive herself if anything happened to Carl, if he was hurt in any way, hurt inside, she meant. Later on, when they got to know each other better, they could decide

how to handle it. Couldn't they just go out on a few dates and see how it went? She didn't mind meeting him in the city. She just had to take the train in to Penn Station. It was easy. They could meet there. Or in front of the movie house. It was perfectly all right with her. She just told her parents she was staying over at her girlfriend's.

Carl had gone to work for his father, for the summer, just for the summer, he hoped, because in the fall there would be school, although he was beginning to worry about that, because if he hadn't heard by then... well, it wasn't a good sign. She was, though. She was the best sign he'd had in his life so far, he told her.

Her father had gotten her a summer job too. In the city, with New York Life Insurance, a filing job. The first job she'd ever had. The first summer she hadn't been sent to camp. She had refused to go away; even before she'd met Carl, she had refused—and how happy she was she had. It was fated that she should have refused going to camp that summer. She felt it in her bones that it was. She loved Carl, and no matter what happened, she wasn't going to be forced to stop seeing him. She'd kill herself if she was forced to do that.

A lot of evenings after work they would meet and eat at the Automat and then just walk around the city. They walked everywhere. All the way up Fifth Avenue. All the way down to Washington Square. And in Central Park. And Times Square. Up and down Park Avenue and Madison Avenue and to Rockefeller Center, where they could sit on the low marble wall that went all around the perimeter of what was in winter an ice-skating rink and in the summer a restaurant with the statue of Prometheus gushing water. It was so beautiful. She had read up on Prometheus in a mythology book. She told him the story of the fire and how Prometheus had the courage of his convictions....

And he told her how he felt about her. He was absolutely certain how he felt about her. So what if they were so young? He was going to go to college and become a scientist, and she would get a job, and eventually they could get married, no matter what their parents said. His parents would be all right, though. He felt certain about that. His father didn't care about anything religious. He just did things for Carl's mother. "And even my mother doesn't care that much. She does it for my grandmother's sake. My father's a reasonable man. Easygoing. He wants me to take over the business. My older brother doesn't want it. But neither do I. I'm just not

71

interested in women's blouses, although I like the one you're wearing all right...." She was sitting on the marble wall; he was in front of her, and he kissed her and said that he was absolutely certain he loved her. She was so delicate and pretty, and he'd never met anyone like her before.

She felt the same about him. She was absolutely certain she loved him too, and would, no matter what. She smoothed his hair back from his forehead; instantly it slipped back. She would never forget that kind of night, absolutely never. How his hair was and his dark long lean face and his almost perfect nose. Almost. It had the littlest bump at the very point of it, a little pimple of a bump, hardly noticeable unless you were up close, which she was and wanted to be, forever and ever.

[4] His not getting into City College that year was the first upset. He continued working for his father. She still had her senior year at Our Lady of Sorrows anyway. He was going to take some courses at night school, at City College, some English courses maybe, because that's what they told him he was weak in.

The next upset was that her father found out, through her best girlfriend, that the guy Missy was dating was not only not Catholic, he was a Jew, and that her girlfriend thought it was her duty to tell Mr. Riordan the truth, because it was weighing on her conscience and the priest told her at confession it was a sin for her not to tell him, so she just had to. Her girlfriend, Valerie, at least had the common decency to tell Missy what she had done so that when Missy went home that day from school she could prepare herself to face her father when he got home from the office.

It was horrible. Her mother and her three younger sisters and her brother all had to be present when her father forbade and forbade and forbade, and if she so much as spoke to her...her Jewish friend on the telephone, he was going to send her upstate to his mother's in Rochester, and did she understand?

She understood, but she was also going on to tell him, right then and there, nothing was going to stop her from seeing Carl Geiger, no matter what her father did to her, she would see him because eventually she was going to marry him, even if he and her mother disowned her. She didn't care because she loved him and he was one of the most marvelous people on the face of the earth. Couldn't he understand that Jews had a right to live too?

He could. Indeed he could—but not with his daughter. So she had better put that into her head and remember it.

She would. She would always remember it. And it would hurt her, because she was going to have to disobey him, and that would hurt most of all, because when had she ever disobeyed him? Never. So he had to realize that this was a different matter altogether. It was.

Indeed. He knew it was, and that was why he absolutely forbade... And had she confessed any of what she had done? Had she?

No. She had not. What would have been the point? How was she supposed to stop feeling what she felt just because a priest told her she had to?

So that's all going to church is for you? Being told to stop doing something you want to do? That's what Jesus means to you?

Her mother had started to cry. Her father was waiting, waiting for her to break down too. To cry. To ask to be forgiven. To apologize for loving someone.

No. She would not. She would not cry. She would remain quiet and calm and show him and her mother and her sisters and brother that she felt something so deeply and completely and beautifully, felt it without any shame—she had done nothing to feel ashamed of—felt it in a way that made her also feel so happy to be alive and so peaceful. It *was* like a peace that passeth understanding, and it was the first time in her life she had ever felt that way. After all those years of going to church, after all those years at Our Lady of Sorrows, finally she felt at peace because she felt love for someone real, someone she could touch, someone she would do anything for... when the time came for that. And it would. It had too. No matter what else she might have to give up.

Her father was waiting.

[5]   And was still waiting.

So, too, just then, was the priest. He was waiting for some commotion at the back of the church to subside. He was angry, offended. She couldn't turn to see. The boys were fast asleep on either side of her. Teresa was asleep in her arms. Better let sleeping children sleep.

The priest waited until silence, Sunday silence, church peace, Jesus silence, resumed.

"Sanctus, Sanctus, Sanctus Dominus Deus Sabbaoth..."

Definitely no Communion this morning. She couldn't face having to deal with the children. They tended to get cranky when she forced them up to the front. The following Sunday. In Rockville Centre she'd take Communion, with her mother and father. She would go to church with them, and Carl could either come along or not. Whatever he chose—but he would be able to help with the children in any case. That's how she would persuade him to drive to Rockville Centre: so he could help with the children. They were his children too. No matter what he said, when he got annoyed, about how she had done things with them. About how she had requested she be allowed to take them to church every Sunday. Sometimes when he got angry about how things had gone in his life, about how his own mother and father had treated her in the beginning, about how he had reacted to that... well, she would always say to him, he hadn't fought her very hard. All he'd said was that he didn't care about religion one way or another. Neither did she, she had said, just so long as there *is* one or another....

So he had no complaints now. If he had said he wanted them to go to a synagogue every week, she might have gone along with it.

But no. He said he didn't care about religion. She could do what she wanted. He didn't believe in anything like that. Since the war, what little he had thought about whether there was a God or not, was gone, for good, he thought.

But if she wanted to play that game, it was okay with him. He didn't care one way or another. Whatever made her happy. He wanted her to be happy. He always wanted her to be happy.

[6]   Carl had enlisted in the Army when he was almost twenty. He didn't know what else to do. He hated being in his father's business. He hated having to sneak around Rockville Centre waiting for the chance to meet her for an hour or so. He didn't want to live that way. Maybe they should just give up, go their own separate ways, because he couldn't figure out what the hell he was going to be able to do with his life. College was out. His father's business was out—and maybe she should be too, because what was he ever going to be able to give her except a rough time of it?

She wouldn't listen to him talk that way. They were going to stay together forever. That's all there was to it. She'd help

74

him. They could get married and she would work—wasn't she working already? Wasn't she slowly saving up money so she could go off on her own with him? It wouldn't be long, either. And then they would get married.

So he decided the only unselfish thing he could do was to enlist and force her to forget him. That's what he wrote her, to forget him, to find some nice eligible Catholic guy her father would like, a guy with a future, because he sure as hell didn't have one.

No. No. No. Never. She wrote back, day after day she wrote back, that she loved him and that she was never going to marry anyone else. As far as she was concerned, they were married already anyway, because once two people have done together what they had done, as many times as they had done it, that was the same thing as being married. He should remember that. Otherwise she was really going to be damned.

It was after Pearl Harbor, the early part of 1942, when he was sure he was going to be sent out to the Pacific as soon as his furlough was done with, that they were married. She wanted it that way.

He was afraid of it. What if he never did come back? What then. What if her mother and father wouldn't accept it and he was so far away he wouldn't be able to help her? What then?

None of that was going to happen. She was sure of it. Absolutely certain.

So they were married without anyone from either family knowing about it. She lied on the license that she was twenty-one. The judge never questioned it.

And afterwards, after it was a fact no one could do anything about, she took him home to Rockville Centre to meet her family.

They were all so shocked, even her father was speechless. And Carl, after all, was a soldier, not just a Jew. He looked so beautiful in his uniform, she was sure her father would have to like him. Her sisters and brother did instantly. Her mother was cautious, waiting for a sign from her husband. "It's a good thing there's a war on, miss!" And then he realized what he had said. "But from now on it's Mrs., isn't it?"

Her reception by the Geigers was very much the same. They just wanted Carl to live and be well and to come home from the Army and the war safe and sound. His mother cried a lot. How could he go off like that, without so much as a

75

word? Don't a mother and father deserve that much honor? Have we been so terrible to you? "We haven't, Melissa. It's the God's honest truth. I've always done my best and tried to understand ... I don't know how he could ... do ..." She decided better not to finish that particular statement. She sighed instead, and her husband took hold of her hand. They nodded together, and Carl and Melissa left that house in Manhattan—forever, as it turned out.

Because by the time that Carl was badly wounded and shipped back to the States for treatment, the Geigers were living in Mamaroneck, no longer Washington Heights.

Melissa was in Rockville Centre. Donald was a year old.

Carl was sent to Fort Sam Houston, and Melissa and Donald went down there to be with him.

He was going to need a whole series of operations and skin grafts, and even so it wasn't a hundred percent certain he wouldn't finally lose his leg just above his left kneecap. It was touch and go for a long time, she wrote her parents. Carl had had a very bad time of it, she wrote. He's so thin, and even quieter than he used to be, "... and I keep telling him how lucky we are, myself and Donald, that he's alive and home and we'll never be separated again. Never again. It's certainly God's will at work here, Daddy...."

It was down at Fort Sam, surrounded by all those men who had been wounded in the most horrible of ways, that she found herself back in church every Sunday. She felt lonely and depressed and it seemed as if the only consolation she had was to sit in church with Donald and pray that Carl's leg would be all right, that it would all be all right, her life with Carl, the choices she had made with Carl, for Carl and herself, because she loved him so, and what would be the point if, after all they had started to work out together, they couldn't be together for the rest of their lives? What purpose would it serve? Whose purpose?

When he was discharged, when he was able to be with her in their bedroom of the little apartment she had rented in San Antonio, when she looked down at his leg, saw all those scars, all that raw red skin, when she looked over the rest of his long, now too thin but to her still beautiful body, when she saw the beautiful made ugly, she gave in to a truth made flesh to her, in that instant. She cried and cried and couldn't stop herself from crying for what had happened to him, what had happened to so many others like him who didn't deserve to be used so horribly. Why? Why should such things go on

76

and on? Why should human beings have to suffer at the hands of other human beings they didn't even know? Why were there those concentration camps and people being gassed? Why was there someone like Hitler? Why was she so simple-minded, so innocent, so optimistic about a future that was always, from then on and for the rest of her life, going to include this image of how horrible the world was? Why?

Because she had fallen in love? Was that any kind of answer?

Because she had prayed that Carl's leg should be saved? And it was?

There had to be some reason for love in the world. Human beings had to have something to believe in, in a world that could suddenly turn into a madhouse. Oh, Jesus. Oh, sweet Jesus. Some peace for a while. Some quiet. Some calm. She stared down at his leg and she cried over it, and then she leaned lower over it and kissed it where it was most red. She would take care of him. She would make sure he never had to suffer another minute in his life.

[7]   The fact of his wound worked one miracle: her parents and his parents cooperated. The four of them did everything they could to help get Carl back on his feet, literally.

They lived with the Geigers for a while.

They lived with the Riordans for another while.

Once more Carl's father urged him to take over the business, when he was ready for it. The business had done very well throughout the war. Mr. Geiger had even gone into the manufacture of uniforms for servicemen and women. That had been very profitable.

And Mr. Riordan was willing to stake Carl to a business, a small business, like a clothing store, if that interested him, farther east on the Island, because Mr. Riordan happened to know that that was where land was going to be developed for housing, as soon as the war was over. If Carl went into a business now, before the building got started and if he was patient—not that Carl or his daughter was known for patience—but if he was patient, in a few years he could have a gold mine out there.

Carl didn't know. He didn't know what he really wanted to do except feel better, recover enough for Melissa and Donald, and now Adam, to get started on their own somewhere, and, yes, maybe farther east on the Island. Possibly out there. But he'd have to get loans and things.

Mr. Riordan could see to those things. Lawyers could do those things with much less trouble. But Carl would have to decide what kind of business he wanted. As far as living quarters were concerned, Melissa and Carl and those beautiful children could go on living in Rockville Centre forever and a day.

[8] They lived with the Riordans until Levittown. Missy's father loaned them money to make the move. They bought their house.

Carl never opened any kind of business. He never went to work at his father's again, either. He wanted a job. He wanted to work for someone else. He didn't want the headaches or the responsibilities that having your own business was always about. No. He had seen what it did to his father. Headaches and ulcers and the rest of that stuff. He got a job working for *The New York Times* in the circulation department.

Every morning he took the Long Island Rail Road into New York City. Every evening Melissa picked him up at the station and brought him home to Spiral Lane.

As far as he was concerned, he'd be happy to go on doing that for the rest of his life.

So would she, she told him.

The only minor problem they had was when Teresa was born and Missy insisted on using that name for her. The next one would be his.

[9] When she stepped out of the church, the sunlight dazzled her, so she wasn't able to see them right away. Everyone coming out of the church was stepping slowly. They saw her, though: Rita and Abe Moskowitz, the Rogerses and their two girls, Evelyn and Loretta and Corinne. They were across the street. Policemen were holding them back, preventing them from crossing over.

And then the whole scene came into focus for her. Rita and Abe seemed to be shouting. The police stood their ground. Impassive. Hands on their hips, near their guns. Behind them, in the street, St. Bernard's churchgoers for the nine-o'clock Mass were shouting too, things like why couldn't people honor Sunday, why couldn't some people stay where they belonged, and of course: "Nigger..." and "Commie Jews...Commie Jews..." So that's what all the noise at the
78

back of the church had been about. That's why the priest had hesitated during the Mass.

The Rogerses. Those two sweet little girls. They were Catholics. It had never occurred to her to think that yesterday, helping the Rogerses unpack their belongings.

And why not? Because they weren't white? Because everyone she had so far met in Levittown she liked was Jewish—except Loretta? Was there such a thing as a Negro Jew?

The boys tugged her to attention. They were pulling her coat, and she felt like she was going to fall forward down the flight of steps. She shifted Teresa to the other arm, steadied herself, told Donald to stop that pulling immediately. And they started down the steps of the church and into the crush of people in front of it.

She would go over to them, to her friends. She was on their side. What was the point of a church that wouldn't let certain people into it? And in Levittown. In a place built especially for veterans of the great war to make the whole world safe for democracy. Disgusting. Repulsive. Such hatred on the faces she passed. The faces on their way into church, on their way out of it. She was ashamed. That wasn't what Jesus had meant. That wasn't at all what he had meant, then or now.

She was crying by the time she reached them, and Evelyn, seeing her push between the policemen, met her, took Teresa from her, just in time. She was going to faint, collapse, give up.

But she couldn't. Donald and Adam were frightened. They were crying too. They had a right to cry. She didn't. She had other things to do. She had to help. "If only you'd told me," she said to Calvin, "I would have asked you to come with me this morning. We could have been together."

"Never mind that now, Missy," Loretta said. "We all better get out of here." The crowd seemed to be pressing closer around them. Even the police were beginning to tell them to break it up, let's go, break it up, the Mass's started in there. Let's go. And then to Rita and Abe, one of the two policemen said, "I'm warning you to get outta here, alla you, you're causing an obstruction here and you got these kids here, let's go, break it up...."

Calvin and Maryellen and the girls moved away first. They walked slowly. Calvin stared at the space in front of them. He wouldn't see anyone, so if someone stood in his path they'd better just get the hell out of it. There was no mis-

79

taking that in his eyes. None whatsoever. If only she had some courage like that. Her car was only down the block. She would follow them, offer to drive them home. She took Teresa back from Evelyn, told the boys to hold on to her coat, and the four of them followed the Rogerses. She was going to be calm. She was going to smile. A smile of conviction. And if something happened, she'd let it happen—to herself, not to the children. She would just keep on walking to her car.

Evelyn and Loretta stayed back there with Rita and Abe.

Corinne was behind her. Corinne was catching up to her. She took hold of Donald's free hand. "Want to skip, Donald? Go ahead, sweetheart, skip."

The people on either side of their path looked on; they didn't say a word.

A strange silence. A strange feeling of peace too.

Corinne helped her into the car. She was going back there. She was sure Lionel would be coming for her. He'd told her if she went with Loretta she shouldn't bother to come back, but she was sure he'd be coming for her. Any minute now, and, no, Missy should just drive home, they'd all be all right because the Rogerses had already driven off. She should too. Get home. The kids look all frightened. Tell Carl hello....Corinne moved away quickly, moving back to the rest of them, although by then the crowd was breaking up.

And, yes, there was Lionel, and stopping his car in the middle of the street and yelling for Corinne to get the hell inside it: "Goddamn broad, get the hell inside this car, will you!"

Very calmly, she did. Missy could see it all in her rearview mirror as she drove off for home.

8

Corinne Feuerstein née Grossman

[1] "You got a kid sleeping at home in a goddamn crib and you go off just like that to be with a bunch of coloreds? What the hell is it with you? You got all your marbles, Corinne? Those people could've killed you out there. Do you know that? I told you once, I'll tell you a million times, they aren't going to let coloreds into Levittown."

"We'll see. And in case you forgot, that kid sleeping in his crib is also your son. If he gets up and I'm not there, you could feed him and wash him up the same way I do."

"It isn't my job to do that. I get one morning off, I want to relax. I want to get up and have a breakfast, have my wife there giving it to me."

"I'll give it to you, all right. A piece of shit I'll give you."

"Shut your hole, Corinne, I'm warning you, you open that dirty mouth of yours once more and I'll shut it for good. I'm not kidding around."

"Neither am I. And I'm warning you too." That stopped him. That always stopped him. Standing up to him did. Giving him back what he tried to hand out. She had his number. She always had it—but he had hers too.

They drove the rest of the way in silence. And what she hadn't been able to observe until then was that it was a very beautiful morning. More spring in the air finally than winter.

Their house was on Spiral Lane, next door to Cynthia and Sandy Klein. Cynthia's house was barn red with white trim. Theirs was yellow with white trim, same as Evelyn's.

The Klein car was not parked out front. They were still, very conveniently, away for the weekend. To Sandy's parents' in Connecticut. An emergency, Cynthia had said. Sure! Some emergency. You can take the girl out of the South, but you can't...

"And no fighting in front of Greg, please?" Lionel said after he turned off the ignition. He put his hand on her leg, brushed the gray flannel, pinched the crease of her slacks, patted her. "Okay?"

She said nothing. She pushed out of the car, rushed up the walk, rushed between the rhododendrons on either side of the front door, rushing because Gregory was crying.

He was standing in his crib, holding on and screaming.

He was wet. He had a load in his diaper. He wanted his Mommy. Sure he did. Her sweetheart. She hugged him to her. Her poor little baby boy. She loved him. Sure she did. "Sure Mommy loves you, sweetheart. Mommy's here. Ssh. Ssh...." And if she went to Lionel then and told him he shouldn't have left Greg alone like that, crying in his crib, a child who wasn't even three years old yet shouldn't be left alone, he'd blame her. He'd blame her for everything, for anything, for breathing, for every lousy goddamn thing that ever went wrong with the world. He'd tell her if she would only just stay home and do what she was supposed to do, everything would be perfect with everyone everywhere. You and your Loretta Massi, he'd say. And your Evelyn Selden. You want to reform the world, do you? Well, start at home first, he'd say. Stay at home once in a while, like you're supposed to..... But unless he stuffed it into her when she was drugged asleep, the one thing she was never going to do again was to have another child. That was final. No matter how much she loved Gregory—and she did, he could never accuse her of that, she'd kill him if he ever so much as implied that—she did not want another child.

"I'm starting coffee," he called from the kitchen.

"You want me to give you a prize?" she called back. That was the way they were best together, calling to each other from separate rooms. And if their house was a mansion, they'd be better off still. If they could get more distance between themselves, they'd be the best off. Like Loretta said about Joe, she could say about Lionel and herself. But she would only say it to herself. She wasn't ready to say it out loud. Not yet. "...yes, sweetheart. Yes, my sweet little boy. Mommy's here."

[2] Corinne hadn't wanted to move to Levittown. She'd wanted to stay put in the Village. Her basement apartment on Horatio Street would have been big enough for three. Which was the point involved in thinking of a move in the first place, the fact that there would be three of them, where before there had been one, and then two.

Not only that, she didn't see why, just because she was pregnant, she automatically had to marry Lionel. Why did she have to?

Because he said so.

"That's a reason?"

"All right. You want a better reason? I'll give you one. The war's almost over. I'm going to be discharged soon. We've known each other how long? Three years? We've had plenty of good times here. I don't say no to that, but there's no reason we can't have plenty more if we're married. I want you to. You're pregnant, and I want you to marry me. I want to get going in some kind of business. I want us to live in a house or a real apartment, not this toy box you call an apartment. It's like playing a game living here. You go out to that shitty nightclub to play the piano, to sing, and no one's listening to you. Do you realize that? When I come to pick you up, I look around, and no one's listening to you. So what good is that? And what the hell am I doing every day? Nothing. Not a goddamn thing. It's time, Corinne. My parents are offering me their store to take over. My other brother's a *shmegegge* and my parents want to retire, to relax.....Is that enough reasons?"

"Enough, but not the right one among them."

"You want me to tell you I love you?"

"I want you to stop sounding like my mother and father telling me what to do. I left the Bronx to get away from that kind of crap."

"Okay. So I love you."

"You're very convincing. I could have an abortion, you know. I have a friend could help me get one."

"Never mind that shit. I'm telling you what you're going to do. That's that."

"That's not that. 'So I love you,' you say, and I'm supposed to fall at your feet for that? It's only my second period I missed. I could still easily get an abortion."

"No, Corinne. I'm serious now. You'll marry me because we should be married. That, I know. That much. The rest I'll convince you about. If you give me a chance, I'll convince you."

That he could do. He knew he could. He was built for it. No one she'd ever slept with was as good. And he was right: they had had plenty of good times in her basement apartment. Plenty. That night was no exception.

In some ways that night was the best, because he was

83

trying harder to please her. He was lingering over her, touching her, over and over, all over, in the darkness of that big room in her big bed, sprawling all over it and her. He was big and he was gentle, tender when he tried to be, which was about as close to love as he was ever going to come. She was the same way. When she touched his back, when she pulled him into her, she tried to put everything she felt into that touch.

And she was pregnant.

And it was time for her to stop trying to be what she'd never be. This was how she could entertain. Instead of in a crummy nightclub. She could entertain him for a long while more. It was time to start that part of her life. He was right about that, too.

He wanted her. She wanted him. That was enough.

It would make his parents happy. It would certainly make her parents happy. They had about given up hope. A nice Jewish girl living in Greenwich Village. Alone. Working in nightclubs. A *shondeh*. Shameful! So, all things considered, "Yes, Lionel... only, slow. Go slow... good... that's good...." She never even felt the weight of him. He lifted her to him. It was the one thing he did best, fucking better than anyone she'd ever known, better than she'd ever expected anyone could.

[3] Levittown was not exactly her idea of heaven. But at least it was nowhere near the Grand Concourse. Her parents would have to come to her. As for living on Queens Boulevard on top of, next to, or in the vicinity of Feuerstein's Paints and Hardware for any time more than a temporary few weeks— also a never. The Feuersteins should all live and be well... at a distance.

So, it was Spiral Lane. A yellow house with white trim and with not one room in it big enough to accommodate even a baby grand, not if you wanted to put anything else in the room like a sofa and chairs. She, personally, would have preferred a piano, but, no, not for the new her. The chanteuse part of her life was over. Corky Cummings was at an end, she should only rest in peace. Corrine Feuerstein née Grossman, late of the Bronx, was giving birth to a new and better her. She had already given birth to an heir for Feuerstein's Paints and Hardware. She had insisted on naming him Gregory, after Gregory Peck. Gregory Peck in *Gentleman's Agreement* she had fallen in love with. Surprisingly, her
84

mother liked the name Gregory too. She had had a brother in Minsk who was killed in a pogrom; just before her family left Russia, her brother was killed. Grischa, they called him. So Gregory was perfect. A good Jewish name: Gregory Feuerstein.

[4]   Next to playing the piano, Corinne loved the movies. Her mother gave her the piano. At the age of six Corinne began lessons. Her mother decided it. She saved money out of her food allowance and bought an upright for her darling daughter. She herself had always wanted to play, so when the teacher told Mrs. Grossman that her Corinne had talent, she felt that her scrimping was a Commandment from God. God's work, the piano. The movies Corinne found for herself. She got money from her father for those. Her father was a shoe salesman for A. S. Beck over on Walton Avenue. His salary was small, but Corinne was an only child, and whatever he could give her, whatever it was sensible to give her, he would, but not piano lessons—what could she do with piano lessons later on in life? Playing a piano? A woman? *Meshugge,* he screamed at his wife; he wouldn't pay for it. She could grow the money on a tree somewhere. But ten cents for a movie, sure, whenever his darling wanted.

Corinne would go after school. She would get some woman to take her in as her daughter.

At home, playing her lesson, she imagined herself playing on the screen, for an audience. The movies had just turned talking when she started going to them. There was no singing, no music, not right away, but she imagined it happening. If it was on the radio and on a Victrola, it was bound to be in the movies soon, and she would be one of the leading stars. She would sing and play the piano for millions of people all over the world. She would look like Pola Negri. She did, a little bit, anyway, although her hair was lighter. It was red, actually, and getting redder. And then she thought she looked like Norma Shearer. She didn't. Then Jean Arthur. No...but Ginger Rogers? Yes. And Ann Sheridan definitely. If Ann Sheridan could play the piano in a nightclub in one of her movies, that's who Corinne would be.

By then Corinne was in Taft High School. She was popular. She could see for herself she was *zaftig.* Boys were always wanting to take her for a walk to feel her up. She loved it too when they did that, which none of them could seem to understand, so she stopped telling them, because as

85

soon as she said she liked the feeling, they wanted to go all the way, and all the way was decidedly too far for her. No thanks, little boy. Another time. When you're older and understand more how to do it. Saying things like that only got them hotter. But she knew how to handle them. She knew how to take care of herself. She knew what she was doing. She was biding her time until graduation; then she would move away from the Concourse, with or without her parents' blessings. She would get a job and some kind of apartment down in the Village. She loved the Village. She loved going down there with her girlfriend from school.

She and her best friend, Roberta Goldstein, went down there together on Saturdays, in the late afternoons, just before it got dark. They would walk around and then go to a movie, to the Loew's Sheridan mostly, because it was so big and beautiful and the screen was huge and Judy Garland's face singing on it, singing her heart out on it to Mickey Rooney—that was the way she wanted her life to be. Roberta Goldstein did too, but Roberta had no special talent, except maybe her body. Roberta was going to be a great lay, the boys at Taft told her, right to her face, while they tried to pinch her tits.

One Saturday afternoon Corinne went down to the Village on her own. She was a senior, and it was May 1940.

She was walking on Greenwich Avenue, looking into stores, just sauntering along, and a guy who's about to go into Harrington's, a bar-restaurant near the corner of Christopher and Greenwich, stops right next to her. He's much older. She sees that right away. About thirty. Tall. Heavy, but muscular. Not good-looking, not ugly. Curly black hair. Nice. A great smile and perfect white teeth, and he doesn't hesitate for a second. He just asks her how she would like to have a drink with him, in Harrington's.

Sure. She'd love it. She was nervous, out-of-her-head nervous, but she'd do it, and she'd do it nonchalantly, like Ann Sheridan would. She had done her hair like Ann Sheridan that day. Soft. Fally.

The bar was long and dark, dark wood everywhere, and a long mirror behind the bar. At the end of the bar was a piano, and on the other side of the piano were tables, the restaurant part.

They sat far down the bar, near the piano. She would have a Tom Collins—it was the only drink she knew. His name was Jack O'Brien.

"Like Pat O'Brien," she said.

"I guess. We're both Irish anyways."

She told him her name was Corky Cummings. She was always going to be Corky Cummings anyway when she moved down to the Village after graduation.

She had two Tom Collinses too quickly, and by then it was 5:30 and a lot more people were coming in for drinks at the bar. They had a pianist who started playing at six. She asked the bartender if she couldn't just play the piano until then. She'd do it softly. She wouldn't disturb anybody, and she did play well—that she could assure him of. Jack O'Brien loved the idea. He was already telling her he loved her too and that she should have dinner with him, and afterward, he had a room over on Horatio. She wouldn't say yes, she wouldn't say no, but she did play the piano. The bartender loved the idea, "...anyone who looks as good as you do and who can play the piano too is all right in my book." He looked at her as if he might like to take her home to his little room somewhere too.

She played and she sang, first, like Judy Garland "You made me love you/I didn't want to do it/I didn't want to do it...." And they applauded so she sang an Irish song her mother always hummed at home—why her mother hummed an Irish song, she never knew: "With someone like you/A pal good and true/I'd like to leave it all behind/And go and find/A place that's known/To God alone/And let the rest of the world go by...."

They applauded some more. They wanted more. She sang "The Masquerade Is Over" and then it was six o'clock and the regular pianist was there and he was angry because she was going to be a hard act to follow, Jack said. Jack said, "Let's eat."

They did, and she was so ecstatic she never could, when she was remembering, remember what she ate that evening.

But she did remember what she did afterwards. She remembered getting into a cab with him, going over to Horatio Street, where he had a small apartment, and she remembered how gentlemanly he was when he got undressed and she told him she had never done anything like this before and she wasn't going to be able to stay late because she had to get back up to the Bronx where her parents would be wondering where she was by now it was so late and maybe she should just leave and catch the subway—very gentlemanly. And she liked the way he looked undressed as well as dressed.

He helped her. He calmed her down. He told her there was nothing to be afraid of. It happened all the time, every day, to everyone. It had to happen to her sooner or later, and it might as well be sooner, because he was sure she was going to enjoy it.

He treated her in a gentlemanly fashion all the way through it. Too gentlemanly. It was over too fast. She was just beginning to really enjoy it when he was finished. Too much to drink, he said. Lost control, he said, because she was so goddamned beautiful. Loved that red hair of hers. First girl he'd ever done it with had red hair, too. Next time, he said, would be better... for both of them. He'd been worried about her being a virgin and everything.

[5]   The next time was better—but not that much. Jack was just as sweet to her, though. She saw him a few times before graduation, and then afterward he helped her find a place to move to, a basement apartment down the block from him.

She hadn't prepared her parents for her moving. At first it made her nervous to think about the whole thing and what it really meant. She didn't stay down there a lot at first. Not until after she told them she'd gotten a job as a secretary down on Twenty-third Street, for a lawyer.

Then, when she had Jack sleeping over, she told them she was going to stay with a girl from the office who lived down in the Village.

By the end of the summer she did tell them she'd found a small apartment of her own down there, near her girl-friend's. She was glad not to have to lie, finally. She hated to lie.

She got her friend Roberta Goldstein to tell them what a great apartment it was. Plenty of room. Room for a piano, even. If Roberta's parents would only be as understanding as the Grossmans were, she'd love to move in with Corinne. But Roberta knew her parents, all right. She almost went too far about building up Corrine's lie, because she started talking about Corinne's friend who recognized her real talents, her talents on the piano, a man friend that was, who was trying to get her jobs playing for parties and weddings... and bar mitzvahs.

Jack did get her a job. In a nightclub over on Eighth Street. Then—it couldn't have been more than a week later—Pearl Harbor happened. Right in the middle of one of her songs, Pearl Harbor happened over the radio the bartender was playing. He had it turned down low, but he raised it soon as he realized what was happening. Everyone in the bar got very quiet and listened.

Jack was there. It was the afternoon. He sat down next to her on the piano stool. He didn't say anything. He just kept stroking the backs of her hands, which were at rest on the keys.

He stroked and he stared down at her hands, and they listened to the radio announcer describing the scene of destruction at Pearl Harbor, and then he said, "You know what, Corky? Maybe we should get married."

She lifted her hands from the keyboard, touched his cheek, a heavy cheek, too heavy from drinking too much. "Thanks a lot, Jack, for asking"—she was sounding like Ann Sheridan, she hoped—"but no thanks. Maybe another time."

[6] Jack enlisted in the Navy a few weeks later, about the same time she left the place on Eighth Street for a better spot over on Charles Street and West Fourth.

Jack wrote to her.

She wrote back to him.

She fixed up her apartment. Lots of pillows and soft things. And when she could afford it, she bought a secondhand baby grand. The basement could handle the piano and a big double bed and sofa and chairs. It had a little kitchen, but she could cook enough in it so she could even invite her mother and father down to it—on her night off. She played the grand for them, and they were proud of her, of how she was working and still stuck with the piano. Her mother was especially proud of her. "You see, darling, how sometimes a little sacrificing pays off? All your life you'll enjoy the piano, and what if I didn't insist, Morris? What then? What if I didn't say she'll take lessons if I have to get down on my hands and knees and scrub floors? Sometimes, Corinne, it's right to insist on what you want. You shouldn't let your husband tell you everything to do. Some things. Not everything. When you'll get married you'll see what I'm telling you..... You're seeing someone, effsheh? Your boss? He's married?"

"Yes, Ma. He's married." She wasn't lying. He was married. But he wasn't a lawyer.

And she was seeing someone. She was seeing someone—and anyone else she happened to like. Servicemen, lots of servicemen she was seeing. They were always hanging around her piano and asking for this song and that song, "On the Banks of the Wabash," "St. Louis Woman," "California, Here I Come." She was good. At the piano. In bed. Some of them were good too, in bed. But not often. Most often they were too drunk to be any good to her at all. Then, those times, she was supposed to be understanding, they told her, understanding, because they were lonely, they were missing someone, someone special to them.

And what was she? she wanted to know. A piece of shit? Those kind she let go to sleep. She let them sleep and then got rid of them as fast as she could in the morning.

Lionel Feuerstein was different. Of course he was. He was from New York City. From Queens. He was Jewish. He was serious about everything. He was serious about his fucking too, and he was good at it. He was built for it. He was built for the long haul, for the duration, the way they used to say it. Like a truck he was built. Big and heavy and overwhelming, once he got started.

And he always felt good.

[7] Lionel was stationed over in Brooklyn at Fort Tilden, in the Quartermaster Corps. He had it knocked up, he said. He could get things, things no one else could get. He kept arriving at Horatio Street with things.

He would arrive before she had to go to work.

He would pick her up when she was finished.

He would spend part of the night with her and leave in time so he could get back over to Brooklyn for roll call.

That was 1943.

And then it was 1944. Lionel, she supposed, was going to be it. There wasn't any real competition, although she made a big show of this guy Jack O'Brien whose letters she was always getting. She wrote to him once a week, faithfully. He wrote to her, sometimes three letters a week. He missed her. He still wanted to marry her. He hadn't met anyone like her...to which she would answer, that's because there couldn't be two like her, thank God.

In the early part of 1945 Jack's letters stopped coming, suddenly. And when she went over to the place on Eighth Street to check on what, other than the worst, might have happened, she found out that it was the worst, that Jack's ship had been torpedoed in the Pacific. One of Jack's younger brothers—she remembered he said he had four or five—was home on furlough and had come down to the place to see if maybe some of his old friends were still around.... Not every-
90

one on the ship had been killed, but Jack's part was the part that got a direct hit from the torpedo.

So all the bad, sad things considered, when she realized she was pregnant and Lionel wanted her to marry him...why not? She might as well. She was only twenty-two and if it didn't work out with Lionel, she'd still be young enough to go back to her...her what? Career?

Some career. Some talent. Not that she was bad. No one during all the times of her playing had ever said to her she was bad—but no one ever told her she was great, except that first time in Harrington's. She would have had to put a lot more into it to become great. A lot more work and a lot more money to maybe develop an act, a real professional act, which, even then, how sure could she be she'd ever make anything more of her life than she could with Lionel? She couldn't be sure. And if she even had to ask herself that kind of question, she might just as well marry Lionel and forget the rest of the crap. At least he had security. At least he was inheriting a paint and hardware store; and when the war was over, which it soon was going to be, paints and hardware were going to be good things to have inherited. She'd had her fun. Plenty of fun. And even Susan Hayward had to give up her career for love and children and a happy future. It happens that way. That's the way it happens, even in real life.

At her own wedding she sang and played the piano. It was a big wedding, at the Concourse Plaza. Her father insisted on it. His only daughter, his darling child, was getting married, and even if it took his last penny, she was going to have a wedding to remember for the rest of her life.

Both her parents liked Lionel, although her mother wished he had been a professional. She was convinced Corinne should have married her boss, the lawyer, the one Roberta Goldstein talked about, "...but this is good too. He'll provide, and you'll be happy."

Roberta Goldstein was her maid of honor. Roberta was still a good lay, so good no one wanted to marry her, she told Corinne, they just wanted to keep her fixed up; one in particular did, a married man. That one, wouldn't you know it, she loved.

Lionel wore his warrant officer's uniform. He looked as handsome as he was ever going to look, which was somewhere between Johnny Weissmuller and Wallace Beery, only darker.

After the ceremony, after the meal had begun, when everyone was sloshing into the half-pineapple fruit cups, she went to the piano—the band was on a raised platform—and she began to play. No announcement. Nothing. She just started, "You made me love you/I didn't want to do it/I didn't want to do it./You made me love you..."

By the time she finished the first verse, everyone was quiet, a hundred and fifty people, listening. It was her finest moment.

It was also the last one like that for a long, long time, maybe for the rest of her life. She was almost four months pregnant, but she didn't show. Her gown was full. A full skirt of satin and lace, and with a long lace train trailing after.

9

"Jell-O again. This is Jack Benny..." Lionel was set for the evening. Jack Benny. Then Fred Allen—and Lionel would doze off and on in his club chair next to the radio, listening and feeling himself up and at some point he'd get up and say, "Come on, Corinne. Let's hit the sack. I got to get up early."

And what was she supposed to do with this lovely Sunday evening in March? Now that spring was in the air. Now that Gregory was fast asleep. Although, if Gregory would only get up he'd be better company for her than Lionel was.

She couldn't play the phonograph, not while the radio was on.

She couldn't play the piano because she didn't have one to play. The nearest one was Arlene Zweig's and Arlene Zweig's *yenta*-ing was too high a price to have to pay for her art. Sundays when Arlene and Max took the boys to her parents', then Corinne went there to play, but this Sunday Arlene was home. It was a matter of principle Arlene was home. She wasn't going to run away from the Rogers situation—not the way Cynthia had. So Corinne was doomed to *The New York Times*—maybe she'd try to do the crossword puzzle once more. No. Too humiliating.

She read. The oil burner went on. The temperature outside was falling fast. Lionel was playing with himself harder. In a few more minutes he'd stand up and tell her it was time to hit the sack.

Sunday evening—and a lot of other evenings just like it. What did she expect? Life wasn't an Ann Sheridan movie. So, okay. But did it have to be so boring?

She'd rather face a Calvin Rogers kind of crisis every day than have to sit in her living room every night listening to the radio. Yes. *She* would. And Lionel would rather not. Lionel would rather not think about anything deep or hard, unless it was his prick getting hard—and that effort didn't last very long, and neither did it do very much to stimulate

93

him to think about anything else. It was always more of the same. Over and over. The same—and the longer they were married the more he did his fucking the same way. Exactly the same way, time after time, the same. More of the same...and when she tried to talk about how disgusting it was for the Rogerses to be treated the way they had been that morning and the day before and probably all their lives before they ever moved to Levittown—*that* he didn't want to hear about or talk about. No. Knock it off, he'd said when they were eating supper—but she hadn't. She had gone on talking. "As a Jew," she'd said, "I don't understand how you can just turn your back on what's been happening here the last few days as if it's been happening in another part of the world. You got discharged, and that's that? Everything's perfect? They made Israel, so there's nothing else for you to worry about? Is that it? Is that how you look at things? Is it? As long as they don't kill any more Jews, they can kill anyone else they want? Tell me, Lionel. Why aren't you interested in anything else but fucking?"

"What the hell you screaming for? I told you to knock it off. You wake Gregory, and so help me you'll have something to scream about." And that's when he grabbed a piece of the Sunday *News* and pushed away from the kitchen table, pushed so hard she thought the table was going to turn over on her—and then the next thing she knew he was in his chair listening to Jack Benny, reading the *News*, set for another Sunday evening as if nothing had ever happened.

And so what was she supposed to do, after she did the dishes? Of course she had to do the dishes. And then what but the *Times?* And after that, maybe the *Women's Home Companion?* And her book after that? For the third time she was trying to read her way inside *The Magic Mountain*, without understanding a third of what she read. But trying, anyway, because she had seen Cynthia reading it and heard her say to Sandy Klein that it was probably one of the greatest books ever written, a masterpiece, so if it was a masterpiece, why couldn't Corinne Corky Cummings Grossman Feuerstein understand more than a third of it? A graduate of Taft High School. A talented musician. And she couldn't understand words printed on a page in English?

And she had the nerve to criticize Lionel? At least he read what he could read.

She read what she thought she should read. Because someone else was reading it, someone she didn't even like. Except

Cynthia had a little college. Two years. She knew something. She was close to being a bitch, but she knew something. She even knew something about music, the music that Corinne was supposed to know about but didn't, the music Corinne's first teacher had told her was what music really meant, music Corinne should study, her teacher had told her, because when a person has a talent for something they should honor it by nourishing it with the best there is—Cynthia knew about that too. Cynthia was the only one of their group that had any kind of what Corinne hated to—but had to—call real culture.

And Corinne could have had that kind of culture too. But no. Of course not. As soon as she could, she had told her teacher she didn't want to study the classics anymore. Later she would. When she was older she would, because she also had a good voice and she wanted to be able to accompany herself. She wanted to play Irving Berlin and Gershwin and Jerome Kern and Cole Porter and sing for hundreds of people, different people all the time. She wanted to travel and play and sing. So her first teacher had gone to Mrs. Grossman and told her to please look around for another teacher for Corinne, because if someone was so talented and wanted to waste her talents on garbage...well, she, Miss Spivack, was not going to be a party to it.

Mrs. Grossman had agreed, yes, it was a *shondeh*, "...but still and all, Miss Spivack, Irving Berlin is not garbage. And George Gershwin is not garbage. The others? Who knows. I wouldn't say one way or another. But if my daughter *says*, well then, that's something else, because in the long run it's my daughter who will do the playing. True? And it'll be my daughter who gets married eventually, anyway, and who knows if she'll even play the piano then? Now is now. So I'll look around, Miss Spivack, like you say."

Now is now, too. And now, sitting in her Levittown living room, riffling through the pages of the Entertainment section of *The New York Times,* scanning the listings of concerts and plays and art shows, now is when she would like to get up, go over to a piano, and play something worthwhile. She would like to do the one thing in the world she could do that no one else she knew could do.

And she still could learn. She could teach herself. She could study Bach and Mozart and Beethoven and Brahms all over again—but this time really study, and learn. Not just fool around. She could get rid of most of the furniture in the

95

room—she looked up, studying the space, and Lionel saw her; Lionel smiled, squeezed his hand down the front of his pants, feeling himself up for her benefit—and, okay, if that was the way she was going to have to convince him she needed a piano, she would. A small grand.

She would start with Bach. Every afternoon, for at least an hour. She could work on her technique...except what would she do with Gregory? She couldn't play if he was taking a nap. He was such a light sleeper. Well, she'd work it out. Somehow she'd work it out. Maybe she could start teaching Gregory how to play so at least then all her mother's money spent on her wouldn't have gone down the drain. Gregory could carry on the Grossman hope. And he was a boy. He could amount to something.

Not like herself.

She was pathetic. With her clothes that were more like costumes and her hair that felt like straw from all the dyeing of it redder than it really was these days underneath. She was nothing. Not even a Cynthia Klein. Whatever that was. But at least when there was a crisis to face, Corinne could face it. At least underneath her dye job and her costumes she was as honest as she could be about her stupidity—at least to herself and to Loretta and Evelyn. She didn't lie to people she respected. She didn't put on airs. She had, after all, performed before people and they'd liked her. And she'd been there yesterday and today, at the Rogerses' when it counted. So, for all Cynthia's real culture, when the chips were down, she was gone with the wind...the bitch!

"How about maybe we'll hit the sack? How would that be? How about coming over here and sitting on my lap, honey? How about that? And then we'll hit the sack?"

Why not? What else did she have to do? At least she wouldn't feel so bored for a while.

And he opened his arms for her to nestle inside of, and when he squeezed her inside them that way, for a while she felt special. She was sure a lot of her friends never felt that with their husbands. She was sure Cynthia never did. And Loretta...that was something different. And Evelyn? Evelyn was special all on her own. So would she be again. She'd get Lionel to buy her a piano, even if she had to blow some life into him. If she couldn't get what she wanted one way, she'd shock him into life another way.

One way or another she wasn't going to spend the rest of her life being bored to death.

10

Cynthia Klein née Berk
(née Berkowitz)

[1]   Cynthia asked Sandy to drive down Division Avenue.
She had to see if there was evidence left of some kind of
trouble.

"At ten-thirty, Cynthia? On a Sunday night?"

"Never mind the time. Won't you just do as I ask?"

"When don't I?" But he didn't raise his voice. Annoyed or
angry, one thing Sanford Klein never did was raise his voice,
even when he was as tired as he was from their long drive
down from Hartford.

And she knew he was tired...and angry. It had been her
idea to visit his parents. He hadn't wanted that at all. He
had wanted to just stay home and read and plant some flowers
and start a slate walk from the front door down to the street;
a slate-lined walk he wanted. She wanted it too, but not this
weekend. "The following one," she had told him, once more
that morning. "The earth's softer as soon as it's April."

"Since you know everything, Cynthia. How is it you don't
know by now how I feel about my parents?"

"I know how *you* feel, but don't you think it's important
for Melanie to see them? Grandparents are important for a
young child. I know how important mine were when I was
growing up. My Grandmother Berk was one of the most beautiful people I ever did know in my whole life." And once she
started on her Grandmother Berk or any other person she
remembered from down home when she was growing up, well,
she knew that was a sure way of getting Sandy to say nothing
at all so that eventually he would end up doing precisely
what she wanted, like just then. "Business like with these
coloreds goes *on* at bight. Back home that's when the worst
of it went on. I do know what I'm talking about when it comes
to things like this, so just drive down Division Avenue. Melanie's fast asleep anyway."

She was. Her head was on Cynthia's lap, her long coal-dark curls splayed every which way, her legs stretched out onto Sandy's lap. Sandy was smoothing the soft skin of her leg just then. Melanie stirred, shivering. Sandy stopped. He didn't want to wake her. She sank back into sleep.

There was a police car opposite the house, and a group of people standing in front of it, conferring it looked like to her. She asked Sandy to slow the Pontiac so she could really tell what was what. The house was all lit up. Some of the windows didn't have any shades on them yet, only the living-room windows did, and she was sure that's where they would be. As if shades would be any kind of protection! "They'll be in there, all right, in the living room. You can be sure of that, and if something starts to happen, they'll turn all the lights off in a second. It always happens the same way. I don't know how many times I've seen—"

"This is Levittown, Cynthia"—he speeded up again—"not South Carolina."

She turned to look out the back window. A man was crossing over. He was throwing something toward the house. "It's started, Sandy, in your lovely Levittown. I just saw it start."

He didn't respond. Even when he turned the Pontiac down Spiral Lane, he didn't respond. When he stopped in front of their house, he motioned for her to get the valise in the back. Carefully, wordlessly, he lifted Melanie. He would carry her inside himself. She didn't so much obey as give in, for the moment give in, because once inside, she would have her say, no matter what *he* said—or didn't say, to be more precise. Because he would say nothing, or very little, especially when he was tired, especially after a day with his parents.

No lights on in Corinne's and Lionel's.

So if she wanted to know what was what over on Division Avenue... "Take her right into bed, Sandy. I'll undress her there." If she wanted honest information at this time of night, she could call Evelyn. Evelyn told the truth, all right. And that's because she had convictions about things. Like Missy did, too. But Missy'd be sleeping by now.

Sandy put Melanie down on her bed, so gently she barely stirred. He smiled down at her. He removed wisps of black hair from her mouth. Her mouth was open. She breathed heavily.

Cynthia was sure Melly was going to need to have her adenoids out sooner than later. Maybe before the summer, before the polio season started. When Cynthia was younger, everything back home was measured by when the polio sea-
98

son started, by when her mother started making her wear the necklace with a camphor bag attached, "...to ward those bugs off, Cindy." No one called her Cindy anymore.....Sandy did not move away from the bed. He wasn't smiling, just staring down. "What is it? Something wrong with her?"

"With her? No. Everything's right with her.....Notice how little she looks like me?"

"True, but she does favor your father. She's got your father's exact coloring. In your family you're the one looks like he didn't belong. You're the odd one. No one else in your family's as fair as you are. No one even near to it. Your brother's got the darkest, kinkiest hair I ever saw outside a nig...excuse me, Negro. You're the queer one in the family."

That stood him up, got him moving back. "I'll put water up for tea."

[2] She'd wait until tomorrow for news. Too tired to talk to anyone. She'd just sit with Sandy, sip her tea, snip at the honey cake his mother'd sent home with them. It was good. His mother's a fine baker. Not as good a cook. Not anywhere near as good as her own mother'd been, may she rest in peace.

Her mother'd have hated this Levittown kitchen. Too small for any decent cooking or entertaining the way they did in Charleston when she was growing up. Dear God, how she hated Levittown. Everywhere the eye looks, there's something ugly. Every house just about the same. Ad infinitum. Ad nauseam. No touch of beauty in it or anywhere really very near it. Except perhaps Jones Beach, and who can be hightailing it over to Jones every day just to see something beautiful and natural! Ashamed how people get cheated. Herself, especially.

Except there was reading.

There was music on the phonograph she listened to with Sandy.

But day to day there was no one to talk to. Not really. Just the same jibber-jabber about what to make for dinner or someone getting a new living-room suite or putting up new draperies...and, of course, politics, politics, and more politics. From Evelyn and Rita and Loretta...as if any of what they do's going to make a dent in anything. Injustice is just part of the way the world works. Take it or leave it. If Evelyn'd had the littlest bit of college, she'd know that. Evelyn's the one should go back to school. Do her good. She'd be less naive. She trusts people too much. . . . "Some more tea, Sandy?"

"No, thank you, Cynth." He didn't look up from the *Times*. His first chance to relax all day—and he goes right to the Entertainment part. He loved opera. He loved to read the Hemisemidemiquavers paragraph. He loved music and any news about it. She did too. Which was one of the reasons they had met in the first place. He had come over from Augusta to their synagogue in Charleston for a Friday service and a recital afterward, Schubert lieder, sung by a young baritone, a friend of his as it turned out, which was why he had come over from Augusta. The baritone was stationed at Camp Gordon too, and he had gotten Sandy time off from their company commander to travel with him to Charleston. Sandy was Jewish. Paul Sykes, the baritone, wasn't, so Sandy could show him the way around inside a synagogue. They were staying with the rabbi's family for the weekend. They wanted to see Charleston. The rabbi introduced them to Cynthia Berk and her sister, Marlene. He was sure the sisters would enjoy showing them around Charleston. . . . . How beautiful Sandy was then. Lean and blond and blue-eyed. How could he have been Jewish?

He was still beautiful. One of the few servicemen she'd ever seen who looked better out of uniform than in. His uniform had hung on him, he was so lean. Civilian clothes, on the other hand, had been made for him. Custom clothes. His mother had insisted on that. "A graduate of MIT must look the part," his mother told Cynthia she had always told him. "And even if we have to pay for them to be made—my husband and I will insist on paying for his clothes—he *will* wear them. I'll see to that." She still did, too. Quite a mother. And even at that moment, as he leaned down over the *Times*, his shiny blond hair falling onto his forehead, Sandy's rep tie was still in place inside the button-down oxford blue collar, his gray flannels, after hours of travel, were creaseless, his loafers were still on. By now all of that was his habit. His clothes, his manner, his silences at times of stress, all habits of style he had accepted as proper, his mother's wish, a way of doing things now without thinking about them, like never undoing his tie until he got undressed for the night. His mother would have told him that when she sent him off to Andover. Keep your tie on at all times and never undo your neck button. And he had obeyed. He had accepted his tweeds and his flannels and his blazer with the crest, and when the time came for him to go to MIT, he had been accepted there without so much as a flutter of anyone's doubt, certainly not his mother's: she had seen to everything. Over and over again, whenever she had the opportunity, she would tell Cynthia about Sandy's boyhood and how responsive and thoughtful and sensitive and instinctively good he had always been— and was—and always would be. Cynthia could count on that. She wanted Cynthia to marry Sandy. She approved of Cynthia and her family and its position—Mrs. Klein's word to describe financial sufficiency, "Yes, Cynthia, your... position... is admirable." She approved; therefore, Sandy accepted. The marriage took place mid-war up in Hartford. Mrs. Klein saw to everything. She even saw to Cynthia's gown, since there wasn't any Mrs. Berk by then... she should rest in peace.

Paul Sykes, Sandy's baritone friend from Camp Gordon, was best man. Marlene, Cynthia's sister, was maid of honor. Paul and Marlene were no longer dating, and that night, when asked when he might marry, Paul told Mrs. Klein, "I've been married once, and now I'm... not anymore. I doubt that I'll find anyone else to love again for a long, long time, if ever."

"Certainly you will. You're too handsome not to." And immediately she whirled around, studying the other dancers, looking for a likely candidate for so handsome a young man.

Paul, however, was staring at Sandy, not at Mrs. Klein. Cynthia had seen and heard it all. She'd always remember that peculiar stillness in Sandy's eyes as Paul answered Mrs. Klein, that peculiar glazed look, revealing nothing, accepting everything that was said, accepting everything that was done around him and for him, with equanimity. All the same to him. Accepting his style from his mother. Accepting Cynthia because his mother said to. The only time he'd ever resisted was when he told his mother they would not live in Hartford after they were married. His mother had even gone so far as to rent a house for them, and Sandy had told her, gently, firmly told her, to *un*rent it because they were not going to be living in Hartford. He had been doing some scouting around on his own. When he was discharged, when he was sure of where he would be working—

"...certainly you'll want to work here in Connecticut, Sandy."

"Why is that, Mother? I'd much prefer being closer to New York City, or perhaps right in it. I love the idea of a big city. I'm sure Cynthia does too."

Cynthia didn't. Cynthia told him so, but on that one issue, Sandy would not be dissuaded. He had many job offers; he took the one in New York City with Royal Electronics. He moved them out to Levittown, where he insisted he wanted to live, "—no matter how it offends my mother. She'll just have to get used to it. So will you, Cynthia. It'll be a fresh beginning for both of us here. We'll be the same as everyone else here. One of the masses. And wouldn't you prefer this Levittown to the one outside Philadelphia? Wouldn't you prefer New York City?"

That much had been true: she preferred Levittown, New York, to Levittown, Pennsylvania—if that was all she could have to choose between.

It had been. Sandy insisted. It was the only time he insisted on anything since they had been married. "I want a house that looks like everyone else's."

"Sandy?" She hated to break into his reading of the *Times*, but just then she hated more the fact that he seemed so separated from her. And what was it she wanted to ask him? What? "Sandy?" He looked up, waiting. "Do you ever hear from Paul Sykes anymore?"

His eyes glazed over. A blue glaze. Very blue. Very tired. All the driving tired them. "Seldom . . . but occasionally," and then he changed the subject. "There's a notice about a Toscanini Beethoven concert. At Carnegie Hall. The NBC Symphony. I'd love to see him once more."

"Who?"

"What do you mean, who? Who else? Toscanini."

"I thought you meant Paul Sykes."

His gaze shifted down to the paper. "Sometimes, Cynthia, I wonder what goes on inside your head."

"Just sometimes? I wonder what goes on inside your head all the time, Sandy. Sometimes I even look at you and wonder why you married me."

He stared over at her. He was tired. He sighed. "You're feeling guilty, aren't you? You're feeling guilty about not staying here today. You're sorry you didn't join Evelyn and the others, aren't you, Cynthia? Why not admit it?"

"No. Absolutely not. I don't agree with handling it their way. You know how I hate forcing people to do what they don't want to do. I was thinking of something else entirely. I was thinking about you. And about myself. I was watching you read, I was appreciating how handsome you are, and that just led me to think about myself by comparison."

102

"By comparison you're fine. How would you like to go to bed? It's late. We're both tired. I've got to go up to Glen Cove in the morning early. A new installation....Okay? Bed?" He stood up. He reached for her hand. She was as tall as he was, and bigger-boned. It embarrassed her standing next to him just then. What *was* wrong with her tonight? "I'll just put these things into the sink. You get into bed. I'll be there in a minute."

He liked to undress alone. He liked to be in bed, in his pajamas, first. That was his habit. And if when she joined him and found that he had no bottoms on, then they would have sex. That was his habit too. They didn't talk about it at all. There was no need to. As soon as she slipped into bed, she would find out.

That night he wore no pajamas. No tops. No bottoms. Enough moonlight in the dark room to see the fine features of his face. And his fair hair.

She removed her nightgown. She rolled toward him, leaned up and over him the way she always did. She brushed the hair on his chest back and forth, and he remained still beneath her. She so seldom had the chance to do that to him. Usually he didn't like any of that kind of play. Usually, in his pajama tops, she would simply get on top of him, fit him into her, jump on him a few times, and that was that. Sometimes he wouldn't even have to move.

So why was he this night suddenly pulling her down onto his chest? Why was he holding on to her this night? Why was he suddenly behaving as if he wanted something more from her? He was trying to move her down, to move her down lower on his body. Why that night? He'd never tried to do anything like that before. She wouldn't. No. She sat up. She straddled him, got him fixed inside her. His eyes were closed. He was so beautiful. Lean. Boyishly muscular. A child. A beautiful child whom she loved. She would never be loved the way she loved him. Never. She was too big. Too big. And too plain. Plain. Plain. She pumped. Plain. Plain. Plain...and in a few seconds he shuddered and was done.

She rolled off and away, panting.

She went to the bathroom: her habit, cleaning herself immediately.

When she returned, his pajamas were on. He was on his side, his back toward her. He was breathing regularly. He would say nothing.

Neither would she. Not even in the morning.

103

She lay there in the darkness trying to think of nothing at all, trying to get her mind to go blank. She heard Melanie cough. Once. Twice. Three times. And the silence. Quiet. Sandy's breathing. A low gentle whistling sound against his pillow.

She wished she were back in South Carolina. She missed her father. Maybe she would take Melanie down there for a visit. Sandy couldn't object to that. He wouldn't even care.... That was unfair. He loved Melanie. He did. She had no doubt about that. It was just that he didn't know fathering. He had no habit about that. His own father had stayed out of that role pretty much. Sandy didn't know how to father. And he didn't know how to brother Melanie either. And how to husband? Did he know that?

She turned toward him. She wanted to smooth his back, to touch his skin again.

She heard a siren, far off. And then a fire engine, far off. And then another siren. They were oddly comforting sounds, as if things in the world out there were going on as usual and would go on, no matter what happened to her or to Sandy or to Melanie. There was comfort in knowing that they were inside, protected, sealed off for the night. A sense of order to the way things worked, even in a crisis, even when a house was on fire somewhere..... Maybe she would try to get tickets to the Beethoven concert, to the Toscanini Beethoven concert. Maybe she would try to locate Paul Sykes and invite him to the concert. Maybe she should just close her eyes and let her mind go blank and sleep and not ask questions anymore about anything at all.

She concentrated on sleep. She heard the oil burner start up. She turned on her side, away from Sandy.

She heard another fire engine, racing somewhere, far off.

[3] The front door was closing, very quietly closing. Seven-fifteen. Morning. Sandy was leaving.

Melanie was up. In her bedroom, playing quietly with her Raggedy Ann doll. Cynthia could hear her talking to the doll, telling it to be quiet because Mommy was sleeping.

"Melanie, sweetheart. Mommy's up. Come say good morning, sweetheart." And she was there, even before Cynthia could sit up. She was in her plaid flannel nightshirt. Warm enough. "Did Daddy give you juice, sweetheart?"

Yes, he had, she nodded, and slid into Daddy's place in

bed. "Mommy, I want to stay home today from nursery school. I want to stay in bed here. I have a cold, Mommy."

Cynthia felt her forehead. "No you don't. You're faking, miss. I know you by now. You just march yourself into the bathroom and wash up, and I'll do your breakfast. Just march now," but instead of letting her go, Cynthia hugged her, squeezed her, kissing each dark eye, smoothing back her curls. And then she nudged her away. "Now, get in there and wash up good."

Almost before she could get her robe on, the telephone was ringing.

Corinne. Had Cynthia heard the sirens and fire engines through the night? Well, what it was was the Rogers house had been set on fire. They'd tried to burn it but it didn't go that far. The Rogerses went to Rita's for the night, "...and as soon as the kids are taken care of, we're all going over there. To Rita's. Maybe now you'll realize, Cynthia, just what this is all about. Maybe now you'll be willing to wake up to reality, Cynthia."

[4] She went to Rita's. She didn't want to, but she forced herself to do it. Evelyn had called right after Corinne had. Evelyn had persuaded her to at least come and listen. "We're talking about human beings, Cynthia. Very human beings. We're talking about injustice, Cynthia. A man and a woman and two little girls. People tried to burn them up, Cynthia, to kill them...."

So she went, and when she got there and looked at the Rogers family sitting in Rita's living room, sitting beneath the Van Gogh *Potato Eaters* and *The Bridge at Arles* and the *Postmaster,* Cynthia felt something slip through the iron doors of her will. She felt like she would start to cry and never stop, unless she turned away, unless she turned away from the sight of those little girls asleep, one on Calvin's lap, the other on Maryellen's lap. She would turn away. She would not cry. She would retrieve from her past the absolute knowledge that to go about doing things the way Rita wanted to do them was wrong, was bound to end up in tragedy for everyone concerned, especially the coloreds. Rita just wanted to take the law into her own hands. And it wasn't even a question of law anyway. Colored people are different, and not until they change themselves to be more like white people...One of the little girls shuddered, opened her eyes,

105

reached for her father's neck, frightened. Tears rushed back into Cynthia's eyes.

She brushed them away. She sat down between Loretta and Missy on the sofa opposite the Rogerses.

Evelyn and Corinne were standing behind Rita. Rita was talking to Calvin. She was trying to convince him to stay on, to please hold out a little longer, to give people in Levittown a chance to find out what was going on, because she was sure that once more and more people in Levittown found out what had happened, they'd support Calvin; she knew they would, they had to, just wait and see....

He didn't want to. He wouldn't. He wasn't going to risk any more. If anything happened to Maryellen or the girls, he'd kill those bastards. He would. He'd done enough. He wasn't going to do any more. She'd have to find someone else. Enough was enough. "Even after the fire was out and we were standing there in the cold night, they were still calling us nigger. From the other side of the street they were..."

Cynthia watched him. He stared straight ahead. Not up at Rita or Evelyn or Corinne. He was looking at something inside himself. She knew that look, knew what he was thinking about and seeing in his head. He was imagining how he was going to get even. Growing up, in certain streets in Charleston she had seen that cold angry look. It had frightened her then. It frightened her more now, because all Calvin Rogers had to do was reach out, get even with *them*—but he wouldn't. Not Calvin Rogers. Someone else would. Sooner or later someone would. And it was going to be terrible...unless there was some kind of orderly change. Cynthia was sure that was the only way. Not Rita's way. Orderly. Over a period of time. A long, long time. And not by breaking the law. The Levitts had a right to do what they wanted with their property.

"I don't want my family to live in Levittown," Calvin patted his daughter's back. She was crying out, suddenly sobbing, then whimpering again. "No. Not in a place like this. I don't think it's ever going to be any better than what it is right now. It's yours. They gave it to you. You can keep it."

Rita moved back, and then Evelyn tried. Evelyn knelt to take hold of the child, but Calvin wouldn't let her. No, he nodded. She stood up. He wasn't seeing her anyway. Cynthia knew that. Calvin Rogers wanted nothing from any one of them anymore.

And then Abe Moskowitz came in from the kitchen to say

that maybe the best thing for right then was for him to drive Calvin and Maryellen and the girls back into the city, he'd drive them up to Calvin's mother's apartment on 116th Street, "...and from there you'll decide, Calvin. Give it a few days and see."

"Nothing to see more than I've seen already, Abe. You can drive us to the station. We'll take the train back into the city."

Loretta stood, and then Missy, and they clustered around Corinne and Rita, and Evelyn was still holding out a hand that had already been rejected, a rejection she seemed unwilling to, couldn't, accept.

That's Evelyn, all right. Needs to be slapped in the face before she realizes what's what—Cynthia knew Calvin's kind, and if Evelyn didn't step back from in front of him...

But Calvin just stood up, holding his daughter, motioning for Maryellen to come on because they were going, they were getting out before worse happened, and Rita kept on muttering for Cal to please stay, to see, to wait, because there were lots of decent people in Levittown, lots more than not, she was certain of it, absolutely certain, people, men, who had gone through the war and understood what suffering was all about, they did, they just needed to be pushed a little, they just needed to be made to see, "...and if you would stay, Cal, and let them see the injustice..."

It was Abe who stopped her. He held her, awkwardly; he was too tall and round and she was so small, and just then, she seemed smaller and smaller.

Cynthia watched Calvin and his family step out of the Moskowitz house, Abe following. A gorgeous morning out there, Cynthia could see from where she sat, arms folded, on the sofa. Tightest little buds on those pathetic excuses for trees. Take years before they looked the beginning of respectable. She felt sustained. All her carpings were correct. She and Sandy had to move Melanie out of Levittown just as soon as they could.

The door closed. "You see," she found herself saying without meaning to, "you see what happens when you interfere where you shouldn't. Things have to take their course."

"You've decided that, have you?" Loretta lit up, poked her cigarette at Cynthia's face. "And it's your course they have to take? Well, I say bullshit to that."

"Please..." Missy reached for Loretta's arm. "Not now."

"Why not now?" Corinne wanted to know. "Now's as good
107

a time as any. Maybe now's the best time for Cynthia to face the music a little bit. What if one of those little girls was Melanie? Then what would you say, Cynthia?"

Cynthia wouldn't dignify the question with an answer. She looked away, toward the window. The venetian blind was up. Sunlight—but no curtains on any of the windows. No real paintings on the walls. Copies. And sketches tacked up. Of people. Loretta's sketches, and not very good. It was all so barren, without any style. Just little pots of struggling ivy and a house the shape of a box. Ugly. All of it—but nowhere else for any of them to go.

"No answer, Cynthia?"

"Not now," Missy persisted.

"Yes, now," Evelyn said. "Now's the time to get started."

So naive, all of them, Cynthia thought. They'll see what's what..... And then she was up and out of that house. She had other things to do with her life than to sit around feeling sorry for other people. She had herself and what was becoming of her life to feel sorry for.

PART TWO

1956

Evelyn Selden
Loretta Massi
Corinne Feuerstein
Melissa Geiger
Cynthia Klein

11

Evelyn Selden

[1]   The ladies were astir on the grass in the backyard. Mid-morning, and too hot to think. "Ladies! Please? A few more minutes and we can all go to Jones...." Evelyn waited for some listening silence, for some serious silence, which the occasion certainly deserved. It was now or never. If she couldn't get the block captains enthused, then it was hope-less—and it was the beginning of August already. "Ladies...I think we all realize this is Adlai's last chance. If he loses in November, if he loses for the second time...then he's lost to us for good. Therefore, between now and Labor Day we need to organize a conscientious canvass of each block here in the W section. At party headquarters I've been trying to convince them to bring him out here for Labor Day weekend. They're receptive—but only if they think he's got any kind of chance to carry some part of this district...if not the country...." Hopeless! They would not be still. Fanning. Leaning. One side. The other.

"Usually the party gives up on Nassau County. They did in fifty-two, some of you may remember. Republican terri-tory, they say. But we know that's beginning to change."

Some beginning! Some changing. She had all she could do to corral forty ladies to do a little canvassing. She could have accommodated one hundred in her backyard. In fifty-two it had been different. They were still on Spring Lane in fifty-two, but now she had room. Now she had a corner plot and a big backyard with mature trees to sit under. A willow. An oak. A maple. Their third Levitt. A ranch. Taupe-beige with white trim. "...and I hope by our effort to convince the Na-tional Committee..." The wrong approach: wheedling and whining in the heat of an August morning. Some changing!

Nineteen-fifty-six was going to be worse than fifty-two. Even more apathy, and Korea was behind them. More of them liked Ike than they were willing to admit. Cynthia did. Southern Pedestrian, that's what she said she was. And Missy was above politics. Missy was a fanatic about being above politics. . . . Evelyn stopped speaking altogether. She was staring out at the ladies stirring on the grass in her backyard—because the baby was suddenly kicking.

She put her hand on her stomach. She wasn't showing yet, but it was coming alive. Whatever it turned out to be, it was coming alive.

Loretta, the only one of her friends she had told, was coming over to her. "You all right, Ev?"

Corinne, stretched under the willow, sat up. So Corinne knew too. Probably Arlene knew, and if Arlene knew, then everyone knew. Arlene was smiling over at her. Sure she knew. No one could keep a secret for more than five minutes—including Loretta. "I thought I could trust you, Loretta." She whispered, but through the still morning heat her voice carried.

Loretta was nimble. Loretta was quick. "Sure you can trust me, Ev. I'll work my ass off for Adlai. See if I don't. All of us are going to, aren't we, ladies?"

Instead of responding vocally, they began standing up. They were leaving. The meeting was over, and Evelyn felt the baby kick again. Poor Adlai!

And then Corinne was on her way over, Audrey and Edna trailing her; Missy and Cynthia came from another side. "Whose car today for Jones?" Corinne wanted to know.

There were enough so that Audrey offered her station wagon, but Evelyn thought maybe she'd drive herself, because her father was coming out on an afternoon train and she wanted to be home in time for when the boys came from day camp. Audrey assured her they'd be back in time, because Evelyn didn't look so hot; she looked a little peaked. Loretta thought so too. And Corinne did. . . although Corinne didn't look so hot herself.

So, okay, they all knew!

[2] Levittowners had their particular spot at Jones Beach. On Beach 6. The parking lot was close to the sand. During the week there was no trouble getting onto it. Weekends they had to go very early, for breakfast. Sundays, Evelyn would pack bagels and cream cheese and tomatoes and three different thermoses—milk for the boys, coffee for Harold, tea for herself—and they would get to Jones by 8:30. Sundays, everyone was there at Jones; Sundays, all the Originals from the old S section would get together for breakfast on the

beach, and all the children would be there, and the husbands—minus one now, minus Ken Halpern now, Audrey's Ken, a heart attack last winter, shoveling snow, one two, three, gone...the first of the Originals.

Evelyn was sitting behind Audrey. Audrey the *shtarke,* the strong! She had begun laughing again only during the last month. Before Ken died, she had always laughed and kidded and sworn she was going on a diet to end all diets, because ever since Deborah was born...Audrey drove in silence this morning. Too hot for laughing. Too hot for going to the beach, as a matter of fact, but habit was habit.

Weekdays at the beach were a different matter altogether. Usually, there were few if any children. They were in day camps or regular sleep-away camps, and so weekdays the ladies played bridge or Scrabble or lined up against their backrests and just stared out at the ocean. Weekdays Evelyn enjoyed most of all. She needed days like those. Since her mother had died this past winter, she needed days like those more than she would have expected. At thirty-four she was tired, and her father was coming out again for a visit that wasn't really a visit at all, because what he did was sit in the living room and read, reading one book, two books a day, reading and not knowing or talking about what he had read, in a daze, waiting to come out of it, to come out of his loneliness, not paying any attention to his grandsons at all—and now she was pregnant again. A third child for their third Levitt...

Strange how, without ever planning it, all of the Originals had moved from their Cape Cods into the W section. The W section didn't have a Levittown mailing address. Their mail came through Wantagh, a fact which the old-time Wantagh residents resented. Too bad for them. Too bad about their higher school taxes. Anti-Semites! Most of them she'd met were, anyway....The houses in the W section were bigger than the Cape Cods. Theirs even had a finished second floor with two bedrooms and a separate bathroom up there. Big rooms—so they had decided to have another child. It hadn't been any mistake. Loretta had just assumed that was the case when Evelyn told her about being pregnant, that day in June when the two of them had driven over to Jones because Evelyn wanted to tell Loretta something important, something that her closest friend should be the first to hear, and hear from the source itself.

"Okay. So mistakes you can correct, Ev. You want me to

112

help you get an abortion? Because no one in her right mind would have a baby nowadays."

No, Evelyn assured her, she didn't want any help with an abortion, not that she was antiabortion. She wasn't. But she wanted to have her baby, "...just because things in the world are so horrible. I can add one more to our side, to the decency side."

"You have another kid at your age, Ev, and you're starting the whole thing over again. You'll be starting from the beginning again. You'll be chained back in the house all over again. After being active so many years out here. Why do you want that? You should be going into politics now, Ev, now that things are beginning to change."

"Where are they changing, Loretta? We still don't have any Negro families living in Levittown. And no matter what we do for Adlai, Eisenhower's going to win. Out here especially."

"I thought you wanted to start college? I thought we were going to concentrate on that, Ev. Going to school."

"I'm not ready yet. I wanted another baby. So did Harold. In a few years I'll be ready for school."

"I don't know whether I'll be able to hold out for a few more years, Ev."

At that moment Evelyn wasn't sure she was going to hold out until they reached Beach 6. She was sweltering. She should have stayed home. The baby was kicking again.

"You okay, Ev?" Loretta, seated next to her in the back of Audrey's car, look worried. But Missy was on the other side of her—just in case. Just-in-case Missy! Missy was the best in an emergency. Loretta went to pieces. When the news came about Evelyn's mother having cancer, Loretta broke down. Missy had been there too, having coffee, talking recipes that day last winter and the snow outside—fortunate that Missy had been there. She got Loretta to stop crying; she made some tea for Evelyn. So if Evelyn were to pass out right there in the back of Audrey's car, Missy could take charge. She would, or Cynthia, up front, between Audrey and Gladys, could. They could all take care of each other: her closest friends. Plus Corinne. Next to Harold and the boys—and her father?—they mattered the most...now.

"A parker," Audrey shouted, "up front. *Gott se danken.*"

[3]   No waves at all.

They sat at the water's edge, talking, lolling. The second

113

carfull had arrived, Edna's car, with Rita and Sally and Arlene and Corinne.

Corinne couldn't go in the water. She was having her
period.

And Evelyn was having her mood.

As usual Loretta was having her problems. With Joe, who
else? "Always, Joe. A man who's willing to just go on selling
railroad tickets as a profession, day after day, in the same
station...what's the use. It'll never be any different, our
life...unless I make it different."

"You're different, Loretta. You're very different since we
met. About fifteen pounds different." Corinne could do it and
get away with it. Corinne had rights with Loretta that Evelyn
knew she was the only other one in the bunch who did. Just
let Arlene try to say something like that, and Bingo.

"Why the hell not? What's to be thin for?"

"For your own self-esteem." Gladys Ginsburg had just begun grapefruit. The famous grapefruit diet. Wherever she
went, she went with a bag of grapefruit.

"Bullshit."

"Must you, Loretta!" Missy let the sand slide through her
delicate fingers. "We're out in the open air. There are children
all around you."

"Bullshit. Self-esteem is for when things are going well,
you feel it. When they're not, how the hell *can* you feel it?
I eat because I *don't* feel it."

"And when you get philosophical, Loretta, I..."

"You what, Cynthia?"

"Frankly, I want to run for cover."

"So run, why don't you?"

"Why should I? I do have self-esteem, Loretta. Even if you
insult me, I still have self-esteem."

"Aren't you lucky. You better count your blessings. You
never know how long they're going to last."

"Loretta? Must you?" Evelyn had to heave up; they all did;
a surprising wave had rushed the water up on to the sand
beneath them. She felt heavy. She wished she could jump up,
jump up and away, into the water. She should have followed
her instinct, her first impulse, which was to stay home.
Everyone was out of sorts.

Corinne was having her period.

Loretta was having her problems, but she shut up anyway.
For Evelyn.

Because Evelyn was having her mood. Nevertheless she

was glad to be pregnant. Probably she would be the last of the Originals to have a baby. Certainly none of the ladies with her were going to. Except maybe Missy. Missy might. Missy might do anything Evelyn did. Loretta too—except a baby. That was definitely out. And definitely out for Cynthia. Cynthia was lucky to have her one. So was Corinne. Although, why lucky? And why no more for either of them? Because of Sandy? Because of Lionel? Because of time . . . because the time for having one was really over with. Thirty-four. Thirty-five. Thirty-six. Too old. And Audrey would have to find a new man to have one. Edna, Arlene, Sally, Gladys—they all had what they wanted. Two. Enough. Stop—and they had. They'd said it just that way: enough; stop. And Rita had always said at those confessionals, "I'll take another principle. If you don't mind. I'd rather have another of those than another baby."

Evelyn had felt just the opposite, even before her mother died.

Harold couldn't have been happier. "It'll keep you home at nights more." Which almost made her change her mind: his attitude about her "causes," as he liked to call them. Her SANE work. Her joining the Library Initiative Committee. Her helping to form a theater group. Her continuing activity for the Democratic party. And the latest thing—she would have to give up on that, running for the school board. She'd been asked; she was weighing it. Harold was against it. "Too much, Ev. You're not home nights enough as it is. What's wrong with staying home more? We'll have another baby. You'll join Missy's sewing group." No. No baby for a while— but then her mother's dying tipped the argument. She wanted a girl. She wanted to replace what she had lost, to recreate that . . . love. She'd name the baby Ellen. Ellie, she'd call it. She'd continue something that way. She cared about continuity, continuing what mattered for her—and that way Harold would get what he wanted. Each of them would be satisfied.

Loretta was extending her hand, to help her up. So was Rita. Gladys was telling her to come on, up, into the water. They were blocking the sun and the ocean, but she had seen nothing anyway. She had seen nothing, heard nothing, felt nothing—except just then: the baby, kicking. Loretta and Rita helped her up. They were laughing. "You all know, don't you?" She laughed too, forcing it, for them.

They huddled around her, hugging her. "I'm feeling a little ... blue. I'm sorry." They moved closer: Loretta and Rita and Gladys, Cynthia and Missy and Corinne. And it helped, for a while, all those warm feelings, all that understanding ... from friends.

[4] But when she got home, the mood deepened and the afternoon darkened, as if it might storm. She would have a rest, a nap, on the sofa in the living room, before the boys got back from camp, before her father and Harold arrived, before seeing to dinner things. They were going to have a simple one. It was too hot to cook. Her father would just have to understand. Maybe tonight they'd tell him about the baby. Maybe then he would understand her not cooking something for him the way her mother might have, the way she was expected to every time he came out.

She stood next to the sofa. She leaned down to rub up the soft cotton nub of its surface, a short velvety cotton nub, a beige-ivory fabric she had fallen in love with and had to have when they moved into this new house, and Harold had said, yes, they should get a new living-room set, and, yes, they could afford the fabric she wanted, now that he was set with the jewelry company, selling, a solid connection.... So why was she finally crying now?

Why?

Not crying hard or deeply or sobbing. No. Not that way. Quietly crying. Why?

There wasn't any one thing in particular she could name as a reason. She had everything to love. Her husband. Her children. Her friends. Her house. She loved her house. She loved the cool breeze through the living room. She loved stretching out on the velvety cotton nub of the sofa and being able to look through the room, through the shade and cool to the screened-in back porch and out into the backyard and the mature trees, the shrubs, the rock garden she was starting there far back against the fence the next door neighbor had put up. She didn't love that fence. She loved open lawns and free fields. She loved the print hanging on the fireplace wall, her favorite, of the golden wheat field, the gold under a gray, lowering sky; and the sketch of a Central Park hill under snow cover; and a little boy who looked like Danny seated at a table reading from an oversized book, the kind of book Danny liked to hold and read and disappear behind; and the Modigliani print of the little girl with pigtails.... Herself. Except when had she ever been that

116

skinny? Never. Still and all, there was a similarity. Something. . . .

The fireplace wall was, if anyone were to ask her, her prized spot in the whole house. The prints, the photographs, the arrangement of shapes on texture, the arrangement of what was real and how the view of it touched hidden, private memories of people, events, places, into something more than life. Her grandmother most of all. In her white hotel apron, stopping as she stepped out of the kitchen door, surprised by the Kodak. Her mother and father in front of the Spring Lane house, dressed for winter, her mother in that ratty muskrat she never wanted to give away, her father in his old cableknit cardigan that was too small for his stomach, the always closed buttons straining. He was smiling. And another one of them—with the boys, on the porch of the two-family in Brooklyn. That house, over with. And Harold, sitting on the steps of his barracks in fatigues, a pipe clenched tightly in his teeth. Still managing somehow to smile and look handsomer than she had ever seen anyone look. That would have been. . . in 1940. When he was stationed in Panama. Sixteen years ago. Sixteen years, over with, and to prove how fast that passage, the last picture to go up on that wall: Danny, almost twelve, Morty, nine. She'd put that one right beneath the Eleanor Roosevelt print, the one of Eleanor, her hand curled beneath her chin, smiling down—on them. . . . Almost time to decide about Danny's bar mitzvah. Whether yes or no. . . to decide! Not if her mother were still alive. No ifs, ands, or buts then—which made no sense whatsoever anymore, either, to do something no one felt anything about, certainly not Danny, but to do it anyway, for the sake of custom, for continuity's sake, for the memory of someone loved and lost who would never know what you did or didn't do. . . for them. Never. . . .

That's why she was crying. Of course that was why. For the loss of something she didn't know how to shape into words. Something she felt. Something she remembered. A picture. Not on the wall. An image. Inside. In her head, forever, of her mother. In a summer dress. Dark blue pima cotton with big white polka dots all over it. A pocketbook of white shell held at her side. A white turban wound tight and high. She was so short, not quite five feet: an image that didn't fit and never seemed to fade. It made no sense whatsoever anymore, remembering that.

But nothing made any sense.

117

Nothing that most people did made any sense. Still and all, they—she—kept on doing them. What else could they do? Other than get married, have children, buy a house, pay off a mortgage a husband works a whole lifetime to finish paying off. Long after the children have grown up and moved out of the house. Sensible? And what did that have to do with being pregnant? Or with her mother's dying. What?

Why couldn't she think out one thought clearly?

Why was she so incapable of thinking clearly? Logically. Sensibly.

She felt stupid.

She wasn't. She was feeling sorry for herself. She was indulging herself. She should be up and doing. She should be "All the Way with Adlai." She should force herself up. She should bake something for her father. She would not cry again for the rest of the day—but she would stay put. For another fifteen minutes. She would just let her mind go blank until the boys got home, until Harold arrived with her father.

She closed her eyes. She clasped her hands on top of her stomach. The baby slept. She slept.

[5] "Okay, boys. Put your baseball gloves in the garage. The steak's ready." Harold's voice reached her from outside: her signal too, to load the tray. The baked potatoes, the salad, the salt, the pepper, the butter, the bread, the pitcher of iced tea.

The table was set on the screened-in porch. A perfect evening. Not too hot. An unexpected breeze. A bonus. A glow of sunset colors. Only the glow, never the sunset visible at the back of the house. "Dad? Harold's ready with the steak. Didn't you hear him?" She stepped back into the living room before setting the tray down. He didn't hear her. "Dad?" He was reading. He was sitting at the far end of the sofa...or was he sleeping? "Dad?" He looked up then, surprised. "Dad? The steak's done."

Harold was coming in from outside.

The boys raced in from the garage.

"Wash up first," she told them.

Danny objected, making that *tsk*ing sound she absolutely hated. "Do I—"

"You do."

"Grandpa's not."

"Do as your mother says, Danny." Holding the steak platter, Harold joined her in the doorway. "Morrie, ready.... Let's

118

not let things get cold.... None of that *tsk*ing, Danny. I told you before about that. You see? Morty's back already. You're wasting time."

"Grandpa? You take me."

She let that one pass, because Grandpa was at least getting up. He took hold of Danny's hand. He led him off into the bathroom.

The meal began in silence. Harold filled each plate with steak slices.

She opened each baked potato, moving around the table, buttering each one, giving to each his salad, telling Danny, when she came to him, to remove his hand from on top of the salad bowl because he was going to have salad or there would be no ice cream later from Grandpa, period, and no ride in the car to the carnival; she didn't like to threaten him that way, but he left no alternative, and did he understand?

He understood—but he *tsk*ed and Harold told him to stop that *tsk*ing or to leave the table, "...and we can also do without the frowning. Smiling once in a while wouldn't break your face."

A quiet *tsk*, almost unheard, half a challenge.

"Danny, I don't like—"

"Harold, please, not now." If she started crying again, she... she didn't know what she'd do. She pleaded silently for him to just start eating; they would take care of Danny later, please. "Dad, do you need anything else?"

He had never stopped eating, once his plate was set in front of him. He chewed on dully, uninterestedly, his mind somewhere else. He was seated, alone, on one side of the table, the boys opposite him, watching him just then, waiting for him to respond. He hadn't heard her. He was leaning over his plate, as if he didn't have the strength to sit up straight. Always an ample man, tall, full, commanding, now he had seemed to give up, to cave in, to move slowly. He needed to be told what to do next or he would just go on doing the same thing over and over again, like chewing.

"Grandpa?" Danny called across. "Grandpa?" louder. "I have to ask you an important question."

"What?" But Morrie did not look across at Danny. His gaze shifted to the outside, to a chair under the willow tree, where her mother, when visiting, had liked to sit, reading—and then he realized who was speaking to him. "Sorry, Danny. I was thinking of something else."

"Grandpa, did you ever have a bar mitzvah?"

"Did I ever have a bar mitzvah? Of course I had one."

"Why?"

"Because I was Jewish and I got to be thirteen and I had one."

"That's why?"

"Isn't that a good enough reason?"

"No, Grandpa. Mr. Rothstein, who was my home-room teacher last year, used to tell us a person should understand the reasons for doing what they do."

"Was Grandma alive when you were bar-mitzvahed?" Morty asked. He knew the answer. Evelyn knew he knew the answer. He just wanted to make them laugh instead of getting angry at Danny. Morty had that way. He had his one dimple, like hers, and his black curly hair, like hers, and her round face. Danny was more a mixture. Luckier for Danny to have more of Harold in his face, but unlucky for him not to know how to laugh at anything. Even her father was then, fortunately. Well, he wasn't exactly laughing. No one had reached that point yet, where thinking about her mother could evoke the joyful sense of her. But at least he was smiling, a rueful smile, appreciating Morty's attempt. Good—and then the baby kicked again. She dropped her fork, the clang a call for attention.

"What, Ev?" Harold started out of his chair.

"That's the third time today I felt it."

"What, Ma?" Morty the jokester was frightened. "Felt what, Ma?"

But, answering, she kept her eyes on her father and his sad smile, "The baby," and then she shifted her gaze to Harold, to his eyes, happy eyes, agreeing, that this was a good time to tell them.

"When are you going to have it?" Danny asked, matter-of-fact, as if he had known right along, as if he understood everything there was to know about having a baby.

"In December."

Morty seemed frightened. She reached over to him, smoothed back his hair. "I'm all right, Morty. There's nothing to worry about."

Her father was still smiling, but he was also crying now. "You'll name her after your mother...."

"What if it's a boy, Grandpa?" Now that they had stopped eating, Danny had begun. Morty was still asking if she was sure she was really all right.

When she brought out the lemon meringue pie, "like

120

Grandma's," only then would Morty be satisfied that she would not have to be rushed to the hospital immediately. "For you, Morty. I made it for you and Grandpa—but Danny can have some if he's willing to be bar-mitzvahed.... Regardless of what Mr. Rothstein said."

[6] They didn't get to bed until after midnight, and then she wanted to talk, about the whole day, about everything, the meeting that morning, the election that Stevenson couldn't possibly win, and about her father, and how the boys had reacted to news of the baby—she had also forgotten to send his suit to the cleaners, she suddenly remembered. She could remember so many things from years back, but sending his suit to the cleaners, that she had forgotten to do, sorry....

He nodded. She saw that, watching him in the darkness. He was tired. He had every right to be.

But she wanted to talk to him. She needed to talk to him, to try to explain and describe how strange she'd been feeling all day, and then too. "Right now, Harold, I feel ... like crying again. For no good reason I understand." Was he listening? She raised herself over him to see. His eyes were closed.

"Sorry, Ev, but I'm really bushed. I did so much driving today."

Never mind, because she was the one who should be sorry, she should just let him go to sleep. She would, except for this strange feeling she'd had all day, "... about us, Harold ... about our life ... our whole life. Our future. I get these pictures in my head. This one is of us. It's almost like a dream. We're walking along a road. I recognize the road. It's the one in front of the hotel. Only, it isn't curved. It's straight, and I can see to the end of it, and the end looks exactly like where we are right now. Exactly. We keep walking and doing things, but the end looks exactly the same as where we are right now. It doesn't make any sense, Harold. I don't believe life should be that way. Harold? Do you?"

"What way?"

"The same. Always the same. No matter what you do. No matter what you accomplish."

He sat up then, but he didn't say anything.

"Harold? Remember what you promised my mother? About school? Remember that night?"

"I remember it. Sure I remember it. But what do you expect me to do about it now?"

"Nothing...now. As long as you feel...happy. As long as you still love me. You do, don't you?"

"I do." He held her. "I don't want things to be different. I have everything I want. Our children. Our house. I'm happy that you're pregnant. I'm . . . happy . . . about everything. I'm lucky to be alive. I'm lucky to love you." He kissed her. "Someday, you can go to college . . . for both of us." He kissed her again, smoothed the hair back from her forehead, as if she were a little girl.

And then, for no reason she understood, she found that she was crying again. Not sobbing the way she had that afternoon. Not out of control. Not anything like that. Just crying, quietly, as Harold held her inside his arms.

He lowered her back onto her pillow. "What you need most of all is a good night's rest. You'll feel better in the morning."

He turned on his side, away from her.

She listened in the darkness to his breathing, to that even, safe sound. He was lucky. He always fell asleep fast.

12

[1]   Heavy...with child. The seventh month was no time to be rushing around from meeting to meeting. Oh, how she had wanted to just plain stay home. But when Loretta said, "You've got to go, Ev, otherwise they'll eat him up alive, those Nazis," and then Danny told her, "You got to, Ma. Mr. Rothstein's my favorite teacher I ever had. Daddy can go to Morty's. Come on, Ma." So, no choice. She went, with Loretta and Rita and Missy, from the final preelection block captains' meeting to Open School Night.

And, yes, Mr. Rothstein did have gray hair, but he wasn't old. Danny thought he had to be old. He wasn't. Evelyn was sure he wasn't even thirty yet. Prematurely gray. Thin. A skin-and-bones type. But ruddy. Like a thin Indian head topped with lots of wavy, shiny gray hair. It was his hair that had changed most since that day he'd introduced himself to her. She'd never forget it. She was taking Morty to school, day after Labor Day, 1952, and she was wearing her biggest "All the Way with Adlai" pin and this slim, undernourished young man came up to her, brownish hair then, smiling, excited, and said, "I'm Aaron Rothstein. This is my first day teaching here, or anywhere, and seeing your pin makes me feel welcome." "Well, if you're on our side, you're certainly welcome, Mr. Rothstein, but the truth is, it's an uphill battle for Adlai," she had said. "All important battles are uphill, Mrs....?" "Selden. Evelyn Selden." "...Mrs. Selden. But you just have to take a deep breath and continue." And what had changed since then, as far as she could tell, was only his hair—and Adlai was about to lose for the second time.

Aaron Rothstein was taking a deep breath. He leaned back along the edge of his desk, folded his arms, smiling. "Welcome, parents. I'm sure you're not very comfortable in those children's desk chairs, but those are my orders from above, from the high command. You sit in alphabetical order at your children's desks. You're uncomfortable. I'm uncomfortable watching you—and that's how you're supposed to get to know me. Silly idea. I tell you that because I received tenure last year. I'm free to criticize with impunity. Also, I'm being promoted to seventh and eighth-grade English. I'm moving to the Jonas E. Salk Junior High. I would have been there this year if they had finished the building in time, or if Dr. Salk had discovered his vaccine sooner. You have a question, Mrs. Massi?"

"A comment, more than a question. I'll get around to a question. Anyway, first of all, we, a group of us, I'm speaking for a group, we're all glad they didn't finish the Salk building sooner. Our kids love you. This school's going to miss you, but this school's loss'll be the Salk's gain, because, as far as our group is concerned..." Loretta was doing an Academy Award performance, doing it exactly as they had planned it, using up time, stalling, frustrating the enemy. Because the enemy was most assuredly there and ready to explode. Evelyn knew those faces. "... our group, by the way, is called the Levittown Ladies Education Support Group—"

"Ask a question, lady, or shut up. This is Open School Night, not a public debate. We got fifteen minutes, and you're using up my time."

"If you'll shut up, mister, I'll get to my question. I was recognized. I've got the floor. This is a democracy, don't forget." Hands on hips, Loretta glowered down at the enemy. A Mr. Bauer. Evelyn knew him from school-board meetings. He wanted bigger classes. He wanted reproduction out of the biology curriculum. He was seated up front; overflowing his child's desk. He was a Joe McCarthy leftover. They were taking second breaths too. "So, as I started to say, and speaking for our group, we want to thank you, Mr. Rothstein, for being the inspiration you've been for our kids, because without inspiration, there is no education, and without education, what kind of society are our kids going to inherit?"

"Goddamn it. Either ask a question or shut the hell up. This is some kind of plot here. You people—"

"What is this 'you-people' routine?" Rita was up and at 'em, next to Loretta, leaning down over a Mr. Reilly, whose wife—Evelyn remembered Missy pointing her out—was president of the Holy Sodality Society at St. Bernard's. Missy was even then catching Evelyn's eye and nodding, yes, the very same. "So, mister? I'd like an answer."

"You know what I mean. Either ask a question or shut the hell up."

"Ladies. Mr. Reilly. Please. Calm." Mr. Rothstein unfolded his arms. Time for him to intervene. Evelyn checked her wristwatch. Eight minutes to go. "We're all reasonable human beings here. I think it might be helpful if we turned our attention to the work your children have done so far this term and what they will be doing in the future. That way we can—"

"That way, Mr. Rothstein, I don't get a chance to tell you what I think about your so-called inspiration."

"Why don't you, Mr. Bauer—if Mrs. Massi will relinquish the floor?"

"Whatever *you* say, Mr. Rothstein, because I for one resent the kind of remarks being made here tonight. This is still a democracy." But Loretta did sit down then. Clearly, Mr. Rothstein had everything under control. He only looked defenseless. A surprising man, Evelyn thought. An old-young man. It was his eyes. Dark. Brown. Like the color of his worn brown corduroy suit. When his gaze settled on anyone, it stayed put. The longer he looked, the larger he loomed. Strange, how some people had that quality, how just by being silent and listening or waiting, some people made you pay attention to them. Aaron Rothstein had that... that...thing about him. He was sensitive and he was strong. He hadn't needed their protection. He could take care of himself—and them too, if they needed it .

"Mr. Bauer? You wanted to say..."

"I wanted to say that my kid tells me you're always giving your personal opinions in class about everything and anything. I don't think the classroom is any place for personal opinions. Everything you say to them is some kind of influence. You're supposed to be impartial."

"I'm supposed to be...human. I'm supposed to think. I'm supposed to teach other human beings *how* to think. The way I do that is by telling them how I arrive at a personal opinion. I always tell the students my opinions are personal. I always shall."

During the next stretch of silence, Evelyn felt the baby moving. Danny was lucky. She hoped Morty would have Mr. Rothstein for a teacher. And oh how she wished she had had that kind of teacher when she was younger. And then the bell rang. God—or something—help you, Mr. Rothstein, she thought. God help any honest, sensitive man in a darkening world, if they want to ban reproduction from the curriculum and Adlai loses again.

The enemies rushed out of the room. The ladies formed a ring around Mr. Rothstein's desk.

[2] "Harold!" Screaming. She heard it without realizing she was doing it.

A nurse was there, holding her hand, checking her pulse. "Not quite yet, Mrs. Selden, not quite ready, but if you want a little gas...if the pain..."

"No. Nothing. I'm all right. I was just remembering..."

The nurse moved off, away.

Remembering...when Danny was born...and Harold was still overseas, and the labor went on and on, and she had to be sent home from the hospital to wait it out at home for a while longer, because she was screaming so much and so loud and, at home, in the two-family, her mother had stood next to the bed, holding on to her hand, telling her not to be afraid, to let it happen, to let it go, not to hold on to a part of her life that was done with. "So let the baby be born, Evelyn. Harold will come home. He'll be all right. He'll be safe and sound and you'll be a mother and his wife, and no matter what, to me you'll always be my daughter, always, so don't be afraid. Just let the baby be born."

Finally, she had listened to her mother, like a good girl, a good daughter, and Danny was born and everything her mother had said had been true, had come true.

Then Morty, and now she was alone here, and soon she would have another baby, because the water had broken already. "Mama"—she heard it. She, making believe her mother would come....

Make it a girl.

It was going to be now. She pushed, screaming, screaming: "Harold!"

He was right outside. She knew he was. And her father too. Together they had brought her. December 26, 1956. Stevenson had lost. They were in their third Levitt. In the W section. She was thirty-four. Facts. Evelyn Selden born Evelyn Howard. "Let the baby be born"—whatever it is...boy...girl...

She pushed. The nurse was there, and the doctor this time, so it was now, and there was the head, sliding through, sliding free, staying there in the air, reaching out into the air.

She fainted. She remembered blacking out and then coming to again and seeing that it was a boy. She insisted on counting its toes and fingers. He was all right. Healthy. Complete. And alive.

126

[3]   Elias Selden. Eli, for short. She liked it. Harold liked
it. The boys liked it. Her father liked it most of all. They
were all there, around the bed, watching the baby, watching
her.

Out in the kitchen she heard her friends preparing the
luncheon. Cynthia's idea: a coming-home-from-the-hospital
luncheon. They were all there, her closest and dearest and
not-so-dearest. Plus some others, from the schools she'd
worked with on the PTA, principals, teachers, and some from
the party, even though Stevenson had lost: a houseful. But
around her bed just then, her family.

Her father was handing her something. A photograph.
The boys were tugging his sweater sleeve to do more, to say
something. "They coaxed me into giving you this." They were
laughing. Her father sat on the edge of the bed. "I had it
blown up."

A photograph of herself when she was... "How old was I,
Dad?"

"You were nine. Do you remember how your mother and
I were standing behind the photographer telling you to do
what he asked you? Remember?"

She remembered. She was in a crepe dress. A birthday
dress. Her grandfather had made it for her. Her mother's
father; dead, both of them now. Both her grandmothers and
grandfathers, now her mother, dead. All dead. The dress had
been made of the heaviest crepe. It was tan with ruffles all
around the neck. The photographer had told her to bend one
leg beneath her, to sit on it, to lean forward, so that her curls
would fall in front of the ruffles, and to smile, smile and hold
it, smile so that her one dimple would show better, and to sit
still, very still, still.... She remembered it.

"Is that really you, Ma?" Morty couldn't believe it,
wouldn't believe that was his mother. And he couldn't believe
Eli and how small he was. "Were we that small? Danny and
me, Ma."

"You were."

Eli began to cry, and then from the kitchen came sounds
of the group out there moving toward the door of the bedroom,
crowding it, wanting to see in, wanting to come in, the ladies
first, but first of all Missy was there with a bottle for Eli,
which Harold took from her, gave it to Evelyn to give to Eli.
He leaned down over her. He kissed her. "I couldn't be happier," he whispered. "I love you."

127

Then there was Loretta, pushing through with a pile of presents. Evelyn didn't see Corinne. Why wasn't Corinne there?

Her father turned away to leave the room. He was wiping at his eyes with the back of his hands.

Some of the others, acquaintances, waved from the door.

There wasn't even a moment long enough for her to sigh into, to sigh into and remember the nine-year-old girl living on, alone, inside her, because just then Eli, in her arms, was sucking hungrily at his bottle. He needed her attention.

[1]   Better Evelyn than herself. That was for sure.

Because her own life, if it was going in any direction, was surely going in the opposite direction from having a baby, another baby. As if two weren't enough!

Evelyn surprised her. Evelyn always surprised her. And one of these days Loretta was going to surprise Evelyn. But not with having another baby. One of these winter days maybe, when it suddenly got beautiful enough to think about its being spring again, she was going to drive Evelyn over to Jones Beach, she was going to sit Evelyn down on the sand in the cold sunlight and just come right out and tell her how much she admired and respected and cared for her, how if it wasn't for Evelyn's being nearby she would have, a long time ago would have, turned herself in the opposite direction from where she was going right then, over to Whisper Lane, where it was almost time for the girls to be coming home from school—which is why she had left Evelyn's when she had, before the other ladies had left: because she had her own two beautiful daughters she loved and who needed her...and they were the other reasons she stayed in their house on Whisper Lane: her own two daughters she loved. Not only because of Evelyn's being nearby.... Goddammit! How tired she was of burying everything she felt. Burying it all. Except when it came to Joe. To Joe she could say everything. Over and over again she could tell him it was just a matter of time. A few years, just until the girls were old enough, and then...then what?

She wouldn't tell Evelyn. Not after watching Evelyn handling the baby and kissing Harold. Evelyn wasn't ready to hear what Loretta wanted to tell her. And what did Loretta want to tell her anyway? What did Loretta Massi know about anything she really felt? What was she ready to say? What would she ever be ready to say? And if she ever became ready, what made her think Evelyn would want to hear anything like that from a Loretta? Maybe...No maybes about it: Evelyn liked the way her life was.

Whisper Lane was only three blocks from Willowood Drive, hardly a long enough walk to wonder through the whys of anything important, and as she was walking the weather distracted her. It did a typical January thing: sunny and clear one minute, and the next minute thick clouds, gray-white, mother-of-pearl gray, a sudden wind rushing them, the wind stopping just as suddenly, the clouds thickening.

It was going to snow. She shivered beneath her plaid mackinaw, although it surely was warm enough. More like a shudder than a shiver. A shudder of resignation, about where she had come from, where she was going next, now. And now the color of outside expressed it. That's what she'd like to paint. Colors that were about her feelings, her thoughts. But every time she tried to do that, to get it just right, the colors were dead gray, lifeless, depressing, without the feelings underneath, without how she felt right now...which snow might help relieve. She could take the girls for a drive over to Jones, let them watch the whiteness disappear in the ocean. That would be a sight. That would be a painting she could do. For them. So when she wasn't around they could look at it on the wall and remember the time she had taken them over to the ocean to see...They would hate it. The ocean. The painting. Her, by then. All they cared about was going up to the candy store on Jerusalem Road and hanging around with their friends. Especially Angela; Mr. Rothstein said that was Angela's best subject: hanging around. Like mother, like daughter. Loretta remembered how she loved to hang around...with Connie. But they'd have gone into the city. They'd have hopped on the subway and gone into Manhattan, to the Paramount, to the Automat....She didn't know anymore where Connie was.

The sun again. Through a sudden break in the clouds.

Levittown: in sunshine and in rain; in moonshine and the dark of night—a series of watercolors by Loretta Kovalic Massi....Actually, the only drawings of hers the girls liked were the ones she'd done of Levittown. It was like a photograph album for them. They'd drag her sketchbook out from the closet and go through it slowly. Their history: her charcoal sketches of their first house in the S section. The mound of dirt behind it. The earth before it became a lawn. The emptiness—that's what she had seen, and loved, then. Emptiness to fill up however you wanted. And the quiet. Before
130

the world started to creep back in on them, on all of them. The Korean War. The Rogerses giving up. Senator McCarthy. The same old shit, over and over and over again. . . .

And trying to pick a path for yourself through it all. Some path that was a little decent, that expressed the best thing about yourself. Something that was honest and open, that wasn't corny. Like the paintings she had done of people. Like the one she'd done of Corinne. That was far and away the best painting she'd ever done of anyone or anything, and that was because she could talk to Corinne. She could tell Corinne anything and Corinne didn't sit there, judging. Even Evelyn did that. Judged things. Evelyn took positions on things. Evelyn had opinions. Evelyn read. Evelyn had goals . . .

And Loretta Massi? What have you got, Loretta Massi?

Problems. A lot of problems. And without the courage to go about trying to solve them. Without the brains to solve them. Stupidity: that's what you've got plenty of, Loretta Massi.

[2] It did start snowing, but much later. It was 10:30 when she realized it was. Putting her paints away, cleaning the brushes, thinking about nothing at all, when she walked to the window of the garage—some place to have to paint in—and looked out, there it was: light snow on everything. A covering. She never thought about what might be going on around her when she painted. She could have been in a studio in Greenwich Village, not in her garage in Levittown. The garage wasn't even heated properly. Authentic cold. The authentically cold studio of a struggling, hungry—but aging—artist.

Joe was playing chess in the living room, playing against himself. He stopped when she came in. "How's it going?" The pale green lampshade cast eerie shadows on his face. He looked masklike. She should have changed that lampshade before she ever put it on that ugly lamp. Why did she do things like that, anyway? She knew ugliness when she saw it.

"Snowing out. I'm going to take a short walk. To clear my head."

"Want me to come? I wouldn't mind a fast walk in the snow."

"No. I'd rather go my . . . You're in the middle of a game. Finish it. I'll be right back." Only, she knew she wouldn't be. She would walk over to Corinne's, see if she was up, sit with

her for a while and shmooze. But if she told that to Joe, if
she said: Hey, Joe baby, I'm going over to Corinne's, for some
life, Joe, because, Joe, you're dead but you don't know it...

He turned his attention back to his game. He didn't even
look up when she went out the door. He knew where she was
headed. He knew a lot more than she was willing to give him
credit for. Might as well admit it. At least to herself she could
admit the truth.

Corinne's latest house was on Wing Lane. Two blocks
away from Loretta's. Corinne had chosen it because she could
place her piano right behind the big bay window in the living
room. Visible to anyone who passed. Visible to Loretta, looking in from outside through the quickly falling snow. Corinne
was bent forward, probably studying some music. The light
around her was peach-rose, warm, a glow. Loretta watched,
separating the scene—Corinne, the light, the piano—from
everything else in her mind, trying to. And then the cold—
it was the cold this time—made her shiver.

She couldn't see if Lionel was there in the room with Corinne. Probably in bed by then, although, if he were, Corinne
wouldn't be playing the piano. He's probably still out. No car
in the garage. He was out. Good. And Gregory had to be
asleep. Or watching television. Corinne would naturally be
the first of their group to buy a television set. Like, with her
doorbell, Corinne was the first. Her doorbell was chimes.
Loretta listened. Loretta waited.

Corinne's face would tell her. As soon as she opened the
door, Corinne's face would tell her: I'm alone, I'm annoyed,
I'm drunk. Or maybe Corinne would be glad, happy to have
company. "Loretta? What the hell are you doing walking
around on a night like this? You all right? What a nice surprise. Lionel's doing inventory at the store tonight. I was
just—"

"Playing. I saw you. I was watching you."

"How about a drink? Some Scotch? That'll warm you up.
I was just having a nightcap. I wouldn't mind another."

"Love it." From the look of her, Corinne had had about
three or four nightcaps. What damage could one more do?

The Feuerstein living room—no matter how many times
Loretta walked into it—was a shocker. There was that enormous grand piano. Such dark wood it almost looked black.
And the draperies were a deep rose velvet. And so was the
rug. And the sofa. One club chair, Lionel's favorite, with an
ottoman to match, was black leather. Real leather. The other
132

was a plush fabric, blue, a quiet royal blue. End tables were that same black as the piano. And gold was everywhere. The lamp bases. The ashtrays. The ornate claws under the end tables. It was like walking into a nightclub—which was exactly what Corinne wanted. Intimate lighting. Peach-rose. Even warmer seen from inside. At least from inside the light softened the glint of gold. Only at the piano was there real light. A little pin-spot lamp, to light up the keyboard, to light up Corinne's inimitable way with her makeup, which was a heavy Pan-Cake base; to highlight her hair color, which was tawny-red and upswept, even in the dead of winter upswept; to heighten the glint and dazzle and sparkle of necklaces and earrings. These days Corinne remained forever Forties. The intense light from the pin-spot hid the hard edges of her face. She handed Loretta a drink. She placed hers on a coaster at the bass end of the keyboard. "I'm doing Beethoven. The Pathétique. I love it, Loretta. I'd play, only it's too late. Gregory's sleeping. So I was just fingering some passages to amuse myself. Lionel won't be home for hours. What's with you? As if I don't know." She sipped, her diamond rings clanging against the heavy glass. She swirled the ice. She drank a long pull, almost draining her drink. "I drink too fast."

"You drink too much."

"That too. But only at night. When I practice. I never drink during the day. When I start to do that, then I'll worry." She stretched her fingers over the keys. Thin, long fingers that trembled over the keys. She stared down at them and then up at Loretta. "But we all get screwed up. One way or another we do. You included. Look at you. Look at the way you look. Joe's old shirt. A cardigan sweater. Smeared-up khakis. No makeup. And your hair's a mess. You look like a bum, not like a lady. What is it with you, Loretta? Why do you let yourself go like this? Why do you go out into the world looking like this?"

"This is the world?" So tonight it was Judgment Day. Corinne's in her cups.

"I'm afraid so." She got up, reaching for her drink as she did, moving into the softer aura of the peach-rose light. They sat at either end of the rose velvet sofa, turning so that they faced each other. Corinne kicked off her fur-trimmed mules, bent her legs beneath her, her long burgundy silk robe billowing and settling around her, covering her completely.

"You are something, Corinne. I have to hand it to you.

133

You can't even sit down on a chair without making a production out of it."

"That's me. That's my nature. My own original nature. I perform. For you. For anyone who wants to watch. Isn't that how you grew up? Didn't they teach you how to do things for everyone else but yourself? Didn't they?"

"You're drunk, Corinne, aren't you? Admit it? Aren't you?"

"I'm not. I'm just goddamn disgusted."

"Why didn't you come to Evelyn's today? Everyone wondered where you were."

"Including Evelyn?"

"No. She didn't say anything but she had other things on her mind. I was surprised you didn't show, and of course Cynthia said something bitchy and Missy looked her high-and-mighty compassionate look. You know that way she gets. All suffering. Every bone in her body suffering for humanity, you included. And me too. She suffers for me too. She does a lot of suffering, but she makes a goddamn good chicken salad." The Scotch was beginning to bubble up to her head. She was tired. She wanted to give in to feeling untied, loose, the way she most of all enjoyed being when she was with Corinne. But Corinne always had to be first of all stopped, stopped dead in her tracks, stopped right in the middle of her act. At least that's how Loretta had to handle her first of all. Put her on the defensive. Slow her down. Get something real to show in her face—and then they could talk. Woman to woman. Under the skin, under the Pan-Cake, a person. Under her own getup, a real Loretta, ready to bubble up and burst out. "I have this feeling, Corinne. I have this feeling about myself. I feel as if something very important's going to happen to me. As if I'm going to discover a way out. I'm going to open up the trap I'm in and get out."

"They won't let you."

There it was. That thing in Corinne's eyes. Instead of staring dead ahead at nothing, they shifted. A door opened in her that was usually closed, shut tight, locked. She looked at Loretta, looking with what she saw suddenly inside her head, rousing herself to reason. "You fight them, Loretta, and you'll pay for it. You'll pay plenty. You want to do it your way? You want to be different from the rest of us? Try it and see what happens. Don't say I didn't warn you. You have to be unique to really do it. You have to be so unique they can't keep you in the trap anymore. For Christ's sake, why don't you take the easy way? Why don't you have another baby? Like Evelyn did."

"She wanted it."

"Sure she wanted it. Like I want another drink."

"She did. It's her way of being who she is. She sees it that way. I don't. You don't. No one else of us does except Evelyn. So it's her own unique way of getting out of her trap. Can't you see that?"

"No. I can't. In fact"—the door in her head had closed again, suddenly. She was staring dead ahead at nothing— "all I can see is that my glass is empty. You want another? Because I most assuredly do. You're talking bullshit, Loretta. Pure bullshit."

Loretta did not want another drink. Loretta didn't know what she wanted from Corinne or Evelyn or anyone. She would leave. She would, just as soon as Corinne returned from the kitchen. She heard an ice tray being banged against stainless steel, and then Corinne was cursing.

Loretta went out there. She took the tray from Corinne. She put some cubes in her glass. She walked her back out to the living room. She sat her back down on the sofa. She held her under the chin, stared down at those eyes, dull green, the whites gray and bloodshot. Corinne was a mess. Corinne was a friend. Loretta should help her. Loretta should find some way to help her. She and Evelyn could maybe find some way together to help Corinne... if she'd let them. "Why don't you go to bed, Corinne, instead of having another drink?"

"Why don't you go home, Loretta. I'm waiting up for Lionel."

"It's your life." She let go of Corinne's chin.

"That's right. It's my life."

"Don't be such a goddamned fool, Corinne. I'm your friend. I know what's going on. I want to help."

"Help yourself first. And then we'll see what's what." She swirled the ice in her drink. She stared at it. She would not look up at Loretta. "Let's see how far *you* can get away from here...on your own."

[3] It was snowing harder. But it was a wet snow by then. About to turn to rain. She buried her chin inside the top of her mackinaw, pulled the ski cap down over her ears. The walk would be good. Clear her head. Fuck Corinne. She was a hopeless case. Absolutely hopeless.

And there was Lionel's Cadillac turning in.

Loretta quickened her pace.

Not that she wanted to be home faster. Joe was sure to be waiting up. He was sure to say: How about a good hot cup of tea? Sometimes he acted more like a housewife than she ever did. He liked doing that kind of thing. Why the hell doesn't he just stay home and take care of everything, then? She'd go out and work.

No she wouldn't. That's not what she wanted. She didn't want any job nine-to-five, five days a week. No. Never. All she wanted was a chance to do what she wanted to do. All she wanted was the same chance anyone else had. The same chance any other man had.

That stopped her. Dead in her tracks.

She looked up at the wet snow falling. Slush. But even so, what she wanted more than anything else in the world was to keep on walking. To walk away from everything she knew. To walk away and disappear into another life entirely. Neither snow nor rain nor anything...

Not even her daughters would miss her, and Joe could take better care of them than she ever could.

Nothing was stopping her. Just herself.

14

Corinne Feuerstein

[1]   She had to prepare herself. But between the slam of the car door and the house door slam, there was too little time for anything more than just standing up.

She would have liked to be without a fresh drink and to be seated behind the piano.

Instead, she greeted him with her drink raised, standing, prepared only for the slam of his voice.

"What the hell is this shit, Corinne? You drunk again?"

"Do I look drunk?"

"You look like shit. You're bleary-eyed." Then, in a sudden whisper, "Where's Gregory?"

"In bed, of course. Where did you think he'd be?"

"Don't start with the sarcasm routine." He took the drink from her hand. She did not resist. He grabbed her roughly, held her shoulder, squeezing it, moving her along that way toward their bedroom, stopping, as they went, to switch off the lights. He went slowly. She did not stumble. His hand at her shoulder was a steadying strength. Almost pain. Almost becoming a point of pain. Tolerable. The big fuck. He knew what he was doing. Like suddenly whispering, "Where's Gregory?" controlling himself, squeezing all that he was into that control, into that hand squeezing her shoulder, moving her toward their bed, pushing her down on it.

"Get in it, you bitch." Hard. A hard whispering control. "You drunken bitch. Get in it and get undressed. You're going to get it for doing this. I told you before, didn't I? I'm not kidding. You think you can get away with this kind of crap? Well, you can't. You hear me? You goddamned bitch."

He was leaning down over her, lowering himself, right above her, so that she could smell the smell of him, the sweat, the cigarettes, the Old Spice from his shave that morning. It was in his hair, hidden in the curl of it, grayer now than black. She opened her eyes to look. She saw his hand lowering over her breast, saw it push the silk robe away from over it, saw it grab and squeeze and pull—and that was pain. That was a focus of pain. She would scream.

But he knew that. He always stopped. Just in time. He read her face. He knew her limit. He always brought her to it. Always stopped. Just in time. She didn't hate him, though, for what he did.

She hated herself.

She wanted to get up and ask him to listen to her play Beethoven.

She wanted to have that last drink he had taken from her. "Lionel? Can't I have that drink you took?" Like a little girl she sounded. I want. I want. I want.

"You're kidding. Give you a drink? You must be nuts. Out of your mind." He stood up, beginning to undress, dropping his tie, his shirt, his pants, his underwear, stepping out of them, naked, lifting his prick to her. "You thirsty? Drink this." Laughing, he sat to take off his shoes, his socks. And then he opened her robe completely, used both hands to smooth the skin on the inside of her legs. Starting slowly. Very slowly. Building. Moving up her body, across her breasts and down the length of her to her feet. Going faster and rougher. From the bottom of her to the top of her. She closed her eyes.

The room was spinning inside her head.

His hands were at the middle of her. They squeezed into her there, steadying her, controlling her. She liked the feel of that, that holding on to her, as if she were pinned to the bed, unable to move, that feeling spreading through every part of her, feeling herself to be everywhere at once alive, and it was a feeling that he had made happen by holding her at the center of herself, by steadying her, by controlling her, by wanting her.

He did want her. He still did. She opened her eyes and saw how much he did. He was taking her all in. He leaned over to kiss her...and stopped. "You stink from liquor. You bitch. You got to stop that drinking." Low. Hard sounds. At her ear. Slamming the words into her ear.

He rolled away, switched off the bed lamp, rolled back again, this time back on top of her. Her arms were still in her robe. She wanted to be out of it. To be free of it. But he wouldn't let her. She tried. He pushed down harder. The big fuck. Big. And heavier now. Twenty pounds heavier since the beginning, since the times he hardly knew which end was
138

up. Now he knew, all right. Now he knew everything. But that was all he knew. How to fuck.

And that was her trap. She had taught him how to set it, and now she was caught in it with him. If there was a way out of it, it would have to be a way out for both of them, and she would have to show him how to find it. She would have to help him and herself. She wanted to. She wanted him still, too. And just thinking that, somehow he sensed it. He lifted enough for her to free herself from her robe. He helped her.

The room wasn't spinning so fast when she closed her eyes again.

"You got to stop drinking so much. You hear?" But his whisper was not hard-edged anymore. His breath in her ear was an urgent sound, like pleading. Slowly he pushed inside her. He held her, squeezed her, but she felt no pain. "You got to stop," he whispered again, "for both our sakes. No need for it. None." He was still, inside her. "You got everything you want. What else you need?"

Beneath him, she managed to move her head to the side. It was very dark in the room. But he was holding her, squeezing her tighter and tighter—and then slowly he began pumping, and rocking, pumping and rocking her, rocking both of them, back and forth, back and forth, slowly, in the darkness.

[2]   Suddenly she was awake.

It was still dark. She heard the rain. She heard Lionel snoring.

Gregory? Had she heard Gregory calling for her?

She listened. No sounds other than the rain, Lionel's snoring, the electric clock humming peacefully on the end table on Lionel's side of the bed. Everything orderly in her house in Levittown in the middle of a January night.

And in the morning she would get up and make breakfast for Gregory and then for Lionel. She would send Gregory off to school. This year he went eagerly. He liked his homeroom teacher and his English teacher. Both the same, that Mr. Rothstein. A lot of their kids had him for English. Evelyn's and Missy's and Cynthia's. They all seemed to like him. Gregory certainly did. Gregory had even started to read more. At the next parent-teacher conference she had to remember to tell that to Mr. Rothstein, that at night, these nights, Gregory would pick up a book, go into his room, close the door, and read. Didn't care to watch television at all. He liked reading better. He liked going into his room and closing the door—and she liked playing the piano and drinking—if Lionel wasn't home. She wouldn't tell that to Mr. Rothstein, about the drinking or about being left alone at night too much.

A lot of evenings Lionel wasn't home. Or if he came home, he was always going out again, for something, to play cards, to bowl, anything—but not for sex. Not him. Not as long as he had his store and...her. He was at the store more than he was home, evenings. Which was why she drank. Had to be the reason. Being left alone...too much...evenings.

She slid lower under the quilt. She was naked, but it was warm under the quilt. Her mother's quilt, her mother's hand-me-down, which Corinne had salvaged after her death. Her father had been willing to give it to junk. He wasn't going to need it in Florida. So Corinne had taken it and recovered it in patchwork squares. She enjoyed doing that. She enjoyed sewing. She enjoyed making things. She enjoyed putting things together. She enjoyed cooking and playing the piano and playing bridge...and having sex...and drinking...

And after Gregory went to school and Lionel left for the store, she would clean the house and shower and call Gladys to arrange their bridge schedule for the rest of the week. She should also call Evelyn and explain why she hadn't been there yesterday. Evelyn would understand. She should also call Loretta and apologize for the way she'd behaved last night. Loretta would understand too. Any one of the ladies she called would understand why, when it got dark, she had one drink, then another and another: even when Lionel was home she did. He didn't understand why, but the ladies would. Before she had met Lionel, when she worked in the nightclubs in the Village, she'd never been that kind of drinker. She'd sing and play without the slightest bit of trouble, so when did it start? What made it start?

She couldn't trace it back to any one thing. She couldn't pinpoint it. Except she knew for sure she wasn't that way before they moved to Levittown. And she wasn't that way afterward, not right away. That she was sure of....So the trouble was that Lionel began not to be home a lot at night. And she began to feel lonely with nothing to do except play the piano, practice, get better and better—and then end up having no one to play for.

When she turned on her side, she heard her heartbeat through the pillow. It was loud. Much too loud. Her heart

140

wasn't strong. Like her mother's had not been strong. And drinking would make it worse.

So she had to stop.

She had to stop killing herself.

She had too much to live for. She had a son she loved. She had good friends. She had all kinds of ability, to do anything she wanted to do, anything. But she had to get out of the house. She had to get out of Levittown to do what she wanted to do.

She wanted to live in Manhattan. She wanted a job. She wanted...When Gregory went to college she would move. Five more years. She could last that long: 1962. She'd be forty. Just forty. That would still be young enough to do anything she wanted to do.

Life begins at forty....If you can survive that long....If you can live beyond all the things that keep on failing before you ever get to forty....

And when had she begun to feel that things were failing? Could she trace it back? Could she pinpoint it? After that first year in Levittown? Was it then? Nothing had worked out the way she wanted it to after that. Even Evelyn admitted that that was true. Nothing the ladies worked on won. Nothing would. Even their school-board candidates lost elections. Too radical. Too left-wing. Better to have a baby like Evelyn had and hope for the best....Or believe in something about to happen, like Loretta. Or play the piano. Or fold your arms like Cynthia and say: Everything's fine the way it is. Or look for a modern God like Missy did. Or...Or turn on your side and try to sleep while your husband snores next to you and your heart beats louder and louder into the night....

15

Melissa Geiger

[1]   She certainly had been tempted to tell Evelyn, at least her. And yesterday would have been the perfect time: Evelyn darling, you and Harold...you inspired us. Do I show anything yet?

She was going into her fifth month...and nothing.

Vanity. She smoothed her stomach. She was standing before the full-length mirror in their bathroom—but she was proud of the fact that after all these years, after three childbirths, and now midway into her fourth, she weighed the same as she had when she and Carl were married fifteen years before.

Fifteen years. Fifteen years come October. And by then she and Carl would have their fourth child. A girl. She wanted it to be a girl. She wanted it to be Agnes. St. Agnes. Agnes and Teresa. Donald and Adam.

Agnes and Eli. It was fated to be. They would grow up together. They would go to school together. They would live in peace together.

In fifteen years...she would try to keep her stomach as flat as it was now. She would exercise. In fifteen years she would be exactly fifty and there would be peace in the world for each and every one everywhere on the face of the earth. Amen....

Prayer was a habit of her life. No getting away from it. She thought of things being one way or another, and before she knew it, her thoughts had become a prayer. It was just her training. You can't be trained to do something day after day when you're growing up and just suddenly forget it. Especially if there's a need in the world for it. And how could it hurt? Even for those people who didn't believe, how could it hurt? Nothing wrong with being on the safe side. Nothing wrong with going to her Scarsdale in-laws' and turning one cheek. Or to her parents' in Rockville Centre and turning the other. It cost nothing, and decency generates decency. One love-giving idea generates another love-giving idea. One inspirational idea generates another inspiration.... So, by May, there would be an Agnes Geiger. A girl. Had to be a girl— in Scarsdale they will be happy, in Rockville Centre, peace that passeth understanding...peace in our time...for all time.

No more wars. None. No Korean wars. Stupid. An absolute blunder. Truman's war—and he shouldn't have been president in the first place.

But trying to remember who she thought should have been...she couldn't anymore....

Too long a time ago. Once upon a time...Still, she could remember exactly what she was doing the day FDR died, and the fact that she was about to chew a piece of veal roast when she heard about Pearl Harbor, or that she was holding Donald in her arms when the telegram came telling her that Carl had been wounded in action. She could remember personal, specific...well, then shouldn't she start remembering that in fifteen minutes she had a dozen ladies coming to the house. Yes, indeed she should, instead of admiring herself in the mirror.

Vanity. Vanity. All is vanity.

She should have been dressed and ready long before.

She powdered. She fluffed her feather cut.

She chose a flannel skirt. A full skirt. Shirred at the waist. A silk blouse. Rose. Pale rose. Muted. A string of pearls.

She was ready. She approved. She didn't show.

[2]   No W-section Levitt house was without its remodeling, its personal stamp. But, vanity of vanities, she thought theirs was the best. It was Carl's doing. Her design, her planning, but still Carl's execution. She had wanted to recreate the flow of open space, room to room, that Rockville Centre had had. It had had open space. Maybe not such open minds to match, but, at least...So Carl had cut through the wall of the kitchen, making the space there seem bigger than it was, and once the kitchen wall was opened up and an eating-serving counter was put in, for informal eating and to hand things through to a dining table just in front, or into the living room leading away from that—the living room was enlarged too, because they were on a triangular plot, right at the curve of the wishbone on Wishbone Lane—then it was all she dreamed it should be.

And she was the first in their group to decorate with Early

143

American. Before Evelyn's version, there was the Geigers'. Lots of shiny maple and rugs she had hooked, and chintz prints on pillows, and a corduroy cover for the sofa. Brass lamps. And pewter. She loved it, loved every piece of it, loved to keep it looking...lovely. Loved to invite people into it. Loved to cook for people. Loved being hospitable. Loved to be helpful and needed. Loved to show people how to do things, things that she seemed to be able to do with such ease—the women that were there that afternoon were there for instruction, knitting, sewing instruction, a knitting bee. They each paid her a minimal fee. They met once every two weeks. She gave them coffee and homemade cake and instruction. She would love to expand it, make it into one of those *salon*-type events she read about in books. Invite speakers. Maybe teachers. Maybe invite Mr. Rothstein to talk about...books and things. While they sewed. She'd ask him when she had her appointment with him about Adam's school work. She'd ask him if he'd like the idea—but even so, the ladies liked things as they were, Cynthia most of all. She told Missy it made her feel as if she were back home, a little girl again in South Carolina. Just the way they all sat around the living room, knitting away, busy buzzing, and Missy always had a fire going in the fireplace if the day warranted it, of course. It was so "civilized" is the way Cynthia liked to put it. Cynthia was working on a three-colored knit dress.

Audrey Halpern kept trying argyles, kept trying and failing, because she forgot to pick up the colors or forgot to attach another bobbin to the round needle. She didn't give up, though. Missy admired Audrey's fortitude. Missy was on the lookout for another husband for Audrey. Audrey should be married. She was the oldest of the group. In the prime of life, as they say—and she shouldn't be alone, and soon she was going to have to find a job to support her two children and herself, in the middle of her life. It wasn't fair. Sometimes God...a lot of times God...look at Edna Leventhal. Her Bud wasn't going to last much longer. It was a matter of weeks. At the most, a month. Probably by the next time they were supposed to gather together, Bud Leventhal would be dead at the age of thirty-seven of cancer, and yet there was Edna working on a scarf for him, trying to finish it that afternoon so she could take it to him in the hospital when she went. In an hour.

She wouldn't be done with it. Even Missy, sitting with her most of all, to help her finish, couldn't have done it in an

144

hour. But they were trying. Edna was just not a natural knitter. Never would be. Fortunately, four of the ladies hadn't been able to make it, so Missy was able to devote more time to Edna. Even so, and even though nothing could be easier than knitting a scarf, no matter how many colors she used, Edna kept doing the wrong stitches or inventing so many variations that the scarf was ending up looking like a web for air to pass through and not at all to keep it out. Edna apologized. Edna always apologized. No matter what she tried to do, it was never as good as anyone else's. Edna apologized for being too fat or being a sloppy housekeeper or a terrible cook or undereducated or not well enough informed—and yet there wasn't once that Missy had ever heard any of the ladies say anything other than how much they loved Edna, how much they would do for her anytime she needed any help whatsoever.

When Missy told her that, Edna would look out from those wide-open surprised blue eyes, from out of that moon-round sweet face of hers, each feature of it a perfect gem, but in the wrong setting, an over-large setting of too much flesh, too much protective flesh that was supposed to soften the blow now when it came—and those eyes would fill up. Missy could remember meeting Edna the first time: there was no excess flesh then. That was recent. That was since Bud had started to die. Sometimes God...She felt a feather touch inside. Under the skin of her abdomen. A feather's brushing there. She smiled.

Arlene Zweig saw it. Arlene smiled. Arlene was making a triangular shawl. Green. Yellow. Blue. Pink. Ugly. That was Arlene's taste—but she meant well. Her glasses kept sliding down her nose while she worked away, working ferociously, talking a mile a minute, to Sally Plotkin on her right, to Ina Silverstein on her left. The three of them had chosen the same projects. Sally's was a solid, a forest green, a gorgeous color that would set off her blond-red hair to nice advantage. Ina's was a serious brown, maroon, tan. Ina was mostly silent these days, now that Burt was in and out of hospitals so often. Arlene would talk a mile a minute and Ina would nod yes, nod no, and continue knitting at her own determined pace.

Gladys Ginsburg, the bridge entrepreneur, was doing a smallish caftan. She could knit, "...from before," as she put it. She knew what she was up to, always, and about everything. Yes, sir, she knew.

145

Ruby Rabinowitz was doing mittens for her younger sister's new baby. At the rate she was going, the mittens would be done by the summer. Ruby would never be a knitter. Some people just didn't have it in their fingers. Little Ruby Rabinowitz just didn't. She was too nervous, too used to being told she didn't do things well enough. Edna was the same way.

If there was one thing Missy wished she could redo—there was only one—it would be school. She'd love to be a teacher, a teacher of anything. She had the patience. She loved to be helpful. She loved to create pockets of contentment where before there was just trouble after trouble. She loved to make people feel more self-confident. "You've got it now, Edna. Just follow that line down to the end with that same stitch. That's it. Keep going. I'm going to get the coffee and cake." Now, Missy thought, if only she could have gotten Loretta to join this class. Or Corinne. Corinne badly needed something like this.

On her way to the coffee tray, Missy stopped to survey her lovely room once more. They were all at work and talking quietly. There was warmth in the room, and peacefulness. The bright afternoon sun, a cold January sun, laced through the ferns at the living-room windows, arranging dots and curves and dust lines on the wooden floor. For this moment here, as she stood there, stopped, watching, listening, captured by the loveliness of her room, as she glanced toward each head bent over active hands or turning to talk softly to a neighbor, as she lifted her gaze to study her own needlepoint samplers hanging in a row alongside the bookcases that Carl himself had built and hung, as she played with, stroking, clicking, her string of tiny pearls, her tiny gold cross, seeing all that, feeling all that, she also felt more and more how happy, how pleased and proud she was to be pregnant. She looked forward to that day in that month ahead when she would give birth once again. She looked forward to her next fifteen years. The next thirty years. Surely she would live to be sixty-five. She hoped so. She passionately hoped so.

In the kitchen everything was ready, set out on her best pewter tray. The coffee had finished perking. She would prepare the teapot.

Her dinner was in the oven. A stew.

Two-thirty. The children would be home in an hour. Maybe then she could get over to Evelyn's again, see if there was anything Evelyn needed.

146

She should also call the other missing ladies. She couldn't remember whether it was Esther Aronowitz who had gone in to Brooklyn to visit her mother, who was sick, or whether it was Rose Newman. One of them had gone, and one of them was having a terrible period. Toby Margolies had a cold.

And then there was Edna Leventhal saying that she thought she should leave for the hospital before the coffee. She had this terrible feeling.... "And I told the children if I wasn't home when they came home from school they should come over here. Is that all right, Missy? I couldn't think straight this morning." She was looking up at Missy. She was going to cry. Missy helped her on with her coat, held her round. "You know it's all right. Just don't worry about them. If they don't come, I'll send Donald after them. Give my love to Bud."

Sometimes God does terrible things; sometimes God does beautiful things. Sometimes...sometimes she even thought she understood why.

[3] A little pimple of a bump at the end of his nose. She touched it, rubbed it for good luck. They were in bed. He had been reading, and suddenly he had stopped. She had done the same thing, at the same time. They had turned to stare at each other, to smile. And then she had reached out to touch the little pimple of a bump at the end of his nose. "You've changed so little, Carl."

"You have. You've gotten better." He dropped his *Life* on the floor next to the bed, slid closer to her.

She smoothed his hair back. That had changed in fifteen years. His forehead went up higher, the hair more gray than black. It was thinning. Not on his chest. That seemed thicker. He never wore pajamas. Not even in the dead of winter. But his body, still as lean, was almost as perfect—except for his leg, of course—as their first time. He moved her closer to him. He rubbed her back, slowly, gently. He wanted her to take off her nightgown. That was his signal. He meant business.

She sat up. She removed her gown. She switched off the bed lamp. She slid back down inside his arms. "I felt the baby today. A feather brushed across my stomach. It was so beautiful, Carl."

He didn't answer, but she could feel his response in his arms. That was enough. Carl would never say much. It wasn't his way. He didn't trust himself with words. But he did

147

things. He had silent signals. He showed her and the children how he felt by doing things. Anything he could do for them, he did. Anything he could build or make or put together, he did. That was the habit of his life, doing things around the house, for them, for her. Some marriages are, yes, made in heaven. Some marriages are fated. Theirs was. Of that, she had no doubt. In the darkness she traced the features of his face. What if something were to happen to him? Like Bud—God forbid. Please, no, God. Bite your tongue. But what if? What if like Bud Leventhal? No, God, please. But at least, touching him, touching his face, his skin, tracing his features, the feel of him would be there, in her fingers. A memory, in her fingertips, for as long as she lived.

A pity most people couldn't get to know Carl. He was too quiet for them. Quiet frightened most people. They thought his quiet was anger. They thought he was angry all the time. She felt the corners of his mouth. That's where they thought his anger was: in the corners of his mouth. Indentations. Deep pinpricks of anger. But all it was, really, was his habit of looking, was his habit of being silent.

She kissed the end of his nose. And then his eyes. And then his mouth. Holding him, smoothing circles of pleasure all over his back. "I'm so happy we're having another baby, Carl," whispering in the dark room, afraid to say it louder, afraid to disturb the darkness. So perfect their lives. Now. Everything proceeding. Peacefully. A gliding time. Time gliding. Fifteen years. So fast. Because they were happy. After the war. After his leg healed. After they moved to Levittown. Happy. Their marriage...only Evelyn and Harold had a marriage that came close to being as happy as theirs. "You're glad now about the baby, aren't you? Because we will manage...about money, I mean...whether you get a raise or not, we'll manage. I know we will. I promise we will. And I promise it will be a girl. I even picked a name for her. And a husband...both subject to your approval, of course. Agnes...and Eli Selden."

He kissed her. They laughed quietly. They listened for the familiar sounds of their house. Stillness—and then he moved inside her.

16

Cynthia Klein

[1] "Melanie has a fever, Sandy. I put her to bed. I came home from Missy's... this was our knitting afternoon... Here I am going on like this before you've even had a chance to take your coat off." She helped him with his raincoat. It was a new coat, a brand new Burberry, with a zip-in, zip-out pile lining. His mother had sent it, a Christmas present. From Florida. Cynthia loved the coat more than Sandy did. She loved his cashmere scarf, too. And his rain hat. She took each item from him. She followed him to Melanie's bedroom.

It was on the other side of the living room. Their living room had been expanded, and Melanie's room was an entirely new addition to the house. Their bedroom was the old master one, only enlarged. It was farthest away from Melanie's. That way everyone had privacy. Cynthia liked that. She had grown up with privacy.

Melanie was sleeping. The light was on. "I gave her some aspirin." Cynthia moved nearer to the bed, tiptoeing, whispering. "She needed the sleep. The fever had gotten to her."

Sandy stood next to the edge of the bed, across from Cynthia. "How much did she have?"

"A hundred and one."

"Shouldn't we call the doctor?"

"If the aspirin doesn't break the fever, then I will, Sandy."

"She gets sick too often, and right now... I don't like her color. It's awfully yellow."

"Fever does that." But he was right. Even before the fever, her coloring had been off. Since even before the cold weather started. And she'd had one fever after another. She wasn't the strongest child to begin with. Always did seem paler than most. Even though the doctors kept telling her it was nothing. Nothing at all. Slower metabolism. Just her nature. Nothing wrong with her—and if three doctors tell you the same thing, you have to believe it. So why didn't Sandy? Why did she feel when he said what he did that he was accusing her, blaming her for the fact that Melanie had too many colds? Or that her coloring was off. Why did he make her feel it was somehow her fault? She did everything in her power...but there she was, standing there thinking about herself. Not really about Melanie. And not really about Sandy. She hadn't even given him a second to go to the bathroom. She had hardly let him take off his coat. What was it about her? Why was she so selfish? She wasn't the one who just got off the train. She wasn't the one in bed, sick. Her daughter. Her own sweetest daughter was—again. Third time in two months. Something had to be wrong. It frightened her to think what. Because if anything happened to Melanie, she'd...she'd what? Kill herself? Go crazy? That was what was crazy: thinking things like that. Sandy wasn't accusing her of anything. She was accusing herself, and for no reason. No earthly reason.

Sandy was staring down at Melanie, just as she was, staring down; arms folded, worried, just as concerned as she was. Melanie was their daughter, not just hers alone. They were both responsible for whatever went wrong, whatever went right. Things did go right, too.

Cynthia leaned down closer. Melanie was having a hard time breathing. She was sweating. Her black curls were glistening; beads of wet lined her upper lip. Her lips were so dry, so white and pink. Stuck together. Maybe it was the lamplight that made her skin look so yellow. Like ivory yellow. Smooth skin. Like Sandy's. Without a blemish. Without a rough spot anywhere. The scrubbed-clean, innocent sheen of it—when she had no fever. A glow of white silk. A rich cream color. Just like Sandy. But that was all. That was all there was of Sandy in her. The rest was pure Berk...Berkowitz. Dark. Dark hair. Dark eyes. Startling dark dots on white, white silk: Melanie, when she was healthy. Not really pretty, not really plain. Like mother, like daughter. Not like father.

Which was sad. Because Sandy was the beauty in the family. Most daughters looked like their fathers. If she thought about the daughters she knew...Teresa Geiger. Exactly like Carl. Ellen Leventhal. Exactly like poor Bud. She must remember to call Edna later. And Evelyn too. See how the baby's...Angela Massi. Maria Massi. Unfortunately, just like Joe. Maybe people say the same thing about Melanie. Poor Melanie. How unfortunate that she favors her mother instead of her father. Daughters usually look like fathers; sons look like mothers. So what happened in the Klein case?

Nothing happened. Nature does what it wants to do. Some

things go wrong; some things go right. Like with Sandy. He looked so beautiful in his concern. Staring down at her, his jacket still buttoned, his tie in place. Tweed. Silk rep. Oxford-blue button-down. So handsome...and her husband. She gestured for him to come out of the room, to let her sleep.

[2] "...Gladys and Gordon. They're coming about eight-thirty. Don't you remember? I told you this morning we were going to be playing bridge." He didn't remember. Because he didn't listen. Half the time he didn't hear a single word she said. But he always said he did. No. Not said. He nodded. Yes. He remembered now. Nodding, not actually saying a word. Not while he was eating. He sipped some wine. Carefully he sliced a small sliver of roast beef. He chewed it slowly, gazing around the kitchen, probably seeing nothing of it at all. Saying nothing. Hearing nothing. Except what he wanted to hear, what he wanted to see, saying only what he wanted to say, and then only to the people he liked—not that he was ever impolite to the people he didn't like. It was not in Sandy to be rude. He just never paid attention to, never seemed to concern himself with, whether or not people liked him. Beautiful people, handsome people, gifted people. they make up their own rules, behave any way they want to, and get away with it. Without half-trying, they seem to. Sandy never tried: he just was who he was. That frightened some people off: that streak in him some people called indifference, some people called snobbishness. His interests and pleasures frightened some people off too.

He liked wine with his dinner.

He liked music to be playing while he ate; he didn't like conversation then. He liked Mozart. He liked Schubert. He liked Brahms piano music, especially the Intermezzi. He played the Glenn Gould recording of the Brahms Intermezzi during dinner more often than any other recording he owned. "Idiosyncratic," he called the performance.

He liked their glass dining table, their aluminum cabinets, their dark Formica countertops.

He liked a cigarette with coffee. He never smoked more than three cigarettes a day, one with each meal, at home or at the office.

He liked neatness, order, schedule, dark things...the fair-haired boy!

They had reached coffee. He lit a Pall Mall; he had always smoked Pall Mall. When they first met he was smoking Pall

Malls, but a lot more than three a day in those days. In the Army he had smoked a lot. Not until after they moved to Levittown, about a year or so after that, had he cut down on his smoking, and as soon as he did, he cut down to three, without half-trying....

"I'm worried about Melly." He blew the smoke to the side, away from her. Considerate. Always considerate. "Something more than a cold must be wrong. Her resistance..."

"Why do you say *must*? You aren't a doctor, Sandy. And it isn't as if we've neglected her in any way."

"Why are you getting so touchy? I'm not even remotely suggesting that we've neglected her. But facts are facts. She gets sick too often for nothing to be wrong. That's all I am saying. Not that something terrible is wrong. I don't mean that."

"Then what do you mean?" She wanted to collect the dishes. It was 7:30. She didn't want to enlarge the discussion—if there was to be one. So, then, why was she? Why was she challenging him?

"I mean that her resistance seems to be much lower than it should be. Maybe she's anemic...but I assume every doctor has checked that out first thing."

"You know they have. They're forever taking blood from her to check on that. You know that. You just never remember from one minute to the next. You don't remember anything. You get lost in your own thoughts."

He stamped out his cigarette. He was looking across at her. He was annoyed. "What's gotten into you, Cynthia? I'm trying to talk to you about Melanie, not about my idiosyncrasies. Why don't you try to keep them separate, at least for Melanie's sake? How about that?" But then he checked his wristwatch. He too saw that it was getting late. "The worst part of it all is that I have to go down to Washington tomorrow."

That brought her to her feet. "Thank you for telling me, finally!" She began scraping, and even she was disturbed by all the noise she was making. Why was she making this...this scene? "What's gotten into you, Cynthia?" That tone. That damn tone of his. So superior. Even over at the sink, with her back to him, she felt it, felt the cold control of it. "Nothing has gotten into me. Nothing at all. Which is..." She couldn't be so vulgar. "Why couldn't you have told me about going away, before now? I wouldn't have had the bridge game." She had turned by then. She was at the sink. She stayed there.

152

She wanted some distance. She wanted to see him at a distance, even those three feet. Which was all it would take for her to see what a fool she was making of herself. Just creating a scene, when so many other things were so much more important. Obviously, he was telling the truth about going away. He wouldn't make up a lie like that, not when Melanie was sick. Poor Melanie. Somehow she got lost in the shuffle. "I'm sorry, Sandy.... How long will you be gone?"

"For the rest of the week. Probably until Saturday. The Defense Department man can't see me until Friday, and I have to do some contract research down there first.... But maybe I could do that on the telephone. Maybe I could stay home until Thursday. By then Melly's fever might break. I might be able to do that. I'll see how..." But the record was finishing. He was getting up. "I'm going to change my clothes. I'll look in at Melly."

Out of the room. With not even a touch for her. Not a smile. Nothing for her. Except the dishes.

[3] "Frankly, Cynthia, if you want my opinion, I'd take her into the city. Levittown's got a lot of things, and one of them's lousy doctors." Gladys Ginsburg fanned her cards, tapped them, counting. She was the dealer—she was, she wasn't, going to bid?—but she was also the world's leading authority on everything, in addition to bridge. On doctors. And on coffee. She sipped some. Made a face. Put the cup down loudly. Squinting. Scrunching up her pretty little nose. It was pretty. Her whole face was. Puffy, but pretty. "I'm afraid I'm just going to have to pass...just."

"You're shameless, Gladys." Said in what she hoped sounded like jest, Cynthia meant the touch of tartness. "Why not tell Gordon you've got twelve points?"

"Because I don't." She closed the fan of her cards emphatically. She sipped some more coffee, scrunching up her nose again. Puffy. Especially in slacks, Cynthia was happy to observe. "I pass too." Cynthia hated Gladys's bridge manners. Actually, Gladys had none, but she was always lecturing everyone else about how they must pay attention to bridge etiquette: when cards have been shuffled, they must be placed just so; cards must be breasted; when one made a bid, that's all one had the right to say, no qualifiers such as she had just added to her bid. Tacky, that kind of behavior. Still, according to Gladys, she was the world's leading authority on everything, including her husband and his *doings*—

153

Gladys's word for it—and how to handle him and them. She was sure she knew how. She had confided in Cynthia over and over again how she just ignored what she had to ignore....

Gordon tapped the edge of the table with his cards. "Nothing to worry about, Cynthia. This time all Gladys's messages are wasted. I've got even less than she has." He sipped from his Scotch. He liked a tall weak Scotch when he played bridge. He liked making fun of his wife because she was a much better player than he was. In fact, she really was the best player of the four.

At that moment, however, the fourth player, Sandy, was not there in the den. He had gone to check on Melanie... for the hundredth time, Gladys whined. "Where is he already?"

"His mind is not on the game tonight." Cynthia knew it seldom was. Sandy was an unwilling bridge player always. He played because she wanted to play.

They waited, listening. Cynthia heard the refrigerator opening, then closing. He was pouring something. "I'll be right back."

Sandy was taking a glass of juice to Melanie. "She was thirsty." Cynthia followed after him, wanting to check for herself.

Melanie was sitting up. She was even smiling.

"Drink it slowly, sweetheart. Daddy just took it from the fridge." Cynthia felt her forehead. Definitely the fever was down. "You're feeling better, aren't you, darling?"

"Yes." But her eyes were following Sandy's hands reaching for the quilt, which had slid off the bed. "It always slides off, Daddy. Why do they have to make it so slippery? I don't need it anyway now. I feel too hot in here." And she was pushing the blanket back. She was in a red flannel nightshirt. Cynthia felt it. It was wet with perspiration.

"Her fever's broken, Sandy. Why don't you go back out there to the game, and I'll change her... her nightshirt's too wet to stay in... and then I'll straighten the bed. Would you like that, Melly?"

"Who's out there, Mommy?"

"The Ginsburgs."

"Daddy? Please? Before you go?" She held out her arms. She wanted Sandy to lean down and kiss her. Her nightshirt sleeves fell back. Her arms were thin, pathetically thin, but she clutched Sandy's neck as if she were the strongest twelve-year-old in the world. "I want to go to school tomorrow,
154

Daddy. I feel much better, and tomorrow my English project for Mr. Rothstein is due. I've done so much work on it, and—"

"I'm glad you feel better, sweetheart, but no school tomorrow. Rest tomorrow." He smoothed her hair back from her forehead. Her skin did look less yellow. Cynthia thought so anyway—but maybe Sandy was right about that. Maybe another kind of test.... Cynthia moved behind Sandy, touched his back, as if to alert him to the fact that she shared his concern, his worry. She left her hand on his sweater. She wanted to keep it there. The sweater was soft, cashmere-soft, but his back stiffened. "Mommy's going to take care of you now." He stood up, alongside the bed, next to Cynthia, unwilling to move away. Melanie looked so much like one of those waiflike Anne Frank photographs, only not as pretty as Anne Frank had been. No. But as thin. More pathetic. Cynthia felt like she was suddenly going to cry. The two people she loved most in the world. Neither one of them really wanted her.

But just then, as if he had read her mind, felt her sudden hurt, Sandy put his arm around her shoulder. "Mommy's going to make you feel like a new little girl. And then you go back to sleep. You need sleep." He leaned down to kiss her.

The fair-haired boy. The dark-eyed little waif.

Her two treasures. Her two prizes. "When you go back out there, there've been three passes to you."

"I'll wait here with you, Cynthia. Okay if I do, Melly? You won't be embarrassed?"

No, Daddy. I won't be."

But he was. He went to the window. He pulled the drapery back. "It's snowing again. Very lightly. Pretty, Melly."

She was in a fresh plaid flannel nightshirt by then. Cynthia was washing her face with a cooling cloth, drying it ever so gently, puffing up the pillows, settling her back against them. "I'll leave the juice here too. On the night table. Okay?"

Melanie nodded, smiling. Her eyes were closing. She was tired.

They each kissed her again, and then they left her. They went back to the den together. Sandy kept his arm behind her waist. He even helped her back into her chair. "She's feeling better. Wants to go to school tomorrow. That Mr. Rothstein must be quite a teacher. He has them mesmerized." Sandy picked up his cards. "Now, if you'll just give me a

155

moment, Gladys...." Very slowly he fanned the cards, with all due deliberation. They all watched.

Such a strange man, Cynthia thought. His moods change with the speed of a thought. Gladys was exasperated. Gordon sipped more Scotch. He was patient, contained. Whatever his wife was, he was the opposite. He had been reading from Sandy's copy of Einstein's *Mozart*. It had been on the end table next to the black leather club chair, Sandy's chair, where he always sat when reading. Gordon resumed his reading of the book. Gladys began humming, louder and louder.

"So, three passes to me. Correct?" Sandy's eyes opened wider, considering, their blue darker in the glow of the lamplight.

"Yes, correct." Just being able to say something saved Gladys from exploding. She and Gordon must have been at it, some kind of fight—and now Sandy was going to bid. It was all too much for Gladys, especially since she held an *almost* biddable hand. "Now, Mr. Klein. What's it to be? Gordon! Can't you put that book down. We're supposed to be playing bridge. I hate it when someone's playing bridge and they insist on doing a million other things. When you play bridge, either you concentrate on bridge or you shouldn't play."

"Well, maybe if you would just shut up for a minute, Sandy *could* concentrate." Calmly Gordon closed the *Mozart*, replaced it on the end table. Deliberately he sipped loudly from his Scotch. Gordon was a big man. Heavy. Tall, but dainty, precise, every movement controlled, thought out, very much like Sandy. Among all their friends, Sandy seemed to feel most at ease with Gordon. She had always wondered what it was between them. A secret pact perhaps? If Gordon said nothing about Sandy's *doings*, then Sandy would say nothing about Gordon's? Except that everyone knew about Gordon's doings. Gladys was always talking about them. And not just to Cynthia. Also to Evelyn and Audrey, even to Corinne, and always in private, in "strictest confidence," one after the other, about Gordon's current affair. But no one, ever, said one word to her about Sandy. There was no secret pact between them. Gordon and Sandy both liked good music. That's all—and they weren't afraid of periods of silence. Men weren't. Almost all of the husbands in their group were...still waters. Maybe not deep. But still. Silent...secretive...secure.

Sometimes, however, Sandy could be silent for too long. Like then. "Well, Sandy? To bid or not to bid." Cynthia was ready to throw in the cards. Bridge was very much beside the point tonight, very much beside the point she hoped—oh how she hoped—to make with Sandy later, tonight.... And she'd seen enough of Gladys for one day. Gladys and her caftan at Missy's earlier had been enough.

"I'll say one heart."

"The blond god has spoken. Hooray." Gladys fanned her cards, closed them, tapped the tabletop with them. "I'll say one spade—which I hope my darling husband is listening to."

"Two hearts." Cynthia's response was quick. Get things over with.

Gordon looked up and across. "Your darling husband passes."

"And god says four hearts." A famous Sandy Klein smile: vanilla ice, a demand for quiet and peace.

Instantly Gladys led the jack of clubs. It was ten o'clock, and they had managed to play only two rubbers.

Cynthia laid out her hand neatly for Sandy to study. His fingers rose to smooth back his fine shiny hair as he planned his strategy. He would go down by one trick, she thought, unless a finesse in trumps worked. If she looked at Gladys's hand she could tell yes or no—but Gladys never let anyone look. Never. It could reveal too much. In the eyes, Gladys always said. Even when a person tried not to, they showed something in the eyes. Just a flicker was enough for the partner to see, if he was looking. So fastidious when she played bridge. Any other time Gladys was willing to reveal every nook and cranny of her life. Poor Gladys, expert at cards and knitting and cooking, but unlucky at love, unlucky with her children, neurotic. It was Levittown. Whenever Cynthia felt herself looking for reasons to explain anything, it was always Levittown. The place was empty, empty right down to the empty heart of it, with no tie to anything worthwhile from the past. Not a shred of history to it. A person had to leave it to find anything worthwhile. As soon as Melanie was finished with high school, they would move. She had promised that much to herself. No matter what Sandy said about Levittown's being the great leveler! It hadn't leveled him. He was, he always would be, more than anyone's equal.

Sandy was just saying that he was surprised to have made an overtrick.

"Because my husband played stupidly. Why didn't you lead a club back? Why do you think I led the jack?"

"You bid spades, didn't you?"

"So what? Can't you use your imagination?"

"I don't have any." Gordon was smiling. He spoke softly. He was being insufferably calm and controlled.

"Before you two go any further"—Sandy was about to decide something for all of them, Cynthia knew that expression all right—"I want to call it a night now. My mind is definitely not on the game and I've got to go down to Washington tomorrow, early." He didn't wait for rebuttals. He made the rules, for his house, for his life. Noblesse oblige. And no matter how much Gladys wanted to continue playing—and she did—she knew if Sandy said no more, Sandy meant no more, and there would be no discussion. He was standing. He was smoothing down the front of his chinos, straightening the cuffs of his beige cashmere sweater, pulling them down over his oxford-blue sleeves. Sandy Klein! Neatness and order personified. Where did he keep his passion hidden? damn him.

She went for Gladys's and Gordon's coats. Sandy was busy with the glasses and cups.

[4] Every room in their house had a connecting theme, a single motif, a carefully worked-out design plan: modern, austere, muted, absolutely uncluttered, the only real color—real, indeed—in the natural green of the plants. Sandy loved his plants. He never let Cynthia water them or move them. Their position was part of the scheme of things. Except in their bedroom, everything in the house had its position in the scheme of things. He had let Cynthia do their bedroom, the way she wanted it, with Southern comfort.

In there were the frills and flowers, chintzes and dotted swiss and tieback curtains on the two windows. The chintz draperies could be pulled closed for the winter, when it got very cold. Like that night. The snow had stopped. The sky had cleared and a strong wind had started up. She was happy to be in bed under her quilt. She would have preferred most of all to have been in Sandy's bed and under him. She needed that more than anything else she could think of. That's what had *not* gotten into her: him.

Not for a long time. Not for too long a time. She had to talk to him. She had to. And he had to be willing to talk to her. About that. And not only about that. About a lot of other things too. About a headful of things she'd been storing up. He had to. He had to want to as much as she did. He was

158

human, after all, so beautifully human, when he wanted to be. "Sandy?" Quietly. On a breath, calling out, "Sandy?"

He didn't—or he wouldn't—hear her. "Sandy?" Louder, because sometimes, if she started it, if she began a conversation in a quiet, calm way, he would seem to want to continue talking, he would seem to try to struggle to say something important—if she began it. Only if she began it. But sometimes it was hopeless. He wouldn't respond. Just wouldn't. He would act as if there wasn't a thing wrong between them. Maybe there wasn't. Maybe she was imagining everything. Maybe she was expecting too much from him, from her marriage, from life. "Sandy?" Full voice. She had to. Otherwise she would go crazy. Her headful of things she'd been storing up would burst. "Sandy!"

"What? What is it?" He sat up suddenly. He really had been sleeping. "Melly? Is it Melly?"

"No. It's me."

He fell back, pulled his quilt higher. "These damn things are always sliding off. What time is it anyway?"

"One. You fell asleep so fast..."

"I'm tired and I've got to get up—"

"—early. I know. You have to catch the early plane to Washington. I know all that. But I have to talk to you about something. I have to—"

"Do we have to talk now? Right now? In the middle of the night? Can't whatever it is wait?"

"It's been waiting. For months now...even longer. It's been...waiting for a very long time. For...for years, for maybe all the time we've been married it's been waiting."

"And you want to talk about something like that, something that important, right now? In the middle of the night?" He had a right to sigh, to be exasperated. "All right. What is it? What's been waiting all these years?" He sat all the way up. Even in the darkness she could see he was staring over at her. His pajamas, that white-on-white silky-cotton-white, from Saks, that his mother always made sure he had a supply of, glowing, and his hair, his skin, glowing. Why couldn't she just say it, just say, very simply: You, I've been waiting for you. All these years. Waiting. And folding my arms in front of me, squeezing myself to stay together, in one piece, waiting, for you to open them, for you to want..."Sandy? Couldn't you just come over here? Get into bed with me?"

"Is that what you woke me up to say? That's what you want to talk to me about tonight? Why didn't you say so in

159

the first place. Sure I'll get in bed with you. Sure. That's easy enough."

She held her covers up for him to slide under. Her little fair-haired boy. He nestled in, against her breasts. She smoothed his hair; she rubbed his back; she loved him so much when he gave in this way, when he didn't fight her, when he didn't turn silent and sulky and distant. "Sandy?"

"What?"

"Sandy? You're not...unhappy? Are you?"

"No. Not as far as I know I'm not."

"Then why do you...why do you look...sometimes you look as if you are."

"That's because sometimes I am." He murmured, still pressed against her. Simple. So simple. There wasn't anything else to ask. Not then, anyway. Not in the middle of the night. Not when she had him in bed with her, inside her arms. The headful of things she thought she had to say or burst had dissolved. Her trouble was, she imagined too many things. If Melly were well, she wouldn't be so on edge all the time. Neither would he be. Apart from that, what did she really have to complain about? Sandy was there. Sandy was staying just where he was, where he had been for a long, long time now. Why didn't she just relax and accept their way of being together? It was as simple as all that. And all she ever managed to do was to make simple things more and more complicated. Did she have to talk? Couldn't she just act?

She put her hand inside his pajama top, touched and smoothed his skin. Silky. Like Melanie's. But cool. Well, that was their way, and he said he was happy. That was their way together. She could do what she was doing. She hadn't ever wanted it to be that way, for her to begin...things. She hadn't ever expected it to be...but it was. It always had been, for them.

She could accept it. She could stop being embarrassed by it. It was just between the two of them anyway. Just them. She had to accept it. She loved him. She wanted him. She wouldn't go crazy. She was always imagining things. Always. That's what was wrong...if anything was wrong. It was her fault. What had he done? Nothing. Nothing at all...that she knew anything about...knew anything real about...like a fact...a real fact.

She moved her hand lower. He wasn't hard, but he wasn't

soft either. She held it. There was life in it. And in her too. There was no need to talk. It was dark and they were alone in their own bedroom in their own house in their own world.

He didn't resist her touching him.

PART THREE

1965

Evelyn Selden
Loretta Massi
Melissa Geiger
Corinne Feuerstein
Cynthia Klein

17

Evelyn Selden

[1]   Between Danny's telephone call and his, "Ma?...I need
to speak to you," and Eli's faltering, "Ma...nish-ta-naw..."
there was just enough time for Evelyn to give in: "Why not,
Harold? What's the difference if we have seders again or we
don't?"

She didn't really have the heart for it; for all the people,
for all the work it would mean. Passover 1965 could come
and go—fast, faster than 1964 had, which was the first one
she'd missed since her mother died. Even the year after her
father died, she'd had one. The boys had coaxed her into it.
And Harold. "In his memory, Ev. Come on. Do it." So she
had—1958—in his memory.

In 1964 she didn't have the heart for a seder, or for anything, for that matter, after Kennedy's death. Not that anyone's death stops anything. A mother's. A father's. A president's.

But then, there was Danny's telephone call from the city,
from his "pad." "Ma?...I need to speak to you."

"Not to your father?"

"To both of you. I want to come out there. Next Friday
night. I'll come for dinner..."

"Next Friday night is the first seder night."

"Are you having one? You didn't last year."

"Last year I didn't have the heart for it. After Kennedy—"

"Don't have it this year either—as far as I'm concerned."

"But if I give one, will you come, Danny?"

"If I have to."

"Then I'll have it....What do you want to speak to us
about?"

"You really are something, Ma." He *tsk*ed. That sound.
How she hated it. "At least call Morty, Ma. Get him to come
down from Boston. I'll bring my new woman."

"What happened to the old one?"

164

Tsk-tsk. "Will you cut it out, Ma?"

"I'll cut it out.... What do you want to speak to us about?"

"I'll tell you when I get there."

Harold was glad she had changed her mind. So was Eli. His Sunday-school class had been studying the Four Questions in English and also in phonetic Hebrew. He'd do it in Hebrew. He liked that idea. He liked learning things there was a reason to learn. He liked being authentic. At nine, he liked the truth. He liked people to tell the truth about everything. About why Kennedy was killed. About why he was the only one of his friends that didn't have any grandparents. Not one.

So, "In the final analysis, Harold..." That was her current phrase. "I guess it's right we have the seder. For Eli's sake, if for no one else's.... I just hope it's not too late to get people. Gladys is giving a seder. Everyone went there last year. Remember?"

"Yes." But that was all he said. They were in the den, after Danny's call. Harold was watching a basketball game, sitting at the edge of his chair, biting his nails, leaning toward the TV. He always sat that way. He never relaxed, never leaned back, unless he was in bed and ready for sleep. "Are you listening, Harold?"

"I'm listening. I heard every word you said."

"If the game makes you so tense, why do you watch it?"

"This is the way I like to sit. You going to start in with that again? You want to make a list? So make a list. How many people you want? Decide. Tell me and I'll get capons from my meat-salesman friend. I'll help you with the cooking, I told you."

"Do you have to raise your voice?"

"Yes. I have to. Do you want capons or don't you, or should I go upstairs and wake Eli and ask him to make up your mind for you?"

"I can do without your sarcasm, Harold. I know my mind. If you knew your mind as well..."

"I know what I have to know. Sometimes knowing too much isn't healthy. You're always reading and discussing, and for what purpose, may I ask?"

"Ask. Ask all you want—" But then the telephone was ringing again. Cynthia, calling to see if they wanted to play some bridge. And so Evelyn had the chance to ask about the seder. Could Cynthia and Sandy and Melanie come?

"I've already accepted Gladys. Why did you wait so long,

165

Ev? You didn't have one last year, so I thought...Why don't you do something afterwards? Because if Melanie finds out Danny was there and she didn't get to see him, I'll never hear the end of it."

So, not only was she giving the seder, she was also going to have an *afterwards*, "...and, yes, Harold, let's have capons. I'll let you know how many. As long as *you* roast them. Do you have any idea what Danny's up to now? What he wants to ask us for now?"

[2] One black dot along the border of white faces: Clarice, Danny's *woman*. That's how he introduced her, "my woman," and she didn't seem to object. A total of twenty-six, for the meal, plus how many *afterwards*? A question mark.

So be it, as long as at the moment of sitting down to the seder table there was relative calm. For her part in the activities, Evelyn knew she was prepared: the food, the setting, the silver, the glistening glasses Harold was filling with wine, the dishes—white with the gold rim—reserved for special occasions, the Hagaddahs, the burgundy-and-blue-emboidered white satin case for the *afikomen* to be slipped into, for the Passover symbols to rest on, and Elijah's silver goblet with the delicate filigree work around its curving surface, an heirloom. A one and only. Which her grandmother had brought from Minsk and which she had given to her daughter-in-law, Ellie. Evelyn had saved that from among the many things of her mother's: Elijah's goblet—and also the damask tablecloth big enough to cover the three bridge tables pressed up against the dining table, a huge white, aged cloth with matching damask napkins. Evelyn treasured those. But the pieces she cared for more than anything else in the whole house were her mother's four candlesticks of burnished gold, gold columns with dark dents, wrinkles, crease marks her mother had tried to polish out of existence each year but never could. Evelyn toured the table. She had lit the candles before everyone was seated.

Harold held up his Hagaddah. "Welcome. Evelyn and I welcome you all." Watching him, her eyes filled suddenly. That winning smile of his. She stood behind Danny and Morty, watching. She touched their shoulders. Only Morty turned to smile. She went to her seat at the far end of the table, the part that extended into the living room. Harold was coaxing Eli to his feet. "I don't plan to read the entire Hagaddah, only the essentials before dinner. And the main essential will be done by Eli." Far away, she felt far away, at the end of the table, waiting.

And her dark-haired nine-year-old pudge of a son was clearing his throat, was beginning. *"Ma-nish-ta-naw, ha-li-law, ha-zeh..."* he had memorized it, had practiced it all afternoon while she set the tables, but now he was reading it from the book. All those eyes watching him, he would tell her later. She was sure he'd say that. She knew her baby son, all right—but it *was* frightening. All those eyes, watching.

His father, right next to him. His two older brothers. His two uncles: Uncle David, alone, and Uncle Irving, and next to him Aunt Beth and Cousin Sheila, Cousin Rachel: so much for the remnants of the Howard family. David, still, and probably always to be, unmarried. Irving had daughters. Therefore the end of the Howard name.

And she had invited Mr. Rothstein...Aaron. He wanted her to call him Aaron. She had gotten to know him well during the years she was president of the General MacArthur High School PTA. She hoped...Aaron...remained in the English Department long enough for Eli to get there. Aaron was seated between Irving and David. Aaron was alone too.

And the Feuersteins: three. Corinne sipped her wine, without a blessing! For shame.

The Massis: four. Angela and Maria were already playing with their bracelets. Bored. Joe was glum. Loretta was...was lighting a cigarette. Infidel! She palmed it.

The Geigers: all six. Donald, in his ensign's uniform, was home on leave before being shipped out—to the Far East, he thought. Adam was going to enlist in the Marines. He was dropping out of Hofstra. Didn't want school. More the village smithy type, a blond village smithy. And Teresa, every inch Carl: dark, laconic, distracted, and now a senior at MacArthur, in the same English class as Gregory Feuerstein—Aaron's senior English. Teresa and Gregory were pals. Gregory had managed to squeeze between Teresa and Agnes. Aggie was laughing then, laughing while her particular pal read his Hebrew. Funny. Everything was funny. Missy was clearly annoyed with Aggie's laughter. She held a warning finger up to her lips. Carl did too, and then he opened his palm in front of his face. He meant business.

Across from the Geigers, Danny and his woman, Clarice. Next to Clarice, Morty's girlfriend, Patricia Johnson. She and Morty were, "...hangin' in at B.U.," is how she put it to Evelyn. Morty! Jet-black glistening curly hair. And tall.

Taller than Harold. Taller than Danny. Handsomer too now, as it turned out. Tall and dark and handsome. Another Gary Cooper—and good, decent, loving in a way that Danny wouldn't allow himself to give in to being. No, Danny wouldn't give in to loving. Lean and angry Danny.... At least, that's how old Ma felt about her Danny.

Harold didn't feel that about Danny. Harold said he understood Danny and that she just didn't, couldn't.

She closed her eyes on the scene spread before her. She was listening to Eli, thinking her thoughts, wondering her way through time gone, time now, back and forth, the way her mind always seemed to work, on a pulse, on a rush of memory—coming, going away. Useless, here, now, memory, her thoughts. Once upon a time...Far away. Far away at the end of the table Eli was finishing in English, politely, the way he had practiced it that afternoon, "...and so, dear Father, please give me an answer to my four questions. Please tell me why this night is different from all other nights."

Down he sat, blushing, embarrassed, waving his fist at Aggie.

Harold kissed him.

His brothers began the applause. Everyone joined in, and then Harold was saying that he was going to skip to the Plagues, "As I read them off, just dip your finger, your pinky, into the wineglass, drip a drop for each plague...on the plate. Try to miss the tablecloth." His smile then, his winning, weary smile.

[3]   Judging from Harold's skipping, it was almost time for the hard-boiled eggs. The bowls of salt water were already on the table, but she should go out to the kitchen and check on the *tsimmis.* "It shouldn't stick, so check, darling," her grandmother would have said just then at seders long since gone and all but forgotten, except by herself—and, she supposed, by her brothers.... And had she forgotten to turn on the burner beneath the chicken soup?

She had not forgotten. The soup was simmering beautifully. The matzo balls were ready to be lowered. Bombs away! She hoped not bombs. Make them light, someone, whoever, up there, she prayed to herself. The capons were cut and resting under foil. Harold's work. His hotel training. And he had set out the plates for the gefilte fish. Store-bought Rokeach. Some of what they would eat she could never have

168

prepared. Harold could have. She? Never. Certainly not gefilte fish, no matter how many times she had stood next to
her mother, watching, or next to her grandmother, watching,
up at the hotel. And she had, watched, especially that first
summer Harold came to work there—and forever afterward,
watching her grandmother lower those grainy ovals of grated
fish into the boiling fish broth, watching as Harold passed
in and out of that hotel kitchen calling out orders, reaching
for this, for that, and, eventually, for her. In and out...of her
memory: Harold, then, and all the others, then. All those
others, dead, gone, and with them a part of her life, gone. At
forty-three, certain places, certain people...and
pleasures...gone. The daughter part of herself...gone. No
other home to go home to but her own.

And her own children...going now: two out of three.
Danny, who would never finish school. She felt it in her bones
he wouldn't. A two-time dropout from Syracuse ("They won't
take you back, Danny." "Don't nag, Ma. I hate when you nag
and question and advise. Don't.") Morty? He'll follow in
Danny's footsteps, wherever they lead, even nowhere, even
into the Army—if it comes to that. And Eli? When she turned,
looked over her shoulder, into the other room, his face was
the first she saw. He was gesturing for her to come back
inside: Come on, Ma—in his eyes. Anxious eyes. Worried.
Waiting. For words about the world. (Ma, "...why does it
work the way it does? It doesn't work right. Why? Tell me
the truth, Ma. When Daddy was in the Air Force bombing
places and people, what did you think?" "Think? Nothing—
except that he should come home safely. That he should be
alive and well and...")

And there came Eli with Harold out to the kitchen to get
her. "Come on back, Ev. We're waiting for you. To dip the
eggs." He led her back to her seat. Everyone did seem to be
waiting for her before they would go on.

[4] She and Harold doled and delivered; Corinne and Missy
collected after each course. Missy even scraped and rinsed.
The dinner was a success. Her severest critic, Danny, said
so. Her brothers loved the *tsimmis;* Harold loved the *kugel.*
Conversation was low-keyed, neighborly. No fusses. No
fights. No differences of opinion. Not yet. They might just
get through the pass without an ambush.

And after the main course was cleared away and the children were requested to reseat themselves, please, for a little

while longer, everyone, patience, she urged, a little while longer, "One more glass of wine, please. One more to go.... That's all we'll do tonight."

The glasses were refilled. Elijah's silver goblet was moved directly in front of Harold. He indicated the place in the Hagaddah and when they were ready, he asked them to stand. Evelyn went to open the door to their house. She stood next to it while Harold read. She watched Eli watching Elijah's cup to see if the wine stirred, to see if the level decreased, to see if the prophet had entered their house.

"Boruch...ataw...adonoy..." Harold recited, "...elohenu...melech...ho...lum...." He lifted his wineglass. They all did. They waited until he finished the blessing, "...boray...pre...ha...goffen." They drank. Evelyn closed the door. She went to Harold. She kissed him and then Eli and then around to Danny and Morty, and the seder, which had been, until then, quiet, burst into spontaneous laughter and sound and life. Evelyn wanted to sing some songs with her brothers, the ritual songs that ended all the old-time seders, the Orthodox seders that she could remember lasted until one in the morning. So they sang "El Bene" and "Hagadyaw-ha-gad-yaw," and Corinne joined in and then everyone listened to her, to the pro, losing herself in the joy of suddenly singing out, her voice, these days, though, straining. She pushed it, pushed it to the limit, the way Evelyn watched her doing everything—extending herself too much, Corinne did, with too many cigarettes, too many drinks, too many fights with Lionel. It was all there in her voice. Lionel was embarrassed by all the attention she was getting. He asked her to, "Quiet it a little, Corinne, will you? You'll wake the dead."

That stopped her. That got Gregory up. Not embarrassed. Not angry. Evelyn couldn't tell what. Ivory-skinned pencil-thin Gregory was a riddle. Growing up, he had been at the house all the time, a friend of Danny's—and then he was never there. He was leaving the table, "...for some air. All the smoke in here..." Angela and Maria followed him, and that was the signal for Eli and Aggie, Cousin Sheila, Cousin Rachel, to go too, to play somewhere where there was an inch of space left.

Loretta and Missy and then Corinne, recovering some touch of her composure with a sip more, a little sip, of some more wine, all of them wanted to get to work in the kitchen— "Before the afterwards begins, Ev"—Loretta was stretching high, higher—"because I'm so stuffed I've got to do some-
170

thing, and if Cynthia gets here and you're not cleaned up, there'll be hell to pay."

Missy suggested that maybe Loretta was overstating the case a little. Loretta thought it was an understatement; Evelyn thought they should just sit where they were because, "It's only all of nine-thirty. Years ago our seders lasted until one, sometimes two in the morning. When my grandfather, my mother's father presided—"

"Years ago!" Danny sucked behind his teeth. That nasty *tsk-tsk*. "Years ago you lit candles for light." Spiteful. He needed a haircut. He needed to wash his dungarees. He needed to stop picking at her. He needed to tell her what he wanted from her instead of trying to pick her to pieces. "Years ago! That's all you ever say."

"Danny!" A Harold warning.

Quiet, briefly, and then a general shifting of everyone's gears, a scraping of chairs and benches and glasses tingling against silverware and china. Some sighs. Her brother David staring across the table at Danny. Aaron, too, staring across. Aaron, surprised. One of his prize pupils. Had Aaron overpraised him? Disappointed, his eyes said, as he stared across.

Encouraged by Aaron's expression, Evelyn went on, "I was only stating a fact about the past, about *my* past."

"That's my point. What you want to talk about isn't exactly relevant to this moment. There are other considerations..." But he stopped. Whatever had been on his mind to say, now was not exactly the moment he chose to say it. His *people*, his *side*, hadn't arrived yet. He was outnumbered. She saw him taking in Donald Geiger, in uniform, and Adam Geiger, soon to be in one, a marine soon: his friends, and now his opponents, his enemies. So was Carl. So was Lionel, probably, if anyone ever bothered to ask him an opinion about anything. The irony of ironies was that she, his mother, was almost always on Danny's side in every discussion.

"Years ago isn't a disease, Danny." Reasonable. Be reasonable, Evelyn told herself. Be reasonable with your eldest son and he will be the same with you. "Years ago things happened to us...some very important things happened to a lot of us..."

"Sure they did. And what good came from it? Who learned anything from World War II? From dropping the atomic bomb. It's happening all over again. It's about to happen all over again to us now, isn't it?" But before anyone could take up Danny's challenge, the door was opened and Melanie

171

Klein rushed in. She was all over Danny, hugging him, kissing him, and then Morty, and she made her way around to Teresa and Donald and Adam, and then Gregory came back to the dining room. So did Angela and Maria, because now the *afterwards* would begin: Danny's forces had arrived— Bruce Rabinowitz, down from Cornell; Laurie Halpern from Buffalo; Gary and Fern Leventhal, he from Northwestern, she from Sarah Lawrence, scholarship; Penny Plotkin, the University of Pennsylvania. And all of them seeking out Aaron to tell him what was what out in the big world beyond Levittown.

And meanwhile there were the assorted parents to greet and seat: Roy and Ruby, Audrey, Edna, Sally, Cynthia and Sandy. As long as the conversation had been interrupted "...we were about to have an intense one, Cynthia." Said during their greeting interval of brushed cheeks, "I could tell by the look on Danny's face." She would do, it was a good time to do, some tea and cake....

So, it was another half-hour before Danny was able to take up from where he had left off. He was determined. He had to, before it got any later, because Clarice was urging him to get to it, they were going to have to leave pretty soon— and Morty was saying that he and Pat might just go into the city with Danny and Clarice, if Evelyn wouldn't mind.

She did, but she didn't say that, not just then, because Danny had finished lighting up another of those foul-smelling French cigarettes for himself and Clarice and was already saying, was saying it out loud, "...and purposely, in front of all of you, so you understand that what I said before about no one's learning anything from World War II, had particular relevance to me. I wasn't kidding, either. You fought in your war and it was supposed to be all solved." He paused, he rolled the end of his cigarette around in his ashtray; he was weighing, it seemed to her, the wisdom of doing what he was about to do—whatever it was; and there was little derision left in the sound of his whispery voice, that child's voice filling up with trembling anger, anger about to overflow now—he was drawing deeply on his cigarette, then smashing it out in the ashtray he held in his palm. Anger. Anger—and for all kinds of reasons she didn't, she never would, understand. What had she done to him? What had Harold done to him? Harold, still seated at the head of the table, drew Eli to his side, holding him there, protecting him there, ready to, from whatever Danny might say. Everyone else was wait-

172

ing too, waiting patiently. So, do it, Danny, she thought. Do it and get done with it already. "The horrible truth is that nothing's been solved. All the deaths of World War II have solved nothing. Twenty years later, and everything's worse than it ever was. I know you won't think so, Donny. Or you, Adam. Or you, Mr. Geiger. Or Mr. Feuerstein. Mr. Massi. Maybe I'm wrong about that part. I don't know. I don't even know about my own father's feelings about Vietnam. But I sure as hell know my own. I'm supposed to be inducted ...inducted...into the Army, and what I wanted to talk to you about, Ma"—suddenly it was Ma, not Ma and Dad, but Ma—"what I've decided is that I'm not going to do it. I'm going to leave the country." Instantly, he was reaching for another cigarette. Silence, suddenly, deepening, lengthening.

Evelyn lowered her gaze, smoothed her hand back and forth over the wine stains that had seeped through the white damask tablecloth in front of her setting. How many wine stains, how many drops from the pinkies of how many people remembering the Plagues had it sopped up, had it had washed from it, restoring its whiteness? How many arguments had it been witness to? If a tablecloth could talk...She should. Harold should. And say what?—You're wrong, Danny? Do as you're told, Danny? The law? It's the law of the land?

"I wish," Harold began; he did not let Eli leave his side, "you had told us this...before, Danny, instead of at the seder table."

"I would have if I could have. There wasn't any time. Anyway, everyone here's a friend. Like part of one big family." His voice grew louder. He drew himself up straight. "We've all shared the same experience, the same kind of Levittown experience of being sealed off from the rest of the real world. Here everything's reduced to narrow interests, to good guys and bad guys. The Commies are bad and the Americans are good; meanwhile, innocent guys are getting killed again. Now they're getting killed because Lyndon Johnson says it's right. It's all bullshit. I, for one, am not going to do it. You agree with me, Mr. Rothstein, don't you? I know you do."

"I do," Evelyn yelled out, at the same time Aaron responded, and so his firm, but quiet *yes* was all but buried under the sound of Evelyn's determined "I do" and Loretta's thumping of the table and her shouting out, "It is all bullshit. Danny's right. Goddammit! He's absolutely right. Bullshit!" Joe tried but couldn't stop her. "And what about you, Donny?

173

You're ready to go off and get killed? You too, Adam? Do you have any idea why? To prevent the spread of Communism? Like Joe McCarthy used to say? Remember that, Ev? That crap? It's all such goddamned crap, for Christ's sake!"

"Must you, Loretta?" Missy joined the tips of her fingers beneath her chin. She was seated next to Donald. She was straining to remain calm, cool, collected. Carl was hunching lower, was turning pale. Donald wanted to go. So did Adam. Teresa didn't. Teresa was on Danny's side. Melanie was too. All the kids were. And the adults? Evelyn should do an instant poll—if she weren't so tired, from cooking, from serving, from collecting, from caring, from being compassionate and having a conscience and trying to continue to do what was worthwhile when all the while all of them all their lives were being made fools of. Now it was Danny's turn to play fool, to lie down and let them step all over his life—but he wouldn't do it. No. Not her son. Not Harold's—except when Danny wanted approval, wanted agreement, he hadn't asked Harold for it. He'd turned to Aaron and gotten it: instantly, firmly, quietly. Harold had said nothing. Harold was saying nothing now. He should, before everyone leaves....

Because they were leaving. Everyone wanted to. An exodus: the beginning all over again, history always going back to the same beginning, to the same victims—except that now, a few minutes ago, Danny had said no—and now also there was Carl telling Danny, "You're a traitor. That's what you are. A traitor to your own country," and then he was poking through the stampede to find Aaron, and finding him, he was telling Aaron next, "You are too. You're not fit to teach in an American public school."

Quiet then, a sudden and total quiet, during which Aaron seemed to assess the moment, the place, the people, looking out at them, at Carl particularly, at Missy too and her pained expression, pained, embarrassed, her eyes trying to convey her apologies for Carl's cruel words, which she was sure, her eyes said, he didn't mean, couldn't mean, not her Carl, no; and as Aaron looked out, he loomed larger, Evelyn thought, his gaze shifting slowly from face to face, from former students to friends to Danny, deciding that it was Danny who counted most of all at this moment. "It's your life to live out— or lose." And then Aaron's eyes closed, briefly. When he opened them, he seemed to be looking inside himself, at something there, something private, no longer at them, at any of them. Evelyn took hold of his arm. The quiet dissolved, became noise once more. Danny and Melanie and Teresa circled Aaron. Missy was apologizing to him. Gregory reached past her to shake Aaron's hand. So did Cynthia. So did Sandy. "Not true, Mr. Rothstein, none of what he said. We don't feel that way at all. Not at all...."

But Aaron was not paying any attention to anyone then but himself. He was even, surprisingly, smiling, and it was then that Harold approached him to tell him to pay no nevermind to Carl, because he was sure Carl didn't mean a word of it, and for Aaron to have a good holiday and to forget any of it had ever happened.

Aaron's smile broadened, became a laugh. "Yes. Right. None of it matters...for us. Only for Danny," and he was gone, out the door, into the darkness. Evelyn watched him until he had driven off in his old Triumph.

[5] They came out of the den, Danny and Clarice, Morty and Patricia, and Eli, into the living room, where she and Harold, in silence, were finishing the dismantling of the seder tables. Harold whispered to her, "Please, no more discussions. Let them leave. Let them take the car. Let them drive the girls into the city," going on to repeat what he had been saying over and over again before they all entered the room, that he and Evelyn would talk to Danny alone, tomorrow, when Eli wasn't around—Harold didn't want Eli to be part of the discussion; it wasn't necessary for him to have to go through that—and when they were alone with Danny, they could convince him *not* to do what he wanted to do. She agreed—to wait. She didn't agree with Harold. Enough talk. She was hurt. She was angry. She was tired.

But Danny wanted to talk. He gestured for them, for all of them, to sit down. So Harold couldn't accuse her of *starting in*.

Maybe a fire in the fireplace would be nice. Maybe some kind of warmth would be nice, a blazing fire on this chilly April night that was, indeed, different from all other nights of her life, and sitting finally, lowering herself to the ledge of the fireplace, facing Danny and Morty and Eli, her sons, and her Harold, and the girls, how tired she was hit her, like the proverbial ton of bricks it hit her. Tired. Tired...of everything. Everything was too much, just too much, especially that look in Danny's eyes was, that accusing look, as if somehow she was responsible for his dilemma. She. Not Harold. Only she.

175

And she had better not say to Danny: I told you so. Because she had said it before this night. Long before it, he would be quick to remind her. Stay in school, she had said and resaid and said again. And he had answered and reanswered and answered again that staying in school was not the way to face the real issue. The real issue was what was important. To go or not to go, that was the issue. To make your own choice. She had agreed with him each and every time it had come up—but then, on each and every time she had also said: "...but facts are facts, Danny, and are you prepared to face the consequences?" He was then.

He still was. More than ever, it seemed. He was in control. Slow. Cool. No *tsk-tsk*-ing. Just anger. Specific anger—and directed at her.

And, also directed at her, an invitation to an argument, "...so just get it into your head that I'm going to leave the country. Because I'm not going into the Army. No way they're going to get me. All I'm going to need, though, is a little money. To start out with." And then he leaned toward Clarice, asking for yet another Gauloise. They lit up. He smokes the most expensive cigarettes he can find, and then he asks for money to leave the country. Logic! Some logic!

But, as Danny would be quick to point out, what has logic to do with an army, or a war or killing other people for no reason that makes any sense? With that too she had agreed, and told him so. She agreed with him now; so she said, "I understand how you feel, Danny. I do. I just think—"

"*You!* You just think!" Quick. Hot. No longer controlled. "Why don't you give Dad a chance to think something? Why don't you let him say something? You never let him say what *he* thinks."

"That's not..." but she never did say "fair" out loud, because Eli moved then, moved across her vision of Danny and away from Harold's holding protection, to her, and Morty was telling Danny, "Hold up. You're really coming on too heavy. Much too heavy for right now." Morty stood up. Tall. The tallest. Standing. Just standing there. Still. In between. Not knowing what, if anything, to do next.

But next had to be Harold, because she wouldn't say anything, not another word, until he stirred himself to speak out, to speak up.

"Sit down, Mort." Harold waited until he had. But he didn't rush to speak. Usually he did when he was worried. Usually he would start to talk, raise his voice, fill up the silence with a lot of words that meant nothing at all... until he reached the place where he understood what he really felt. This night was different. He didn't do it that way. He remained silent.

She would too. Just as she had promised Harold she would. She would say absolutely nothing at all until Harold had spoken up. It was his turn to be the villain—if that's what Danny wanted one or the other of them to be. She eased Eli inside her arms, held him tighter, for comfort, for affection. She didn't want to cry. That would have been the easiest thing to do. Her habit. But Eleanor Roosevelt up there on the fireplace wall wouldn't have cried. Her Catskill grandmother wouldn't have. Her mother certainly wouldn't have. And so, now, Harold? What now? No longer was he that Harold looking down at her from the photograph. Not that Harold in his fatigues, with the pipe in his mouth, looking down at her like a movie star. No. Not that one. The real Harold, the now Harold, was waiting to speak, the one who was forty-seven years old. What now? Now that your oldest son has said he will not obey the law. And if Danny doesn't neither will Morty when it comes his turn. A mess: the whole world was more of a mess than anyone would have thought possible when they had moved out to Levittown, hoping for the best. Much worse... and all these years of joining this committee and that committee, of signing one petition or fifteen petitions, all that effort had ended up accomplishing nothing at all. For all that wasted effort, for her son's hatred—yes, it was hatred—she felt like crying. Effort and time and hope wasted, if, in the end, Harold says to Danny: You can't break the law. Even if it means that maybe that's the only way Danny can save his life from being wasted, destroyed.

But that's what Harold did begin to say. "You can't do it that way. I won't give you money to do it that way. I won't, because it doesn't make any sense to do that. If you want to prove your point, you can't run away to prove it. Who's going to listen to air?"

"Who's going to listen if I'm dead? You heard Mr. Rothstein. I'm the one who loses."

"You're exaggerating, as usual. So was he. Johnson's not going to let a war happen there."

"You believe that man? You believe his shit?"

"That's enough!" Harold jerked his head in Eli's direction. He didn't like that kind of talk in front of Eli. "Do you understand, Danny? And no Mr. Rothstein talk either. No Carl. Understand?"

"I understand. Don't worry. I understand, but I don't accept any of it. No way that I accept it." Danny was ready for another cigarette. For once, Clarice wasn't. She returned from wherever she had been drifting. She bent forward alongside Dan. "I think we should split. I mean, I got to go away from here."

"In a minute." Danny rested his arm on her dirty dungarees. His black turtleneck had specks of the beige shag rug all over it. Absorbed by them, Clarice pulled at them, one at a time, until, overwhelmed by their number, she sighed, leaned back once more inside the wings of her chair. "It's not going to help, Danny. Your black sister knows whereof she speaks."

"Don't say that, Clarice." Evelyn's promise to remain silent didn't include answering someone else's accusation. "You could try us harder. None of you seem to have the energy to try harder, though. You all seem so dazed and defeated before you even begin to try."

"We're stoned, Mrs. Selden." Morty's woman surprised herself more than anyone else. She hadn't connected two words together all evening. She covered her mouth, laughing. And then, embarrassed, she began to laugh louder. Morty tried to stop her by smothering her inside his arm. That didn't help. She had to laugh it out, Morty explained, embarrassed himself, but his embarrassment was guilt. "I'm sorry, Ma. But we are. Not Danny. The rest of us, though."

That brought Eli to his feet, in front of Harold. "I saw it, Dad. Before, when you were taking the tables down. It looked just like one of your cigarettes. That was all."

"You didn't give him any, did you, Morty?" Harold made Eli sit back down.

"No, Dad. I didn't give him any. But it's only a matter of time."

That did it for Evelyn. What she wanted to do then, was just ask them all to leave, to get out of the house, do whatever they wanted to do, but please to leave them in peace. Here they all were, trying to talk about something serious, about what she thought was a matter of life and death, about Danny's future, and that's all they could find the ingenuity to do? Smoke marijuana? "I think what you've done here is
178

just plain insensitive. Is this the only way you can deal with us?"

"I'm not stoned. You heard Morty. And I'm still waiting to get an answer to my question. It's my four questions in one. You actually think Johnson's different from any other president? You think I'm supposed to risk my life to find out?"

"I don't think your father has to answer anything at all tonight. He's not on trial. Neither am I. I don't know what it is you have against me, or him, but whatever it is, I'm not going to be treated like your enemy. I've had enough of your stepping all over me. I try to be fair with you. I try to be fair with all of you. I try to make sense out of whatever you say that I don't understand...but I don't think we have such a different point of view about the world. So, at least we can discuss things. We don't have to fight. No one here wants you to have to risk your life. No one wants you to do what Donny Geiger did. Or Adam. I certainly agree with Mr. Rothstein. You must know that. But you have to remember there are people who feel that way. Your way of doing things isn't the only way."

"You feel the same about that, Dad?"

"What I feel is that you shouldn't have let them smoke marijuana. Not in front of Eli."

"I don't stop people from doing what they want to do. I don't have that kind of right—but I'm asking about the other thing. The important thing."

"I don't want to talk about it now." He stood up, but he didn't move off. Just standing up had always been enough to demonstrate the force of his control. He was tall enough to seem to take charge. He could raise his voice louder than anyone else if he had to. The boys knew that. She knew it. "As far as I'm concerned, that's all we're going to say for now." And if he chose not to raise his voice, then it was his silent treatment he used: they were expected to keep their mouths shut, to look up to him and realize that he meant what he said. So was she, because he was angry then. But he wasn't so dark and angry anymore. His hair had thinned and grayed, and when he stood up he leaned, as if he were looking for some kind of support—but he was still in control. So handsome. People looking up at him had to be disarmed by that. They always had been. She had. When he said no, it was no.... Only, tonight, she wished he wouldn't use that approach. Not with Danny. Danny needed some strong statement from him—if not from her. Danny needed some help. The marijuana issue was, really, secondary to the fact, to that request implied in the challenge he'd been directing at her all evening. What was marijuana compared to that?

"Harold, I think—"

"Whatever you were going to say right now, Ev, don't. It's enough. I don't want any more talk tonight. I'm putting Eli to bed." Without looking at her directly, he gestured for Eli to leave her side, to come to him because he meant what he said.

Eli didn't want to. She could feel that in the way he burrowed closer to her, but she nudged him to go, go—and then he did.

And Danny stood then too. No *tsk-tsk*. A sigh. An old sigh from a young man. He stood next to Harold. They were the same height. Morty stood up too, moved across the living room to say good night to Harold, to take his place between Danny and Eli, the three of them facing Harold. No one paid any attention to her.

No one paid any attention to Clarice or Patricia, either.

Danny asked for the keys to the Chevy. He'd drive everyone back into the city. They were going to a party, and in the morning he'd bring the car back out, first thing, for sure, he and Morty would be back out, a promise, "...before you're even finished with breakfast, Dad. I promise."

Harold was shaking his head, and then he was smiling. He was grabbing Danny behind the neck, pulling him close, and next Morty was hugging Harold, saying how he was sorry about the pot, Dad, he wouldn't do that again, a promise, he apologized. Eli was smiling up at them, caught inside the grip of all that brotherly affection.

"You are something, Danny. You really are something. You'd make a good salesman. Better than me." Harold handed over the keys.

Not once had he turned to ask with his eyes how she felt about the car, or about the way he was handling Danny or Eli's going to bed or what Morty had done—or about anything at all. He still wasn't going to.

Instead of being hurt by that, instead of crying the way she ordinarily might, all she felt was...anger. New anger. She felt somehow insulted in a way she couldn't remember ever having felt. No one was paying any attention to her. Not even those two girls. They were impatient. They stood

180

up. They wanted to leave. Clarice walked from Danny to the door.

And while that was taking place, Evelyn got up, left the room, went into the kitchen, where dishes and glasses and silverware and platters and pots and pans were all waiting to be cleaned and scrubbed and scraped and put away, where so much disorder was waiting to be restored. Every dish they owned had been used. Every glass. Every piece of silverware. Everything they had ever collected in twenty-three years of marriage seemed to be on display and in disarray. Not only things they had bought for themselves, but also the things that had been her mother's and her grandmother's and that she treasured. It was all there in front of her, waiting to be set back in order. She stared at it all, stunned and tired and angry. Very angry.

And made even angrier when she heard the front door slamming. They had left, Danny and Morty and their...their women...had left without saying good night, without the simplest thank-you.

She turned away before Harold and Eli could see her start to cry. They came into the kitchen just as she rushed out of it.

And in her bedroom, in the darkness, she fell on top of the chenille spread, buried her face into it; she would not let herself break down, would not let herself give in to her oldest habit of sobbing, of sobbing herself into an acceptance of the belief that somehow what had happened was her fault, that in some way she could never quite understand, she was responsible for Danny's hating her or Morty's behavior tonight or Eli's fears of "out there." No. She wouln't let herself. Dammit. Dammit all. She wasn't alone in her life. Harold had had a hand in it, too. Why doesn't he accept some of the fault? Some of the responsibility? Why was it always her fault when something went wrong? Why was she always being blamed for having joined one organization too many; for not being home when she was supposed to be, for being too fair, too capable, too interested in too many causes and not interested enough in what was going on in her own family? That would be Harold's argument later. That was always his argument when he got his angriest. Otherwise, when he wasn't angry, he was proud she was involved and interested and concerned. Then he would praise her. Sure! He would praise her because she could invite thirty people to their house and feed them and entertain them. Of course! Dammit! Dammit all! She would not cry. It was her life "to live out—or lose" too.

She heard their steps going upstairs. Harold would get Eli ready for bed. She listened. She listened to each of their movements upstairs. She told herself to be calm, to stay right where she was, to wait, to see what he would do next.

She lay in the darkness of their bedroom and waited.

He was in the kitchen next. He was running water into the sink. Dishes were being scraped. He was clearing the dishes from the double sink. She recognized the dull pong of stainless steel. Like an old coffee can she had collected soda-bottle tops in, that same kind of sound when she used to shake the can. She liked that sound then. Distant. Different. Mysterious. When she was a little girl in her grandmother's hotel in the Catskill Mountains and she had searched around the grounds for soda-bottle tops, collecting them, her secret treasure.

Harold was not coming into their room.

Harold was going to do the dishes.

She listened to the bang and clatter and dull metallic pong against the stainless steel.

[6] She had fallen asleep.

Harold was bending down over her. He was kissing her. She had felt it. In her sleep she had felt it ... as fear. She had drawn back, afraid, and when her eyes opened and she saw him up close like that, relief was what she felt first of all— and then anger and hurt and three million different feelings racing through her sleep-roused, angry head. She would never be able to sort through it all and tell him, unless he helped her. She needed help too ... and then, without wanting to at all, she was crying, a little girl, hurt.

"Don't do that, Evelyn. Please. Not now. Just get undressed and get into bed and sleep, and tomorrow we'll talk about all of it. I did all the dishes. Everything's put away."

"Thank you." She moved him back, away, so that she could stand up, get undressed, just as he had ordered.

Their backs were to each other. Without looking at him, she slid into bed. And when he had done the same she reached up and switched off the bed lamp.

In the darkness again, she was waiting again, for an explanation. And no more crying. That had been a momentary lapse, that crying out for help. No more of that. She wasn't a child. God knows. She could handle whatever had to be
182

handled. Alone she could handle...whatever...if she had to...if she were forced by situations to handle...whatever. But he had to talk too. He had to say something, not just, "I did the dishes. Everything's put away." Didn't they make a promise to each other, right at the beginning they had made it, never to go to sleep angry?

So, she was waiting. And she deserved an explanation from him. It was his responsibility to offer one, to tell her why, all of a sudden, he had left her, literally and figuratively, alone. Why? Dammit. Why? All of a sudden, before, he had put an end to any discussion. All of a sudden...

But it hadn't been all of a sudden. Nothing was all of a sudden. Danny wasn't suddenly deciding he wouldn't let himself be drafted. No. He must have thought about it. He must have been thinking about it for a long time, and then, *suddenly,* there it was and he was faced with making a choice. He had thought about what he would do, and when the time came for doing it, he acted according to what he believed. Nothing sudden about that. And nothing sudden about Harold's putting an end to the discussion. He didn't believe in talking. He never really had. He didn't trust it...or maybe it was himself he didn't trust. Maybe he didn't trust himself to say what he actually thought about...things. Things generally. Maybe he didn't know. What did he really know for sure? Maybe he just acted on instincts. Maybe he just stood up, raised his voice, turned silent, disarmed people with his silent treatment, his dark and angry look, his commanding control of any situation, always expecting to stare people— their friends, their children, herself—down. To win out that way: by being handsome.

But his hair had grayed and thinned, and when he stood up he leaned, needed something to hold on to...like everyone else.

"Ev? You asleep?"

"No."

"You're angry. You're angry at me?"

"Yes. I'm angry at you. And at them too."

"Why at me? I didn't start it tonight. Danny did. And then Morty, that...that I'm not going to put up with. You can rest assured on that account."

"That's the least of it. As far as I'm concerned, that's the least part of what happened tonight."

"Not to me. To me that's the most important concern. What Eli sees them do—"

"Is that all Eli has seen them do? And what about us? What has Eli seen us do?"

"What are you talking about us for? What has that got to do with anything we're saying?"

"Why do you have to raise your voice?"

"Because you're talking nonsense."

"I don't think it's nonsense."

"Well, I do."

"And so that's that, Harold? That's the end of it? You call what I say nonsense, and I'm supposed to accept that as the final word? Just like my mother did when my father said the same thing to her? Nonsense! Only my father used worse than that. At least you haven't started cursing me yet."

"And you're not raising your voice now?"

She was—and she wasn't going to let herself do that. No. Absolutely not. She wasn't going to say another word. Not until he did. She wasn't going to end up doing all the talking...the way she always did. She always did because she always had to. According to him, nothing was ever bad enough to need all the talking about she believed in. She. She believed in it. She. What about him? What did he believe? She was waiting to find out. Just as Danny had done earlier. Until now she had always thought they believed in the same things. There'd never been a reason to think otherwise. Not a really important reason. At least not important to her. So why couldn't he just open his mouth and talk to her? They weren't exactly strangers.

She was going to wait for him to say something. She was going to wait all night if necessary. It was too important. As far as she was concerned, it was one of the most important things that had ever happened between them. And for once, she knew why. Finally, she thought she knew why and could explain why.

She turned her head so she could see him. Until then she hadn't let herself do that. It would have been too easy to turn toward him, to have moved closer to him, to have let him soothe her toward sleep or toward sex. More sleep than sex these days....It was light enough in the darkness to see his face. He was on his back. He was staring up at the ceiling. He was listening too. He was waiting too. He was waiting for her to speak, because that was their way together, that was their habit together: she talked; he listened. He was afraid to have it any other way.

She didn't think she was afraid to.

184

He sighed. He turned his head. He saw that she was staring at him. "It's not nonsense. Okay? I agree. What you want to talk about isn't nonsense. Only, can't we let it go? For now, can't we? I promise I'll talk. I promise. I won't forget." He reached out, touched her face, left his hand on her cheek, smoothing it. "I promise."

"Do you remember what you called nonsense? Do you remember that?"

"You. What you said."

"That's right. And how you treated me tonight. After this whole day of preparing for tonight by myself, that's how you ended up treating me. Eli saw that too. Not just smoking marijuana. Eli also saw Danny. He listened to Danny. He's afraid. He's afraid something will happen to Danny and to Morty and to himself and to us. He's afraid there'll be a war and they'll use a bomb. He's afraid he'll be watching television and someone will shoot Johnson like they shot Kennedy. He's afraid."

"That's why I didn't want to talk about it in front of him. I didn't want to have an argument with Danny in front of him. And I just got finished telling you I didn't want to talk about any of this now. I'm tired, Evelyn. Don't you understand what I'm saying? I promised you I wouldn't forget—"

"I heard you. You always...promise."

"Don't you believe me?"

"No. I don't. Tonight I really don't. For the first time, I have to admit to you, I don't."

He didn't answer immediately, but he did withdraw his hand from her face.

She rolled onto her back again. Her body ached. She felt heavy and old and at the same time wasted, thin. Somewhere inside her the substance of herself was undernourished, anemic. Beneath the roundness, beneath the heaviness of her breasts and the fleshiness of her thighs, there was still that little girl alive, not dead, not dying, the thin little girl from the Modigliani print was still alive inside her. She wanted to be fed too, that thin little girl, waiting there. She wanted to grow up too. She wanted a chance to speak up, to be heard, to find out, to learn more and more. She didn't want to be suffocated beneath layer upon layer of useless, protective fat. It was unattractive. It was unappealing. Harold didn't like it.

"Okay. I admit it, Ev. I didn't want to face it. I didn't want to have to face it tonight. I also didn't want to let anything
185

spoil the seder for you. I swear that was part of it too. You worked hard. I wanted you to enjoy it, to have pleasure from it, to—"

"Why did you give in to Danny so quickly? Why didn't you at least ask me what I thought? Why did you make a fool out of me?"

"Because I don't know what to do about Danny. I don't. I admit it. It isn't like anything I ever had to face. Things happened to me and I did what was expected of me. That's all I know about, and now, suddenly, it's all different for me. I don't know how to deal with...it."

"Harold, Danny is my son too. He's part of my life too. You don't have to deal with him alone. It's my problem too. And none of it suddenly happened...to you. Or to me. Or to Danny. But Danny doesn't want to be the next...victim. He's going to make a choice."

"I never had the chance to do that."

"Neither did I."

"That I don't understand at all. What have you got to do with the Army or being drafted? I was drafted right after the war in Europe started, and ever since then there's been the draft, and Danny..."

"And ever since I was born I've been a woman. Do you understand that? It's simple enough for you to understand? I'm a woman and Danny's mother and your wife and...oh, what's the use." She was sitting up. She was staring down at him. She was confused by what she wanted to say to him— and he was turning on his side, away from her.

"Harold?"

"I'm tired. I told you to let me alone. Let me alone, goddammit. I don't understand what the hell you're talking about. I'm too dumb...I'm too stupid to understand, so leave me alone. Just go to sleep. At least you've got a bed to sleep in. At least you've got a house that's your own. You've got food. What more do you need? Why are you blaming me for everything that's wrong with the world? What did I do that's so terrible?"

"Can't you turn around? Can't you face me and let me try to explain...to myself as well as to you. Can't you? Won't you?"

"You've explained plenty already. You want to deal with Danny? Then deal with him."

"We both should deal with him. Together, we should—"

"I don't know how. You told me already I was too dumb

to understand how. So why don't you do what you want to do. I'll just go on doing what I *have* to do for all of us to keep going." With that, he did sit up. "And that's the real difference between us, isn't it? You want to pick and choose. You want choices. You want other things more than you want me."

"Why are you saying that now, Harold?"

"Because it's true."

"It isn't. It isn't true at all. You know it isn't."

"I don't know anything at all. That's what you said." He fell back against the pillow. "And it's true. I don't. That's what's wrong with me. I don't know how to think, so how can I say what I think? And that's what you want from me. To say...something. I can't. I can't even change. I don't have time to...to think."

"Neither does Danny. But he's going to make some time for himself. We can too. We can change too."

"I'm too old."

"You're not. Neither am I."

"You don't have to change. You always...keep up with things."

"And what good has that done? How has it helped Danny? What's going to happen next to him? If he leaves the country...what does that mean? What's going to happen to all of us?" She leaned over him, rested her head on his chest, listened to his breathing, to his heartbeat, to the wheezing sound—a new sound—she heard these nights when she settled against him, searching for some comfort, some warmth, because she did love him, no matter what came next, no matter how much she changed or...kept up with things....She loved him. She needed him. And he still wanted her. No matter what he said...or didn't say. She reached higher, to kiss him.

18

Loretta Massi

[1] As soon as they got home from the Seldens', Maria and
Angela announced that they were going out again. They had
late dates, double dates, with brothers. The brothers were
home from college, for the holidays, one from Cornell, one
from Penn State. They were Jewish.

Joe did the questioning, of them, and of Loretta after the
girls left. "What could they be doing so late?"

"I can assure you not to worry. Maria's almost twenty-one,
for Christ's sake, and you're still worrying about her getting
knocked up. Don't. She's protected. So's Angela. I took care
of that with them already. We talked plenty. They know more
than I ever knew when I was their age. Believe me. More
than you ever knew too. So whyn't you just go to bed? You'll
be getting up before you know it—and remember, Joe, I got
the League tomorrow night, so I won't be home early. I might
even have dinner with Aaron Rothstein afterwards. He lives
in the city . . . downtown. Manhattan. He told me to call him
if I came in. I'm glad Ev invited him tonight, no matter how
dumb Carl acted with him . . . and I can see from your expression you're not so happy about him either. What I say to that
is, it's your problem. Because I like him. And the kids like
him. So I think I'll call him, and maybe I'll stay in the city
with a girlfriend from the League. I'll see. . . . For now I'm
going out to the garage. I want to finish something for the
class." She didn't. She had finished it before they went to
Evelyn's. But she wanted to look at it again, because she was
sure it was the best painting she'd ever done. The teacher
had better think so, or she'd explode. "Go ahead, Joe. Don't
worry about the girls. They'll be fine. What are you looking
at me like that for?"

"I want to talk to you, Loretta."

"Again, Joe? We have to go through this again, tonight?"

"Yes. Because I got to understand what you're trying to
do. I don't understand it. You tell me, but it don't sound like
188

the truth to me. And I'm just supposed to go along with anything you decide to do? Just like that? 'Now that the girls are old enough,' you're always saying, which is supposed to make whatever you do okay? Is that it?"

So, instead of going out to the garage, she went into the living room. They both did. They went to their respective corners, she to her Eames swivel chair, Joe to where his chess game waited. He had kept the old end table for it, a maple piece of ugliness that she had wanted to throw the hell out when she finally redecorated the room. But no. He wouldn't let her. He'd take the modern chair and foam-rubber sofa and the electric-bright dots of color on the Scandinavian rug and the hanging chrome lamp over his head. Okay. He even liked the white room now, and all the plants, all her paintings on the walls, but he was going to keep that goddamn end table if it was the last thing he did. So, she let him.

And she'd let him take his seat, let him begin again to try to convince her to reconsider her plan. He could try. He could try from now till hell froze over and he wouldn't be able to—but let him try.

She hated it that she felt sorry for him. She hated it that she guessed she always had. Feeling sorry for him only meant that she felt sorrier for herself. All these goddamn years wasted on waiting. He was pathetic. Going from one shitty job to another. Going from his mother's death and his father's death and selling off the grocery, for peanuts, to depending on her completely, especially now that the girls pretty well went their own way. Which they did. And so would she. No way to stop it anymore. Absolutely none. Now that what she knew to be the truth about herself wasn't anything she was going to be able to hide anymore.

And, anyway, why should she even try to hide it? For whose sake now should she? As long as Maria and Angela wouldn't be hurt by it? Or her own mother? Her own mother wouldn't understand a word she said to her. Her mother! Her mother was the biggest part of it, in a certain way. Having to see her, how she was now. Watching her. Who knew what she heard or understood? Strapped into a wheelchair. Paralyzed. At sixty-seven. In a nursing home—but with the nuns, of course. With the biggest cross hanging around her neck, and she can't say a word, one way or another. Just staring out at nothing at all. So, if she went to her and said: Ma, I want to tell you something about me, something that may come as a shock to you... What could shock her now? And

189

maybe a shock would do her good. Shock her out of a stroke and back to normal. Maybe a shock would do Joe good too. He knows a lie when he hears one. Maybe lying to someone so as not to hurt them is the worst kind of hurting, especially when they know you so well they can see right through you. Like Joe was doing right then: looking at her and through her in a way he never used to be able to do. He didn't want to be treated like a goddamned idiot. He was a human being too. So was she. Everyone was. Everyone got hurt in some way. If you're alive, you get hurt....

"Joe? As long as you want to talk, let's really talk. Let's be honest. Let's clear the air. We go over the same ground all the time, and what it's really all about, neither one of us ever says. Isn't that true? Just answer that one point. Isn't it true?"

"I don't know if it is. I know I say what I think it's all about. I tell you the truth. I'm simple, Loretta. You know that. I'm a simple-minded guy. So I figure, okay, she's bored with me. So I say to myself I should do something to improve my mind a little. I should read about painting, for example, so I can talk to you about it, so you'll know I'm interested in what you do—but you don't pay any attention to what I do...for you. Even chess. That's to improve. And as far as the other thing is concerned..."

"What's the other thing? Why don't you say what you mean for once? For Christ's sake, you're a grown man, Joe. What the hell do you mean when you say 'the other thing'? Can't you say 'sex'? You afraid of the word? Your daughters are out screwing around, and you can't even say the word 'sex.' You're forty-four years old, for Christ's sake.... And I'm raising my voice and I don't mean to. I'm sorry. I don't want to hurt you, Joe. I swear it."

"Well, if you don't, then why don't you tell me what you think it's really all about? You could help me a lot if you did. Because, to tell you the truth...and it is the truth. I swear it is, Loretta...I don't understand what's happened. As far as jobs are concerned, as far as money is concerned, I'm the first to admit I'm a failure that way. But you know as well as I know, I never had a chance to do better. And as far as ...sex... is concerned, I'm willing to do ... whatever you want. I'm not a very ... passionate guy. I admit that too. But you're not ... perfect ... on that score either."

"So what do you think that means? What do you think that's all about? Answer that one, Joe, and maybe we can really talk to each other the way you want us to do. Do you know how long it's been since we had sex? Since we even tried to have it? Two months? Three months? How the hell do you stand it? Don't you need some kind of outlet?"

"That means you have an outlet. Doesn't it? You having an affair with someone? Is that what it's all about? You're having an affair? If you are, why don't you just say it? Say it out loud, Loretta, and then maybe we can get somewhere from that point. You're always screaming at me to tell the truth, to clear the air. Well, why don't *you* clear the air? If you're the one having an affair, you talk. Not me. I don't have anything to say." He looked down at his chessboard. The pieces were all jumbled together. He poked at them, waiting. He was going to wait for her to say...whatever.

And she knew she was going to. Finally, she was going to say...whatever there was to say. No matter how it turned out afterwards, it couldn't be any worse than it had been for all these years. Wasted. So much time wasted. From her life. From his life too. Only, what happened next was going to be a hell of a lot harder for him to handle. Because, after all, what else was he but decent? Not good-looking. Not a man with a job he liked. Not educated. And with a wife and daughters who didn't really need him for anything. So, she had to feel sorry for him. She couldn't help it. "I am having an affair, Joe, only it's not exactly the kind of affair you're expecting."

He flattened his hand over the chess pieces and then he gathered them into his fist. That big hand of his. Everything about him, big. And all of it wasted. Like his body was now. Too thin. Emaciated almost. A cadaver almost.

Pathetic. So, she couldn't just blurt it out. "Don't say anything for a minute, Joe. Just let me say what I'm going to have to say. I don't want to hurt you with any of this stuff, but facts are facts and they might just as well be out in the open before it's too late for both of us to do anything about ourselves. We never should have gotten married. We...I...I should have known better. About myself, I mean. I felt something. I always did, I suppose, but I didn't really want to admit it to myself. Now, it's all I *can* admit to myself. I'm about seventy-five percent sure, anyway, that I'm meant to live my life as a lesbian. And the affair I'm having is with a woman. When I go in to the Art Students League, I see her afterwards. That's where I met her. She..." She had to stop. She could hardly breathe. She was going to faint. Unless she stopped. To breathe. To take deep breaths. To calm herself.

191

To settle down. She was shaking. Her heartbeat filled her ears.

Joe had let go of the chess pieces. He was watching her. That much she could tell. But nothing else. His face was a blur. His features seemed dissolved, disappearing, melting under the bright light shining down on him from the chrome lamp. Wasted. So thin. So distant. So far away. She couldn't see him at all. Gone. A line...moving away.

[2] She was on the carpet. He was kneeling beside her. She had fainted, and he was trying to help her. He was rubbing her hand. He was crying.

And then so was she. It was all a mess. The whole thing. Their whole life. A mess.

"Loretta? You okay, Loretta? You fainted. You just fell right onto the carpet. Slid right out of the chair. Just like that." He was on his knees, trying to get her to sit up, to lean against him, between his legs, to hold on to him.

Which she did, because she was frightened. And they both were crying, quietly crying. She had said it out loud. She was sure she had, and then she had fainted. So why didn't he look as if he had heard it? Why was he being so good to her? So decent. Why was he rubbing her back that way?

And then he was getting her to stand up. He was leading her out of the living room and into their bedroom. He didn't turn on the light.

He sat her down at the edge of the bed. He was undoing her blouse. And he was helping her out of her slacks. As if he were undressing Maria or Angela when they were little girls. The way he used to take them into their bedroom and settle them into their beds. He was doing that for her. His little girl.

Some little girl! But she let him. He wanted to. He wanted her to be all undressed. He wanted to run his hands all over her skin. Up and down. Up and down. Some little girl! She was too fat. Dumpy. Anything but sexy. So what was he doing it for? Why? Why was he playing with her nipples? Why was he leaning down to suck them? One. Then the other. Why? After she'd said what she'd said. She didn't want him to do that. No.

But he wouldn't stop. He pressed her back down. He played with her pubic hair, brushing it, rubbing it, acting as if he hadn't heard what she'd said.

192

"Don't play games, Joe. Don't fool yourself. You'll be sorry. Sorrier than me, Joe. I know what I'm talking about."

But even as she said that to him, her voice filled with an anger new to her, anger at not being listened to, not being paid attention to, as if what she had said, he would never believe—even then he was getting on top of her, still in his clothes, even then he was pulling his prick out of his pants, he was trying to push it inside her, pushing it because it wasn't hard. It was big, but it wasn't hard. And it wasn't going to be.

"I told you, Joe. I told you not to." She tried to move him off her. He wouldn't budge. "That's one of the facts. Sex between us is finished. It's over. Do you hear me? You can't with me and I don't want you to try. You hear? You want to help yourself? You want to help me? Then listen for once. It's going to be different from now on. Life's going to be different for us. Do you hear me, Joe?"

He heard. He lifted himself. He fell onto his part of the bed. She heard him. His breathing. A drawing in, in, deeper, a silence, and then release, as if in a moment he would sob.

But if he did, she wouldn't turn to him. She wouldn't try to soothe him in any way. They were going to have to try to begin to sort through all the tangled junk of their lives. They were—she was, with him or without him—going to begin to get out from under. Before it was too late. Some can. Some cannot. That's the breaks of the game. Because in the end it ends the same way for everyone. But at least she didn't have to, she wasn't going to, wait for her end on Whisper Lane in Levittown.

19

Melissa Geiger

Carl insisted Agnes had to go up to bed. Before they talked about anything that had happened at the Seldens', she was to go right upstairs. No stalling. No excuses about Donald going away. No. None.

She was trying to hide inside Donald's arms. "I won't wrestle with you, Aggie." Missy reached for her. Donald let his arms drop. "Your father wants you to go up to bed." Missy tugged at her arm. "So do I. I also want you to say good night to Donald the way a grown-up young girl should. You'll hear everything that's said down here. You know that."

"Aggie! Now!" Carl's raised voice shocked her, shocked all of them into stillness. He was angry, all right. He was different tonight, on this night that was supposed to be different from all other nights. Missy took hold of Aggie. Aggie kissed Donald, and then she shook free of her mother. She would not say good night to Carl. She raced to the stairs. "You don't have to come upstairs with me, mother. I don't want you to. I'll take care of myself."

"Have it your way." Missy went back to her seat next to Carl on the sofa. Teresa was alone on the love seat, brooding. Donald and Adam were in their club chairs. Theirs. Each of them had a special place. Donald's was corduroy, chocolate, a color, a tone that had always seemed to match his manner. Just as Adam's tufted bright challis print suited his. Muscular. Not too heavy, not too thin. The blondest, most lustrous hair she had ever seen on a boy his age. Donald was handsome, but Adam was beautiful. And Teresa? Teresa was angry and hurt and alone. So much like her father, really. Dark-haired, tall, his nose. The little bump at the end of it....

Agnes, upstairs, was dropping her shoes louder than she had to, was slamming the bathroom door louder, was galumphing back to her bedroom. That door she left open.

And what would she hear?

"So now you want to tell me why I'm so prejudiced, Miss High and Mighty?"

"Just talking that way shows it, Daddy. Because Danny Selden has ideas that don't fit in with yours doesn't mean he's a punk or dumb or spoiled or anything like that."

"What if I call him un-American? Like I said about your Mr. Rothstein. How about that? Will you accept that?"

"I don't know what that means. And you just don't... understand Mr. Rothstein. All I know is that Danny Selden has his own ideas about things. He thinks about what he's doing."

"Meaning I don't?" Donald had jumped up. "I can't stand that kind of garbage from my own sister, especially when I'm leaving here tomorrow morning and—"

"You asked for it, Donald. You enlisted. You couldn't wait to be drafted. You too, Adam. And so now you call Danny a coward. You too, Daddy. It's just... unfair. You call Danny a Communist, and of course you're supposed to kill Communists, aren't you? What if you had to kill Danny Selden? Would you do it, Donny?"

"If it was the law... if it was the law of my country and I was supposed to defend the law."

"I think that's just plain crazy. I really do—and unchristian too, isn't it, Mother?"

"That's what I meant before, Teresa." Carl was leaning forward and then down lower, looking down at the carpet. "That tone. I don't want to hear it in your voice. I don't want you speaking to your mother that way. Or to Donny and Adam. I don't like it. Do you hear me, miss? Because your two brothers are going to be out there somewhere fighting to defend your right—that punk's right—to go on disagreeing. They're going to risk their lives—"

"That's exactly what I don't want them to do, Daddy. I don't believe in a war to settle things. It never does. Even Mother agrees with me about that. She's told me so a thousand times. But I can understand how you might feel differently about that, Daddy. I can. I really can. I—"

"You can't understand how I might feel about anything. Not if you have those attitudes." He began kneading his thigh. He sat up, extending his leg.

"Is it bothering you, Carl? Does your leg hurt?"

"Never mind my leg, Missy. Better pay some attention to your daughter and what she's saying. Next thing you know, she'll be eloping with Danny Selden somewhere."

"Must you be so unfair, Carl? That really is unfair. And must you raise your voice? We're all civilized people in this room, and Teresa does have a right to voice her own opinion."

"Not that kind of stupid opinion." This time Adam jumped up and began pacing, stopping in front of Teresa, staring down at her, his fair skin flushing with his anger. Intimidating Teresa. Trying to. The way he usually could most people who tried to stand up to him. So beautiful. Charisma, they called it in him. Like John Kennedy had. Had. Adam had it too, and he was telling his sister to stop shooting off her mouth. Teresa was sitting up, at the edge of her chair, sweeping her long black hair from her forehead defiantly, trying to stare him down. "...always shooting off your mouth about what you don't know anything about. And now you're even trying to tell Dad that you understand how he feels. What do you know about a war or getting wounded? Nothing at all. So why don't you for once just shut up?"

"Never. You'll never get me to shut up. Not anymore. You probably can't wait to get wounded. Is that why you had to rush to enlist in the Marines?"

"If you weren't my sister, I'd...I'd..."

"You'd kill me, wouldn't you?"

"That'll be enough." Missy stepped between the two of them, getting Teresa to sit back down, leading Adam back to his club chair, gesturing for Donald to sit back down. Everyone obeyed her. Everyone usually did. She too sat down before she spoke next. Calm. Calmly. "I don't like those kinds of thoughts. We're not animals. We're supposed to be reasonable human beings. Must you treat each other like enemies?"

"I have to, Mother, because she's crazy. She's a certifiable crazy. You better take her to a psychiatrist."

"You, Adam. Not me. Mother better take you first."

"You're asking for it, Teresa." Adam started up again, but Donald pulled him back down. "I'll remember how my loving sister appreciates what we're doing for her—and her friends. For Danny and her Melanie and her Gregory Feuerstein. The Commie, the creep, and the fag."

"Donald!" Missy's voice rang out. She leaped up. "That is so disgusting, Donald." Absolutely disgusting to hear her own children talk this way to each other. Why doesn't Carl say something? She didn't want to stand there in their living room and deliver a lecture or a sermon about understanding, not again. That's what Donald would say next. Mother's on her soap box again, Mother's turning the other cheek again, Mother's being Jesus again....But now, just when she hoped Carl would join her in her indignation, when she hoped he would express with her some sense of being offended by Donald's use of those words to describe friends, people, human beings they all knew so well, what was Carl doing? He was sitting back down in his easy chair. He was surveying the plants in front of the living-room windows. He was acting as if he had heard nothing at all; the whole evening was about to be blotted out. That was disgusting too—and depressing: to think he would suddenly leave her out on a limb, in the lurch. They were all expecting her to say more. They were all certain she would. She always had in the past. The first time Donald had said "shit," she had scolded him. And when Adam had said "fuck" and Teresa had said "bitch," she had felt it her responsibility to say something to them about using words that hurt people. Like "fag." What a hurtful word! So was "queer." Why were people so cruel to one another? It seemed to her they were crueler here in 1965 than they ever had been when she was growing up. They don't care. They don't feel. They don't want to learn about differences. Not even Carl, for that matter....They don't want to read. They don't want to know about how some people have to suffer through their lives. All they want to do is sit in front of the television set and stare....That's what they expected her to start saying. Well, they've got another thing coming. Tonight she wasn't going to say anything at all.. Let Carl do it. He had started it, anyway, at Evelyn's. Let him finish it here, in *his* home now. It was all too depressing to listen to her son—their son—say "fag" and not even think about what he was saying or about whom. Depressing. Doesn't he have a conscience? Teresa wouldn't use a word like that. Never....Missy would be damned if she was going to open her mouth, to be the only one to open her mouth, to defend Gregory or Melanie. Or Aaron Rothstein. Damned if she did....Damned if she didn't. Because she did have a conscience that would bother her. She was glad she did, dammit.

Sure enough, Carl was not going to say another word. He would not even look over at her standing there behind the sofa. He'd even lost his anger about his war, his wound. "Carl?"

"What?" At least one word, but he did not turn back to look at her, to join in her outrage.

"What are you staring at? Didn't you hear what Donald said?"

"I heard."

"And?"

"It's probably true. Donald'd know sooner than I would." Donald laughed. So did Adam.

Teresa didn't. Teresa was on her feet. "I think that's just plain disgusting."

Thank God Missy wouldn't have to say it for once.

"Don't make such a big deal out of it." Donald got up too. And then so did Adam.

Everyone was standing except Carl. He covered his face with his hand. He brushed his hair back from his forehead. He stared up at the ceiling. He would say nothing else.

Neither would she.

"You're both so big and brave. I'm really proud of my *he*-man brothers, my *he*-roes. The Church really taught them, didn't it Mother? I can tell you one thing for sure, I'm glad I didn't let you drag me to Church. I'd rather learn about the world from Danny and Melanie and Gregory ... and Mr. Rothstein. If this is what Jesus does to people, you can have him." But then, instead of backing away from Donald, Teresa moved toward him. Before he realized what had happened, she kissed him. "I hope you'll be okay. Take care of yourself." She didn't rush up the stairs. She didn't slam the door to the bedroom she shared with Agnes—not that Agnes would have been sleeping.

And then Donald went to Carl. He put his hand on Carl's shoulder, roused him from whatever reverie he had lost himself in. "No matter what she says, Dad, I still feel I'm doing the right thing. So does Adam feel that way...." Adam was nodding, agreeing, letting Donald speak for him. "Teresa just has to exaggerate everything. She doesn't really know about what's going on in the outside world. Neither does Adam, for that matter. That's the one thing about growing up in Levittown ... but we can talk about that another time."

Then he went over to Missy. "Don't pay any attention to what Teresa said about the Church, Mother. She was just all heated up. She doesn't really mean anything she says. That much I know." He embraced her. He leaned against her for the briefest of moments.

She wanted to tell him how wrong he was, and not just about Teresa. But there wasn't time. And she was too depressed. Just too depressed about the whole turn of events.

The evening certainly had become different from all other evenings—and it was Donald, after all, who was shipping out. It was Donald whom they wouldn't see for so long. And then Adam....So she kissed Donald instead of saying just how right Teresa was. She hugged him, kissed him again. "You'll take care, Donny? Won't you?"

"I will, Mother. I promise."

Donald and Adam started up the stairs together, as they had on so many other nights—but not again, never again she supposed, after this night, would they share their room. Donald waved down. "Don't the both of you stay up late."

Her two beautiful sons! Their two beautiful sons! They knew how to take care of themselves. They weren't going to be needing her anymore. The door to their room was closed quietly.

She stepped in front of Carl's chair. He stared at nothing. Still far away. Remote. Donald's good night hadn't really roused him, and neither was she supposed to. She was supposed to be a good mother, an understanding mother, and a dutiful wife. When hadn't she been! Tonight, especially, when she felt least like being one.

She knelt down in front of him. "What is it, Carl? Tell me, please." But he continued to stare out, past her. The shine of brass and copper was in his eye, the sparkle and gleam of cut glass, the joy of print and pattern; there was order everywhere his gaze rested. She'd worked to get it that way, for him, for herself, for the children—and, yet, look what had happened anyway, in spite of all her efforts.

He lifted his arm, moved it through the air above her, let it down gently on her shoulder. "Doesn't Teresa see what I see in here? In this house?"

"She sees, Carl, but that's not the point."

"And Donald and Adam? Even you said you agreed with the idea of enlisting early. Getting it over with. You said—"

"That doesn't mean I don't have doubts. I do, Carl. I understand what Teresa means. I understand about Danny, too. I'm only surprised you don't. It's one of the few times we've ever had a real difference of opinion. Aaron Rothstein is a fine teacher and Danny isn't a monster, Carl. Doesn't he have a right to decide to risk his own life or not?"

"I didn't have any rights. I just did what I was ordered to do. I didn't have doubts about that war. I was too young to have doubts—and I loved you, don't forget. And about you

199

I still have no doubts." He smoothed the back of her hair. She looked up at him, watched his eyes watching her. His fingers moved across the skin of her face, trembling fingers, tracing memories on it. She felt it in his fingers. She sensed all the movement of his mind back and forth, back and forth, from this moment back to their beginnings. Only people who had lived together for as long as they had could press into a touch a whole lifetime of how they think together, how they feel and fit together. He was sorting out how he felt. She sensed that in his look, in the beginnings of an embarrassed smile, in his mouth opening to speak. Clarity for a moment: something remembered that lights everything up. Something about himself he was seeing. "I was remembering how I was at Eli's age, at our seders, and about how my mother and father used to be." His face flushed with the pleasure of an old picture reseen. "I suppose I should have called my mother in Florida." He paled, guilt, old guilt, overtaking the flush of pleasure. Clarity receded. The smile was gone. Reality jumbled the old facts into new disorder. "You know, we've been together longer than the ages we were when we met? Do you realize that? I know you longer now than I knew my mother at the time we met. That's a funny fact." He nudged her head beneath his chin. He wanted her to lean there, to lean against him, to let him take care of everything that needed to be taken care of, for her not to worry, about the boys, about Teresa and Aggie, about anything at all. She sensed all that in the way he held her.

She didn't doubt his feelings for her.

She had no doubts about her feelings for him.

But she just couldn't also help feeling saddened, because no matter how tightly he held her then, no matter how gently he whispered in her ear not to worry, not to be concerned about anything at all, she knew she was. She knew she had reason to be. Things were not right. Not at Evelyn's. Not here in her house. Not at Loretta's or Corinne's. Not even at Cynthia's. Not anywhere in Levittown or the rest of the world were things really right.

Not anywhere in the world! Humpty-dumpty...the world...and was there anyone anymore who could set it right?

What she wanted to do just then was to get up and go to their bedroom, to get undressed and to fall asleep inside Carl's arms, because doubts or no doubts about the rest of the world, the one feeling she didn't doubt was loving Carl—

even if he had acted strangely at Evelyn's or if he hadn't said anything to Donny when he should have. He had his reasons. She was certain of that. "Let's go to bed, Carl, and in the morning we'll both give Donny his breakfast before he leaves. All right?"

He helped her up. He nodded. He led her to their bedroom.

20

Corinne Feuerstein

[1] Gregory was going to keep on walking, right through the house, to his bedroom, and then he would shut the door behind him, shut her outside, the way he usually did.

Lionel would do the same. Even though he didn't have to go to the store in the morning, he would just keep on walking, right through the house, to their bedroom, where he would yell for her to come on, it's late, so come on to bed, and then he too would shut the door behind him, not even waiting for her to get there.

Why?

What had she done to deserve that kind of treatment? From either of them.

She wasn't drinking very much anymore either. Helped herself. Fortitude. Bootstraps and all that shit. They both knew that. Nothing stronger than wine. Those four glasses of sickeningly sweet Manischewitz—they would stop anyone from drinking. But it was more the kind of thing Aaron Rothstein had said at Evelyn's, about living out your life or losing it.... "Gregory! I want to talk to you. Lionel! You too."

Going in their separate directions, they both stopped, startled. She had probably yelled out much louder than she realized. That happened a lot these days. Yelling louder, to shock them. That's how much she needed to talk to them. She did. She felt so goddamned lonely. Especially this night, this seder night. It was the singing. It was how useless she felt. She played bridge. She played the piano. She belonged to as many groups as she had time for. She went to concerts everywhere, and she knitted with Missy, took French cooking lessons, was even then organizing a theater reading group with Evelyn, and taking German lessons at Hofstra so she could study and sing lieder; therefore, could anyone please tell her why the hell no one would take her seriously? Not her son! Not her husband! Probably not even her friends!

"Greg! Please. Please come back here. I need to talk to
202

you about something. I want to tell you. About those songs I was singing before. You don't know what they mean, do you? Your father does. Your father used to be able to read Hebrew. Why don't you come tell Greg about that, Lionel? Why don't you tell him about your seders, Lionel? About his grandmother and grandfather. He hardly knew them. Wouldn't you like to hear, Greg?"

"It's late, Corinne; I'm going to bed." Lionel continued on out into the kitchen, through it, to the front of the house and into their bedroom. He didn't slam the door. At least he didn't do that.

"Greg?" She hated to plead, but she did it anyway. On this particular night she did it anyway.

And on this particular night Greg was listening to her. At the other end of the living room, on his way to the back of the house, where his bedroom was, he had turned around. He walked back to the rose velvet sofa. He sat down. He was really a good son. He had had a hard time of it growing up. She knew that. She wanted to make it up to him. In any way she could, she wanted to make it up to him. He'd been alone too much of the time growing up. It showed in his face. A sensitive face, people called it. Not handsome like Donny and Adam. Not as secret, as seductive a face as Danny's. An in-betweener, her Gregory. Pale smooth skin. Wavy dark healthy hair the lamplight made lustrous. Dark deep-set eyes. A long face. A prominent nose. Long, like Lionel's. Big hands. Tall, like Lionel. But thin. Narrow-boned, as if he had been stretched out from birth to grow taller, never wider. He sat with his big hands between his legs, looking up at her, waiting. Tell me a story, he might have asked next. Like a child might. Only, he never had. And he had never asked her to sing him a song.

"You didn't really know I had such a good voice, did you?"

"Yes I did. Lots of times you started singing when you played the piano. How would you know if I was in my room listening? I did that a lot. I listened to you all the time. You've got a great voice."

"That's one of the nicest things you've ever said to me, Greg." She sat at the other end of the sofa. What he'd said was just what she'd needed to hear. She was touched. She relaxed for the first time in she couldn't remember how long. What a difference it made to hear just the simplest word of approval. She had been trying. And he must have realized it. "I appreciate it, Greg."

He looked down at his hands. He squeezed one inside the other. He had become tense—or maybe he always was these days. She wasn't sure. She couldn't remember how long it had been since that last time she'd gotten him to sit with her and talk. She couldn't remember a lot of things from her more recent past. From her past past she could remember everything... and that's what she had wanted to talk to Greg about. That's why she had called out to him and to Lionel. She'd wanted Lionel to tell Greg, too, about the past, not just herself. Lionel never wanted to talk to Greg about himself. Lionel sometimes acted with Greg as if he hardly knew him at all. Why did he have to take out on Greg his anger with her? That was going too far. And why couldn't Lionel just pay her one simple compliment, like Greg? Greg was so good. In spite of everything, he was. And when he went away to school next September... Oh, how she was going to miss him. That's when the real test was going to come. That's when she'd really find out what she was made of. "You're looking forward to going away to school, aren't you? But are you sure you had to go so far away?"

"You call Michigan far, Mother? Your sense of geography isn't one of your strongest points!"

"No. It's true. It never was. I knew the Bronx and I knew Greenwich Village."

"Do you know where Mr. Rothstein lives? On Bank Street? Did you live near there?"

"Not far. I lived on Horatio Street. When your father and I first met, I was living there. I had a big basement apartment down there. I used to love that apartment... Well, never mind about me. So, you're glad to be going away to Michigan? You're sure it's the right place?"

"Mr. Rothstein thought it would be. It has a good writing department. Mr. Rothstein thinks I have writing talent. Mr. Rothstein is the best teacher I've ever had. He stresses the positive qualities of a person, but he's also honest. He doesn't lie. Teresa and Melanie—especially Melanie—they both love him too. Maria and Angela—they never were good in English. But Danny... Danny thought he was great too. So did Morty. All of us were lucky to have Mr. Rothstein for—"

"Why did you and Danny stop being such close friends, Greg?" Too strong. Too direct, she realized. Once more he squeezed one hand inside the other. His shoulders sagged forward, were thrust back. That was his answer. A shrug. He didn't care... but he did. That was in his face. He stared down at his hands. He squinted. He was unhappy. She supposed he had lots of reasons to be, and she supposed that whatever they were, he'd never want to talk to her about them. Why should he? She'd been too involved with her own unhappiness to have any time for his, and now he was going to be going away to school and she wouldn't really have the chance to get to know him, not the way she should have and could have. She could have been more of a confidante; he could have been one with her, instead of Loretta and Evelyn. Her son. A friend who would have listened to her.

But she at least had had people to talk to. He hadn't. And, still, he didn't seem to be falling to pieces. Tense, yes. Unhappy, yes, but not about to have a breakdown. He'd be able to take care of himself. Like she had done for herself. "Greg? Do you feel I've been a terrible mother to you? Do you feel your father's been a terrible father to you?"

Again his shoulders bent forward and back. Another shrug. He didn't want to talk about any of that. She did. She had to. Now that she was trying to reform, she had to try to ease her conscience. Greg could understand that. He was sensitive to those things. He must be if he was going to write. She could have said things to him, he could have said things to her, that most mothers and sons might not ordinarily say to each other. They could have been different from the others. They could have been special to each other. She wasn't exactly the ordinary run-of-the-mill mother. How many Levittown mothers had actually been singers in a nightclub in Greenwich Village? How many mothers had been talented enough to perform before people and be paid for it? Not too goddamned many! "I'll bet, Greg, if you're interested in becoming a writer, I'll bet I could tell you some stories you could write about. I'll bet things have happened to me..."

"Things have happened to everyone, Mother. Even to me." He looked over at her. He wanted to. He wanted to look at her and talk about what had happened to him, not about what had happened to her.

It made her nervous again, his way of looking at her. He wasn't afraid. Whatever had happened to him, he wanted to talk about it, whatever it was. She wished she were in one of her caftans. She felt bloated and bulgy and old in her wool pantsuit. Red wool. How could she be a mother in a red wool pantsuit with her hair streaming down the side of her face? It's a wonder he was as contained and controlled as he was. And with a father whose only thought was to get into bed

205

and fuck. A father who grunted and groaned and farted and made fun of everyone and everything....

"Greg? What could happen to an eighteen-year-old who lives in Levittown?"

"Not much. Not much at all. Not here. If there's one thing I wish I could have changed about growing up, I wish I could have done it in the city. Not here. That's why I'm happy about going away to school. There's nothing here in Levittown. Only houses and streets and people and kids, and at night there's nothing to do but leave it and go into the city to do something that...that means anything...at least to me. I got tired of watching television night after night, and thanks to Mr. Rothstein I felt inspired to go into the city and do things there. I like plays and music and going to museums. That's one thing about you, Mother, I never really understood, how it's only in the last year or so you started going to concerts. A person who loves music like you do. How come it took all this time to stop...to stop...wasting your time and start doing things? Who inspired *you?*"

"You did. Watching you do things did."

"That's certainly a lie. You never paid any attention to me. You know that."

That's what she had been afraid of hearing from him, that and more. There would be more, now that he had gotten started. There'd probably be a whole catalog of things he hated about her. They'd come pouring out of his mouth, now that she'd managed to get the floodgates opened.

"Not that I'm holding that against you, Mother. Because I'm not. I swear I'm not. Maybe you didn't pay attention to me, but I never once felt that you didn't love me. You did everything you were supposed to do for me every day, even when you were...drunk....I might as well say it, right? I never felt you neglected me. As far as Daddy is concerned, well, that's another matter....Anyway, I asked you a question. I don't mean to just ramble on."

"Ramble. Ramble as much as you want." All of her fear had drained out of her. How fortunate to have a son like him. And he'd been there all along. If only...he'd even said *drunk* without sounding like he wanted to kill her. Why? Why had it taken so long? What a waste! He was right. He was so right. Eighteen and he understood more than she did in her whole lifetime of living her forty-three years....He didn't accuse her of anything either. He just understood. About herself. Not about Lionel. Maybe about that she could help

206

him. Maybe she could get him to understand why Lionel seemed to be so cold, even though that was the last thing in the world he really was.... She wished Lionel was sitting there alongside her and listening to their marvelous eighteen-year-old son it had taken so long to discover. "I'll tell you what inspired me, since you asked. Since you were kind enough to ask." She wanted to laugh, she felt so happy. Even though what she had to tell him about was anything but happy. Ironical. That was the word. That was how she felt about it. "It was when Kennedy was killed. That weekend. Remember that weekend we all sat there watching it? The three of us together? I didn't have a drink that entire weekend. His dying and the shooting...it inspired me. And, of course Loretta and Evelyn. They helped me. And being active and all. All my activities helped me. The activities you probably resent."

"I don't, Mother. I used to. For a while anyway, until I had my own things to do. I had some friends. Teresa. Melanie. And Maria too. I was a close friend to Danny...for a while." For the first time since he had started talking, he shifted his gaze away. His shoulders hunched forward and then back. He wasn't shrugging this thing off so easily. But he was determined. Even if he couldn't just blurt it out, he was determined to continue, to say something, something more.

She could help him along. "Friends are more important than parents past a certain age, I suppose. You can get to know a friend. A parent...My own mother and father I couldn't have gotten to know. Not really know. They were a different kind of generation. Their concern was to survive somehow. With very little. Our generation only knows how to survive with too much." And then she heard herself rambling. She couldn't seem to stick to one strand of thought. "When I moved down to Greenwich Village, I couldn't tell them. I couldn't tell them what I was doing down there without...hurting them. And I never wanted to hurt them. I told them...lies. I told my friends the truth. That's why...that's why I started talking. About friends. I wanted to say something about friends and losing Danny's friendship."

"It wasn't so much a question of losing it, Mother." He looked down at his hands as he spoke, not at her. "It was more a question of me thinking it was one thing and he...it was just a different kind of friendship for him."

"How different?"

He was trying. She could see the evidence of that. He was
207

forcing himself to sit up, to look up and then over at her. He wanted to be able to see her and tell her...what? She remembered those days after Kennedy was killed, when she would walk through this house aching for a drink. It was always there, at hand, a bottle, anytime she wanted it. The trouble was, she wanted it anytime—and she wouldn't let herself do that. For a whole week she didn't touch a drink. And then it seemed easier and easier not to, and then it became easier and easier to say to herself: Yes, one, no more than two. To keep it under control. Control. She was under control. Greg was under control. Every sane person trying to stay sane was under control. Her closest friends were. Greg's were—and Greg himself, trying to tell her something that was not easy to say, was under control. "Maybe if you start to say it Greg...maybe one word will lead to another..."

"I can't, Mother. I just don't know...how you'd take it. Or Dad. He hates me as it is." His face had seemed to shut down suddenly, its wide-eyed self-confidence gone in a second, gone for the day, gone fishing. He stared ahead, out across the room to where her piano was, through the dim light to the pin spot there. More like a nightclub than a living room. She'd redecorate it first chance she had. Brighten it. "One thing I wish, I wish you'd had another child. I wish I had had a brother or sister I could have talked to. Why didn't you, Mother? Have another child."

"I...I didn't want to. I thought I'd take up my career again. I thought I'd leave—"

"Aren't you ever coming to bed, Corinne?"

They had been so absorbed, they hadn't heard Lionel enter the room. He was behind them, standing there in his pajamas. If he had been there long enough...well, if he had heard what Greg said, and what she had said, so much the better. Better late than never for a father, even a Lionel, to hear that his son thinks he's hated. Her words he'd heard before, but it never hurts to repeat.

"I'm coming. I was just talking to Greg about...some things."

"That I can see for myself. What kind of things? Not about Danny, I'll bet. He won't have Danny's problem. The draft he won't have to worry about."

"How do you make that kind of statement? You know something about how the draft works I don't know? If he's in school, if he stays in school, he'll be all right. At least for a while he will. I checked on that. I know I'm right about that." She had turned, so that she could talk to Lionel directly, so that she could watch his face while she talked. He was annoyed, exasperated, his hand was moving through the air dismissing her words as nonsense or beside the point. Why was he being so nasty? Didn't he know how to be a human being for a few minutes? What made him so angry all the time? Even though she was acting better and better, even though she was never drunk anymore, he was still angry with her. Or with Greg. And with Greg there was no reason, absolutely no reason for him to treat that boy that way.

"I don't want to talk about it now. I want Greg to go to bed and I want you to go to bed."

Greg didn't have to be asked twice. He seemed relieved. It was a matter of seconds: he kissed her, he walked across the living room, he closed the door to his bedroom behind him. Final. Gone. Gone fishing.

"Come on. It's late." He moved off. Of course she would follow! The bastard.

[2] "You can talk for a few minutes. It won't hurt you to talk for a few minutes. You don't have to get up early tomorrow. So why, Lionel? Why are you so stubborn? We can talk quietly and sensibly like two mature adults, right? Just answer one question for me. Either you sit in front of the television set or you go out to play cards or you go to bed. That you consider a life? You look forward to living like that in five years from now, let's say? In ten years? And if I suggest going on a trip that's farther away than Las Vegas, you get so excited I think you're going to have a heart attack. What is it with you? You're not exactly a senile old man. How about for once going to Europe? Or California instead of Las Vegas? Evelyn and Harold had three kids to deal with and a lot less money, and they go all over. Why not us?" Enough said... by her! She would wait for a reply. She would wait all night if she had to. She would keep him up while she waited.

He was on his back, trying to sleep, his hands folded on top of his chest. In the darkness of their bedroom she could see the even rise and fall of his breathing. Fatso. He was getting fat and bushy-haired and slow. The bastard was relaxed, or making believe he was, because when was he ever so quiet? He even looked a little sad, as if he were being laid out for his coffin, but with something left over on his mind, something he had wanted to say and didn't have enough time for. Okay. She was giving him the chance to say it, whatever it was. "How about it, Lionel? Can't you say something? After all, comes September and Greg goes off to school, it's going to be the two of us alone again. What then? What's going to happen to us then?"

"You'll start drinking again."

"Thanks a lot. You're really something. You want to drive me crazy?"

"Drive you? You always were. When were you anything else but crazy?"

"And when were you anything else but a nasty fuck?"

"That's why you're here, sweetheart. Because I'm a nasty fuck and that's what you like, fucking. Isn't that right? Am I right or wrong?"

"Wrong. If you'd look at something other than your prick once in a while, you'd see some changes. In me. In my attitudes. In my behavior...not a whole lot, but enough so you'd notice—if you looked. You've changed too, you know. Even now, you're a little different."

"Bullshit."

"Lionel? Why are you doing this now? I'm trying to talk to you sensibly. I'm turning the other cheek, like Missy tells me to do. So why are you taking out after me? What did I do to you? Because I wanted you to sit down with Greg and me and talk? Is that something to be angry about?"

He sat up suddenly. He had made up his mind. Whatever was on it, left over on it, he was going to say. He wasn't going to look at her while he said it, though. He was staring toward the window. Dark there, some moon. Profile. A silhouette. Not bad. Puffier than it had been, his nose. His bushy hair like shredded Brillo pads. "I heard what he said before. He thinks I hate him. I don't. That's bullshit. But there's something...something between the two of us..."

"How can it concern the two of you and not me? I'm his mother. Why, if you knew something...why wouldn't you tell me? What could be so terrible that you—you of all people—would want to keep it from me?"

"Okay, Corinne. You asked for it. You'll get it."

"That's news? Ever since we've been married—that's twenty years already, remember; chew on that fact for a while, big boy—you've been saying that to me. You asked for it; you'll get it. Okay. I'm waiting."

"It's Greg. It's about Greg...and what I saw."

"What did you see? Where?"

"Greg...and Loretta...Greg is the same as Loretta."

"The same how, Lionel? As far as you know, how? What else is Loretta except Loretta?"

"Queer."

"You know that about Loretta? You know that about Greg? How can you know...?"

"I've got eyes, haven't I? I can still see, at least."

"See what, goddammit? What did you see? Tell me already, because if you don't, I'll go get Greg and ask him myself!" She was half out of bed. He pulled her back, held her right where he pulled her to, up close to himself, so that he would say what he had to say right to her face. No matter how she twisted away, he held on to her.

"You see how it is, Corinne? When it's Loretta, it's one thing. When it's your own son, it's another, isn't it? Then it's a different matter altogether, isn't it? You and your goddamned principles about things. About being fair to everyone. About treating everyone the same. Bullshit! Goddamn bullshit. I saw Greg. With a man. An older man. My age. On Third Avenue in the city. Near Bloomingdale's. I was coming from the Queensboro Bridge. Around Christmas vacation. I was going in to a plumbing jobber for parts, and I saw them—I saw him first and I automatically pulled over to ask him what he was doing there and I'd drive him back home if he wanted after I made my stop, and then I saw this man next to him and it looked like both of them were going to collapse, Greg especially. He turned white as a sheet. So I just drove off. I didn't even get out of the car. I never even said a word to him. I still haven't. Three months already. Neither has he. He treats it like it never happened. So do I. Maybe it didn't. Maybe I misunderstood it. Maybe I just imagined the whole thing. It was too coincidental. It couldn't have happened. And as far as I'm concerned, that's how I'm going to leave it."

He had let her sit up, and this time she made it out of bed before he could grab her.

She went out to the living room, but the lights were on already. Greg was there, standing there in his bathrobe, waiting. "You were both yelling, and I heard you. I figured it had to be about me. It is, isn't it, Mother? Dad told you...why don't you go get your robe? It's cold. I won't run away. I'll stay right here. I promise."

She was at the piano. She was holding on to it. And then Lionel was alongside her with her robe. He helped her into it. And now that she was supposed to be warm, now that she

211

had supposedly wanted this opportunity for the three of them to be together and talk it all out openly, now she didn't know what to say. She felt so many things all at once, it was impossible to pull one thought from the pack and hold on to it. They all rushed through her head at a speed greater than the speed of light. It was all dark to her. It was all jumbled together in her head. She would have loved a drink. She would have loved to sit down at the piano and to play the "Pathétique." No...ladies and gentlemen, I have been asked instead to play the "Appassionata"....From some Bette Davis movie that was, the "Appassionata." The thing was, also, she could have played either. That was almost the funniest part of this crazy situation.... "Is what your father is saying true?"

"That it's a small world? That he saw me in the city? Yes. That's true."

"Also, that you were with someone? That it was a man...and that the man was...was...different?"

"Queer? That was the word you were yelling before, wasn't it, Dad? Queer? He was. He was asking me to go with him. To his apartment. But I didn't go. Not that I didn't want to—I'll tell you the whole truth, Mother, nothing but the whole truth, whatever that is. I don't think I'm a great-looking guy. Being tall helps, but I'm not the average great-looking guy. So when someone appreciates me in a different way, I can't help but feel a little flattered—but I didn't go with him."

"Bullshit!" Lionel was stepping toward him. This time she had to hold *him* back. "Just stay where you are, Lionel. To you everything is bullshit except what you say. Why don't you believe him? You think he'd be standing here telling you this if it wasn't the truth?"

"I don't know what he's saying. You're so goddamned smart, suddenly you understand everything. He was flattered but he didn't go. He is, he isn't? What is all that but bullshit?"

"It's the truth, Dad. I don't know, but I'm not going to be ashamed of what I thought. I didn't do anything. I didn't do anything with...with Danny either, Mother...but I thought it. So maybe I am and maybe I'm not. I don't know. If I lived in the city, maybe I'd know, but does a person know everything at eighteen?" He moved then, for the first time since he had begun to speak. He covered his eyes with those big hands of his. He was shaking. He began to cry. "I didn't do anything wrong. I didn't."

By the time she reached him, she was crying too. As tall as he was, she still managed to hold him as if he were a little boy, her baby.

He bent to make himself smaller. And then he was sobbing.

She got him to the sofa. She sat him down. She let him cry. She looked up at Lionel. He had remained just where she left him. "He's your son too, Lionel." She said it softly. "Your son. My son. Ours, Lionel."

"That, yes. That much, okay, I'm responsible for. And because he is, I'll pay for whatever he needs. I'll send him to school. All of that shit...but no more than that. Because no matter what he says, he's one of them. All I have to do is look at him to know it. Look at how he is right now. Look at him crying." And with that Lionel came over to them, pulled at her to get up, to get away from him, to leave him alone, "...because he doesn't deserve any help." She pushed at Lionel. She pushed at him with all her strength, but she couldn't budge him. He took hold of her arm. He pulled her to her feet. "He's going to get what he needs, and no more. If he wants to go to a doctor, I'll pay for that too. Whatever he decides to do. But I'm not going to decide for him. I'm not going to tell him what to do. He can make up his own mind. He's old enough. He never came to me before to ask me anything. He's not going to start now."

"I won't." Greg kept watching her, not Lionel. He wanted her to see that he was all right, that she shouldn't worry. He'd be all right now. He was in control of himself now. He was okay. She didn't have to hold on to him. He wouldn't collapse. He wouldn't go to pieces. "I'm used to deciding things for myself. I've had years of training. I don't have to go to a doctor for help. I'm not sick, Dad. I know why I never went to you to ask your opinion about what I wanted to do. It was because you never acted as if you wanted me to. You never seemed to have the time to listen. You were always so busy doing...nothing...." It was so easy for Lionel to raise his free hand and slap Greg. The sound of it stopped them, froze them.

And then Lionel let go of her arm. He seemed to crumple. He was going to fall forward, against Greg.

But Greg moved first and fast and away, saying, over and over as he went, "It's okay. It's okay. It's okay," as if to convince himself that it was okay, really. He convinced Corinne. She was, somehow, sure he would be, but maybe she

213

wouldn't be. Maybe Lionel wouldn't be. He was on his knees in front of the sofa where Greg had been sitting. "I'm sorry," he mumbled. "I'm sorry. I didn't mean to hit him. I didn't, Corinne. I lost control. I didn't mean it. Explain it to him. You can explain it to him. He never gave me a chance. Never. He never has, Corinne. You know that. He never even wanted to come to the store with me. Not once did he come."

"When did you ask him?"

He looked up at her. He was still on his knees. And then he lowered his head onto the sofa. "He never wanted to. I could tell that." He would have stayed there, his head resting on the sofa pillow. Pathetic. Pathetic, what was going on. With them. With all of them. Something. Everything. Everything everywhere was going wrong. If she only had the intelligence to name one thing out of that everything, to give it a name, call it something...what? A father slaps his son. That's something. Sure. But what?

"You should have asked. You should have taken him."

"He wouldn't have come."

"You're still so sure now, after what he said tonight? You still can be so sure?"

"I'm sure." He stood up, but he didn't turn away. "I'm positive. He thinks I'm a piece of shit."

"You're a fool, Lionel."

"That too. And I'm sorry for that too. But that you always knew. I wanted to help you, and I didn't know what to do for you either. And with Greg...I don't know how to talk to him. I don't know...you'll explain? Tomorrow, you'll explain for me?"

"I'll try. But I don't understand either. I'm a fool too. And I'm tired. I'm exhausted."

She stepped around him and very quickly he was following her. Tonight, however, one thing he was not going to get was her.

21

Cynthia Klein

[1] "Personally, I don't see why we couldn't have gone to Evelyn and Harold's to begin with. All you had to do, Mother, was to call Gladys and lie a little. You can't make me a friend of Myrna Ginsburg by putting me in her company more. Myrna and I have nothing in common except the fact that we both live on Wisdom Lane, which is pitifully little. Terry Geiger is my friend. Greg Feuerstein is my friend. And, what you really don't like, Danny Selden is my idol. That's why you really made us go to the Ginsburgs'. Because you knew Danny would be there, wasn't it, Mother?"

"I don't like your sarcasm, Melly."

"It's not sarcasm. It's the truth. And if Danny were to ask me to come live with him and be his love, I'd do it in a second."

"Sandy? Did you hear her? Are you listening?"

"The truth? No. I was trying to listen to Wagner, but raised voices interfered."

"Daddy! For shame. The Good Friday music? On Passover? Sacrilegious! Weren't you going to say that to him, Mother? Haven't you been dying to say that to him since we arrived home? How perverse. Like your always say to him? The last thing you wanted was for Daddy to put on music. You wanted to talk about Danny. You think it's so terrible what he's going to do. You also think it's so terrible I don't want to go straight into college, don't you. Anything I want to do, you won't even begin to listen to. Just because Myrna Ginsburg is willing to toddle off to Boston U. doesn't mean that I have to follow in her footsteps, does it?—and please don't tell me once more how I'm wasting my youth. It's my youth, not yours, and if I've been accepted at Radcliffe once, I'll be accepted again...when I'm ready to go. If they don't accept me then, I'll go somewhere else. The only one who would really hate that would be Grandma Klein, and you, I suppose. You wouldn't care, Daddy, would you?"

"What *I* care about is having to do what I'm about to do."

He slapped his knees, resigned, exasperated, still in his blazer, his collar open, though; he strode across the living room with all deliberate speed and removed the recording from the turntable. "All day I've had a yen to hear this music. Admittedly, this record is scratchy and worn, but it is Toscanini. It is *Parsifal,* and it just happens to be a sentimental favorite. Of course there is no reason in the world why my daughter and my wife have to indulge my wish, not even for fifteen minutes. Of course not. I'm just the order boy around here. I do what I'm told. You tell me we're going to the Ginsburgs' first, for the seder, instead of the the Seldens'? Fine, I say. Sure. Whatever you want, Cynthia. Anything you decide is okey-dokey with me. When have you ever heard me complain? I wouldn't think of complaining. It isn't civilized to complain. It's vulgar to complain, especially in front of your loved ones....Don't laugh, Melanie. I'm not being sarcastic either right now. I'm serious. Dead serious....And as far as your even having a fantasy about living with Danny Selden, I suggest you had better scratch that one right off the great agenda in the sky. Not only will he not have it, I won't. So don't confuse yourself on that particular score, Melanie. You're not, are you? Confused?" Sandy had stood next to the turntable to deliver his speech. It was certainly that. It was meant to be. He remained standing there, for effect, Cynthia was pleased to note. For perfect clarity, emphasis, presence. Like his speakers.

He had placed them, *his* speakers, on either side of the big back bay window. When they redid the room, he designed it, designed the space in the corners for the speakers to be placed in, raised off the shag carpet on wooden blocks, a foot high, AR-3 speakers, facing the length of the living room, lovely rich sound. Perfect clarity, emphasis, presence—and the rest of the room to match, chrome and glass and leather. No draperies. He wanted very little color. He would not let her add any when they redid. Just the green of the plants. The room ended up looking the same *after* as *before,* only richer. Some order boy!

In silence, both of them watching his deliberate pace, he returned to his Aalto easy chair. He had bought that for himself. He had placed that himself too, just so, at the apex of the imaginary isosceles triangle of stereo sound waves he carried in his head. "Instead of God," he had once told her, "I have an image of the ideal sound-wave triangle in my

216

head, and myself at its apex. That's true happiness—that and the best high-fidelity equipment money can buy."

Well, God and Sandy Klein move in strange and mysterious ways. That, she had always known. Without her having to ask him, Sandy had come through once more. Melanie had received the word, and his word was law—even for Melanie it was still the law, fuss and fume as she might.

"Is any of what you—and we, Mother and I—just said discussable?"

"Discussable? Yes. Certainly." He unbuttoned his blazer, opened the knot of his rep tie, slid it out of its button-down tunnel. "Even Danny is discussable. His ideas are, in any case, but not in terms of your fantasy of him. Your personal fantasy, I mean. That I don't want to hear any more about. I really don't, Melly. But anything else . . . yes. As well tonight as any other time. I'm ready. Are you? Cynthia? Are you? Did you hear her?"

"According to Melanie, I've been ready ever since we left Evelyn's." Actually, Cynthia would have been happy to leave things just where they were right then and there. Melanie had received her *No* concerning Danny, which was really what Cynthia had been after. The school situation, her intuition told her, would work itself out as soon as the Danny situation did.

But school was where Melanie had left it, and where, then, she picked it up, ". . . because school really is a basic issue, Daddy, basic to me anyway. Going to college right now seems irrelevant to all the values I feel strongest about. Danny represents a truly moral issue, but all injustice—"

"Before you get deeply into injustice, how about telling me—me, not your mother, so please dispense with that patronizing tone I heard before. Not that I appreciate it when you use that tone on her. It's uncalled for. Your mother is not a fool. Not in any way at all. It's time you realized that. She has her attitudes and opinions thought out the way most intelligent people do. Some of them may be more . . . rigid . . . than you might like them to be, but getting older gives people some rights, you know. Aged people have civil rights too. We most assuredly do—not that I want to get sidetracked. Instead, what I want you to tell me, before you go back to injustice, is what you plan to do if you don't go to Radcliffe in the fall. And understand this, whether Grandma helped you with being accepted there has nothing to do with my question. . . ."

Sandy! How much she loved him. Not in the old way of how she loved him when they met, but in this way, this new way of being married for over twenty years and finding they were in agreement now about almost everything. Mellow together most of the time. They were. Mellow...a word from her own youth. She hadn't used it or thought of it in a month of Sundays. Mellow with each other...except about things like her deciding to go to Gladys's for the seder instead of Evelyn's and Harold's. But why Sandy preferred Harold to Gordon, she couldn't quite figure out. Gordon even liked good music. Gordon went to the opera. Gordon knew the violin, although Sandy thought he looked like a horse's ass on those rare occasions, very rare, when they could persuade Gordon to play it. Sandy was right. She had to admit that: Gordon looked silly. He even had a horsey face...which is probably why Sandy preferred Harold. Harold was undoubtedly the handsomest of the husbands—after Sandy, of course. No one was more beautiful than Sandy....

But she wasn't listening to Melanie. Melanie was talking and stalling simultaneously. She was going on about finding herself, finding her role, her profession, her milieu. Sandy had eased back down onto his Aalto easy chair, listening, staring up at the ceiling, his hands, one on top of the other, resting on top of his flat stomach. Never gained a pound of weight. Never got the least bit flabby. He swam, at a club, in New York. Had, for the last five years, ever since he'd been permanently settled there by the company. No more Washingtons—but he swam in New York regularly. It had paid off. He looked younger than the day he'd married her. It meant a lot to him to look young. More than it did to her, strangely enough. That kind of vanity had never been her problem. "...must I be able to tell you exactly, Daddy? Must I know exactly what I want to do? Isn't it enough at my age to know exactly what I *don't* want to do?"

Melanie, too, was irresistible—when she was controlled, reasonable, calm, in the same way Sandy was behaving. Then her natural intelligence took charge, just as naturally as her natural passion had before. She was—had turned out to be— a marvelous combination of the two of them. Nothing plain-featured about her. Delicate. Petite. Raven-haired, they used to call it back home. Ivory-skinned, they used to call it in South Carolina. An ivory-skinned Southern belle. Scarlett O'Hara. Melanie wasn't quite that...but she was Melanie. And that's why she was, because of Scarlett. That name.

218

Growing up, Melanie had been embarrassed by it—until she read *Gone with the Wind*. Then she hated it. She liked Melly better, much better. . . .

Sandy was considering that last question. He liked it. He said so, ". . . very persuasive." He nodded, appreciating her, his daughter.

Their daughter . . . and spoiled, petulant, willful, vain, now that she realized she had developed her own special look. She sewed up her own clothes. Skirts. Slacks. Bold-colored plaid blouses. Clothes that always seemed to be too big for her small frame, but the force of her personality carried them off. She was searching for who she was. She was making herself up as she went. She wasn't afraid, and she had a conscience. She did care about injustice in her world, ". . . I really do, Daddy, I just don't want to rush off to school and follow a plan that's made up by people whose judgment I don't really trust. I'm not saying I won't go to school eventually. I will. That, I can promise you. I just don't want to go now." She paused. She was not nearly finished. She had a lot more to say, a whole lifetime of things to say. Her expression conveyed that, and also her determination to win, to prove her case, to be convincing.

Sandy waited, attentive. So did Cynthia, arms folded, crushing her silk blouse, holding in all that she might want to say, waiting for the moment when she could.

"What if . . . ?" Melanie's courage faltered—and then rushed around the edge of her fear into the open air. "Teresa and I had a plan of our own. We wanted to travel. To California maybe. Or Europe. For a year. Not any more than that. We both . . . I'll just speak for myself. I feel as if growing up in Levittown, I've been at a disadvantage. In the way you always complained about, Mom. I don't mean that the both of you didn't give me everything I wanted. I don't mean that at all. Maybe it's just the opposite. Ever since I was little, I've never been deprived of anything. During those years when I was sick, I really felt overwhelmed by all the things you gave me, and also by all the love. I'll never forget that. I couldn't ask for better parents. . . ."

Sandy sat up, touched.

Cynthia thought she was going to cry, suddenly, so she just squeezed her arms tighter, to hold that in too, all of herself checked, held in, waiting, always, for the right moment.

"Don't say anything, please, not yet, Daddy, because if

you do, I'm liable to get...sidetracked." Sandy laughed. So did Melanie, and having done that, she couldn't resist getting up, rushing across the room to give him a kiss, rushing back again to her seat next to Cynthia on the foam-rubber sofa. No kiss for Cynthia—but a smile, a warm enough smile, love in it, and then she resumed her presentation, like a lawyer might present his case. That's what she should be, a lawyer, a petite, ringleted, raven-haired, ivory-skinned lawyer. She had the kind of mind that never seemed to get lost. "What I feel is that growing up in Levittown was like growing up on a desert. There was never anything here for us to do. When you started taking me into the city, then I began to feel different. But like a foreigner at first. I don't like feeling that a city like New York is in another country. Not when we live so close. We were talking about that. In our English class. We just finished *The Tempest,* and Mr. Rothstein approached it that way. About being protected and cut off from experiences the way Miranda was by Prospero. Did you ever read the play, Daddy?"

He nodded, intent on listening to his Melanie. Cynthia felt a surge of envy for their closeness. Not unnatural. Really not... and it receded, as fast as it came upon her, because Melanie was going on about fathers and daughters, "...Levittown fathers do, Daddy. They treat their daughters like Mirandas, and the world isn't so brave and new the way they remember it being when they were younger. It isn't. It has atom bombs in it, and a president gets shot on television, over and over again he gets shot. 'Our revels now' are really ended. Mr. Rothstein agrees with me about how unreal Levittown is. And, as you heard, he also agrees with Danny. About the draft. He's going to get into a lot of trouble about that out here. He's even thinking of quitting before they start telling him to cool it. If he was ever fired, what a loss—"

"He has tenure, Melly. Evelyn checked all that when she approached him about speaking to her anti-war group. He agreed."

"You know, Cynthia, you should ask Rothstein for dinner again. I liked him. I liked him a lot. We talked a little bit tonight. He knows his music, all right." Sandy stood up, carefully removed his blazer, carefully folded it. "I want to talk to him about *The Tempest.*" Cynthia nodded: Yes, she would. "And about Melanie too, of course. A very persuasive case you've got, Melly. Very. Your Mother and I will discuss it.

But for right now, I want to tell you that I'm proud of you and that I love you...and that I'm going to bed."

[2] "Carl will never allow Teresa to go with Melly. I'm absolutely certain of that. Can you imagine Carl, conservative Carl, letting his daughter travel with Melly farther than Manhattan? When she gets on the Long Island Rail Road to go to Rockville Centre he has to give her all kinds of instructions. I've seen it, Sandy. I've been there and seen it happening. I've heard Carl telling Teresa what she should do when she goes into Penn Station. Even when she's with Melly he does it." She couldn't sleep. She wasn't the least bit tired.

Neither was he. He was on his back, his hands behind his head, his pillow folded into a mound, a support. Thinking, now, as ever. Quiet. Unapproachable, she felt. Wanting to be alone in his bed to sort out the pieces. The engineer. The analyst. Persuasive. Very persuasive...but apparently he, she, separately and together, had been just as persuasive with Melly as she had been this evening with them. They had done a good job, as they used to say back home. Reared up a good one, they used to say.

"Sandy? You're not sleeping, are you? Can you? Can you imagine Carl doing that? Can you imagine yourself letting Melly...go? Wherever she wants."

"I don't know. That's what I've been thinking about. Can you?" He turned on his side to face her. Perhaps he really did want to talk. Usually he would say that kind of thing to Melly: Your mother and I will have to discuss it—and then they never did, because usually whatever he decided was all right with her. Whatever he said was right. They agreed without having to agree out loud....Mellow now together about most things.

But not, she was afraid, about letting Melanie go. Not mellow about that. "No. And if we have to, I'm not going to find it an easy matter at all, Sandy. I admit it."

"Conservative Cynthia." He laughed. Quietly. With her, not at her. He understood. He must feel the same way.

From whom had Melanie inherited her courage to be her own cause? From Sandy? From her? Cynthia Berkowitz Berk Klein? From the way things were in the world nowadays? The things Melanie had talked about before? Levittown? Aaron Rothstein? Seeing an assassination on television? Seeing it over and over again? Cynthia felt that for herself, seeing those things, admitting their differences from her

221

growing up, what she most of all wanted to do was fight to keep things she had some control over as much the same way as they always had been. She wanted Sandy to want the same thing. She supposed, yes, she was conservative. "I guess so, Sandy. I guess I've become more and more so. You are too, at heart. You are."

"Less than you think. Much less than you know." He rolled onto his back again.

What he'd said, she didn't like to hear. What he'd said was the truth, but he didn't usually just come right out and say it.

The truth was, there was so much about him she didn't know anything about at all. For the last five years she hadn't seen any reason to ask. They had settled into the pattern for their lives together. He was there every time he had to be. He was saying all the things he had to say when he had to say them. Before then she never felt certain about him. Would he be there? Would he go to Washington? Did he care for her at all? Did he approve of how she handled Melanie? Did he want more than he had gotten out of life? And then all of those questions just dissolved in her head. There wasn't any reason left to ask them, and she didn't feel the need anymore to force him to talk to her about what he might be thinking. He was with her. That's what mattered. His actions finally did speak louder than any words he might have used to explain what he was thinking privately. She didn't want to know. She didn't want to know about anything at all that he didn't want to tell her. If he was content, so was she . . . with the way their lives worked. She wasn't even going to ask him what he had just meant. If he had really wanted to tell her, he would have remained on his side, facing her. People tell more about themselves that way than if they open their mouths. When she folded her arms across her breasts . . .

His breathing had a beat in it, a vibrato. He was nervous. She could hear that. It was a distinct difference for this night. This night! Why is this night different from all other nights? At Marcia's seder Marvin Zweig had had to ask the questions. Marvin Zweig? The youngest male there. Nineteen! Yes, the times they are a-changing. Seders. Gone . . . with the wind. The wind outside their bedroom windows was whipping up a freshness. Early spring, 1965. The world would calm down now. Lyndon Johnson would be good for the country. Danny would be deferred at the last minute. Melly would go to Radcliffe. There wouldn't be any big war. Sandy would not be acting as if, suddenly, after all these years of not talking to her, he was going to start. She didn't want to hear it. She wouldn't. She wouldn't answer him. She would listen to that beat in his breathing and be silent. Their life just now was too good to change anything in it at all. She wouldn't let it change.

"But, I guess"—he sighed, still nervous, still determined to speak—"I guess whatever I've done hasn't mattered. Listening to Melly tonight, I realized that nothing else but loving her has mattered very much. I did mean that. About feeling proud of her. Don't you?"

"Yes. I do." That much she would venture. It was certainly the truth.

"Whatever we did, Cynthia, it's very beautiful to feel love coming back from her to us. Very beautiful. When she leaves here, I'm going to miss her so much. We both will. And she will go, whether she goes to school or she goes to California or Europe or wherever, she'll be going. Then what, Cynthia? What about us? I felt...old tonight. For the first time in my life I felt forty-five. I'm forty-five years old, Cynthia."

"There isn't anything about you that's forty-five. I was looking at you and thinking that you looked even younger tonight than you did when we were married."

"Nevertheless, I'm forty-five. You're forty-three. And Melanie's going away. I was just remembering when I went away from my mother how relieved I was. I couldn't wait for it. I was so glad to be drafted finally, so she couldn't say I was deserting her. Which she did anyway, even though she had my father. She had my brother, too, but it was the same way when I went to college without coming home every other weekend, I was deserting her.... I always wondered . . . I still do . . . why, when she had everything she could possibly want . . . materially want..." He stopped, his breathing slowed; she listened, waiting. The wind gusted, dropped, gusted again. "Why, I wonder, did the things that interested me become the only things she was interested in? What has she missed? Personally missed? What . . . have you . . . missed, Cynthia?"

"Nothing."

"You answered too quickly for me to believe that."

"Believe what you want, Sandy."

"Do you mean that? Do you really mean that?"

"As far as I'm concerned, I've gotten a lot more from my life so far than I ever expected to have."

"So far? And what about the future?"

"What about it?"

"You won't help me talk to you tonight, will you, Cynthia? You don't want to face...certain facts."

"About Melly, you mean. I'm facing—"

"About what Melly's going away will mean to us." He was sitting up. He was swinging his legs out from under his blanket. He was wearing only his pajama top. He sat at the edge of his bed waiting for her to respond. White cotton, glowing. His hair, glowing. She would have to say something.

"It will mean that it's going to be very empty here without her. I've faced that. But how else will our life change? Our pattern is set. You're in the city swimming two, sometimes three nights a week? Sometimes I meet you to go to a concert or an opera or a play. Sometimes a whole group of us go. And on weekends we're here. We entertain. We go out to our friends'. That's the way it's been. That's the way, as far as I'm concerned, it'll continue to be...only I suppose I will get involved with some new causes. There'll always be some more. There always are...." As long as she continued talking, now that she had started, everything would be all right. It would be. She felt certain of that again. She didn't want to hear anything else from him about what she didn't know. She didn't need to. "I'll be content that way. I've always been content that way. I like my life. I feel fortunate. I felt proud of Melly tonight too. I admit I want her to go to school, but after listening to her tonight, whatever she does, I'll trust her. I won't give up trying to convince her to go to school, but whatever she does, I promise to go along with it and trust her."

"You're sure? You really mean what you've just said? In five years from now, in ten years maybe, if I remind you that you said this tonight, you won't suddenly point a finger to me and say something like: 'You ruined my life'?"

"You haven't, Sandy. You haven't at all. I love you now more than I ever did."

"Sexually, too?" He leaned into the space between their beds. He held his head in his hands. She thought he might begin to cry. She felt embarrassed for him.

She wanted to help him in whatever way she could, but she didn't want him to say whatever it was he felt he should say. He wanted to relieve his own conscience and, strange to say, he really did seem to care that she didn't want him to, didn't need him to. "Sexually too. It doesn't somehow mean

224

the same thing to me it used to." Then, before he could sit up or react, she slipped from beneath her blanket. She made him sit up. She got on her knees between the two beds, made him open his legs so that she could lean inside them against his body, so that she could make him feel that she did in truth know how she felt: dependent on his affection, and very glad to be. "I'm very content, Sandy. I love you and I'll never have a reason to say that you ruined my life. You haven't, so far. I don't think it's in you to even come near doing it in the future." She put her arms around his waist, waiting, and then finally he brought his hands down onto her back. He kissed the top of her head. "I really am very content this way, Sandy."

PART FOUR

1965–1972

THE LADIES OF LEVITTOWN
WEDNESDAY NIGHT
BOOK GROUP

Evelyn and Aaron, 1965

Loretta and Aaron, 1966

Missy and Aaron, 1968

Corinne and Aaron, 1968

Cynthia and Aaron, 1968

Evelyn: Committee of One, 1972

22

Evelyn and Aaron, 1965

[1]   "Moral turpitude, Arlene? In Levittown? I don't even know what it means. Do you?"

"All I know, Evelyn, is that you're the one who's always saying not to believe everything you read in the newspapers. So in this case, you happen to be right. You have the article in front of you, don't you?" Evelyn did. While she spoke on the telephone to Arlene, she kept rereading it, the article about Aaron's resignation in the Levittown *Tribune,* for May 24, 1965.

"There's nothing in the article about moral turpitude— whatever that means. I'll have to go to a dictionary to find out. But how it can be applied to Aaron Rothstein, I'll have to know facts before I believe it. If you really do know more, Arlene, what more do you know? Tell me? And also tell me how many other people before me you've already told?"

"None—and that's insulting, Evelyn. I am capable of some loyalty, even if you don't think so. Aaron has been as good to my children as yours—"

"Tell me, Arlene."

Arlene did, and after she did, Evelyn called Loretta first; Loretta thought they should meet to talk about, "...the situation that could develop and what could be done." She called Corinne. Evelyn called Cynthia and Missy. The five of them, and Arlene, would meet at Evelyn's as soon as possible to discuss a plan of action to deal with "...whatever," is all Evelyn would call it on the telephone.

[2]   That same afternoon, after Arlene's appointment at the beauty parlor, a Committee of Five—and Arlene—seated themselves around the oak table in Evelyn's kitchen. The teacups were in place. The Levittown *Tribune* was opened to the article about Aaron Rothstein's resignation. Evelyn had placed it between Arlene and herself: all the better to

point to. "Before anything else is said, tell them, Arlene, who told you what you told me."

"The Bauers." Arlene leaned toward her teacup, her beehive, that dyed-black, sprayed-stiff beehive, every brittle strand of it glistening in the late-afternoon sunlight, that *thing* never so much as quivered. That was moral turpitude. That hair was.

"Remember the Bauers?" Evelyn forced her gaze away from Arlene's hair. "Remember that Open School Night? Aaron was still teaching at the Gardiner's Avenue School then, 1956. The Bauers were out to get him that night. We had that plan. To protect him. He didn't need it. Remember? The following year he went over to the Salk school."

They did remember.

Missy went on to remember the first time she and Evelyn met Aaron, "...in 1952. We were wearing our Adlai pins, the big ones. 'All the way with Adlai.' Aaron came over to us and introduced himself. It was his first teaching day. Remember, Ev? He told us the pins made him feel welcome. He'd just been discharged from the Army that summer. He got the job out here the first interview he was sent out on. You remember how impressed we were with him, Ev? He was so . . . natural . . . with us. Even Morty and Adam were won over. It was their first schoolday too. I'll never forget that."

"Which is all the more reason we should try to get the facts, Arlene. The real facts. The ones in the article, we all know. Aaron's dates are like a history of Levittown. You list the three schools he worked in and you have it all. He had a premonition something like this was going to happen. When he went from Salk Junior High to the General Douglas MacArthur High School...I was doing PTA work there then...how he hated the idea of 'General' as part of the name of a school. It couldn't come to good, he told me. To go from the Savior to the Destroyer was a bad sign, he said." Evelyn folded the *Tribune*, rapped the table with it. "Okay, Arlene. Shoot. And remember, we're talking about a human being. Someone we all care about. Our children too we're talking about. For Aaron to resign so suddenly, without saying a word to any of us—it doesn't make any sense."

"Not the story in the paper. That doesn't. They wouldn't print the real story. First of all, the Bauers saw Aaron coming out of a bar in Greenwich Village...not alone, either. With a man, a very young man who—"

"You know he lives in the Village?" Loretta poked her

Camel dangerously close to Arlene's beehive. "Did you tell the Bauers that? Did you? He's got more right to be in the Village than the Bauers have. Did you tell them that, damn it?"

"If you don't mind, Loretta..." Arlene waved the smoke away. "And I'd also appreciate it if you wouldn't use that tone on me. You don't have to be so condescending, especially you."

"What's that supposed to mean?" Loretta leaped up. Corinne pulled her back. "We'll do that one another time. Get on with it already, will you, Arlene."

"Yes. Please do." Cynthia sighed, sipped from her teacup. "I still have a dinner to prepare. We all do." Cynthia folded up, sat back, waiting, ready. Nothing could surprise Cynthia, nothing in the whole world could. She always told Evelyn that. Just the opposite of Missy. Everything surprised her. She fingered her cross whenever she expected the worst. She was hanging on to it then, because Arlene was going on from where she had left off, "...a very young man who was drunk and who was holding on to Aaron's arm—and not just to steady himself, the Bauers said. It was very compromising."

"Maybe Aaron was helping him." Loretta lit up another Camel. Even she was nervous. Corinne kept finger-combing her hair, she was so nervous.

"Anyway, the Bauers also told me—and this is the hardest part to accept. Remember, I'm just repeating what they told me—that Aaron was tutoring a son of a friend of theirs and that Aaron made...advances to the boy and the boy told his parents and the parents went to the principal. The principal of course went to the superintendent. There was a meeting with the school board—"

"With Aaron present, I hope?" Evelyn unrolled the *Tribune*. "I hope someone had the decency, the common decency, to ask Aaron if it...if..."

"If what?" Arlene pushed back from the table, decidedly out of the circle, disconnected, disconnecting herself. "Why do you immediately take Aaron's side?"

"Because, Arlene, I respect Aaron too much not to. I know what his accomplishments are as a teacher and as a human being. Personally, I'd want a lot more facts than all this hearsay. I think we should go to see Aaron—those of us who want to." Evelyn turned to Arlene so that there would be no doubt that the Committee of Five was not going to become the Committee of Six. Not that Arlene really would want

230

that. Never. Right from the beginning, from Spring Lane days, Arlene was always the messenger, the bearer of bad tidings, the Yenta of Yellowtrim Farms, never the doer of deeds. Therefore, "We should go to see Aaron. We should have some kind of plan worked out, some offer, something we'd like him to do for us. Something that would show him we're not against him.... I don't suppose you'll come with us, Arlene, will you?"

For answer, she stood up. She was going. She had other things she had to do. No one else joined her. Only Cynthia thanked her.

[3] "What we have in mind, Aaron, is some kind of group, more like a class of some sort. In literature. Not exactly great books. We tried that, but no one would shut up long enough to discuss anything except the other groups we were in—if you know what I mean." Evelyn wasn't sure she knew what she meant. She knew she was uncomfortable. She was too old for student armchairs. Too old and too fat. She was, and Loretta was. Lucky Missy and Corinne. Cynthia's problem was that she was too tall. But none of that mattered. Not to Aaron.

He was nodding. He sat atop his desk, legs swinging in and out and to the side. A crazy rhythm. Pendulums that wouldn't keep a proper time, a regular time. His gaze wandered from their five faces to the windows of his classroom. He cocked his head to the side. He was listening, but to out there, to beyond those windows, where, although she couldn't see it from her chair, there was only traffic. Heavy traffic. The steady sounds of it. North to Hempstead Turnpike. South to the Southern State—and in between those boundaries, Levittown. Levittown, outside those windows, all grown up, eighteen years old, and very June green out there this afternoon. That's what he was listening to, and while he did, he played with the edges of his beard. He had let his beard grow out. A full beard. Many shades of gray. Like his hair. Many shades of gray, and wavy, long, splashing every which way at the end of this teaching day. He seemed tired. His eyes— they were gray too—were tired eyes. He looked far older than his age this afternoon. Thirty-seven, the article had said. More like thirty-seven going on ninety. Very little meat on his bones. Gray and gaunt. A long hard teaching year coming to a close. Maybe a career coming to a close too.

"Aaron?" She called him back. She felt like she was intruding. "We have the names of sixteen ladies who want to be part of any group you're the leader of."

His gaze returned to her. Again he nodded, but he was not with her, not with any of them. His legs stopped swinging. Thinking. He was thinking. What? She couldn't tell. Had he heard her at all?

Loretta nudged her. Go ahead. Talk. Interrupt him and his reverie. Corinne's eyes agreed. Missy, fingertips touching beneath her chin, was content to wait politely. So was Cynthia. Ladies. Perfect ladies. Anyway, Aaron was getting up, was leaving his desk, was moving slowly to the windows, was turning then, opening his overwashed wash-and-wear jacket. He smoothed down the front of his chin beard. "You may or may not know this, but my current nickname in the halls of this school is 'Graybeard Loon'—among my students, especially, the ones who end up liking *The Rime of the Ancient Mariner*. There are some who do. Even these days. Precipice days, I've started calling them. Perplexing times, these times. Mind you, I'm speaking from personal experience, very recent experience—which I suspect you know more about than you're willing to talk about." He looked out the window, but briefly this time. He wanted to, he was ready to, talk now.

"The story in the *Tribune* about my resignation is just that, a story. But so is the rumored story. Those are lies too, which I'm sure you've heard. That's why you came here. I'm grateful you did. At least I have the chance to tell you the truth. Yes, I go to bars. Not a lot, but sometimes. Yes, I saw the Bauers in the Village. The young man I was with was drunk. He was unhappy. I was trying to be...human. As for the other part of the tale, nothing. I never, in all my teaching years—in all my life here or anywhere—ever sexually...ever abused my responsibility as a teacher or a human being."

Loretta slapped the desk part of her chair. "Well, why the hell won't you fight the case, then? Didn't you tell me you had tenure?" But instead of looking at Aaron, she was searching out Evelyn's eyes. She was embarrassed. "I knew about the article in advance. Aaron told me. I'm sorry, Aaron. I didn't mean to betray a confidence."

"You didn't. I did. I divulged much more than you did. Voluntarily. I wanted to. I needed to...talk to people whose affection I value. Your coming here this afternoon was just what I needed. It makes me feel even more secure that what I'm doing—not fighting—is the right thing to do. And, yes, I do have tenure. The school board knows that, of course.

They can get around that easily enough. They read me the moral-turpitude clause in my contract. They sidestepped the human question. They used a Joe McCarthy tactic from the good old days. Remember them? They didn't ask me if what the Bauers said was the truth. They're smarter than that. They asked me if I was a homosexual. That, I didn't deny. I wouldn't. I am." He moved from the window back to his desk. He sat along the edge of it again. He swung his feet back and forth, back and forth, waiting, watching, giving each of them, Evelyn supposed—she had shifted her gaze to the blackboard behind Aaron—a chance for the meaning of what he had said to sink in, for all of them or any of them to react to the fact he had stated without so much as a rapid eyeblink. Courage. He had that. And pride. He wasn't afraid. He was calm, the kind of calm that only innocence allows. How little she actually knew him. After thirteen years of knowing him, she hardly knew ... how he felt at that moment.

"I also see nothing sick about my admission. Which is how they wanted me to feel. They also warned me not to make the fact of my homosexuality an issue, not to admit it publicly in order to prove my innocence in this particular instance. They would really fix me if I did. Their words, *fix me*. I'd never get another job, anywhere, they told me. But if I left quietly, there would be no problem. They would go along with any reasonable story I told. They would even write letters of recommendation, supportive letters." He stared back toward the windows. He listened again to the outside. She watched him. Levittown out there. Levittown all grown up. Levittown all done up in its finest June greenery.

"So ... I decided I'd rather leave 'em laughing. Let my students call me 'Graybeard Loon.' Better that than 'queer.' Better to have them remember me for what I did than for what others would undo, with one word. Also, frankly, my own survival does matter to me. My future matters to me. I've got only myself to depend on. I depend on my dependability. I'm a decent guy. Honest ... you know the type? Principled and all that. Even served my country in time of strife. Another strife. Korea. No one cared if I was a homosexual then. I told them then too."

"Speaking for all of us here ..." Evelyn had been delegated that right and responsibility, and if any one of them present wanted to, she could object, "Speaking, as I say, for all of us ... that part ... that's not important to how we feel."

"Perhaps not. But my being a homosexual is important to

233

how I feel. It's a natural part of me, as natural as it is for someone else to be a heterosexual. I'm not depraved. I don't perform unnatural acts. Only psychopaths do, and they should be pitied and helped, not hated. I've taught school for thirteen years without a problem—until now. I've dealt with over one thousand students without a problem until now. And now I'm being told I can't teach here anymore. No one tells any of you you can't be something anymore, do they?" He looked down at Loretta. But he smiled. She smiled back. They had, between themselves, an understanding, Evelyn realized. So Loretta had been to talk things over with the "Graybeard Loon." Evelyn wouldn't mind the chance to do the same: to talk things over and out and through with someone who would listen and understand and make her think about new things. She'd like that a lot.

So would Missy, probably.

And Corinne, certainly.

Cynthia? Go know! Who knew Cynthia? The Shadow?—and in addition to the five of them, eleven other ladies were ready to talk things over with him, to start up again from where, before Levittown, we left off our lives. So, "Aaron? What about our group? We're prepared to pay you. No fortune. Mad money. We need you. We need someone to get us...up and doing again with our lives."

"Will you tell the ladies about my being a homosexual?"

"Why do we have to?" Cynthia surprised herself by the question: it had just popped out, the expression on her face said, and because it had, she was obliged to continue, to finish what she began. That was Cynthia's *proper* way. "I mean, doesn't the logic you used before—about your students remembering you for what you did—doesn't that apply to the ladies as well? They'll know you for what you do."

He nodded, thinking it over, thinking it out, thinking it through, and then he said, yes, he'd think about doing the group, he'd let them know before the summer was over. He was going to have a lot of things to think about and decide, but, "...no matter what happens, I'll always be grateful for this visit and why you really came here." He stroked his beard, he smiled, he said, "If I decide to go ahead with the group, how about asking your husbands to join? Would you do that? And would you tell *them* about me?" He gazed down at them. He waited.

Evelyn thought it was time for them to leave. *"We'll* have
234

to think about *that*...over the summer. We'll have to meet with all the ladies and decide...about husbands."

"Well, you'll have all summer, too."

As they left, he was smiling. She was glad for that much.

[4]   For the first time since they had moved to Levittown, Harold and she were alone at home together that summer. Danny had settled in Toronto. Morty was "on the road," he called it. The draft board was starting in with him already, too. Eli, at least, was in camp, safe and secure, for now. The Seldens! Every which where.

But just as true for the Geigers. Donald overseas. Adam gone to the Marines. Agnes in camp. Teresa...how did Missy ever get Carl to let her go with Melanie to Europe? A miracle! So the Geigers and the Kleins were alone, and the Feuersteins too, now that Gregory had left for Michigan. Why he had left so early, Corinne wouldn't say and Evelyn wouldn't ask....So, true, most of her friends were alone together that summer with their husbands. And Loretta wasn't even around much. She was commuting with the girls almost every day. They had jobs in the city. Loretta was going to the Art Students League, she said. She enjoyed commuting. Made her feel young again. Which wasn't at all how the rest of them felt, not even when they went out to Jones Beach: no kids anymore to run after and worry about. Now they could sit still and read and talk, play bridge, play gin, play Scrabble, or just plain stare out at the ocean and say nothing at all. Harold did that a lot that summer. All the husbands did, especially after the way Ken Plotkin died.

He was sitting in his beach chair next to Evelyn. They had decided beforehand, all of them had, to stay late at the beach that evening. It was the day after July 4th. They were going to have a kind of picnic, for the regulars. Harold would do hamburgers on his portable grill and roast potatoes in it too. The ladies would bring a big salad, and they bought watermelon and fruit and cakes and drinks. It was all just about to get organized, just before sunset. Harold had started the fire, the potatoes were in. She and Ken were doing some planning on their project: the ultimate beach chair, with compartments for thermos and ice and storage space for beach blanket and magazines and whatever else, and yet light enough and compact enough to carry easily and to price out modestly. Ken had leaned over to show Evelyn where the thermos could fit in, and suddenly, instead of pointing, he

235

was falling, facedown, onto the sand, just behind Evelyn's chair, so that, at first, she didn't realize what had happened. She thought he was still pointing to where, explaining what...

Sally, on the other side of him, she saw. She reached for his arm. It had gone limp. "Ken, will you please stop fooling around? It's not funny. Come on!" And then Evelyn remembered Sally smiling, a frightened smile. "Ken! Come on! Please," and to Evelyn, "Always has to be the joker. Ken! Enough is enough."

By then Evelyn had turned to see. His face was bluish. His freckles paled, drained of any vivid color. Harold was leaning over him. Sandy and Gordon and Carl were all there and crowding nearer, Gordon trying to help Harold lift Ken up.

A snap of the fingers. One, two, three—and Sally was alone for her lifetime, not just for the summer. Ken Plotkin, gone. Only forty-seven. Harold's age, almost to the day. Forty-seven, most of the husbands. Forty-seven or forty-eight or forty-six.

Penny came home for the funeral. Evelyn wrote Aaron to tell him. He was up in Provincetown, where he usually rented each summer, with teacher friends from the city, women, old friends, he wrote back, asking her to explain to Sally why he couldn't get down in time. He would write to Sally as well, but Evelyn could explain better than a letter. He supposed this summer would be his last one up in Provincetown for a while—unless he could decide what to do next, and then do it....

Evelyn felt as if everyone she knew in Levittown was going through that kind of mood. Ken's death made everyone slow down that summer, slow down and sit still more, at home, on the beach, everywhere. She and Harold did a lot more of that too, just sitting and staring out at the ocean. No kids anymore to run after and worry about. Just themselves to worry about.

FRIDAY, AUGUST 13, 1965

Dear Evelyn,

Thank you for your kindness on my behalf with Sally. She seemed to understand and accept my not coming down for the funeral. In her last letter she even suggested that Ken's not knowing me better was his fault. She had been talking to him about his joining the new book group, if it became a reality.

236

More than ever now, she hopes it will. She is counting on its becoming her prod, "the something that keeps her continuing." The tone of her letter was very much the same as yours was that afternoon the five of you visited my classroom. "To start up again from where, before Levittown, you had left off your lives"—those were your words that afternoon. They have, as you can see, remained with me, a reminder of all the unfinished business still left to complete in my own life.

In former years, just about this time, I would have been receiving news concerning the opening of school. Most of my friends here in Provincetown are teachers. Labor Day and the new term are just around the bend in the bay—for them. I admit to a sense of loss. Their talk is filled with the energy of renewal. Until now and ever since I began teaching in Levittown mine would have been too, just about this time. Teaching has always been "the something that keeps me continuing." It will again, but probably not this next year. I have decided to slow down this next year, to live off my thin sliver of reserve, to work part time, to write ... or to discover if I can. I'll start by giving myself a year. I'll also very happily take on the reading group. It will be an exciting kind of challenge. It will keep me connected to people who have given me so much. I hope I can give back as much—and more. When I came to Levittown, I brought nothing with me other than fresh thoughts of a death that had almost stopped me dead in my own tracks. It was the last of a series of deaths that had kept me spinning like a top for years. Levittown steadied me. Levittown was hope and enthusiasm and a future. Therefore, as Sally says, here's to continuing. In spite of the bleakest evidence to the contrary, here's to continuing!

See you soon. My best to Harold.

Sincerely,
AARON

23

[1]   There were across-the-room conversations and side-by-side conversations and bracelets clicking and clanging as arms were raised and dropped and chairs scraping as they were dragged from one corner of her living room to another. "Ladies," Evelyn tried shouting, "enough already. It's past eight-thirty." Volume dropped lower, and then there was the rush and flash of color across the room: Rita in her printed peasant blouse and skirt from her Mexican trip, Corinne in her almost see-through burgundy chiffon blouse, new from Bonwit's, were moving to places on either side of Loretta. Loretta was under Eleanor Roosevelt's picture. Loretta always sat under Eleanor Roosevelt. Missy always sat under Albert Schweitzer at Evelyn's. Cynthia always sat next to the framed photo of Evelyn's dear dead grandmother. She liked to pick it up, study it, smile at it. Habits. Habits. Old habits... and this night they were beginning something new. "Aaron, you'll have to stop them. You're the teacher."

He leaned forward in his wing chair. "Ladies!" Loud—and there was silence and stillness in the room. Edna, Audrey, and Sally, beneath the hanging plants in front of the big back windows, folded their hands in their laps, erect, ready. Even Arlene, the brittle brilliance of her beehive a black glow, settled back into stillness. Aaron's scrutiny contacted each expectant face. Esther Aronowitz next to Arlene, and then Ruby Rabinowitz, tennis-tanned Rose Newman and tiny Toby Margolies, whispering Gladys Ginsburg and Ina Silverstein; the quieter the others became the louder Gladys's whisper sounded. She was explaining her seven-spade grand slam of the night before—and then she realized the only sound in the room was hers. That stopped her.

Evelyn handed Aaron a list, the ladies, in alphabetical order, "...because after tonight our meetings will be alphabetical, starting next month at Esther Aronowitz's, and when we get to Arlene Zweig—we should all live and be well—
238

then it's back to Esther. We're calling ourselves the Ladies of Levittown Wednesday Night Book Group."

Had to be Wednesday, Evelyn had explained to Aaron when she telephoned him in the city to clear that night with him; Monday was going to be anti-Vietnam night; Tuesday was bridge; Thursday, ten of the ladies were also starting a music appreciation course at Hofstra; and Friday, "...Friday is Friday, for the family, for those of us lucky enough to still have some, and, of course, Saturday is also Saturday, although this year we're beginning a new theater group with real casts and directors and producers. We're going to do full-length readings. Sundays...so it has to be Wednesday."

So, Wednesdays it was, and that night, that last Wednesday in September 1965, the meeting was at Evelyn's, which was out of alphabetical order—Loretta was on her feet telling him—"...because we voted to do it that way. As a symbol. The original idea for the group was Evelyn's, so we thought the first meeting should be at her house. And, as Evelyn would say, 'we should all live and be well,' we hope it'll be the first of many, many more meetings. I've been delegated to explain some of this stuff to you, some of the ground rules. Most of it, though, will come out when it needs to. We've elected officers, but the only one who'll matter to you is Toby. She's secretary-treasurer. Each month she'll send you the enormous check you're going to get from us. Maybe it'll buy you a ticket to something. Anyway, Aaron, welcome, and thank you. Our hearts are in the right place."

A hush then. Expectant. Aaron leaned back within the wings of the wing chair she had asked him to sit in. A central chair. He smoothed the front of his beard. Thinking. He stared ceilingward. He looked...how? Healthier than when last seen. Fit. Sunburned. His gray hair had sunlight left in it. It was longer and wavier. He lowered his gaze, unbuttoned the cuffs of his red plaid shirt, pushed each sleeve up, up, above his elbows. Thin arms, but muscular. He leaned forward suddenly; he retied his sneakers. Settled his dungarees' flare. The silence deepened. He wasn't bothered by it. It was his device, his way of holding them fast—as if they needed that. She was ready. They all were. They were overready, ripe, aging fast. So begin, Aaron, she almost said—and then he did. "We can't begin at the beginning of things. Each of our beginnings was different. Each of our lives, therefore, is different, right now, right here. Each of us has come too far to turn back now. Personally, I find myself at a place of disruption. I suppose I should give you the opportunity to question me about my resignation. Perhaps some of you want to...." He waited. He surveyed the silent faces. No one, it seemed to Evelyn, wanted to do anything but get on with her future. But, at least, Aaron had settled the matter with his own conscience. "In that case, we can proceed, we can begin to discover what common ground we share. You tell me what you want. Why don't you begin, Loretta."

Loretta wanted Freud, "...a perfect place to start." Corinne seconded that.

Rita thought *Das Kapital* would be better for the first year.

Sally Plotkin wanted modern poetry, "...Penny told me to say that."

Arlene wanted to go through all of Dostoevsky.

Audrey thought, what could be better than a year of philosophy, from the Greeks to who knows where? Edna Leventhal agreed.

"Well," Missy thought, "if it's beginnings you want, what surpasses the Bible?"

"Freud," Loretta and Corinne yelled out together, followed by Esther Aronowitz calling for, "Kafka. I want Kafka." And Rose Newman screaming, "Joyce, Joyce, Benjy told me Joyce, so I'll say Joyce. What do I know!"

Ruby Rabinowitz loved reading biographies.

Ina Silverstein thought comparative literature was good because, "...it's international and also Burt's health is so good now he's taking a course like that at NYU. I could read his books along with him. We could read together. It'll be good for both of us. It'll keep his heart steady."

And it was then—and quite naturally so—that Aaron raised the issue of husbands being asked to take part in the group, being part of it "...at the beginning? Next meeting, perhaps?"

"No husbands," Evelyn said. "We discussed it. No, for now." Evelyn saw that the red eye on the giant percolator had just come on. Gladys was leaping up, starting for the sideboard where the cakes and cheeses and crackers were set out. "Didn't we also say no about that, Gladys? Remember? No jumping up for coffee until the meeting is over. No elaborate spreads, either?" Gladys returned to her chair under the hanging fern. "Frankly, Aaron, I think you're going to have to choose the books. I know when I read, if you ask me five minutes later what I've read, I can't remember a single idea. And if I do, I don't know how to connect an idea from a book to my life."

"That's just plain age, Evelyn." Arlene's contribution, which Evelyn could have done very well without, thank you!

Cynthia, who until then had said nothing, began folding up those long arms pulling in for the night, crushing breasts and printed silk—and then a sigh. "We can't agree on anything, Aaron. We never can, which is why you're here: to help us learn how."

"In that case, I'll impose my will. Benevolent despot, that I am. We'll begin with *Howards End.*"

"That's my maiden name: Howard." Evelyn felt immediately elated, special, singled out.

"Even better, because it was what you just said, about connecting ideas, that made me decide. 'Only connect'—when you read the book, you'll see what I mean. And you must read the books assigned. No faking it. So, *Howards End,* by E. M. Forster. In paperback. I'll try to keep them all in paperback. Then perhaps *A Passage to India,* by Forster... I think you should write down the titles. Good practice. An aid." There was a rush for pocketbooks, and then Evelyn had to get Eli, who was upstairs doing his homework, to bring down some pencils and paper. Aaron waited. "Like elementary school," he said. Pencils were poised. "The third month we'll do *To the Lighthouse.* Virginia Woolf. Then *Mrs. Dalloway...*" He was smiling. He was enjoying himself too. "We'll do a book a month. Or longer. We could take a year on *Women in Love.* D. H. Lawrence. He'll be fifth.... Am I going too fast?" Everyone was busy writing. "And then...Joyce. Tell Benjy, Rose. Is he liking Colgate still?" A nod from Rose's bent head. *"Dubliners* we'll do first. We'll end the first year with Joyce. It's altogether fitting and proper.... Also, and for the last time...I promise. No husbands? Now? At the beginning?"

"Speaking for mine"—Missy had on her anguished look—"no. Maybe next year."

"Next year? Next year in Israel, sooner." Corinne fluffed and fingercombed. "That they can pay out money for. For that they have time."

"Speak for yourself, Corinne," but Cynthia was clearly speaking for herself and her Sandy. No one else was agreeing with her. The vote was all in Corinne's favor, sad to say. Evelyn would have said it sadly, anyway. Because it was a matter of time. When did Harold have time to read? When did he have time to sit still and think about what he'd read? Or learn how to? When?...Well, now, as a matter of fact. More now than ever before. Now that the kids were gone and didn't need them every minute of every day. Now that Ken Plotkin had died the way he had. It had to be some kind of lesson. It should have been. It was for a while. But now Harold was—all the husbands were—back at it. Pushing. Faster and faster. To make more and more money. Getting further and further away. Getting more and more ground down by overwork, overeating, understimulation.... What to do? How to stop? How? Questions. So many questions about so many things, and no answer-bringers anywhere. That feeling growing inside more and more, since Kennedy was shot, no answers. Only questions. Questions to ask and ask and ask again, and always the questions ended up being the same question, the one on the other side of Aaron's statement before: How do we learn to live with the fact that we've all come too far to turn back now? That we can't start all over again? Just as Aaron said. We can't. We continue. But what if you're stalled on dead center? What then? What to do then? She wanted to learn, somehow, what to do when the will caved in. They all of them in this room wanted to learn that. Slow learners! All of them. But there, nevertheless. Slow! Slow in the body. Slow in the brain, but there, ready to try. Bone bracelets clunking to stillness; brass and silver and gold bracelets clanging and clinking, and then brought to rest by eager fingers.

Colors flashed. Raised arms were lowered, were settled to stillness across ample breasts and hips and stomachs. So what! They were there. The ladies were waiting in perfect stillness for Aaron to continue.

He took a deep breath—and she remembered, as if it had happened the day before, that other day, in 1952, when he had introduced himself, when he had said to her, to Missy, about Adlai losing, "All important battles are uphill...but you just have to take a deep breath and continue," which he was doing. "The mind, I'm sure I won't be the first one to point out to you, is a miracle of genetic engineering, the most recently evolved piece of human equipment, and the most important, because with its emergence comes consciousness. Out of that comes awareness. But the mind, like any other part of the body, needs to be used and stretched and tested. It needs to be nourished. Ideas do that. Old ones. New ones. Sound ones. Faulty ones. All kinds. All the time. Otherwise,
242

if the mind isn't used, isn't used for the purpose evolution has given it, if it falls into disuse, there's no reason to suppose it won't atrophy, shut down, turn off, be naturally selected out of the evolutionary process... like a tonsil or an appendix. The most recent piece of human equipment could be the first to go."

He paused. He gazed ceilingward, waiting, as if he were waiting for his next thought to arrive. "Perhaps no one agrees with me. Perhaps I'm not making myself understood. If that's true... if that becomes true in the future, please then some-one say something. Tell me."

The ladies remained silent. There was no shuffling, no chair squeaks, no movement. There was almost no sound of breathing. Aaron's gray-eyed gaze shifted from face to face. "What I'm talking about—the mind shutting down—that wouldn't happen within our lifetimes. No. Although atomic holocaust is always possible. That would put an end to every-thing. That would take the skin off everything we've ever said about civilization, wouldn't it?" He laughed... alone.

Evelyn wasn't sure she knew what he was talking about, but she knew she wanted to try to. Some of what he was saying were thoughts she'd never considered before.

"In any case, we here are going to proceed *as if* the mind matters. *As if* it will always matter to most people. That will be our part in the evolutionary process. Too grand? Too pre-tentious? So what? Let's pretend. Let's pretend that when you begin *Howards End*—Evelyn's maiden name, our first connection—when you look at the first sentence, 'One may as well begin with Helen's letters to her sister,' you'll think of it as our beginning. A starting out. You'll meet Helen and you'll meet her sister Margaret. They live in England during a time of great social change. You live in America during a time of great social change. 'Only connect,' the book says. Connect one time to another. See if you can. Try. Start out. Begin...." But that was where he was going to end the first session. He slapped his thighs. "Enough for tonight. I don't want to spoil the pleasure of reading the book by telling you too much."

And then it was time for coffee and cake.

Gladys was first at the giant percolator.

There was a rush of words, of conversation starting up, of movement in the living room, a following of Aaron over to the food and coffee. The ladies all wanted to ask him... things. About his summer and about how it felt not to be in Levittown every day. Not to be teaching. How would he survive? Evelyn handed him a cup of coffee. The ladies circled him, asking, asking, asking. Sally Plotkin, petite Sally Plotkin, alone now, stiff-upper-lipping it, asking Aaron how long it would be before she would understand about... evolution. And Esther Aronowitz asking Aaron how long it would take her to become a teacher, because all her life she had wanted to become a teacher or a nurse or a... something of service... to people. No one asked him anything about his resignation. Polite. Considerate. Kind. Trained that way. Able, most of them, to keep a confidence. Evelyn watched them come up to Aaron, say something like thank you, thank you for this chance, this opportunity, this "new beginning," Rose Newman said, "because now that Benjy and Dolores are at college, it is that. One part of my life is ended and another one begins. You're right...." She didn't want to let him go. None of them did. Everyone wanted to hold on to Aaron for dear life.

He stayed on, talking, answering, turning, to this one, to that one. Polite. Polite ladies, too. Even Arlene. Even she would wait to find out... things... in time. Probably only Loretta knew *about* Aaron. And Loretta wouldn't tell. Loretta wouldn't divulge a confidence either. Loretta was polite. Loretta, for all her candor, knew when to speak out and when not to. Loretta, like the rest of them, had a conscience, respected the rights of others, was kind, considerate, cared. Yes. Trained that way, brought up that way, growing up before the war, the world war to end all wars, number two; a person's business is a person's own business; only speak when spoken to; be honest; act responsibly. They had all behaved that way. She certainly had, and now all she had were questions. Forty-three years old. Or forty-three years young. In between. Middle-aged. With memories to match. Remembering, more and more of the time. Middle-aged memory: it felt like a monster inside her head, a monster with a million fingers, each finger pressing the present life out of her head, forcing her, more and more of the time, to resee, relive, remember, the people she'd loved and lost, the dead of her life alive in her head too much of the time... and what she really wanted to do was start out again. Must be something like fate that Aaron had come along when she, when all of them, most needed him. Yes.

And fate too that when the ladies began to leave, Missy and Corinne and Cynthia and Loretta stayed on. Aaron had asked them to. He wanted to thank them, the five of them,

244

"...because this period in my life has been one of the hardest. The wheel of fortune goes down. It also, fortunately, comes up again. It has to. You've helped it move up faster." He kissed each of them, and then he left for the city.

[2]   When Harold came home from poker, she was in bed, but she was far from sleep. A mind in the middle of the tumble cycle had kept her far away from sleep, and reading had been out of the question too. She had turned out the lamp on her bedside table. She would think. She would lie there in the darkness, listening to the sounds of their house, and to Eli, tossing and turning away from a dream in his bed in the room above theirs, and she would try to think things through: starting from one place, one event, connecting it to another place, another event, just as Aaron had said to do it; tracing one time to another time—but then Harold came in from poker.

He was tired. No, he didn't want to hear about the meeting. Not then. Tomorrow. It was almost one o'clock already, and he had to be up early, to get up to White Plains as early as he could in the morning, for an auction of some jewelry and gold and silver, from an estate. "You'll tell me all about the meeting tomorrow night, at dinner."

"Should I make an appointment?"

"Why're you starting in with me now, Evelyn? At one in the morning?"

"And why do you have to raise your voice? You're right next to me. I can hear you perfectly. Does Eli have to hear too?"

He turned back onto his back. He sighed. "Okay. What happened that made it so great?" From his table he took a cigarette, lit it, inhaled so deeply he began coughing, coughing so hard he had to sit up.

"Harold—and don't start yelling again—will you do yourself a favor? Will you do me a favor and put out that cigarette? You don't need it. You especially don't need it in bed."

He rested his elbow on a raised knee. He stared down at her. "Is there anything I'm allowed to do you approve of these days? Is there?"

"Is there anything wrong with my telling you something that's meant to be helpful? You smoke and you cough and you have trouble breathing, but you still go on smoking. Is that intelligent?"

"Who ever said I was intelligent?"

245

"Why is it so hard for us to talk to each other without fighting? We're not exactly strangers—or maybe we are. Maybe that's what's happening."

"And what's that supposed to mean? Because I tell you it's late? Because I have to get up early? Because I didn't ask you right away about your lousy meeting?" He stabbed the air between them with his glowing cigarette.

"Please watch the ash, Harold."

"Dammit!" He turned away, stubbed out his cigarette, fell onto his side, facing away from her. "I'm going to sleep. I don't want to talk about...anything. I don't know how. I told you I'm not intelligent enough. I'm not your...your Aaron Rothstein."

"Now, that's just plain—"

"Stupid. I know. That's what I'm saying. That's what I'm trying to tell you. I'm stupid."

"You're also being cruel. You don't even really know Aaron. I hardly do."

"I know you think he's smarter than all of us, smarter and more sensitive and more understanding."

"He is. Certainly more than you're being right now. You won't even try to understand me. You won't even try to talk about what interests me or that I want a chance to...to improve myself."

"Why do you have to? As far as I'm concerned, you're fine the way you are. What's made you so unhappy? So discontented? When we were married, what did you expect was going to happen to you?"

"I expected that because I always tried to understand how you felt about things inside, you would do the same with me. That's what I expected. Harold? In a few years Eli's going to be gone too, and then it's going to be the two of us alone for the rest of our lives. What's wrong with trying to learn more or understand more? What would be wrong with going to college if I thought I could handle it?"

"Nothing. Nothing would be wrong with it."

"Won't you turn around?" She reached over. She pulled him around, onto his back. "I like to look at you. I always like to look at you, even in the dark."

He lay there staring up at the ceiling. He sighed, but not out of annoyance now. He was quieter. She smoothed the hair back from his forehead. "Just because I want to learn about ideas I never had a chance to learn about before..."

"I never did either."

246

"I know, Harold. That's what I meant. This should be the time. It's the only time we're ever going to have. Aaron keeps saying the husbands should join our group too. You said no. They all say no. You have no time to read. You told me that a hundred times already. And does that mean I shouldn't? Does it have to mean, if I do, that I don't value all the things we've had together? Because if you think that, you know you're wrong. Dead wrong. I do value them. I love you. But I didn't grow up thinking that at the end of my life my highest accomplishment was going to be that I was a grandmother, especially if the son that's going to make me a grandmother has had to move to another country in order to stay alive. Who even knows if Danny will ever come back here?"

"Who knows anything for sure? No one." He sat up. He put his arms around her. He rubbed her back. "I love you too. You know that. You also know I want you to have the chance to do everything you want to do. I'm proud of all you do, always. You know that. Do I have to tell you I am?"

"Yes. And you also have to try to tell me how you feel inside yourself about what *you* want."

"What I want, Ev...I don't know what else to want. And even if I did, it's too late to change the way I am. It's too late to change the way the world works."

"I don't believe that. I'll never believe that."

"That's why you're you, Ev, and I'm me—and now you've got your reading group. Enjoy it. If you do, I will too. I promise." He lowered her back onto her pillow. He leaned over her. It had been a long time since he even seemed like he wanted to make love.

24

Loretta and Aaron, 1966

APRIL 27, 1966
WEDNESDAY NIGHT

Dear Aaron,

As you can see from above, you've all only just left. You're still driving along the Long Island Expressway into the city even as I write this down. You of all people probably can figure out why I had to write to you. To apologize is one of my reasons. If the ladies were back here I'd apologize to them too. I'm feeling sorry for myself, and what you didn't know and what I want you to know (you should have known before anyone, but I'm like everyone of my generation—I can't speak up about what's most important to me, even tough me can't) is that Joe and the girls are now living with his mother in Astoria. I'm alone in the house. It's up for sale, and as soon as it's sold I'm going to be moving away, to California, as a matter of fact. And I'm going to be moving out there with a woman, a Michelle Isaacson who has just gotten a degree in social work. This is all by way of maybe explaining my behavior tonight. I'm sorry for blowing up. I'm sorry if it caused you any difficulty, because, even though you don't realize it, in lots of ways you've saved me these last few months. Just having the book group, just sitting there at meetings knowing that you knew about me was like being rich all of a sudden. We shared something without saying a word. And then there were all those times I visited you in the city and you let me get things off my chest— that was an act of friendship I guess I've never had from anyone, not even Corinne, who is my closest friend out here. Corinne knows about me. Evelyn I've never leveled with. She never seemed to want to talk about it. She probably would have done the same thing with me that she did with you that day in your classroom when you told us all. She'd say: What difference does it make? You're my friend no matter what, and you can count on me no matter what. Which is fine as far as it goes, but I don't think it's far enough. Evelyn doesn't really

248

want to try to understand how I feel inside. But don't get me wrong. I love her. It's just that she's always ready to talk about Women's Strike for Peace. She's never willing to talk about the kind of piece a woman might want in bed. I hope you can get her to change, Aaron. Corinne, on the other hand, has talked and talked and talked about me—but in the past. She's clammed up a lot recently. My guess is that it's because of Gregory. She won't say and, believe it or not, I'm embarrassed to ask her.

So, you're still wondering, while I ramble on, why did I let Cynthia have it tonight? I'm not one hundred percent sure, but I do know it grew out of Women in Love and our discussion of Gudrun and when Cynthia said for the one thousandth time how she hated the book. For me, when she said it tonight, it was one of those moments people say they'll remember all their lives. Or like you say about some books that after you finished reading them you're never the same again. Well, that's what happened to me. The giant percolator had just stopped its percolating, the red eye was blinking open. Perfect timing, I thought, and anyway, it was my living room in my house on Whisper Lane, and if I want to tell Cynthia she's full of shit, I can. So I did, and while I was waiting for her to come back at me, I kept looking up at those paintings I'd done of all the ladies. Evelyn's and Corinne's, of course, I love. Missy's too, in a delicate way. Rita's is good too. Even Cynthia's is, but I was looking at them in a different way suddenly, as if they were over with for me, that I'd be leaving them—and that I wanted to. And that I'd have to be packing the pictures away with all my other collections, of shells from the beach, and pressed flowers, of buttons and strings, ribbons, rubber bands, shoelaces—and more, lots more I was collecting for the time in the future I was going to start doing collages. I suppose I won't now. I suppose when I move out to California I'll throw away all that junk. Anyway, when Cynthia said that about hating the book and about how selfish Gudrun was and how unwomanly, I had to tell her she was full of shit. I had to say that trying to discover herself as a person was what mattered to Gudrun, not whether she was womanly or manly or whatever. I really thought I understood Gudrun. I don't think Cynthia does, because she doesn't want to. I put in my slave years as a woman. I admit it to myself. Cynthia doesn't. It's been hard doing what I did. Ever since I told Joe about myself, these have been the hardest years of my life. He was always trying to get me into some kind of trap so our divorce papers

249

would say I was a lesbian and then I wouldn't be able to see my own daughters. Can you beat that? But what do they know about lesbians in Levittown? What do they know about anything in Levittown? All of us moved into a housing development—that's what it really was—on the ugliest piece of land in Nassau County, on flat potato land, and we called it paradise. Instant suburb. What did we know? We were Catholics. We were Jews. Schnooks. Victims always. Protestants had the real suburbs. Grosse Pointe. Shaker Heights. Oyster Bay . . . fill in whatever name you want. Protestants aren't giving any of their powers away, believe me. Well, never mind about that part of it, because it doesn't really have anything to do with why I told Cynthia she was full of shit—or does it, Aaron? (I can hear you saying: Only connect, only connect.) And then Cynthia doesn't say anything back to me. She just folds up those long arms of hers and stares at me and tells me, finally, she has a right to her opinion. Which of course she does. And at that moment I felt ashamed of myself. I felt as if I had let you down, as if I hadn't really listened to what you'd been saying all these months about how people had to change slowly, about how they had to be persuaded to change. But then, in the next minute, I felt just as certain that I hadn't let you down at all, that maybe Cynthia had, because I at least was declaring my independence for the first time, that I was trying to act like Gudrun or Helen Schlegel might. Maybe I don't belong to easy categories, but maybe I don't want to. Maybe I prefer being different. I'm no Clarissa Dalloway or Mrs. Ramsay or Adela Quested. But I am a Loretta and I feel cheated and I don't think it's too late for me to get out from under—literally and figuratively. I'm not even menopausal yet. Maybe, I thought during that moment, this is my chance and I better take it now, because if it wasn't now it would be never. So, I did and I am, thanks largely to you, Aaron, for making me get up off my ass and start thinking I was worth something. The girls are old enough. They're also old enough to understand something of what I am. They'll probably never understand all of it, but neither will I probably. They may never think what I did was the right thing to do to them. They may never agree with me—but no one ever agrees with everyone one hundred percent—not even Cynthia has to. I have my reasons. Cynthia has hers. She's got her husband and her own ideas about things. They aren't mine. Gudrun's are closer to mine. So be it—as you often say at the end of an unfinished argument or discussion. So be it . . . for now, for me. To be continued, somewhere else. I keep thinking about that word from Women in Love: *"wohin."* Herr Loerke said it. *Wohin?* Where? Where are we going? Any of us. All of us. Lesbian or straight. Alone or together. Where? Because we all have to go somewhere. Well, for me, for now, I'm going to California with someone named Michelle Isaacson, which was another thing I wanted to tell you in this letter. The only other thing I wanted to tell you was, thank you, Aaron.

Love,
LORETTA

25

Missy and Aaron, 1968

[1]   Her lovely house. Her warm, inviting house....

Even on such a day, even filled with so many people standing still, looking over at her, at Carl, not knowing what they
could do, what they could say, that would help. The ladies,
her beautiful, lovely friends, moved among them all, serving,
coffee, tea, cakes they had made and brought over, and
drinks, a sherry for Missy's mother, who leaned down over
her, stroking her hair from time to time, sighing from time
to time, crying. So many of them were crying.

She wouldn't.

Neither would Carl. He sat next to her on the love seat,
kneading his bad leg through the gray flannel of his pants,
his gaze cast down, absorbed, as if he were in deep debate
with the shag pile of the carpet. And then someone would
break away from a group, would lean down over him, over
her, to tell them both how sorry, how terrible, a shock—and
then move back, away, not knowing what else they could say,
or do, that would help. Nothing would help now. Nothing.
Not even afternoon sunlight, bright in the room, stirring the
colors of its prints, her needlepoint pillows, glinting on her
polished brass and copper and pewter. No. Nothing would
help. Not even Donald over there, looking out through the
back bay window, his arms around Agnes, his uniformed
arms around Agnes, while nearby Eli Selden was trying to
get her to come outside with him, to come away from the
window and go outside. She wouldn't. She wouldn't leave her
brother. She pushed Eli away, back, against Aaron. Aaron
caught Eli as he stumbled, held him upright. Aaron had
driven out from the city, to help too. Aaron was trying to talk
to Donald. She saw Donald's lips moving, but he did not turn
toward Aaron. He wouldn't. Dour, an Aaron word to describe
her Donald. Dour, Donald's eyes squinting into the sun, the
sun glistening along the tips of his crew cut. So close-cropped
that crew cut. So trim his navy-blue dress uniform. Hand-

some. Handsome Donald. But much handsomer four years back, 1964, before the Navy, with long black wavy hair then, his fine features freer, not so stern, not so harsh and set as they were now. Harsh and stern and hurt, hurt and crushed under that mask of anger. That's what it was: a mask. He wanted to cry as much as they wanted to—and wouldn't. A man wouldn't.

The ladies were crying. They moved through the room with trays, asking, smiling, and crying.

A space opened in front of her. Aaron entered it, knelt down before her, hunkering, he called it when they read Faulkner—why would she remember that word just then? All of a sudden. Aaron hunkering. "You knew him so well, Aaron." He held her hand in his. He squeezed it. Two and a half years since the reading group started; two and a half years of thinking and rethinking things. "Today . . . tonight . . . we were supposed to have a meeting tonight. Weren't we, Aaron? It's the last Wednesday in April, isn't it? We were going to do the Nighttown section tonight. . . . This has been the best year so far . . . for the group. Until now." She covered her face. She would not cry. She would not allow herself to cry. She fingered her little gold cross, separated its chain from her strand of pearls. She rubbed the cross between her fingers. "So many times you came to this house, Aaron. In the past. Before the group, I mean. When you came as a teacher, to talk about . . . his progress. His and Donald's. Adam was a year behind him. In junior high. You had them both in English. Donald eighth. Adam seventh. And in 1964 again. Remember? Donald was in twelfth, Adam eleventh. Just four years ago, Aaron. Four little years. . . ." She let go of her cross. She touched his beard. "Even you've changed. Your beard's shaggier. So is your hair. Why do you always look so glum? The only time you don't is when we're at a meeting. Then you come alive. But when we get together in the city, you're always glum. What happens then?"

"I don't know. Maybe it's just the city does it. Maybe I'll have to move from Bank Street to the country somewhere. Upstate maybe. Out here to the suburbs."

"This is no suburb. You're always telling us that. . . . I'm sorry about tonight. We'll make it up. Reading *Ulysses* has been . . . so marvelous. And remember how I was against doing it? Remember how I talked about the Church and Joyce? How I fought it? I'm glad I lost that battle. Other battles . . . others . . . if only I'd won some of those others." Once more she covered her face. She would be as all right as the circumstances allowed. She put her hand on top of Carl's, the one working at his leg. She stopped it. She wanted him to stop. It was driving her crazy to watch him working, kneading, rubbing his leg, all the while studying the shag pile of the carpet.

"You must stop, Carl, darling," she whispered. "You must. Do you want me to get you something? Some coffee, or a drink? How about a brandy, Carl?" He nodded no. "Then I'll be back in a moment." She gestured for her mother to please come sit down next to Carl.

She made her way past the Zweigs, the Silversteins, the Ginsburgs, touching them as she went, trying to steady herself that way, trying to smile too, trying to show them she was in control. She wanted to be over at the window, next to Donald and Agnes.... Where was Teresa? Why couldn't she have come home in time? Why? Why such cruelty? It had to be intentional, otherwise...Not even a telegram to let them know where she had gotten to. Cynthia knew where Melanie was. Why couldn't Teresa...? She put her arm through Donald's. She leaned against him: her only son now.

She stared out at the sun-filled garden. The perimeter of privet hedge Carl had planted when they moved from Spiral Lane to this house: her lovely house. And her herb garden: laid out in a wheel, inside each spoke, herbs; and the rock garden for which Carl had brought in earth so she could create an artificial rise at the back of the yard, behind the herbs; and the extra maples she had wanted, the birdbath, the birdhouses, the rectangle of smooth rich earth that would be her vegetable garden. In another month she would be planting it. "Oh, God," she cried, and Donald turned to hold her. Agnes moved to Missy's other side, looking up, crying too. "Adam," Missy cried. "Adam.... You're not going to go there, Donald. I won't let you. Do you hear me? I won't let you."

"I hear you, Mother. Everyone does. Don't scream, please, Mother. No need to do that. We'll talk later. When everyone's gone. Later."

She quieted down; the murmurs, the whispers, began again, behind her. She smoothed Aggie's hair back from her forehead, Aggie's black hair, like Carl's, like Donald's, like Teresa's. Only Adam's had been blond, like hers. Gold. Gold blond. So shiny, like the gold in her lovely room. Gone. Adam was gone. Forever. Forever and a day. *Lacrimosa dies illa,*

254

the priest had chanted that morning at the requiem service. *Lacrimosa*—and then, as now, her tears came again, quietly. Jesus and tears. Thoughts of a lifetime. Her habit. Quiet. Calm, but not resigned. Never resigned to this death that should not have been. Not at twenty-one. Not in a place she'd never heard of before in her life and that she would never forget now for the rest of it. Khe Sanh. Khe Sanh. Khe Sanh. An ache in her throat. Like her tears. Pulsing. Gushing. "Adam," she cried out again.

Evelyn was there. Evelyn took hold of her, took her inside the circle of Corinne and Cynthia and herself—and Aaron, too.... But no Loretta. Loretta had telephoned from San Francisco, as soon as she heard about...it. Evelyn had phoned her. Loretta. Far away. Far away from their lives.

And on the other side of the room Missy saw Joe and Maria and Angela. Even Maria and Angela had taken the day off from work to drive out with Aaron, to drive back to Levittown for this day. This day....

For this waste. "Adam," she whispered, swaying inside the circle of her friends. But she could see to where Donald was, across the room. She could see him, and then she could hear him. He wouldn't accept Gregory's hand. "Cruel, Donald," she whispered. A terrible waste of feeling. Gregory turned away. He came to Missy. He kissed her. He kissed Corinne, told her he was going into the city with Penny, who was driving in with Mark Moskowitz. Yes, he'd call her before he left to go back to school. Yes, he had a place to stay in the city. With a friend. Don't worry, he told her.

And then he went over to Lionel. Lionel nodded. That was all. Lionel was talking to Harold and Max Zweig and Gordon Ginsburg and Sandy Klein. Lionel was embarrassed. Lionel had no time. Lionel was worried about how they felt about Gregory. It was all over his face. Not Gregory's. Gregory wasn't worried about hate. Gregory was used to it. Missy wasn't. Never would be. Hate killed Adam. "Adam!" A sob then, a crying out. They held her up: her friends, her ladies, in her lovely living room on Wishbone Lane. Morty Selden, down from Syracuse for Adam's funeral, was saying, extending his hand to Donald, "Come on, Donny. I'm your friend, Donny. It isn't my fault what happened...." But Donald moved away, took Aggie with him back to where Carl was, back behind the love seat where Carl and her mother sat, neither of them willing to talk to each other, separate, unaccepting, the way they had always been with each other, resigned, mute, in a state of truce, always.

Morty shrugged. He smiled at Eli. He kissed Missy. He'd take Eli home, he told Evelyn. He'd wait there, not to worry, to take her time. He kissed Missy again, and Corinne, Cynthia. He shook Aaron's hand. He held on to Eli the way Donald had held on to Aggie. They moved off to where Harold was. Morty would go back to Syracuse. Morty would stay in school, like it or not, so that he wouldn't be drafted. He would keep on, he would survive, in his patchwork dungarees, his blue denim workshirt, his antique beige corduroy jacket, faded, shredding at the cuffs. He kissed Harold. Harold held him. Lionel shook his hand, and Max and Gordon and Sandy Klein reached up to tousle his black curly hair. Sandy was losing his. Even Sandy Klein was getting older.

The circle broke up then. She was all right. Missy assured them she was. She was under control. Not to worry.

[2] She asked Aaron to stay. "Carl wants you to as well." Maybe Aaron could talk to Donald. "He wants to volunteer for duty in Vietnam. Maybe if you reason with him, maybe he'll listen to you."

But Donald remained dour. He wasn't listening to anything Missy said or Aaron said. Carl seemed unable to talk. Neither did her mother. Carl got up from the love seat across from Donald and Aggie. He paced back and forth between the fireplace and the back bay window; he stopped to stare outside. The sun would be low in the west, on the other side of the house. Missy went to him. "Maybe someday, Carl, you'll just take the whole house and turn it around so we can see the sunset. Someday you can..." She stopped. He had begun to cry finally. He didn't want to move away from the window. He was embarrassed. She knew that expression. Donald had it too. So did Agnes. Not Teresa. Dour was not all of it. There was another part to it, that part of being taciturn which was about anger held in place, checked, concealed, like unusable passion, a frustration as universal as dying sunlight reflected but unseen, and so Carl was embarrassed and Donald seemed intent on committing suicide. Because that's what it sounded like to her. Donald was telling Aaron, "...yes, now more than ever. Now more than ever I want to go there. For him. For Adam's sake. Now more than ever I want to stay in the Navy, otherwise all of what's going on is unbelievable, Mr. Rothstein. Unbelievable. Crazy."

"But it is that, Donald. It's all that, and it's more, and if you join in it, then you add to it, especially now."

"You were in the Army, weren't you, Mr. Rothstein? And so was my father. My father was even wounded. Almost killed. Why was *he* in it? Why was *he* there? Why were you? And are you going to tell me about how the times were different? How the reasons for those wars were different? Don't. I know all that. I've heard all that. But, still, when you were drafted, you went. All I did instead of waiting to be drafted was to enlist. So did Adam. It was just a matter of time anyway. My father even agreed—"

"Your father..." Carl turned then, turned her too, to face Donald and Aggie and Aaron, all of them sitting still in the darkening light of her lovely living room. "Your father... was very wrong... about so many things."

Like a handkerchief falling, she felt herself floating down to the floor, slowly, ever so slowly, her legs giving way.

Carl caught her. Carl held her up. He got her over to the sofa. He knelt before her, taking hold of her hand, rubbing it.

The others were there too, her mother swaying behind Carl, swaying and crying and clutching Missy's chin, not knowing what she could do anymore for her little girl who was all grown up and who had almost fainted. Her mother! Her mother took hold of Aggie, pressed her to her side, instantly smoothing back Aggie's wisping hair. Aggie was crying. Aggie would not let her father touch her.

Only Donald would she let take hold of her next. Not her grandmother or her mother or father, only Donald. "Don't go 'way, Donald. Stay home here with us. You heard what Daddy said. Please, Donald?" She had her arms around his waist. She looked up at him, tears running down her smooth child's skin. "I don't want you to die too. Please?"

Donald said nothing. He stared down at his father kneeling. She saw his face, because by then Missy had regained her control. She made Carl stand up. She stepped past her mother and Donald and Aggie. She went up to Aaron, who had remained near the back window. She apologized for her behavior. She apologized for the behavior of her entire family. "...and thank you for trying. But it's too late. He's made most of his choices by now. We all do, sooner or later, as you always tell us." She spoke up so the others would hear. "Some of us have to stick by them. Loyalty. That's a way to live too." She embraced him, offered her cheek, turned to return to the remnant of her family.

26

Corinne and Aaron, 1968

[1] Aaron suggested the idea for the party: on Bloomsday, June 16, 1968, in his floor-through on Bank Street. He wanted to give them something. It was altogether fitting. For endurance—after ten months on *Ulysses*. "Husbands too. Let them see where we're at, as they say these days."

Corinne volunteered to work out all the details with him. They would meet in the city. They would plan everything. Some of the ladies would do covered casseroles and they'd make salads, pies, the works. No problem at all. She telephoned to tell him to meet her for lunch in the sculpture garden of the Museum of Modern Art. "Love it there under the trees, in the shadows. Hides me. It's so dramatic. A canopy of trees in the city. And so peaceful. In the heart of the city, that hush..."

Fine. He liked it there too.

Unfortunately, the day they met for lunch, there was no peace anywhere.

On the terrace, under the canopy of trees, silent people, but no peace. They were listening—so was she, so was Aaron—to a portable radio on a nearby table, for a word, for news, from Los Angeles, all of them waiting to find out: would he live, would he die?—another Kennedy.

"Almost two months to the day after the assassination of Martin Luther King..." the announcer said. The volume was turned lower.

The hush returned to the sculpture garden. A hum in the air above them. And from beneath their feet, from under the slate of the terrace, another humming sound, a hum alive at the heart of every silence she had ever heard in the city. Like a distant motor that never shut down. All those years she had been coming to this garden alone—a lot, too many to count—and not really to see art so much as to listen to that distant hum at the heart of the city's hush. Awesome—now that she had been through three years of the book group, she used words like that. She wasn't embarrassed. Awesome, that sound at the heart of every silence. She heard it every time she came here. In those years, years before, when she was drinking too much, when she was always planning how she would leave Lionel, she would come to this garden, alone, and listen and think about what she had dreamed of becoming—and hadn't. In those years, years before, she could have been a contender. Like they said in the movies: she could have been a contender. Not anymore. And it was a person dying that made her think of time, of the time she was living through, living out, and of those years, years before...

"A nightmare," Aaron was saying. "An absolute nightmare. So much for reason and reasonable minds in an insane world. What's the good of reason?"

She sure as hell didn't know. She knew shit. She knew about sitting in shadows and about sunspots on the slate and the breeze moving them. Like walking inside a following spotlight. That she knew. She also knew that now that she had Aaron there across from her she wanted to speak to him about more than the Bloomsday party. Especially on this day.

The radio volume was turned higher, then lower—no further word from L.A.

The breeze died down. The sunspots were still. Sticky hot humid June noon. "You know, Aaron, I've gone through some shitty times in my life. Let me tell you I have. Not that I don't realize we all have. You have. Missy. Gregory. But when is there going to be some end to it? How the hell did we all get locked inside this goddamn toilet?" She looked across at him shrugging, pulling at the edges of his beard. Graybeard Loon! In an Indian kurtah yet. A wild print that she should be wearing. Red. She loved it. She used to have that kind of style, that kind of pizzazz. Now look at yourself. Look at yourself, Corinne Feuerstein. A drab! In a basic orange halter-top dress. And the Ladies of Levittown's nonresident part-time teacher-sage was shrugging again. "Who knows! Who knows anything anymore."

He poked at his salad, because it was there, under his fork.

The portable radio was turned up again. "...and there is still no word. The vigil outside the hospital is being kept by hundreds. The crowd grows in number as the silent waiting continues."

"Maybe we should call off our party, Corinne. Too much dying this spring for a Bloomsday party."

"No. We'll have it. No matter what. Life, as they say, goes on."

"...and doctors are saying that the nature of the wound is such that if he does pull through there will be permanent brain damage. They are not willing to say more than that." Once more the volume was turned low. Once more the hum at the heart of the silence filled her head. She gazed out of the shadows to where the bright sun glinted white on the surface of the shallow reflecting pool. Her mind had gone white too. A blank. And she had things to say to Aaron. Lots of things. She knew—but what? She *was* getting old. Like it or not! Time marches on. Drying is aging.... She was turning into a harum-scarum. Like Molly Bloom. What it was with herself was that part of her brain had been pickled in alcohol. In those years before, it had been pickled. Parts of it were never going to operate again. Permanent damage. The shooting. The party. Yes. She had to talk to him about the party. She wouldn't let him back down. What's one more death, unless it's your own...or one of your own? "Aaron, listen. Listen to me, Aaron."

But he too had turned to gaze out over the reflecting pool, out toward the slim pencil building that turned its back to the museum and garden, its front toward Fifth Avenue, listening to the continuing report. "Claims are now being circulated that Sirhan Sirhan did not act alone but with a woman accomplice. She was apparently in the kitchen of the Ambassador Hotel at the time of the shooting. She was wearing a polka-dot dress..."

Corinne stabbed deep into the mound of salad in front of her. "Aaron, listen, listen to me, Aaron."

"I'm listening, Corinne."

"I have to talk to you."

"Talk, Corinne. Go ahead. Talk."

"I just wanted to make sure you were listening to me, because I need your advice." But first she sipped from her iced tea. She also needed nourishment, energy, courage. She took out her compact. She squinted. She fluffed the edges of her split-end, freshly dyed, outrageously red hair. Outrageous! That red, next to the orange of her dress. She tried to roll the edges of her hair under, into some semblance of a pageboy. It never worked anymore. Still, she kept on trying. "I keep trying to look like Ann Sheridan's sister. An image from my youth. Do you know, I still use the same shade of powder I used to use in the Forties? I even go to Bonwit Teller's to get it. Some habits never die. But some habits don't hurt anybody either....Listen, Aaron, Gregory has moved out for good. Forever. He's not coming home from school this summer. He told me he wrote to you. He told me to speak to you, that you could explain it all. He told me he's fallen in love with a...someone."

"A man. Yes. Say it, Corinne. It won't hurt. Or if it does, it'll only hurt for a second. He did write to me. He told me his plans. He told me—"

"Did he tell you that Lionel went to the draft board in Levittown? That he told them Greg was graduating, and eligible to be drafted? Lionel did that, Aaron. He's willing to see his own son go into the Army. And you know why? Would you believe why? In 1968? Lionel is still saying the Army will make a man of Greg. He'd rather see him a dead man than alive and...a homosexual." She snapped her compact shut. She had been using it to help her say what she had to say, like holding on to a cross or a Star of David or a charm: her past, her powder, her picture of herself as Ann Sheridan. Dead. Dead as a doornail, as they used to say. "It's hard to believe a father would do such a thing. It's hard to believe I would have a husband that would do it—but I do, and I suppose I'm stuck with him. That's because I'm the kind of person that wouldn't hurt anybody else, only myself, which may be why Lionel and I are still together. I'll admit that to you, Aaron. I'll admit that today. Tomorrow? I don't know how I'll feel tomorrow. So don't hold me to it, because I might still decide to pull a Loretta. Who knows? Because Lionel's latest *shtiklach* is really a killer. Maybe it's Lionel who's going through change of life. Even before me. So, Aaron, listen. Please."

"I am, Corinne."

"I've got only one more question, and I have to ask it. Remember, I'm a mother asking. Right? A mother, however, of a son who is also a homosexual. Okay? And what I want to ask is, when you get depressed, when you think about some of the horrible things that have happened to you, say when you think about your friend who was killed in Korea— Loretta told me about that. We all know. The five of us know. Anyway..."

"Corinne, ask me already. Ask your question. Please? What is it?"

"I'm asking. I'm getting to it. In my own way, Aaron. As a mother...of a homosexual son...when you get depressed and you can't stand another second of bullshit about being a homosexual, do you think about committing suicide because you are one?"

"No."

"And?"

"And nothing. Just no, Corinne. I don't. There are far worse things in this world. And what difference does it make to how the world works if every once and again a man and a man or a woman and a woman touch each other tenderly? What vast cosmic plan does it threaten? When my friend died in Korea, he didn't die because he was a homosexual. He probably could have stayed out of the Army if he had told them he was. He chose not to. I did too...at first. But after I was drafted, after I was separated from my friend, I told them. They didn't discharge me. They wouldn't. They told me I had to be caught in the act before it mattered. Would I commit suicide over something so absurd? Never. I loved my friend. I grew up with him. He was dead and there was nothing I could do to make him undead. Homosexual or not. But my father...that's the other side of the story. My father committed suicide. That Loretta didn't know. My father, as far as I know, was a heterosexual. He committed suicide because he was depressed, because when my mother died of cancer he didn't want to live anymore. The memory of love kept me alive. The loss of it made my father kill himself. There is no simple solution to what hurts a person most."

She returned her compact to her purse. She didn't feel relieved. She didn't feel worse. She felt...Lionel. She took hold of her glass of iced tea. All of the ice had melted. The sun was past being directly overhead. The sunspots on the slate under the trees were still. Sticky hot humid June. One-fifteen, her little jeweled watch said—as soon as she moved it far enough away from her eyes for the dial to come into focus. Damn stupid impractical beautiful thing!

"Now it's my turn, Corinne. I have a question to ask you. About me. About the ladies and me. About how they feel about my being the leader of their group *and* a homosexual."

"We never talk about you that way. Not as a group we don't. Didn't the five of us decide that a long time ago? Individually, I think you must know. No one wants to leave the group. That should tell you something."

"It does. And what about the husbands? What about Lio-

263

nel, for example? Does he have some crazy idea that I'm responsible for Greg?"

"If he does, he's never said it. He never wants to talk about you. He never wants to talk about Greg. He wants to forget Greg exists. He doesn't want him around....As far as the other husbands are concerned—and you...well, they never talk to us about you. We...none of us...we never talk to each other about what really matters. We never have. I think we're all afraid to by now." She laughed, even though what she wanted to do was cry. "It only hurts when we laugh. Right, Aaron?"

"Right, Corinne. Let's call off the party."

"No. I'll take care of it. I'll work out all the details. I'll call you. I'll let you know."

They smiled across for one another—even though the next report coming in from Los Angeles indicated a turn for the worse. "Absurd," he said, "so absurd this reality we're all trying to live through now. Beyond our control now."

She tried her compact again. Squinting. Fluffing. Wiping the tears. Back inside, little fools. Back.

[2] Bloomsday, June 16, 1968, fell out on a Sunday, and because it did, plump, *zaftig*, not-so-stately, but certainly thoughtful Audrey Halpern decided the party should begin at five P.M., "...Monday being a workday for the husbands— I can still remember when I had one of those—and if we want to get everything in, we'll need time. Drinks and food and Aaron'll do...something. Who knows what!"

Corinne had chosen a Committee of Four, including her-self: Audrey, Edna, Sally—the merry-enough widows, "...but if they're busy before, during, and after," she told Aaron, "they won't have time to think about who's missing from their lives. We'll arrive at four. Paper plates. Plastic glasses and silverware. Easy cleanup. Ham. Turkey. Salads. Drinks. We've got an overbake of cakes. And I'll have Esther Aronowitz's giant perk, the one you love, Aaron. The monster one. You don't do a thing, except maybe ice, because if we bring it from Levittown, it'll melt."

She also asked him to set up the bar on his desk in his bedroom at the back of the floor-through. He was on the top floor and his back windows looked down into a garden, a real garden with actual trees. Corinne loved the view. "Brings back my past. When I was a Village virgin. Trees and a skyline. A horizon, Aaron....Missy and Carl send regrets.

They're not up to it yet. And I called Joe Massi, according to your wishes. He told me to tell you to kiss his ass. He blames you for everything. You're the devil. You encouraged Loretta. You encouraged the girls to take her side. The girls are going out there. To visit. To comfort Loretta. She and Michelle are breaking up. So it'll be fourteen ladies, eleven husbands. You start at the bar. We'll do the kitchen. They'll drink two drinks tops. Jews, remember, Aaron. Not Irish. Ineluctable, Aaron. Ineluctable, genetic fate, Aaron. Am I right or am I right?" She was pleased. She was glowing with sunburn. The day before, the ladies had made their initial appearance at Jones, "...so never fear, Aaron, summer's here, and it's Bloomsday."

She had done her hair in an upsweep: her Rita Hayworth mood. She wore one of her oldest numeros, a spaghetti-strapped, tight-fitting, plunging sheath of a shiny cotton print, a pima, from her prime, that she was still able to squeeze into. When she was dressing, Lionel hated the way she looked: "Cheap. Like a whore." "Good. That's the Molly Bloom in me coming out. It's always been there. I'm just going to let it out a lot—a lot more—while there's time...." And she had a half-dozen bracelets on each bare arm, and dangling earrings, big golden loops. She painted her lips a deep rose red, like the rose in the print of her dress, "'...like the Andalusians used,'" but Lionel didn't know what the hell she was talking about. "Andalusians? You crazy?" Anyway, Audrey was honking outside, she had to go. "Harold and Evelyn will be picking you up. Years ago we could have done a quickie, but these days, Lionel...your blood's tired." She rushed past him, out of the bedroom—"You've slowed down, Lionel"—and out of the house.

[3]   Aaron gave her one drink.

Harold and Sandy—Sandy insisted they take over the bar, "...to give Aaron his chance to star." Sandy gave her her second, and then she stopped. On her own she stopped. She had too much to do, to supervise, to organize, and Aaron's kitchen was small. It called for precision movements to get that group fed and beveraged and settled into eating spaces. She even had to remove her bracelets. Every time she dipped into the cole slaw, so did her best bone ones. It disgusted Cynthia, and if it disgusted Cynthia, well, then, "...would I ever offend you? Willingly offend you?"

"Yes. Of course you would. So just give me my plate, Corinne, before you dump it all over yourself."

Evelyn was next on line, and Evelyn was complimentary. Evelyn was not now, nor had she ever been, bitchy. "It's all going smoothly. Aaron's helping people find room. If only he had an air conditioner. The noise, of course, we're all used to. Arlene screaming is part of the landscape."

The food line snaked its way, paper plate by paper plate, up to and then away from the kitchen entrance. From there it was every man, every woman for...whom? Themselves? On the floor, mostly, with pillows. In front of the windows under the ficus limb. Aaron had one of those New York City phenomena alive in his living room. "A tree, of the fig family," he told a circle of admirers collecting inside the peninsula his Hershey-brown-corduroy sofas circumscribed— just being near Aaron sometimes made her see things grandly, like a circumscription. She could have been a contender.... "I've had this tree for sixteen years, and all the while this limb has grown out horizontally, toward the western light, to where the sun goes. My ficus is hungry for sun. A natural enough heliotropism, don't you know. Nothing perverse." Aaron, she knew, was working on his third scotch; Aaron was nervous and worried, so she had better get him to eat. Ah, the remembered joys of drunken oblivion—but she beckoned for him, come, come on, come across the room to her, over the bodies back to back, side to side, all over the floor. Instead, he moved to the corner, where the tree's tub stood. He wanted to be locked in there for the moment. He was surveying the crowd in his living room. He seemed reflective, pensive. Ah! He sipped. He spied her watching him, still beckoning from her position just outside the entrance to his kitchen. He raised his glass to her. Eating was in full swing. The husbands were safely anchored. Soon it would be Molly Bloom's hour.

"Come eat, Aaron. Come." She mouthed the words, and he heard.

[4] "We are in Dublin on another June 16. In 1904, instead of 1968. It's a workday, not a Sunday, another quite ordinary day in the lives of some quite ordinary people, the kinds of people you might meet up with on the streets of Levittown— if anyone out there were ever to go out walking anymore...." Pausing, Scotchless, Aaron stroked his beard. He gazed ceilingward. He was in front of the fireplace. Corinne had moved

him there, led him there, settled him there, whispering for him to, "Begin. Talk. Tell them. Tell the husbands what's what," and so he had begun and now he was pausing, stopping, gazing ceilingward. Thinking. . . .

She had taken up his earlier position next to the tub of the ficus tree. Lionel was alongside her, sighing, impatient. Having eaten, he was ready to head back to Levittown. She knew his signals, his belchings, his tiny tooting farts. And not just her lovely Lionel. Most of the husbands were sighing impatiently—so, better get on with it, Aaron, better perform for them, like a trained seal, perform. Wives, husbands, she wanted to sing out into the expectant, heavy-hot silence of this June evening, I come to praise Aaron, I come to praise him for . . . for . . . things I can't put into words. For focusing the machine for me. For helping me put myself at the center of my life. For helping all of us do that—before the inevitable slide into menopause, which she was even then feeling. The heat. The outrageous red of her hair—she was turning bizarre. Corinne Feuerstein née Grossman, former chanteuse, closet pianist, reformed drinker, sex maniac, lousy mother, and would-be thinker, sliding toward menopause, but pausing to think now, nowadays, hoping, trusting the possibilities still left in her life even when faced with the bleakest evidence to the contrary, thanks to Aaron and how he looks ceilingward, struggling to say something helpful, straining to follow a loop of thought somewhere inside his trained head.

"Quite ordinary people," Aaron resumed. "Leopold Bloom, Molly Bloom, and Stephen Dedalus. But we go inside their heads, inside their minds. We hear the unique rhythm of each character's thinking, the words, the flow, the references. It's a great adventure and it's made up out of the ordinary events in the lives of ordinary people very much like any of us here now." Another pause. This time for effect. He gazed down, at the bodies back to back, side to side, on the floor, on the sofas. They were waiting now for what might come next. Even Lionel. He had stopped sighing and belching. She had tried all this past year to talk to him about *Ulysses,* and every time she had, he had waved her and it out of existence. Just like he did Gregory. Well, Gregory had outsmarted him by going to the draft board and telling them, yes, he was queer, so what? So you can't come into the Army. So thank you and good-bye. And now she had outsmarted Lionel too. She'd gotten Lionel into this room in Aaron's floor-through. She'd gotten him to listen to the man he called a queer talking about *Ulysses.* So there, big shot. So there, all these ordinary people so much on guard, so defensive, so ready to protect themselves from what they didn't know very much about. Most of them were. Maybe not Sandy. He was attentive. He seemed secure, calmly listening. He'd probably read *Ulysses.* And Gordon Ginsburg, listening.

"How Joyce did what he did is another matter. That's the lifelong work of scholars. That's like asking how Shakespeare could have written his plays or Wagner could have written his *Ring.*"

Another Corinne Feuerstein project. She had already scheduled it for the autumn at Hofstra: Wagner and the *Ring,* Myth and Mystery. Evelyn might take it too, either that or full-time college. It depended...

"...but for me, for the ladies too, the greatest achievement comes at the last, the so-called Molly Bloom soliloquy. It's late at night of the book's one day. Molly is in bed upstairs. Down below, Leopold is giving a drunken Stephen Dedalus a cocoa, to steady him. Molly overhears them. She can't sleep. She herself has had a very full day, a day of adultery and pleasure and guilt and memory. Everything. The works. Her mind keeps tossing up bits and pieces for her to examine. There is a river flow of thought through her head. Just as there is in the heads of each of you right now, even as you listen. All kinds of thoughts darting in and out and around. About all kinds of things, without punctuation, without censorship, on June 16, 1968, evening...." And still another pause, while he leaned forward, while he pointed. "And if I were to ask any of you, if I were to ask each of you, would you stop the flow, pick up a pebble of thought, examine it, tell it to us, would you be willing to? Would you share a thought or two with us? Would you...Roy Rabinowitz?" A pointing finger. Roy jumped away from Ruby's back. "And you, Gordon Ginsburg? You, Harold Selden? You, Sandy Klein?"

Sandy didn't jump up, or away, or even look away. He smiled. "Yes," he said. "Yes, I would, yes."

Aaron laughed.

The ladies applauded.

Lionel poked her. "What? What's going on?"

"You'll see. Just listen, for a change. Learn something."

"Fuck you." But he whispered it, so no one else would hear. Not that they could have, because Sandy's words had broken the ice, cleared the air. Conversation rose all around

268

the room, and Aaron had to shout to be heard then. "Good, because tonight is meant to be a celebration. And maybe next year we can do it again. All I want to do now is put on a recording for you. It's Siobhan McKenna reading from the Molly Bloom section. And maybe, husbands, before next year, you'll let your wives help you read through the whole book. They're all experts now." Carefully he stepped away from the fireplace, stepping over bodies on his way to the bookshelf wall and his turntable. He had prepared the record. "'...wait theres Georges church bells wait 3 quarters the hour wait...'"

He remained standing at his bookshelf wall, listening and leaning and watching them listening. Corinne listened as if it were all new again, "'...all over you like a warm showerbath O Maritana wildwood flower we sang splendidly though it was a bit too high for my register even transposed...'" Molly, the singer! Corinne, the singer! All over with. Done with! Dead as a doornail! And listening, suddenly there were tears burning her eyes. Cigarette smoke hovering. Hot. Hot. Hot in Aaron's living room. No breeze through the window behind the ficus leaves.

"'...two glancing eyes a lattice hid...'" Eyes. Tears. Blurring all the faces nearby, Lionel's most of all—but she could see his boredom, his fidgets, his fat fingers as he cracked his knuckles. Fuck him. Fuck him for all his fucking ways.... And Sandy's eyes. So different. Sandy's blue eyes, staring at Aaron, darting away, glancing back, attentive to each word, calm in the still air. "'...that lovely little statue he bought I could look at him all day long curly head and his shoulders his finger up for you to listen theres real beauty and poetry for you often I felt I wanted to kiss him all over also his lovely young cock...'" Sandy smiled. Cynthia locked her arms in a self-embrace. She looked over at Aaron, urging him with her eyes to turn it off, to stop it, to explain more, talk more.

Corinne counterurged. No. No. No.

But fidgets and fussings and phews were clearly evident. Max Zweig's eyes were a beady fury. Audrey and Edna and Sally seemed forlorn, alone with their longings. Audrey aflow with her flushes. Rose and George Newman, back to back, hunched over in discomfort, or was it just plain disapproval? Corinne wanted to sing, to sing out, "You made me love you/ I didn't want to do it/I didn't want to do it..."

"And now Leopold has joined Molly in bed," Aaron explained, looking ceilingward.

269

"'I wished I was one myself for a change just to try with that thing they have swelling upon you so hard and at the same time so soft...'"

Shiftings and turnings and muttering then. She heard it rising. She watched for signs of any mutiny. Good thing Missy and Carl weren't there. Harold was having a hard time of it just then. He was preparing himself for flight, but Evelyn pulled him back down. No way out. No choice in Aaron's inn but to listen to Molly's mind making itself known, looping through a spiral of thought, "'...its all his own fault if I am an adulteress....O much about it if thats all the harm ever we did in this vale of tears God knows its not much doesn't everybody only they hide it....'"

The tears fell then—for herself, for the simple truth touched into life inside her. She made no attempt to hide them or stop them. Dead as a doornail, her oldest dream. Dead.

"'...the sun shines for you he said the day we were lying among the rhododendrons on Howth head in the grey tweed suit and his straw hat the day I got him to propose to me yes....'"

Lionel wanted to move away, but he was trapped next to Gladys and Gordon Ginsburg—and the ficus tub. Anyway, Gordon knew they were near the end. Gordon got him back against the wall again.

"'O and the sea the sea crimson sometimes like fire and the glorious sunsets....'"

Sandy, she saw, had closed his eyes. The voice like music mounted Molly's mountainside in Gibraltar as a girl, "'...a Flower of the mountain yes when I put the rose in my hair like the Andalusian girls used or shall I wear a red yes and how he kissed me under the Moorish wall and I thought well as well him as another and then I asked him with my eyes to ask again yes and then he asked me would I yes to say yes my mountain flower and first I put my arms around him yes and drew him down to me so he could feel my breasts all perfume yes and his heart was going like mad and yes I said yes I will Yes.'"

Silence—and the record turning, scratching, round and round, until Evelyn's clearing of her throat roused Aaron to remember where he was and what he was doing there. He checked his wristwatch: late for a Sunday evening. "Perhaps you get some sense of what Joyce was after...."

The crowd was standing and stretching and turning in

circles and she was moving from the ficus to infiltrate, to quiet them if she could, just in case there was something else Aaron wished to say—which she doubted. Everyone was in a rush to get going. The cleanup committee was cleaning up: Evelyn, Esther Aronowitz, who was even then seeing to her giant perk, and Ina Silverstein, Rita Moskowitz. Their husbands helped. Harold, stooping, groaned as he reached for a fallen earring. Grayer in her eyes Harold had suddenly become, grayer and gnawing at the corner of his mouth too much. Older. From one moment to the next, older. Even Sandy, whom Harold was asking about the earring, older. His skin not so baby-behind-smooth, some furrows on the forehead, some thinning of that fine hair. Had Corinne actually seen that—what?—wry smile of his earlier? Wry? Such a word for a former Grand Concourse beauty! Well, why not? Culture comes to the Grand Concourse! Starring Ann Sheridan's sister Sue Sheridan.... She really must be going off her rocker, because the earring Harold was playing with was hers. Her Lionel was accepting it from Harold, was passing it over to her, was saying: How's about it? We going yet? Her Lionel! Her pained, puffy, paunchy Lionel, ruddy with high blood pressure. "It's Monday tomorrow, remember," he reminded her.

As if she needed a reminder of the way the world went! From day to day, went!

And all the while Aaron stood there next to his turntable, watching his record slow its spin.

She got to him, pushing through the crush. "Never fear, Aaron. If there's one thing that you've got, it's your ladies. Need us or not."

He nodded. He smiled. He felt good tonight, very good. "Yes," he said, "very good. Some thinking occurred here tonight. Some. Among some of the men here tonight. The others, those who don't want to practice the skill, do so at their own peril. A loop of new thought will go round and round with them—or without them." No one was listening to him but Corinne. But not true—Rita was there. Rita was retrieving a paper plate from behind a stack of records. Evelyn was there too. And Audrey and Edna.

They circled him and kissed him, all at once, their Graybeard Loon!

[5] Silence in the Lincoln Continental... starring Sue Sheridan. She made him drive down Horatio Street—for old times'

sake—before he turned out of the Village to uptown and the Queens-Midtown Tunnel.

Almost all the way home they were silent.

That was her mood: silent reflection, bizarre silent reflection. Bizarre Corinne Feuerstein! Definitely she was sliding toward menopause, without passing Go, without collecting two hundred dollars. She had a right. She had her rights to indulge her mood, her own particular mood, once in a while, like making him drive down Horatio Street. For the hell of it. Because...she wanted to let a few old memories overwhelm her before they were gone for good. That had been her mood for months now. She'd even started reading Proust. Aaron had suggested it, and she had jumped. A Pavlov dog.

Oh, well. There are worse things than jumping after culture. There is, for example, the heat, the sticky humid night heat outside the windows of the Lincoln, and there is the Long Island Expressway: the ugliest expressway in America, she supposed, even in darkness. An affront to mankind. And it could have been so different. She remembered...she remembered when you took the Grand Central Parkway to get out to Levittown.... Maybe when they got home she would call Greg—except just then she didn't know where to call him. He was on the road somewhere. What a life! "You don't want to talk about tonight, Lionel?"

"No."

"That's what I figured." It was too hot to think, he would have said, if pressed, or he was too full, and besides, who the fuck was she to insist he had to think or speculate, consider, discuss, analyze? If he didn't want to, he didn't want to. But if there were consequences? Would he accept those? That she could ask him. That she should ask him.

But she didn't.

They were headed south on the Wantagh Expressway by then, and in a few minutes they'd be home and in bed in their lovely red-and-pink home on Wisdom Lane. Barn red she'd had it painted, out of perversity, the color of Levittown past, recaptured; barn red with white trim.... What she wanted more than anything else in the whole world when she got home was a drink. She wanted to get into her robe, pick up the Proust, fill a glass with Scotch, go into the den, and be left alone.

Lionel wouldn't let her. Most of all Lionel wouldn't let her take a drink. "I want you to go to bed."

And that's what she did. She got into bed, without her

nightgown on, because Lionel wanted it that way. He wanted her naked under the lamplight. He stood naked over her, staring down at her. Maybe that would help. Maybe if he leaned down, maybe if he got down at the side of the bed and licked her a little, sucked her nipples a little, rubbed her a little—but none of it helped. He couldn't get hard. He didn't know why. He didn't feel guilty. He had nothing to feel guilty about. "If you want to know some guilt, I could tell you some stories about some of your best friends..."

"I'm not interested, Lionel. I don't want to hear. I'm only interested in what's going on with you. What's happening to you? Maybe you should go to the doctor. Maybe it's just prostate trouble. I'm sure it's temporary."

Still at the side of the bed, on his knees, he rested his head on her stomach. She felt sorry for him. She played with his gray curls. Thinner now. Looser. Less substantial. Only his hair was thin, because the rest of him was overweight and underexercised. Even now he was straining to stay in his kneeling position. She better let him up. Or he might have a heart attack on the spot.... My Horatio Street lover grows old. She got him to stand up. She held his prick in her hand: soft. She smiled at it. "You'll come back to life again someday—at least, I certainly hope so."

"It will." He got into bed beside her. She reached over and turned out the lamp. "Give me a chance, Corinne."

"That's all I've ever done all my life with you is give you your chances. And while that was going on, I've used up almost all my own." She rolled on her side away from him. "I'm tired of that, Lionel. Very tired."

27

Cynthia and Aaron, 1968

[1] Thin, yes. Much thinner. She saw her reflection in the mirror over the dressing table. She had sat up in bed so she could see it. Before they got there. She had to see for herself once more. How would Aaron react when Sandy brought him through the door of the bedroom? Would he say: How thin, Cynthia? How waxy, Cynthia? Of course not.

Neither were the corners of her mouth sunken in. A good sign. The light was still good. October afternoon light. Brilliant sunlight all day. Painful clarity. The sky so blue, cloudless, cool, bright. She had cried to see it through the window: autumn. Melanie had come in upon her crying. Melanie had cheered her, made her stop, forced her to take hold of her fear. She would make it through the treatments in perfect order, Melanie said, because the doctor had said so and Sandy too had sworn to her that that was exactly what the doctor *had* said. Cross his heart. Hadn't he promised her he wouldn't lie about anything that happened? He would tell her the truth because she wanted the truth. Yes. Melanie had sworn she would too: the truth. Melanie had come home to be there for the operation. She was going to stay home for as long as necessary, until she was convinced that everything was fine. She almost was, "I'm ninety-five percent certain," she had told Cynthia that afternoon when she came into the bedroom and found Cynthia crying in her sunlight-dappled bedroom. "You'll finish the series of treatments in another week, Mom, and then I'll be a hundred percent and then I'll go back to Italy and in a few months you and Dad can come visit us there."

Perhaps some lipstick? Certainly she should comb her hair once again. Too flat from sleeping. But her arm was paining her. Still sore. She would call Melanie. Melanie would comb her hair. Melanie would...She was going to cry again. She was helpless. She hated that feeling. She hated the stabbing pain. She hated the scars. She hated Sandy's seeing them.

She hated looking at her one full breast and the other . . . gone. Gone with the wind. . . .

She cried, but she wouldn't call Melanie. Melanie had dinner to finish. Sandy and Aaron would be home any minute . . . they were home. She heard the front door opening and closing and their voices greeting Melanie and laughter and before she'd even had a chance to fluff up her hair in the back where it was flattened from the pillow—there was Aaron coming to the bed to kiss her, and then, taking hold of her hands, he took a step back to look her over.

That's what he was doing.

Was it too late? Was it arrested?

"So, my seer, what's the verdict?"

"Mother! Don't do that." Melanie took hold of Aaron's arm, moved him away.

Sandy leaned over her, kissed her. "The verdict is you'll live."

"You look marvelous, Cynthia." Aaron was at the foot of the bed. "You truly do. I'm not lying. I wouldn't. I promised I'd tell you the truth."

She nodded. She wanted to believe him. She hoped what she was doing then was smiling.

"I'll make us drinks." Sandy stood up, unbuttoned his blazer, pulled the knot of his tie lower. "Scotch and water, Aaron? Right?" Aaron nodded. "You, Melly?"

"No, Daddy. I'll have some wine with dinner, which I have to go finish."

"Would you like some sherry, Cynthia? The doctor said it would be good for you. If you felt like some. Do you?"

"Yes. For the occasion. Yes." She motioned for Aaron to come sit down next to her on the bed. Sandy followed Melanie out of the room.

Cynthia wanted, ". . . to *yenta* a little, Aaron. Because I heard from Missy—even Evelyn admitted it—that at the first meeting of the Ladies, in September, Arlene and Rita almost came to blows about the reading list. True or false that most of the reading is political?"

"True, but that's what the ladies wanted. They voted it that way."

"And you didn't influence them any? You and Evelyn and Rita didn't? Tell the truth, Aaron? You didn't say anything about the Democratic convention and Vietnam and Nixon? I don't believe you. Isn't the first book going to be *Wretched of the Earth?*"

"Yes. It is, and yes, I did make a little speech about connections. But it was almost the same speech I made when the group began, and by now everyone knows what I mean when I talk about connections. Arlene thinks we're trying to form a Communist cell."

"And Missy thinks you're antireligious, all of you."

"I'll speak for myself. I am. About that I've never dissimulated. Even Missy can't claim otherwise. I've been trying to get us to read *Future of an Illusion*. They won't. Missy won't read Freud, which proves how much influence I really have. Missy has more. Missy talks more these days. Now that you're not there to intimidate her. Now we need you back to quiet Arlene."

"Yes. I can quiet Arlene. That'll be my epitaph. I quieted Arlene Zweig." But she couldn't smile. She folded the edge of her cotton quilt back and forth, back and forth, staring down at her fingers, her long, now very thin fingers. She raised one hand, studying it, tracing the pattern of veins on it, the veins prominent like rises and falls on a topographical map. Too thin. Much too thin. But there came Sandy. It brought her back from her dying. She took the glass of sherry.

Sandy proposed a toast. "Now that you're on the road to recovery, here's to making it faster." They all sipped. "Perhaps tonight you'll feel like coming to the table, Cynth'."

"Perhaps. We'll see, after a while. Dinner won't be for a while, will it?"

"No. We have lots of time to talk."

But instead, they sipped in silence. It was the light, Cynthia thought. Late afternoon light. Dying into evening. It was the chintz on the chaise longue that Sandy had moved into the room for her, to move to, for a change, its blue floral pattern, the tint of it, the tone, cold in the dying bright light. And the lace curtains she had put up on the windows. It was a back-home kind of bedroom, something so *disconnected* from the rest of the house: it was the quality of something irretrievably lost but foolishly recreated. Melancholy. Nostalgia...of the infinite. That painting at the Museum of Modern Art. "Have you been to the Modern Art recently, Aaron?"

"Not all summer. Not since Corinne and I met there to plan the Bloomsday party. Just before you...took ill."

She nodded. She sipped some more sherry. It grumbled through her stomach. She grimaced. It pained her to feel woozy, to lose her grip of control. She set the glass down on the end table. She listened. Music. Sandy had put on some Mozart. For sanity, as he always said about Mozart: "Something sane in this insane world."

Aaron recognized it. "That's Klemperer's recording isn't it? The Twenty-ninth? I have that recording too. I love it."

Sandy was pleased. His pleasure was in his face, ready, spontaneous, a little boy's pleasure. She hadn't seen that frank, feeling freedom in his face in...in—she couldn't remember how long it had been, but it was surely years and years, before Levittown, she thought, because in Levittown only Gordon Ginsburg had listened to music with Sandy, who was not even his closest friend. To hear Sandy tell it, Harold was his only friend. But when Sandy was with Harold, they didn't listen to music, and she couldn't remember his ever looking as relaxed as he seemed to be with Aaron. They talked on easily. Even Aaron seemed released. He left his beard alone. He didn't smooth down the legs of his crumpled blue jeans, his unironed blue denim workshirt. Aaron the Graybeard Loon, lost in the Sixties; Sandy Klein in blue oxford button-down, silk rep tie, opened and pulled down, his only concession to comfort and informality in the Sixties, his silky blond hair, thinning, yes, but neat, even at the end of what she knew had been a long day because the night before with her had been so long—she had had pain, she had kept him up, she had clutched at his hand: Aaron and Sandy, unlikely friends.

But as she watched, more than listened to them talk, she saw that there was something, a quality of tilting the head to listen, a movement of the hand as it gestured to emphasize a particular point—they were talking Mozart and Beethoven and what happened to the world when it moved from one to the other. She wished she could care. She wished she had always cared...more. That was what Sandy missed in her: that shared sense of interest. Instead, just as he had let himself be lost in Levittown, he had submerged those interests, had made most of his important pursuits solitary pursuits, and now—now that she was going to die—she would, she felt it in her bones—now it was too late to make that up to him. He needed a friend...like Aaron. That much she could somehow arrange to give him before she died. She was crying again. It had turned too dark in the room. She cried very quietly. How beautiful Sandy still was. At forty-seven his body lean, wiry, strong. It was the swimming in New York. It was tennis with Harold. It was the way he nourished what

277

was inside himself and cared for his outside. Only now, now that she was sick, his skin looked sallow, his blue eyes had dark rings around them: he was so tired. Aaron's being there had animated him. She felt good about that. She hoped she was smiling. She turned on the lamp on the end table. She sipped some more sherry. Just a taste, to sweeten her sour mouth.

"Dinner," Melanie was calling before she came into the room, "dinner now, or whenever you want it," because she had seen Sandy and Aaron talking as she entered. She could see how happy Sandy was.

Melanie sat at the head of the bed, next to Cynthia's arm. She smiled at Cynthia. She rounded the front of Cynthia's hair, settling the wisps of it. "Join us, Mother. Try. How about it? There's no reason you can't. You just have to start doing it again. That's what the doctor told us, and tonight's the perfect night for it, with Aaron here. You can show him. You always liked to impress him."

"Melanie! Don't talk that way."

"It's true. We did too. In class." Aaron and Sandy had stopped talking to each other to listen to what Melanie was saying. When Melanie wanted to be heard, she was. She only had to shake free her coal-black hair from her shoulders, and eyes would turn to watch the sheen of it, the soft spill of it. She wore it center-parted—Cynthia loved it that way best, combed out and free-falling, not braided—framing the ivory oval of her even-featured face. She was pretty. Not beautiful, but very pretty. Slight, but ample where it mattered. Like Cynthia...had been. "You can admit it, Aaron. You knew it. You knew we were always vying for your attention. Especially Teresa Geiger. She had such a crush on you she found it next to impossible to talk. You knew it. And in your other class that year it was Maria Massi. We used to get together after school and try to imagine ourselves in the city with you, visiting you. Remember the time we did? You had friends there. You were so embarrassed—but so were we.... Levittown kids. We just didn't know where to go look for reality. I can tell you one thing—meaning no disrespect either, Daddy, Mother has always been on my side about this—living in Italy, I never think about missing anything in Levittown except the two of you...and you too, Aaron. Sometimes." She laughed. She stood up. "Dinner? Okay? How about it, Mother?"

Yes, she would try; with Sandy's help she would try,
278

"...if, Aaron, you would just go on out to the table first, and, Sandy, if you would get me my terry robe? Please? The blue one."

[2]   The glass-and-chrome dining table was set in front of the big back window.

Melanie had lit candles, and as the darkness outside deepened, the nostalgic mood inside deepened too. Cynthia couldn't help herself. The wind gusted. Leaves on the maples in the backyard swirled, lifted, fell back, some fell off and down. She watched them. "Nature it is" as Molly would have it. Nature. Natural for things to fall off and die. She tried to eat a sliver of the pot roast. Melanie had made a pungent pot roast, Italian style, with red wine and marjoram and garlic and some parslied potatoes, crunchy fresh vegetables. She knew it was good. Sandy ate with relish. So did Aaron. She couldn't eat anything. She felt tired. Would they mind if she left the table? Would Sandy help her to the sofa? She wanted to stretch out there and listen to them talk, watch them eat.

Sandy settled her there on the sofa. He put on the "Emperor," quietly, in the background, an old Horowitz recording he had somehow saved from oblivion, he told Aaron. He listened. And Melanie. They all three sipped from their wine. The candles flickered.

Romantic. How romantic! Another romantic evening in Levittown. Sandy's face shone out of the shadows around the table. How she loved him. How she loved looking at him.

While the music played, they were silent. They ate and sipped their way through the "Emperor Concerto," and when it was over, when Melanie had served out the salad, Sandy told Aaron how he didn't think he'd sat with anyone in Levittown, "...except of course Cynthia and Melanie, just sat and listened to music without finding it necessary for someone to speak. You're the first of a kind, Aaron. I'm very grateful. That calls for some more wine."

Sandy was happy. Which made her happy.

And Aaron was too. Aaron was grateful too, "...I don't have any friends who listen to music as intently as you do either. It's rare. Come to think of it, I don't have many friends. Not since I was...not since I resigned have I made many friends. I've turned into an isolate. Except for the ladies...and their husbands...I—"

"We'll have to change all that," Sandy said, refilling
279

Aaron's wineglass. "You can't just write all day and read and listen to music. You have to do more, get out more, exercise. We all do."

"I haven't really cared to do more very much—but I agree. I should. It's a bad cycle. I should change my perspective, perhaps move off to 'fresh fields and pastures new.'"

"Milton?" Melanie asked.

"Yes." Aaron smiled. "Good girl. You remembered."

"Some things. Some people. You."

Sandy said nothing. He began his salad. "Good. Excellent meal, Melly. Your...your roommate in Bologna is lucky."

"So am I, Daddy. When you and Mother come over there, you'll see him and see why."

"How much more time do you have at the university?" Aaron wanted to know.

"He has another year. I have two. We'll stay until I finish, and then...I don't know. We'll see. We'll see what the world's like. He's in medicine. He can practice anywhere. If Nixon's elected, I think I'd rather stay in Italy, or anywhere in Europe for that matter."

"Maybe I'll join you."

"No," Cynthia called out. "No you don't, Aaron. You can't leave the ladies in the lurch."

They all laughed. It was the first time all of them had laughed together that evening.

[3] He kissed her before he turned out the light, and then he got into his bed. "If you need anything, just call out. Remember, Cynth'. Anything."

"Yes." She waited until he had slid under his quilt. Then she waited for his sigh of contentment. "You liked Aaron tonight, didn't you?"

"I did. Very much. I've met him a dozen times but I didn't really get to know him until tonight. I guess that happens with certain people. With quiet, commanding people. He is quiet, essentially quiet."

"So are you."

No answer. Silence. Dark silence in their bedroom. The bedroom that hadn't been used—properly—in so long. She couldn't remember the last time....Her room. The room Sandy had said she should decorate. Anyway she wanted. Please herself. She did. In a way that was *home,* back home, another place, another era. Gone...as she would be soon. And she wanted to be sent home...afterward. She wanted to be buried with her mother and father and Grandma Berk...Berkowitz. She wanted...she wanted to tell Sandy that in so many ways he resembled Aaron. Not obvious ways. Not how each of them looked. Not that at all. "Sandy? You're not sleeping so soon, are you?"

"No. Not at all. I'm very far from sleep. I was thinking...about being quiet. Of course, you're right. You're always right. I am quiet, except that there are all kinds of quiet. There's the quiet that Harold is for example. He's quiet around perceptive people, people who might see through to his inside. Then he becomes the quiet, dark, handsome Harold. All smiles. All charm. Completely on guard. He uses his looks so people won't find out that nothing much *is* going on inside him. He treats Evelyn that way, keeps her off guard. And then there's the Aaron kind of quiet. He can be quiet because everyone knows his life. He hasn't hidden anything. He's secure and strong and accessible. That's the open-book kind of quiet. A listening quiet. And then, of course, there's me."

"Yes. There's you. Who doesn't say anything...out of habit."

"Out of habit. Yes. Mutual habit, Cynthia. I might speak, I might have spoken—if spoken to. If asked."

"Melanie told me something about you. She told me years ago. That you were a Virgo. She said Virgos never tell people directly anything about themselves. They tease others into asking them questions. You never could do that with me. I never was the type to be teased. I never would let myself be. I can't start now. But Aaron...Aaron's different. Ask him a direct question and he responds. You don't have to tease him into talking. He's not afraid of what he thinks. He has convictions about his...about experience. He'd make a good friend. You share interests. You'll have plenty of time...to indulge them . . . together . . . plenty of time . . . for friendship . . . after I die."

"Why do you talk like that, Cynthia? The doctor told you—but of course you won't believe him. Why do you want to believe the worst? I don't know why you do, but you seem to want to. And you'll outlive me. I know you will."

"Whatever you say. But, just in case, having a friend like Aaron won't hurt. Just in case...Aaron would be... understanding. He'd appreciate your . . . situation. He'd value . . . you." And then she realized she was crying again, quietly crying again, without realizing she had begun to cry again.

That's what was happening to her every day. Things beginning inside her, going on inside her, ending, without her knowing they were, without her being able to control them. Like crying—and not out of fear. She wasn't frightened just then. She wasn't...anything. She felt, just then, nothing, not even any pain where her breast had been. She supposed she was crying as much for the fact of that loss of feeling as for anything else she had never had the chance to feel in her life—and never would have the chance to feel ever, now, now that she was going to—she was sure she would—die. So, yes, she was crying about that too, and about what she had never felt *with* Sandy. She never could have done anything about that, being Cynthia Berkowitz Berk Klein. Now, all she wanted to do was to hold on to his hand. She asked for it. She reached for it. It was there.

He had gotten onto his knees alongside her bed to hold on to her hand.

28

Evelyn: Committee of One, 1972

Dear Loretta,

You asked me to begin at the beginning. You asked for the facts. "No bullshit," you said in your letter, but how do I know where the beginning of this situation began? I'm Evelyn Selden, not Claire Voyant. I don't even know how you got to know what you know. Probably from Corinne. And if it was Corinne, why did she write you instead of coming to me, first of all? I could have used her help coping. I still could. So why didn't I go to her? I can hear you asking. Well, she was visiting Greg, out there in your world, when Arlene started doing her bursting-in-on-me routine. I couldn't go to Missy. She's too otherworldly for this kind of confidence. And, of course, Cynthia, being party of the first (second?) part ... well, it's you I needed. You're my authority on these kinds of matters. You would have known what to do with Arlene ... but you're not here. Therefore, this letter, which is bound to sound chaotic. I hate chaos, as you know. All I can try to do is present the facts in sequence, just as Aaron would want me to do. The rest is not my business, he would also say. It's Aaron and Sandy's business.

The beginning ... no. Not just yet. First, last night. Last night was our third meeting on Sexual Politics. It's to be the last of the current season, our seventh as a group. It also happens to be, for Harold and me, our twenty-fifth Levittown year. We moved here October 1948. Remember, Loretta? You were there already. So was Arlene. She came bursting in on me my first morning. She's never stopped doing that since. Bad history has a way of repeating itself. Come to think of it, what history is really good? Never mind. Anyway, last night, immediately after I had finished one of my impassioned speeches about how I didn't think a woman could remain unconvinced about the need for the movement once she had read Sexual Politics and about how I, personally, considered it a kind of Bible for women's rights, right then Cynthia shouts out, without even raising her hand, that she thinks the Ladies of Levittown Wednesday Night Book Group is an idea whose time has passed, too much politics, not enough literature. Well, in view of the information you're trying to get from me, you can imagine how Aaron struggled to control himself. There is Cynthia (we were, incidentally, meeting at Arlene's. Symbolically, it was very fitting. Zweig. Z. The end of the alphabet, etc., etc.) and Cynthia lays her bombshell and waits for Aaron to pick it up. You probably won't remember this fact, but Cynthia is entering her fifth postoperative year. That's the year they say tells the whole story. Remember how Cynthia used to fold her arms and close her mind against any invasion of a new thought in a green world? (See how Aaron—much more than college did—has filled my mind with all kinds of allusions? I don't even know it's happening. The only worthwhile power for a person to possess in this world is the power to educate.) So now that very same Cynthia wants to sever all the connections we've established as a group and, unfortunately, she has placed Aaron in an untenable position.

All of which leads me to the thread in the story you are most interested in: Aaron and Sandy.

So, now, back to Arlene. Arlene saw Aaron and Sandy in what she called "compromising closeness" at the New York State Theater, which is, you may or may not remember—you've been gone from here so long—part of the Lincoln Center complex. Well, this whole situation is complex. The connecting threads are so many shades of gray I find it hard to tell them apart. But, of course, Arlene can. Arlene sees everything. She saw them sitting too close together. That's what she burst in to tell me, along with, "I'm the last one to talk about what anyone does in private, but..." So I said, "Be the last one, Arlene, please." Needless to say, she didn't heed my request. Not completely, but she hasn't been a complete blabbermouth either. She's been selective. She's only told those ladies who would never go right up to Cynthia and say: Hey, Cynthia, I hear your Sandy and Aaron are, you know, friends. Nevertheless, when we sit around the bridge table—without Cynthia—it comes up. From Edna, who wouldn't hurt a fly, and Sally, ditto, and Audrey. The good people among us. Missy says nothing at all, only that she would hate it if the group were to disband. That much she told me on the way home last night, and also how much Aaron means to her, how good he was to her and Carl after Adam died. Corinne has also been closemouthed. I spoke to her on the telephone this morning about the events last night and she thought that probably Cynthia was right. That's all she would say. She's got her own problems to deal with, she said. Who doesn't? You. Me. Each and every one of us—but especially Cynthia has, which is why, I suppose, she wants to end the group. She can avoid the ladies that way. No one can accidentally say something about Sandy or Aaron. Frankly, I don't see any sign that Cynthia is angry with Aaron. Just the opposite. As a matter of fact, right after her operation, she was the one who kept urging the two of them to go to the opera and theater and museums together. She encouraged the friendship. Cynthia's not an Indian giver, is she? Arlene knows that about her. We all do. We also know we owe Aaron something. Just one statistic shows how much we owe him: twelve of us—out of the original sixteen—have gotten, or are about to get, college degrees. And in this farshtinkener world of Richard Nixon, that is at least something decent to point to. Here we are, most of us up to our necks in flushes, and we're still going strong, we're still up and doing, thanks to Aaron.

Therefore, I don't have any hard facts to give you. As long as Cynthia can deal with whatever is going on—my intuition tells me she can—then the rest of it is not mine or anyone else's business. I think we all should try to spare Cynthia any extra problems. Idiosyncrasies or not, Cynthia's been a reliable friend for a long time. I know I could always count on her if I needed her. Any of us could, including you, Loretta. As far as Sandy is concerned, he'll always be an enigma. But he has never been anything but kind to me and Harold and everyone else he knows, and especially to Aaron. After all, Aaron is a semi-enigma too. So, Sandy is a good friend for him too. And what's wrong with friendship? It's reciprocal. True?

And maybe the book group is an idea whose time is over with. We have all, as they say these days, gotten to another place. We should be able to continue on from here on our own. I do plan to speak to Aaron directly, as directly as I can, which probably won't be direct enough for you, but I'll try. As soon as we come back from visiting Danny in Toronto—Harold, Eli, and I are going up after July 4th, as part of a trip to the Gaspé—I'm going to meet with Aaron as a Committee of One (Corinne doesn't want to push Aaron. Neither do I, but I do think he should know what's what with Arlene.), and if he wants to talk about Sandy, fine. I'll be happy to. But, one way or another, it's not going to change how I feel about Aaron—

or Sandy. It never changed how I felt about you, did it? I'll let you know what happens as soon as it happens. For now, I miss seeing you and sometimes I even envy you the simpler life of honesty, direct honesty.

LOVE,
EVELYN

[2] Every time she tried to break through—*break through* was what she felt she was trying to do, but to where, she had no idea, never having been there before—Aaron would re-thread some strand of family intimacy like, "Is Morty going to stay in San Francisco?" or "This Deedee Danny is living with now, she's black, is she?" and she would do the opposite of break through; she would fall, in this instance, against the back of her barstool. They had met at O'Neal's earlier, before the others, *just so* she could talk to him alone. It was a Mostly Mozart night. Ordinarily they were eleven for Mozart, but Corinne and Lionel were in Las Vegas, "for the cure," Corinne called it. Evelyn, she told herself, you're botching it—or Aaron was being willful. "What is it, Aaron?"

"What is what? Whatever do you mean, milady?"

From where she sat she could see across to the fountain in the plaza of Lincoln Center: the water shooting up; the water dropping down, enervated. The air out there was dead. Dog days out there. Air quality unacceptable.

"Aaron, let me tell you again that I appointed myself a Committee of One to speak to you about continuing the book group, with or without Cynthia. If Cynthia has her reasons for not wanting to be part of it, that's her right, but why do all of us have to suffer?"

"Suffer?"

"Be deprived. Of your help."

"Why do you need my help, Ev? And what possible help can a lowly homosexual part-time teacher, would-be writer offer up to anyone in Levittown, USA?"

"What is it, Aaron? What is it with you tonight?"

"You asked me that before. I have no answer for your question, unless you're willing to accept that what I have is a bad case of the human condition. I need more and more Mozart sanity."

"It can't be any worse than menopause, and even that passes, eventually. Your disease you've had a whole lifetime to get used to, so why should tonight be any different from any other night?"

286

"Dayenu! Dayenu! Dayenu! Seeing Sandy *en masse,* I get freakier than usual. It's the repression. Repression does it every time. And that, of course, is what you really want to talk about, isn't it, Ev? About Sandy and me, according to Arlene Zweig. Arlene never learns anything from the past, so she's forever doomed to repeat it. *Pauvre petite* Arlene! I'm talking in tongues tonight. It's the drink does it too. Drink and repression. Corinne warned me, about that and about what Arlene has been saying. Corinne also advised me to let it all alone. Let it simmer down, because now even Arlene has turned on that bitch, Ann Bauer, the one who was always out to get me, right from the beginning of my Levittown days. Remember, Ev? The first Open School Night? It was that anti-Semite Bauer and his wife, Ann? German Levittown Protestants. They saw us together at the ballet. Sandy and I were sitting too close together. Big deal. Big fucking deal. So they tell Arlene, naturally, and, naturally, Arlene tells a selected few, only to have Ann Bauer end up calling her a kike. Protestant hypocrites. Cruel justice! But that's the way it is when you've always had the power, when history gives it to you. Crooks are everywhere, and Arlene spends every waking hour worrying about me and my morals, just the way the Bauers hope she will. She's the indecent one, the vulgar, *vulgaris!* Have you spoken to Cynthia? Has anyone? Corinne informs me, No. No one has, which is good. Not so good is the fact that Corinne didn't speak to you and that you didn't speak to her. That's the saddest part. That's the part that, by now, the two of you—at least the two of you—should be able to overcome. If I'm not embarrassed by the two of you talking about Sandy and myself, why should you be? Or Corinne?"

"It's a habit of a lifetime, Aaron. To let well enough alone. It's the other side of the great divide...the chasm, as you call it. We're from the old school, where conscience and respect for one's privacy have value. Corinne's got her own private concerns. My job as her loving friend is to help when I can, leave her alone when I can. Nowadays they call it being supportive. So, I'm supportive. Of you too I'm supportive—if and when you need it."

"Well said. Well received. But, then, answer one more question before the others get here, because, in truth, the center cannot possibly hold much longer. It's August already. August 1972, mind you. So far, I've had one Scotch. I plan to have a few more before Mozart, and my question is...Evelyn

287

Selden, I'm forty-four . . . you're fifty . . . fifty, Ev, dig? . . . and so therefore what difference can it possibly make to anyone, if a forty-four-year-old life-battered man, and a fiftyish love-coddled, handsome—not vain, remember—and generously decent man are something more than friends? What great matter to anyone else but those directly involved? What difference? I didn't start this thing. Cynthia did, as a matter of fact. Cynthia is more responsible for it than either Sandy or myself. And if Cynthia is able to cope with her imagination, what's it to Arlene? Or the Bauers? As far as the Book Group is concerned, you don't need me anymore, Evelyn. You're able to be on your own. You always were. It was just a matter of getting started, that's all. You'll be back in school in the autumn. So don't worry about a thing, and most of all, thank you for talking...straight to me. Laugh, Ev? You're supposed to laugh. You're supposed to feel good. You broke through....Aha, the first contingent has arrived. Sandy's getting us a table."

And then he was calling them over and ordering drinks and Cynthia was suggesting that they should order sooner rather than later because, "...the air in here is enough to give me cancer all over again."

All the smoke in the restaurant had frozen into an air-conditioned mist, a still mist hovering above their heads.

"Nine, ultimately," Sandy told the waiter, and also that he wanted a Tanqueray martini, very dry. "Red Label, Aaron?" Yes. "Cynthia?" No. "Ev?"

But Ev was just then distracted by a new contingent: Harold and Gordon and Gladys and Missy and Carl. So Sandy began drink orders all over again and Harold complained that it was a "scorcheroo" out there, paying little attention to her affectionate squeezing of his arm—so, yes, dammit, she would so have a Red Label. "Me too, Sandy." To hell with her newest diet for one more night.

And then there were the drinks. She wanted to make a toast, "Health with honor, Aaron!" Only Cynthia and Missy held firm. They drank water. Aaron tipped his glass across at her. She hoped she was laughing. He wasn't. His frizzled Graybeard Loon beard was sweat-glistening, his denim shirt a relief map of wrinkles, his gray eyes glazed over with a staring reflection of his inside repression. She saw it. She knew it. The human condition, he would have said. He leaned—she was not imagining it—absolutely he was leaning against Sandy, even while Sandy went on about the letter
288

they had had from Melanie saying that she and Paolo were coming home for Thanksgiving and that Paolo had just been appointed cancer researcher at a Milan hospital, an excellent appointment, and then Sandy was draining his martini and signaling for another, still altogether buttoned up in his three-piece seersucker, the blue silk rep tie perfectly knotted, perfectly placed within the long points of his white voile shirt collar. How? On such a day. Absolutely unwilted. Not even the faintest sign of sweat. Yellow hair splashing down his forehead. Aglow. From the sun, he would say, if asked—Mr. Neat, Mr. Clean, and loved by Mr. Scruffy. That's who Aaron was. Mr. Scruff and Friz. And Gordon was Mr. Long-in-the-Tooth, with a fringe, a hula skirt of hair around a freckled bare bosom of a head. And Carl was Mr. Hunched-Over-and-Silent and Gloomy. Smile, Carl! But he never did, never would anymore—only for Missy, when she pushed his button, which she did then. She reached over to touch the arm that, below the table, was working his bad leg, kneading, rubbing it.

"Let's order," Cynthia commanded. "The air in here is abominable."

"How many chicken-in-the-basket?" Sandy would handle the ordering: the take-charge Sandy Klein style. Presence! He had it: a powerful, controlling presence. At fifty-two he looked more like a boy than some of those deadbeat kids milling around the bar on the other side of the restaurant. Amazing—and they, all of them, they all submitted to his quiet authority. It was in him to be king. And Aaron was his prince. King Sandy, king among breadwinners, she thought. King of the enriched-white-bread winners, Levittown's aristocracy: the husbands. Men of the round table. Sworn to conceal...everything. The safe way. The brotherhood of getting by, keeping mum, and loose lips sink ships. The leftover way to peace with honor: saying nothing to upset the boat or the apple cart. And, irony of ironies, even Aaron was part of it now. She felt the Nixon numbness in her blood, but it turned into just another flush.

And then Sandy was ordering their dinners, "...eight chicken-in-the-basket and one rare hamburger for our lone star..."

Yes, Aaron—she raised her glass, tipped it toward him this time—hold out for as long as you can. Dare to be different.

289

"But nine salads. Right? We all need roughage these days, don't we?"

"Not me." Gladys poked Gordon for the bread basket. "I want to eat bread and cake. I want to wallow. Today at Jones I started a new diet, until I saw Arlene almost get sucked under a wave. So I thought: What's the point? Missy, you saw Arlene get sucked under, didn't you? You missed it, Ev. Would have done you the world of good."

[3] No, he told them after the concert, no, he didn't want any coffee or dessert. Too tired. After eleven already. Long past his bedtime. Not to worry. He would walk for a few blocks, catch the subway at Columbus Circle. He'd call. He'd call Evelyn over the weekend. Cynthia had already asked him out for the weekend. He was fine. Really.

So, how come, when Aaron kissed her good night, she didn't feel...what? Comfortable about him? His mood was ...troubled. "Why don't you wait until Harold gets the car, we'll drive you down to Bank Street." She held him by the sleeve. She didn't want to let go of him.

"Sandy treats me like his son," Aaron whispered, "and now you want to be my mother. Thank you, but no thanks. Good intentions can suffocate. I need love. Not fathering. Not mothering."

He walked off—but he turned back to wave.

Only she and Sandy waved back. The others had turned away.

And then Harold arrived with the car. Cynthia called out to them to come on, she was tired, Aaron would be fine, he knew his city....

[4] Evelyn leaned lower, over the bed, closer to him, so she could hear what he was saying. Missy was right behind her, and on the other side of the bed Cynthia kept wiping tears out of her eyes.

Aaron's neck was bandaged. Patches of his beard looked as if they had been ripped out or sheared off by the knife that had stabbed his neck, his chest, his left arm. Out of his right wrist were the I.V. tubes, and what he was trying to say was that he was left-handed. "Do I have my left hand? I don't feel it. I can't turn to see."

"Yes." Evelyn cried again, turning her head away—then back, because he was saying something else, forming the words more than saying them out loud. "Am I dying?"

"No. Absolutely not."

"How long have I been here?"

"Two days." But Evelyn had only been contacted that day, that morning. A call from Roosevelt Hospital, where he had been taken after the police found him, just inside a parking lot on Sixty-second Street. He'd been dragged there, the police thought, from Broadway, left there. He was unconscious when they found him, and they'd only found the metal I.D. tag that morning, going through his dungarees for some kind of information, they'd found it. It said in case of emergency to call LLWNBG at KL 5-8842....the Book Group...at her number.

Aaron's eyelids fluttered closed then. He was going to sleep. Just sleep. She waited to make sure. She watched, still leaning over him, waiting to see the certain rise and fall of his breathing.

Missy touched her, took hold of her hand. The two of them moved back and out, to the corridor where Sandy was waiting; when he had been inside the room earlier, Aaron had not yet regained consciousness. "He woke up, Sandy, for a moment, just a moment. He's sleeping again now."

Sandy stepped around them, went to where they had stood, across from Cynthia. He leaned down lower over Aaron.

Evelyn watched. Sandy covered his face. She could see his trembling.

Cynthia went around to stand behind him, to hold him, her bad arm bent awkwardly down his back. Since her operation Cynthia had never been able to bend her arm without pain. Maimed—and now Aaron was.

Some condition, this human condition, Evelyn thought, watching, remembering then those lines Aaron always quoted: "I don't know how humanity stands it/with a painted paradise at the end of it/without a painted paradise at the end of it." She turned away. A mindless act. Pointless. Senseless. Out of nowhere. The air...She and Missy leaned close together, for comfort, both of them crying, each for her own reasons, each with reason enough to be crying.

PART FIVE

1975

Corinne
Missy
Cynthia
Evelyn

29

Corinne

[1]   Corinne handed the letter to Lionel and then sat back on the sofa next to him. She'd just watch him and wait and see. Just wait and see.

SATURDAY, JULY 19, 1975

Dear Corinne,

Gregory has been heard from, and he is fine. He's now settled in with his lover. (Gregory used that word. I use it with his permission. He's aware that you'll probably show this letter to Lionel.) They have an elegant apartment right off Russian Hill. It isn't my style. I'm just your basic simple radical lesbian—but it takes all kinds, doesn't it, Corinne? Who knows that better than you! Anyway, Greg's lover, Ralph, owns a men's haberdashery downtown, in the best location. The store is elegant too. Greg seems as happy as I've ever seen him. He likes his job with ACT. He says they may be playing Off-Broadway very soon. He loves his lover. He's very happy in their apartment. What else does he need! Even if it doesn't last, at least it happened. Which is what I keep telling myself. I'm, as they say, between things right now. It's been rough. I lost my Pat because she refused to have Maria and Angela come out here for a visit. We had a major argument over that and we split up. Now, it turns out, the girls are not coming anyway. Joe's giving them a hard time about seeing me. In any case, Pat was only using the girls as an excuse. We were bound to break up over something. It's been in the works for a while, so I'm not in a state of shock, just depressed and lonely. Having Gregory nearby really helped. Ironic, isn't it, Corinne? Ironic, too, isn't it, that as much as I wish I had enough money to hop on a plane and join the gang at Jones Beach, all I have to do is imagine myself trying to explain my life out here to Arlene or Toby or Rose, even to Missy, and immediately I perk up, count my little list of pluses, and then I feel better. I don't regret what I've done. I came out here because I wanted to be me. I came out here with Michelle because I wanted to be me with her. I was for a while. I'm not sorry I came. (I still see her when I'm down in L.A. She got her doctorate in social work. She's living with the same woman she left me for.) I'm painting and loving it, and even if nothing comes of my serious stuff, I love doing it. Anyway, I've got steady graphics work with an illustration agency. I'll find yet another apartment and another lover and I'll stay active in the women's movement until victory or death. Don't worry about my committing suicide. I won't. Neither will Gregory. Even if something were to happen between Ralph and himself, I can guarantee you he wouldn't. You seem to have a hang-up about that. (Aaron told me you did a long time ago.) Contrary to what the media would have you believe, gays are no more unstable than straights. We even behave like regular ordinary human beings just trying to live out their lives. Would you believe it? We even go through periods of depression—like I am right now. I get over them the same as most sane people do. It's all part of a lifetime, Corinne, as you well know. So, as Molly Bloom says, "No more thinking myself into the glooms."

I had a call from Melanie from the San Francisco airport. She and her man were on their way to Japan for a medical convention. She told me that on their return to Milan, Cynthia, Sandy, and Aaron were going to be visiting them there later this summer. True or false? Every time I ask you about that situation, you avoid a response. What's with you? Aaron does the same thing when he writes, but he is probably under a Sandy-induced hypnotic spell to keep mum. Remember "Mum's the word"? Well, you don't have to clam up. You are, after all, the mother of a gay son. We have shared some confidences in our time, many more than most of our friends have. Levittown was not exactly a revealing community, was it? (Is it?) We all lived pretty much by ourselves, even when we were together. And as long as I'm on the subject of Levittown, N.Y. (I specify, because now there are far too many for comfort, even outside of Paris. Doesn't it feel good to be an Original? An authentic?), how about sitting down and writing me a dishy letter? You haven't mentioned Evelyn once in your last five letters, and her letters to me could come from a perfect stranger. Out of sight, out of mind! Is she still menopausing? Are you? Are you still not drinking? Are you still liking your job? Are you still you?

Goddamn it, I miss you. How about floating me a loan?

Stake me to a round-tripper? You don't have to tell Lionel.
He'll never miss the money. He's got so much of it as it is. And
then, when I get there, we can all go over to Jones and get
caught up on everything—before everything is over with.
Things in the world at large are not exactly going very well.
American and Russian astronauts have lunch in space and
New York City goes begging for money. And they call me and
my kind perverse! So, how about the money? I'll bring home
a picture of Gregory and Ralph for you. Nu?

Love,
LORETTA

"At least you didn't try to hide it," he handed the letter
back to her. "At least you're open about it all."

"When did I ever hide anything from you? Even drinking
I did in the open. In all these years, what did I ever hide?"

"Nothing."

"So why did you say that?"

"I just said it. I didn't know what else to say. I didn't want
to think about what *it* says," but then he did—have to think
about it. He was staring at her. He could see that she meant
business. Whether he liked it or not, she meant business.
"You going to send her the money? You going to let her come
here?"

Damn him to hell! He knew that was the least part of it.

He started to stand up, thought better of that, sank back
down, sighing. He was tired. He was going over to Harold's.
To play poker. To relax. "As far as I'm concerned, Corinne..."

"'As far as I'm concerned,' what? What is it concerns you
far enough?"

"Look, Corinne, if it's a question of money, that's one thing.
You've got your own job. You teach freaks music. You can
spend your money on one. Do whatever you want with it.
That's your business. You don't have to account to me. You
want to send her some...send it. I don't give a shit what you
do. But if you're going to ask her to stay here... then I've got
something to say in the matter. Then I'll say...that when
and if she comes, I'll go. I'll go somewhere else. I'll go on a
vacation somewhere. I could take the time off from the store.
I'll go...somewhere."

"How about San Francisco? Wouldn't that be a nice idea?
Visit our son."

Then he did stand up. He checked his wristwatch. "I got
to go. It's late already. Where's your bridge game tonight?"

"We're not playing tonight."

"It's Tuesday, isn't it? You always play bridge on Tuesdays."

"Used to. Not anymore. We're starting a new ... group."

"What's this one? Advanced ball-busting?"

Say nothing. She would say nothing at all. She would stay calm. She would not reach for a cigarette. She would not finger-comb her hair, smooth it, pull it, pat it, push it back off her shoulders. She would look up at him, seriously, calmly, and say something, when she opened her mouth to speak, reasonable. "We're beginning a C.R. group. Someone from Hofstra's coming to help us start it. It's at Gladys's. Later."

He was shaking his head. He was trying to laugh, forcing it out, as if he might choke over it. The fat schmuck.

"You ladies are really something else again, and you ... you take the goodamned fucking cake. You'd do anything. Evelyn just has to name it and you're ready to do it. How come you don't take a course on how to improve your cocksucking? That you could use. That would be useful." He was leaning down over her, close down, ready to push her back down if she tried to get away from him.

And there was nothing near enough at hand she might just pick up and kill him with. Like her piano. That would be nice. Heavy. Quick. Flatten him out. "Why don't you go, Lionel? You said you'd be late. Go ahead. Go play poker." She was all right. She was under control. The old pro! Once a pro, always a pro! She coulda *tokkah*'ve been a real contender ... instead of married to this fat gray curly-headed schmuck leaning so close to her face she could smell on his breath the sautéed onions she had so carefully done for him to go with his calves' liver, just the way his mother used to make it for him, just the way he liked it cooked, the fuck!

She pushed him back. She found she could do it very easily. He was always a pushover—if push ever came to shove. Only these days it wasn't any fun. When push came to shove in the past, it also almost always had come to sex. Good sex. . . . He stepped back, straightening, waiting for her to say the next *whatever*, because he didn't really want to have a fight. Not before a poker game; there wasn't any time to try to have it come to sex. Trying! His trying! Which is why she had him just then by the short hairs—as they used to say—or by the balls. Either one, and always meaning the same thing: he just couldn't keep it hard enough, often enough, these days.

297

"Why don't you go, Lionel? Your men friends are waiting. And it's too hot to argue tonight. The windows are open. The doors are open. All our neighbors will hear it when I raise my voice. Because I will eventually. If we fight. If I hand back to you some of the shit you've been trying to hand me most of my life, and especially for the last few minutes.... So why don't you go?"

But he didn't move farther back. And what a sight. In Bermuda shorts and short white socks and moccasins and a sky-blue, "Welcome to Las Vegas!" T-shirt that barely covered his belly button. He'd gained so much weight in his gut, gained mostly since he couldn't keep it hard...on command, couldn't keep it hard. Needed to be played with. Fondled, touched in such a way that made him—him, not her—dependent.

"Maybe, Lionel. Maybe when Loretta comes here for her visit...maybe instead of going to Las Vegas...maybe you'll go instead to Reno. How does that suggestion grab you...in the balls?"

Then she was the one moving, moving through the living room and out the front door and into her own car, her very own VW, which she had bought for herself with her own money from her job. Fuck him!

[2] Wednesdays was when they played bridge, during the summer, during the day, at the beach. Corinne could have played any day of the week. The school for retarded children she taught music at was closed all summer. But Evelyn from her Federation interviewing work and Gladys from her UJA fund-raising could only take Wednesdays off—they were out in the field. Missy was the fourth. She had every day off.

 If the day promised to be an ideal beach day, they would try for the earliest start. No fussing with food. Missy was the only one of them not on a perpetual diet. A thermos of iced tea. A yogurt. A fruit. No complicated equipment. No need for any. No children anymore. And no husbands allowed on their Wednesdays at the beach. Wednesday was their day. The Ladies' Day. Always had been. The Book Group. The beach...that Wednesday it was Corinne's turn to drive, and from the moment she turned onto the Southern State Parkway until they arrived at Jones, she was talk, talk, talk. And, yes, she was aware of it—when Gladys asked if she was aware—yes, she was. "I'm aware, and I'm also aware I'm not saying anything that matters. Just be patient. That's what
298

friends are for, to be patient and understanding. The C.R. lady told us that last night. So, if you're really friends...and you are, even you, Missy...don't answer that. It was uncalled for and unnecessary. I apologize, and I'm also willing to examine where that comes from."

"What I would really like, Corinne, is for you to concentrate, please, on your driving. Get us there. Get us on the sand so we can stretch out and relax...and then you can talk for as long as you want and explore every motivation you can find in every corner of your head, and I won't take offense. I promise. You can say anything at all. Anything that comes into your head. It's too hot in this car to talk."

And when they were finally stretched out on the sand— not stretched; they each had their own little low canvas-backed chair—Corinne did then tell them a piece of what was really on her mind, just a piece of the letter from Loretta, just the piece about Loretta.

That bothered her more than anything, that she didn't just pull Loretta's letter out of her tote bag and let them all read it for themselves, the whole thing.

That she didn't, after all these years of knowing each of them in group after group after group and saying things to each of them as a group or individually that were hard to say, about her drinking, for example, or about Loretta's original and honest reason for leaving Joe, that she couldn't blurt out the truth—which all of them knew anyway—about Gregory's moving to San Francisco, or about Aaron and Sandy, or that she didn't feel free enough with any of them, not even Evelyn, to say outright: Look, ladies, I'm thinking that maybe Lionel and I have reached the pits, that maybe we're going to get a divorce or maybe separate...she couldn't do it, mind training notwithstanding, Aaron, wherever you are at this moment, that fact filled her with a genuine, honest-to-goodness profound feeling of loneliness. What courage—she finally understood the magnitude of it—it must have taken Loretta to do what she'd done.... So, instead of showing them the letter, she told them, "Loretta's going to be coming east. I had a letter yesterday...." And then she went on to recite her instant replay of the facts, her filtered version: the truth according to Corinne Feuerstein, queen of the white liars.

Yes, Maria and Angela were supposed to have gone out there...but because Loretta might be changing her job or something like that, she wasn't very clear on that point, she thought it might be easier...this way. And, yes, Michelle was living in L.A. "Did that have anything to do with it?" Gladys wanted to know, asking between dabs of her lanolin skin shield.

No, not as far as Corinne knew. It was more a question of a job, of money, of just how high things were in San Francisco, everywhere for that matter, for the working...person.

"And Gregory? What about Gregory?" From Evelyn, who also then went on to say that she had received a letter from Loretta.

"And?" Corinne wanted to put an end to her recitation. She was ashamed, embarrassed, disappointed in herself, on guard...and with her best friends.

"Later. I'll tell you afterwards. What about Greg?" Evelyn was postponing too. Evelyn was on guard too. Evelyn shielding her eyes from the sun, was staring out toward the ocean, where the waves were lapping so quietly it could have been a lake.

"Greg?...Well, yes..." Settled in. Loves his job. Loves his new apartment. Loves San Francisco. Feels he has a greater opportunity for freer expression of his talent...." At fifty-two, still lying! Corinne covered her straw hair with a big-brimmed straw hat. Hard to tell where one ended and the other began. The life bleached out of her hair, bleached out of her too. What was that line? That line that Aaron was always quoting. Not the drummer line. The other one. From Thoreau? "What was that line that Aaron...?"

"'As if'?" Evelyn was attentive. Staring far off as she was, she was still attentive. Probably thinking thoughts similar to her own.

"No. The other one. Thoreau, I think."

"'Little lives of quiet desperation'? That one?" Corinne nodded, not trusting herself to say any more out loud. "Why were you thinking about that just then? Is Greg desperate? Did Loretta tell you that? Did she tell you that about herself? Was that it? She kind of implied it in her letter to me."

"Must we?" Gladys had finished dabbing. "It's too early for Loretta, and quiet—or even noisy—desperation. Let's play bridge. I'm ready."

"In a minute. In five minutes. A half-hour." Missy was on her stomach, mumbling into her arm support. She hadn't even taken off her jumper. She had spread her towel and fallen onto it, face first. "I'm tired beyond the telling of it," but with that she rolled onto her back, "and if you ask me why, I don't think I could find one word for it that would
300

make any sense at all." She sat up. She took off her jumper, reached for the Johnson's baby oil and then her sunglasses and then her "Nassau, Bahamas" straw, a little-brimmed peek-a-boo straw that barely managed to shield her lovely little L of a nose. "It's a scorcher." Delicately, fastidiously, she began to dab and flutter her fingers, freeing them of excess oil. "The water's so calm there are probably jellyfish. There has to be something to spoil this day. I just know it."

"Nature it is." Corinne pulled at the edges of her brim, shielding herself, trying to hide from everything. "Old Mother Nature it is. You can't fuck around with her. Does what she wants. Does jellyfish on our one day of rest. Outdoes the Lord for being a pain in the ass."

Missy didn't like that. She turned her cheek away from Corinne, however. She said nothing. She passively resisted. Some reflexes, some instincts, never died completely. Like nervous tics. Missy was Catholic deep down until the bitter end. Missy wanted God. She was squinting, looking away, down the beach, for him. On Beach 6. Levittown's. Not God's. Theirs. Always was. Always would be. A beach for people. They were not alone on this Wednesday in late July. July what?

What difference did it make what day in July it was? Only the year mattered. July...1975...and just a few minutes ago it was July 1955.

And a few minutes before that it was 1935—they all went back that far, and farther back. Some comfort in that, that they all shared those years, that history, that they all could remember how things used to be—and not a hysterectomy in the bunch, only one breast cancer...so far.

On Corinne's left, Missy continued to dab, continued to flutter her fingers free of excess oil, flinging the oil out, away from her dotted-swiss, white-eyelet one-piece. Little Miss Missy.

On Corinne's right, Evenlyn, and an altogether different sight: a mound of breast-straining brown Lastex. Year after year, Evelyn bought the same suit: copies from her youth, she'd told Corinne. Only now, these days, the brown Lastex one-piece looked like it might explode, might not endure the strain. And her skin was too dry. Too tan and too dry. Drying is aging! Drying is aging! Once more Corinne should tell her that; for the billionth time she should tell her to put on some more oil, cover up with cocoa butter, because drying is aging, my darling friend, my darling overweight friend who went

301

on diet after diet and who would never, she never could, get thin....

Whereas Gladys wore...not quite a bikini. It was a two-piece on the way to becoming a bikini. A royal-blue polyester number. Gladys was dieting too, but she was still bulging and spilling out over every edge. She could care less! The new Gladys Ginsburg could care less about anything else but her own personal well-being and the new self emerging from her recently raised consciousness. It was Gladys who was leading them all to the raising. Gladys had been an early convert. She had followed Loretta to a group in New York City. Corinne remembered that. It was right after Myrna and Nathaniel were safely away in two safe colleges, one in Maine, one in New Hampshire, and Gordon was safely sure that if he continued his affair with his New York City broad it didn't, wouldn't, threaten his marriage. Gladys could care less even then—well, then, all Loretta had to do was mention that the National Organization of Women was sponsoring a consciousness-raising group and Gladys was Johnny-on-the-spot, ready, "God love her"—Missy's words then. How Corinne remembered that day on the beach when Gladys made Gordon and herself the Scrabble topic and Missy had said, "God love you, Gladys, for not acting hastily with Gordon." And Gladys had answered, without batting a false eyelash, "God? What the fuck has he got to do with Gordon's screwing around? Gordon's been doing it since right after we were married, and God didn't think to stop him right away. Did he? My only regret is that I didn't follow his example sooner. But everyone knows I'm a slow learner, slow but sure." It had been the same foursome that day too. That day how many years ago? Ten? At least ten. The same foursome. By accident, the same—and the force of circumstances and cars and kids and camps and vacations. And by now, today, the foursome was habit, with all the attendant comforts of habit—which, just then, Corinne wasn't feeling. The comfort of familiar friends wasn't comfortable just then. Not for her: Corinne, the liar!

And not for Evelyn, it seemed. Or for Missy. Only for Gladys, who was bubbling away and swathing herself in lan-olin skin shield which also seemed to quick-tan her. How come? And how come she looked blonder than usual? A touch blonder? Aha! No point in asking! She'd say it was the sun. Nothing but the sun. So be it! So, it had to be: her bubbling was that she'd found a new someone to fuck her...God love her!

Which left the troubled trio. None of us would *think* of looking for a new someone. Never. Well, maybe the red bombshell. No. Never.

Why troubled? For no reasonable reason at all. Of course not. Just a mere string of bagatelles coming loose in our heads and bouncing every which way. Corinne'd bet that if she could do an on-the-spot survey of the ladies sprawling all over Beach 6 at Jones—and at eleven A.M. it was crowded enough with umbrellas and chairs and freezer food bags to gather a scientific sampling—she'd bet she'd find that the troubled trio was actually part of the majority, a not so silently suffering majority, only silent on the beach, looking for some peace on this beach, on this their day of rest....Nobody knows the troubles we ladies have seen. Missy with the picture of her dead son inside her head, carrying him there as if she had never delivered him to life—that was how she had said it to them one day, on another summer's day, the summer after Adam's dying, when they had come to the beach for some peace and relaxation and weren't able to find them then either on Beach 6. "...as if I'd never delivered him to life," Missy had said that day, between crying and breathing deeply, trying to calm herself, steady herself. "...as if he's going to be still-born in my head forever...." And now Donald was stationed in Pensacola, teaching others about the new ways for war, not wanting to come home to Levittown, telling Missy and Carl to visit him down there, where, at least, people were honest about America; and Teresa was still camped out somewhere in Colorado, on a farm, camped out, subsisting, and Agnes was on the road to there this summer, wherever, but—and it was consolation, small, but some, for Missy, for Evelyn—she was on the road to there with Eli Selden, the two of them watching out for each other as they passed through "enemy territory," as Aggie wrote home to call it, through the holes of the Bible Belt, the two of them with their center-parted hair and Eli with his fledgling beard that Corinne had laughed at lovingly, rubbing it for good luck before they left together on their trip into the heartland to look for their Sixties brothers and sisters.

And in addition to Eli there was Morty, with his college degree in the history of history—such a sad story; no wonder he was having a hard time selling his goods and living with his woman, who was pregnant and who, under no circum-

303

stances, would consider an abortion, it was her baby too, not just Morty's, so, therefore, it was also her worry to worry about its future and hers and Morty's and the possible use Morty's degree could be in the grand scheme of things. As if there had been a time when to know history was to live free of it, was to be free of the need to repeat it. No one, it seemed, ever was. Not even James Joyce. Not Corinne Feuerstein with her degree in social science and her job with welfare. No way free. And not Evelyn either, social science, a volunteerist, who, in order to see her Danny, her firstborn, had to travel on a plane or a train or drive to the country next door, where, for some reason, the government there didn't think Danny was a traitor or a crook or a Nervous Nellie because he, having found himself alive, wanted to stay alive for as long as he could. Was that such a hard thing to understand? If Corinne Feuerstein née Grossman could understand it, why couldn't Gerald Ford? Why couldn't Bob Hope or John Wayne?

But also why couldn't Carl Geiger? Who still couldn't and wouldn't talk about it to Evelyn and Harold.... Well, that's Missy's problem, one of her other problems, as if she didn't have enough.

And so, now, well, now, will the real Corinne Feuerstein stand up and tell her assorted *oy vays* to the waiting audience gathered, for this special occasion, from the far corners of Beach 6, one of the world-famous Robert Moses bejeweled series of beaches known collectively as Jones, located on the beautiful south shore of lovely parkway-gutted, car-clogged, shopping-center-studded Long Island? Well, yes, since you ask, I will, and I'd also be delighted to stand up and be counted or sit down and play for you the "Pathétique Sonata," which I also prepared for you, should you want that instead, some Beethoven, don't you know, because unaccustomed as I am to public speaking, I do, however, sing, yes, I play piano, yes, and I was, some of you may even remember, a chanteuse, but, alas, I am now the wife of something known as a Lionel, a subspecies, the kind that has stopped evolving in the head but continues to grow in the prick—although that growth is undergoing a phase of crushing reappraisal. Or, if you would prefer, I could also read to you from *Ulysses,* or ... I could stop stalling, gang, and lay it on the line. You see, gang, it's like this, gang, in addition to being a wife, I am also a mother, a mother of one son, a solo, a choice—I wanted, the Lionel wanted, no others, neither son, nor daughter, nor ... not that

I have anything against queers, some of my best friends are queer, but what I really wanted was me, myself, I. I wanted my career, don't you know. I wanted to be a contender. I wanted to be something other than, or in addition to, being a...mother and a wife and a...well, I won't ever be a grandmother, *oy vay*. So, now, well, will the real Corinne Grossman Feuerstein please stand up and speak at length about those forces, both genetic and societal, both timeless and timely, that have combined to shape her life into the minimally acceptable, bleached-red, split-ended life she seemed to have discovered herself living, Bachelor of Arts in music-certified and Aaron Rothstein-approved, notwithstanding....Thank you. I shall. Personally, speaking just for myself, all I know is that I took the road more taken...and I'm sorry. "How about them egg rolls, Mr. Goldstone?"

Only it wasn't an egg roll Evelyn was holding out to her. It was a Dannon yogurt, a totally plain Dannon yogurt, and an accompanying white plastic spoon.

"Take it, Corinne. Take it and be glad. In Africa they're starving."

"And then, maybe, we can play bridge?" Gladys. Gladys. Gladys. "Wake Missy up. We came to the beach to play bridge, not to sleep, not to swim. What's gotten into you all?"

"I'll turn the question around." But first Corinne indulged her faded chanteuse's sense of drama; she slowly, deliberately Bette Davis-ed her cigarette, and then, of course, coughed, out-of-control coughed, spoiling her moment, gasping, sputtering, "What...new...number...has gotten...into...you all?"

"That's all you can think of, Corinne? Fucking?" A fine one to talk, Gladys.

However, having heard the word "fucking," Missy awoke from her cat nap with instructions: Missy was herself again. "Before you start the yogurt, Corinne, let's go for a dip, then we'll eat, and then we'll play bridge for the rest of the afternoon. How does that sound?"

"Peachy, jiminy, lemony, pinkiny, Mommy." Corinne surprised herself by the speed of her leaping up. "I'm taking four giant steps. One for each of us." But first she threw her cig away, pulled Evelyn to her feet, hugged her, for no particular reason other than affection and the fact that Evelyn's brown Lastex one-piece matched her own red Lastex one-piece.

The three flung their hats off. The four held hands, stepping off cautiously, speeding up, almost, but not quite, at their age, running, running, right up to the water's edge.

Gladys was the first one in.

Evelyn next.

Missy and Corinne waited for the water to tell its temperature on their toes.

"Oo-ooo-ooo. Too cold." Missy bent and lifted water to wet down her arms with, and then her neck and face. "Ooo-ooo. Marvelous." And...into it.

Corinne waved. Yes, she was coming in, in a second she'd be in. She twisted, then down, to touch her toes. Up and down and up. Puffing. About to cough. No more cigarettes. No more glooms. The moment was one of Aaron's "as if" moments. Later she'd be Lionel's wife and Gregory's mother. Later. For now...the leap...in...to join her friends...and up...with them...up through the water for air.

[3] She was out in the back, on the patio, stretched the length of the redwood chaise recliner. Dusk. A slow darkening. A slight breeze. Enough for the willow fronds to furl up...down, up...down. She had had one drink, only one, and then she must have fallen asleep, because all the ice in her glass on the slate beneath the chaise had melted. She gathered the folds of her terry robe closer. The slamming of his car door must have awakened her. That's what had done it.

Well, dinner would be simple to put together. Chef's salad. Ready to go as soon as he was. She felt languid. One-drink languid. Too much sun. More than she'd realized. "Corinne?" He didn't sound contrite from last night; but he didn't sound angry, either. In between. Or either one...depending. "Corinne?"

"Out back. On the patio." Depending...on how she would be with him. Good. She had him by the balls. By the short hairs. A little threatening never hurt anyone. She made some room for him along the edge of the chaise.

"You had a drink?"

"You want one?"

"I wouldn't mind."

"Go get it. Get me another one, as long as you're up. I'll be waiting here. I won't go away."

"What's for dinner?"

"Cold. Salad. It's all cut up. Ready whenever you are."

"Maybe I'll take a shower. It was a scorcher today. I feel sticky. I stink." He smelled under his arms. One. The
306

other. Made a face. "These shirts. They hold the smell in. Polyester. Don't get me any more of these kinds. Get cotton. I like one hundred percent cotton in the summer."

She nodded. She had been about to say: Get your own, why don't you?—but that expresssion, that little-boy fear in his eyes, and the lines, the age lines beneath them, gave her pause. He was tired. He was bent back with fatigue, searching along the edge of the chaise for some space to bend all the way back, to collapse there alongside her for a minute or two, "...a few minutes," he mumbled, sinking back, out of her sight line, just his stomach heaving into view then, his head next to her toes, the stiff bristly curl of his hair brushing her toes.

They stared up at the dusk-dark sky through the willow fronds. A little breeze. Gentle. Delightful. The fronds furled up and down, up, and the oak leaves rattled. She shivered.

"You cold, Corinne? You want to go inside?" But he didn't sit up.

"No. I wasn't shivering because I was cold."

"What, then?"

"I don't know what then."

"If *you* don't know..." But even he realized there was no need to say more. He should just shut up. That's what she wanted.

He obliged.

She saw her first star of the evening. She wished on it: an old dumb habit, vestigial Grand Concourse. She embarrassed herself. She squirmed. She smiled to herself. She wished that Lionel would stand up, pick her up, carry her inside—and fuck her, the way he had when he first loved her, when just touching her anywhere, her hand, her breast, her toes, he would have a hard-on he would just have to obey, because when the commander talked—he used to say that—when the commander talks, the troops have to obey....She couldn't remember the last time he had had that kind of hard-on; she couldn't remember the last time she had wished he would have. Must be the sun. Must be last night when she told him to go to Reno. Must be...she felt...old. Tired too. Both of them old and tired and afraid together, for a moment under the first star afraid together, through the wars together, and with a son together who was now, it appears, living quietly and lovingly with his lover just off one of the hills of San Francisco...together.

Well, at least he had someone too. It could be worse. He

could be alone. It could be worse for her too. She could be alone. And Lionel too. He could be alone too. He deserved to be. She should have thrown him out years ago.

Or she should have moved out herself, years ago, even before Loretta had. Out of Levittown. Back to the Village. Corky Cummings, Greenwich Village chanteuse. Ann Sheridan's little sister, Corky. Ha-cha-cha.

And thinking that far back, she went back a little further, not wanting to, really...pointless. Jack O'Brien. That first time. She sang in Harrington's. She got drunk. He took her home....Jack O'Brien. Dead. And her best friend, Roberta Goldstein? Where? Not dead. Alive somewhere. Married. Children. The last address for Roberta was from Fair Lawn, New Jersey. Levittown dressed up. Levittown-across-the-Hudson. Levittown West. A wealthier element, but a ghetto by any other name...and why not? Why not some peace and protection when the will won't work? When it's fifty-two in your head and eighty-five in the shade? Why not take what you've got and make the most of it? Make more out of it than it is. Lie about it and your husband and your son...and yourself. This is your life, Corinne Feuerstein née Grossman. "What about the drink you promised, Lionel?" The whole day this way: down, as they say.

"I'm going." But he did not so much as move a bristle of hair away from her feet. The mound of his stomach rose and fell, rose and fell, in time to the willow fronds, up and down, up, down. "I'm almost too tired to eat."

"We don't have to. We both could lose a few pounds. You could lose fifty. Fifty might make a dent." No response from him. "Evelyn had a letter from Loretta too." That roused him. He lifted up onto his elbows. "No. Nothing about Greg. I read it. Evelyn's sending her money. She's going to invite Loretta to stay with her, you'll be happy to hear." He was. He fell back. He took hold of her crossed feet, held them in the palm of one hand, squeezed them—but affectionately—and then turned his head to kiss them. He licked their soles, one after the other, and again.

She shivered. Dark was coming faster. "Don't, Lionel. Don't do that. I want to talk to you...first." She was not saying no. She was just putting it off, pushing it back to later on the agenda. "I want—"

"I don't want." He sat up. He stood up. She reached up, took hold of his hand before he could move away. She pulled him back down onto the edge of the chaise.

"Either we talk, Lionel, or, so help me God, I'm going to leave you. I'm serious. I want to talk about Greg. I want to talk about me and about...us."

"What about us? You want me to join Weight Watchers with you? Okay. That I'll join. It's a deal. I'll shake on it." She pushed his hand away. It fell onto his crumpled seersucker slacks, slid between his legs: a heavy hand, a heavy sound.

"You really are a shit, Lionel. An absolute, complete shit. Weight Watchers!" Then she sat up, swinging her legs so that she ended up alongside him, so that she was able to keep him seated there until she'd had her say. "An ultimatum. Not just a warning anymore. I mean it, Lionel." No screaming. She was calm. That fact gave her courage to push on, to leap in. "I am not going to spend the rest of my life letting you squeeze out of me the rest of whatever decency is left in me. I may not accomplish like some people. It doesn't show to you. But I do something too. I try. All the time, all my life I try. It's one thing. It's another. I take lessons. I go to school. I work at my job. I stay alive. I stay lively. And whatever I do, you want to make fun of me. You want to ridicule me. Why, Lionel? Why do you want to make me feel like I'm nothing? Like I'm a piece of shit you can just kick out of your way. I ask you, why? I'm asking calmly. I'm not raising my voice, but I want to know why. I'd like to hear you even *try* to explain. Right now. When we're *out* of bed. Say one thing that shows you have some understanding or appreciation of me. Something that shows me you feel something, that you're still alive from the waist up—or even down."

He covered his face. He shivered. He sighed.

She touched his arm, pulled his hands down, away from his face.

All the strongest urges she'd ever had to do, to be, his hardware-store mentality had canceled out of her. He'd filled her and fucked her and forgotten how she'd given up her career, how she'd stopped herself—herself—from drinking too much, how she'd done it all alone, without his help or encouragement. Alone. No more. No more of that alone shit. She wasn't going to live with him and not force him—somehow—to look at her, to see her.

No more.

Period. Finished. Like her periods, finished. They might be, yes, but she wasn't, goddammit.

And if Greg embarrassed him, Greg embarrassed her too.

309

She'd admit that to him, She'd be willing to—but she also wanted to understand. She would try. She would. As long as he would. As long as he would open up his mouth and say something, then they could try to make something together to look forward to, something different from the dead feeling of living in the same house with someone, sharing the same bed with someone who didn't even begin to understand—they went around in a circle, her thoughts. All day long. Around in the same circle. She felt old and wasted and unappreciated. She deserved more. She did!

She got up. She wasn't going to sit there and humiliate herself waiting for him to say something kind or decent or loving. He didn't have it in him; he had it dangling from him. That's all he ever had that was sensitive. Now, even that had gone dead.

She would go get dinner. If he followed, he followed. If he didn't, he didn't. She was going to get on with her life, one way or another, with him or without him. And she was going to have something to say about the how of it from now on, no matter what! That much she would accomplish.

He did follow her. From the patio, through the living room, into the kitchen.

It was when she reached out to open the refrigerator that he stopped her, turned her around, held her, squeezed her inside his arms with such force that all the strength she had couldn't begin to get him to let go. No pushover then. She tried to knee him, then to pinch him and punch him. None of it worked. "Please let go of me, Lionel. You're really hurting me. Lionel!"

He meant to hurt her. He wanted to hurt her. He was lifting her, dragging her, out of the kitchen, toward the bedroom. He squeezed her against him. She couldn't see his face. She went dead. Deadweight inside his arms. It didn't stop him. He could have lifted the whole house.

She should scream...but she knew she wouldn't. She wouldn't give him the satisfaction of seeing her afraid—and she was. She was frightened. She could hardly breathe. He was going to suffocate her.

And she couldn't have screamed. No voice. No sound would come from her throat. No song.

Limp. She went limp. In the darkness of their bedroom, he threw her down onto their bed, following her down, on top of her, pinning her there, beneath him, his face up against hers so that she felt its heat, its anger, its sweat burning through the sunburned-skin heat of her day, her Jones Beach heat, the ocean, her friends, that kind of warmth, lingering, circling inside her head, her thoughts, the sand, the water, the sun—and the wasted efforts of a whole lifetime of trying not to, but always, giving in.

And now, as he rubbed his face across hers, as he roughed her hair, there was no question about yes or no. This was his way of showing her he was still alive. She was pinned beneath him. Speared. He was hard. That was his game. She liked sex, and that's what he'd give her. That was his understanding of who she was. So much for the rest of her! A snap of the fingers for the rest of her that he didn't and never would understand.

So, if he wanted to fuck her right now, she'd let him. Let him do what he wanted. Let him have his way. It didn't matter.

And then, afterward, she'd get up, zip up, put dinner together...and talk. She'd tell him all the things he didn't want to hear. About himself. About Greg. About what she was going to go on to do with her own life—whether he liked it or not, whether with his approval or without it, because she didn't give a shit anymore. She had her own job. Not much. But her own. At least it was with music. She'd make her own way and he could join her or not. If all he ever wanted to do was go to the store, play poker in Levittown, or gamble in Las Vegas...well, sorry, but she had other things to do. She was sorry to have to tell him, but she was otherwise occupied. She'd made some other plans, sorry, one of which was that she just thought maybe she'd mosey on over to San Francisco and visit with their son. Remember him? Their son. Who lived with his...his...lover. Remember? Our gay son. Who moved away to get away from his father...and his mother. Yes. From both of them. But at least about herself she could do something. She could start in with analysis maybe. She could join...yet another group. She could start drinking again...and forget everything, forget she was ever alive.

He was zipping down her terry robe, and then rubbing her breasts. She felt nothing but his anger. That's where his passion was, in his fingers, poking, squeezing, pathetic reminders of a lost, young, urgent skill. Pathetic. The old system wasn't working. Frustrated. But he pushed on. She'd give him credit for that much. Tonight: determination.

He wasn't hard; he wasn't soft.

He was going to need her help. He was going to have to start thinking about doing things a different way, or doing nothing at all. "This is pathetic, Lionel. What you're doing here is pathetic."

He was pushing and pulling and pushing, and nothing at all was happening. The sweat on his forehead had turned ice cold.

"You'll have a heart attack, you keep that up."

He stopped. He lay against her. Deadweight. He shuddered. A spasm of shame—then stillness in the dark room. No breeze. Only a hum through the open windows of their bedroom. A hum from far off. A glow of light from far off, from the kitchen, where she had gone, from the patio to the refrigerator...when? A few minutes ago? A hundred years ago? Before. Just before, when he had followed her inside. She should have stopped to play the piano. She should have stopped and made him sit on the rose-red velvet sofa to listen to her play her favorite...Chopin. Yes. Better that than this pathetic scene. His panting. Like a little boy. "Do you have any idea what you're doing?"

"No."

"Do you want to find out?"

He rolled off her and back onto the bed. "I'm too dumb to understand."

"Maybe, but like I said before...before? Remember? Outside? Under the stars? Like I said before about myself, I try. All the time, I try. And I'm not sure you've been paying any attention. I'm just making a suggestion that maybe you should. Maybe you should try to find out what's going on...with me. *And* with yourself. Because a problem doesn't disappear just because you don't want to talk about it. You...we both have to face it. Maybe we've had it. The only thing we've ever had in common was sex. And look what that's come down to. Look at us." She sat up over him. His seersucker pants were twisted, the fly open. The buttons of his white polyester short-sleeved shirt were straining to the bursting point across his bloated gut.

She zipped up her robe. "If you could give me one reason why we should stay married, just one, other than the time, all this time we've lived together, alone together, twenty-three years, Lionel...we've got twenty-three years invested in each other, and Evelyn and Loretta know more about me than you do. Years ago, I didn't care. Now I do....But, you
312

see? I'm doing all the talking again and you're doing nothing. You talk now. *You* tell *me* what you think."

"I can't. I don't know...the words. You all had your Aaron. All you ladies. You went to school. You...men are full of bullshit. Men are always bullshitting each other. Women...you, you're honest. Corinne? Don't decide against me. I'm not the worst there is. I'm not playing around. That's one thing I don't do. Never did. Plenty of my so-called friends, they did. In the city. Never in Levittown. Never with friends. They still do. Not me. I never needed to. I had you here."

"What if you didn't...have me here...now? What then?"

He raised himself up. Awkwardly, fearfully—she could feel a fear in his fingers, a trembling something, a difference—he held her face. He looked into it, peering through the darkness at her, a sadness in his gaze too, and then he kissed her, roughly, a little boy's kiss, very quickly, then turned away, embarrassed, but still holding on to her chin, as if he was uncertain about what to do next or if he had done enough yet to convince that...that...

"What, Lionel?"

Nothing—because he let go then. Enough for now.

"That was sweet, Lionel. I appreciated that." It was enough—for a start. "And maybe later you'll even try to talk about...things."

"I'll try."

"Good. That'll be a,...novelty."

"Don't get bitchy, now....I was also thinking that maybe we could go to Vegas again and maybe drive over to see Greg...if you want."

"If *you* want. Not just me, Lionel."

"Don't rush me."

"Why not? Who's got time to waste. Your odds are double or nothing. So think on that. I'll get dinner in the meantime. And later, if you want, you can try again. I'll even go that far."

[1] What it was, was the full moon. Midsummer madness.
They sat out in the back staring up at it. Holding hands.
In matching redwood chaises. Side by side. Holding hands.
Hello, old lovers. Just two little people alone and in love in
Levittown. Under a July full moon...so of course the tele-
phone had to ring. Something always happening to spoil a
perfect moment. If it wasn't mosquitoes...

Arlene Zweig. Just back from Israel. Fantastic. Breath-
taking. If anyone should go, it should be Missy and Carl. And
why don't Missy and Carl just come over for coffee and she
and Max can tell them...

"No, Arlene. No, thank you. Not tonight. When your pictures are developed, we can all make a night of it." But
Arlene would not get off the phone. She had to know what
was what about whatever, and just then Missy couldn't think
of one piece of news, one item of interest that had transpired
since Arlene had left for Israel a month ago. Burt's death
Arlene had been home for, and yes, Ina was as well as could
be expected under the circumstances. "Pam and her husband
took her up to the Poconos with them, and from there she's
going to Joe and his wife up on the Cape. I wonder how come
Burt and Ina managed to end up with two such sensible
children?" Arlene immediately took umbrage at that. Her
sons were sensible. Professionals. Not like Evelyn's. Or Rita's
Mark or Edna's Bobby, "...but of course Bobby was without
a father so early, and also Audrey's David. Bobby and David
are so much alike in their ways. In that child psychology
course I took at Hofstra they said that in a family in which
a father dies early..." There was one thing Missy remembered and interrupted to say, "...about Audrey. Your men-
tioning her reminded me. She met someone. A really marvelous man. A widower. A little older than she is. They met
at a singles party for over-fifties at the Jewish Center in
Great Neck. A friend from Hadassah invited Audrey there,

314

and one thing led to another. She sees him all the time these days." So at least she had one item of interest to give to Arlene, and then she really had to get back to Carl. They were in the middle of backgammon, "...and welcome home, Arlene. Say hello to Max."

But, no, not so fast. Not when Arlene holds the phone. Who else was where? she wanted to know. Ruby and Roy she knew were in the Bahamas, but why, in the middle of the summer, they go to the Bahamas, who could understand? Not Arlene. Never.

Missy did. Of course. It was cheaper and that's when they could afford it, and Rose and George could go then too, and Toby and Jack. A good group. They all get along well...and, yes, she had had one card from Cynthia. From Italy. Aaron was well, yes.... And then, finally, the one bit of news that all along Missy had been repressing, she blurted out, about Loretta's visit. "Yes, it's the truth. She's going to stay with Evelyn and Harold.... No, Corinne would have had her, but Evelyn took it on herself...no. No problem about it as far as I can tell. As a matter of fact, we were all together at the beach today...Gladys was the fourth.... She's fine. Actually, Gladys is better than I've seen her in months. She seems better than all of us."

Which led Arlene to conjecture about things that Missy would not, just would not conjecture about, certainly not on the telephone, sex things—and then there was Carl coming into the living room, exasperated, as exasperated as she was; she tried to show him she was. She rolled her eyes down at the phone. "Arlene, I really must hang up. Carl's getting angry. Why don't you and Max come for dinner Friday. You can talk about the trip. We'll play bridge..." That stopped her. That's what Arlene had wanted all along. Dammit!

[2] "...because even if Teresa does come back here, you know it won't be for long, Carl. Maybe our house is too big for our life now? In September she'll go to Vermont and Agnes will be in Buffalo—in school. Let's get her back to school, Carl, please? And so that leaves me. Maybe I should go to school too, like the others. Maybe I should work for a degree, like Evelyn did, and eventually I could get some kind of job.... Carl? Are you listening?"

He had turned away from her toward the window, on his side, staring up at the moon framed in it.

"Are you feeling all right, Carl?"

"I'm too full. You let me eat too much of that pie. Too much whipped cream."

"Let you? You wanted it. Carl? What is it? Really, what? Is it your leg?" She tried to roll him back onto his back. He resisted, which was not like him at all. "Carl?" Whispering. not wanting to annoy him. But needing to talk, needing to talk a lot more about a lot of things. Painful things. Yes. But, after all, they were grown, mature people who had been through so much together, what could be so difficult, so personal, so private they couldn't say it out loud to each other easily? What? In their old bed?

What was bothering him?

It wasn't his leg. She knew how he was when his leg was bothering him. That was a particular kind of moaning and rubbing and moving. Tonight he was still. Very still. Not very approachable, nor responsive, not even in his familiar quiet listening way responsive. He seemed sad, as if he were thinking about giving in, giving up. Hopeless, the round of his back, curving away from her. "Carl?...Is it my talking about a job? Is that it?"

"I'd rather not start that tonight."

"But what if I would rather, Carl? What about that? Doesn't that count at all?"

"Not that, please. Don't start whining like the rest of them. Like Loretta used to sound. Just what we need around here is Loretta's visit."

"That's so unfair, Carl. That phrase, 'the rest of them.' You mean you think I'm different? I'm so different—"

"You are."

"How am I different?" Anger in her voice. Not whining, but real anger. She heard it, and all she ever wanted to be was reasonable. All she ever wanted him to be with her was reasonable. "How, Carl? Aren't you going to answer?"

"Well, for starters, you're not a lesbian. That's one big difference." On his own, he rolled toward her, finally, but he didn't look at her, not directly. Even he was ashamed of what he'd said. The moonlight so white on his face, a mask of white, hiding the real Carl Geiger, the one who never used to say things like that, not to her.

She wanted him to see how disappointed she was. She held his chin, made him turn his face toward her. Her little boy! Her little boy, ashamed and confused and hopeless. Hopelessness in his face. She saw it there. Hopeless...and weary.

316

"I don't know what to say, Missy. I don't know how to say what I'm thinking. I don't know the words."

"Try."

"What's the use? You won't agree with me." He stared up at the ceiling. On top of his T-shirt he extended his fingers, fingertips touching: his little chapel of resignation. "I just didn't think things would work out this way. That we'd reach this stage of our lives and our house would have no one in it. I never pictured it that way."

She lowered her head on top of his hands. His chapel opened. "Neither did I," she whispered. He smoothed her hair, her back, his hand sliding back and forth across the silk of her nightgown. That was exactly what she needed, that smoothing out of things, that soothing, that, tonight, just that. She listened to his heartbeat. Strong. Strong. Strong, and then, suddenly, a difference, a whooshing, fluttery sound she didn't remember ever hearing before. And again: whooshing, fluttery. Recurring regularly. "Carl? Are you feeling well? Tell the truth. Are you?"

"Yes. The truth. A little indigestion, but nothing, really."

Which meant that if she coaxed him, he would talk, now, about that. He would be relieved not to have to talk about the other thing, the Loretta thing. "Nothing, but what? What else?"

"Nothing. I'm just not feeling up to par. I went to the doctor. At work—"

"To the doctor? And you didn't tell me before now?"

"It was just the company doctor. I had that numbness in my arm. He told me no more smoking. Not even a pipe. Watch my diet. That kind of thing. You know. Usual stuff. Circulation..."

She sat up. So did he.

"And the whole evening you just let me talk on and on. Weren't you going to tell me? Without being coaxed into it? I don't understand that, Carl. Shouldn't I be told if you go to see a doctor? Shouldn't I know how you feel? Me? Of all people?"

He took hold of her hand. "Missy, let's not talk about that kind of thing now. Please. And let's not talk about you getting a job. Not tonight. I'm not up to it. I was thinking about other things. I was thinking that maybe, for my vacation, maybe we could drive down to Florida. We could visit my mother and then we could go over to see Donald. He thinks he's going to be shipped out of Pensacola, probably in late September.

To the Near East, probably. Mediterranean duty. In his last letter—"

"What letter, Carl? I don't remember anything about being shipped out of Pensacola in his last letter."

"It's in a letter he wrote to me. To the office. Sometimes he writes to me at the office."

"He does?" Again, anger in her voice—but it suddenly seemed impossible to be reasonable when people, the people closest to her, were not being honest with her, were not telling her what she believed they should be telling her. What's the point of reason in an unreasonable world? How many times had she asked that question in the reading group? A hundred? And how many times had Aaron answered, "None"? And how many times had she refused to accept such an answer? Well, here it was again, and it was her own husband who was being unreasonable. She was damn tired of turning her other cheek. "That's infuriating, Carl. Donald is my son too. I have a right...Did Adam do the same thing?"

He fell back onto his pillow. "Yes."

"And Teresa? Agnes? Do they?"

"No."

"Just your sons....And now, of course, just Donald....What did Adam say when he wrote to you? What did he say that I wasn't supposed to know about?...Carl? I can't tell you how angry...how hurt I am. It's just so unfair. First about the doctor and now this. After so much shared together? You go along with such a ploy? Hiding things from me? What else have you hidden from me? What about other women? What about that?" And she was shouting by then. She didn't care, doctor or no doctor. Heart attack or no heart attack. Dammit all to hell. Herself included. All this sacrificing. All this waiting for things, waiting for life to return to normal. Ever since the war, that war, World War II, the great war, waiting and sacrificing—for the duration, they used to call it. Damn them and their duration. Their duration is my life being used up....And then another war...and son...used up...who had things to say he wouldn't say to me. "Carl? I want to know what Adam wrote to you. What he said to you he couldn't say to me." Rage was what she felt. Rage. Gushing out of her—as tears. Sobbing.

Carl held her. She didn't resist. She couldn't. He smoothed her; he soothed her. He apologized into her ear, quietly, whispering, "I'm sorry, Missy. I'm sorry." Saying it over and over again and then explaining to her, as she cried, cried it all
318

out of herself, telling her about how Adam wrote him about being frightened, about how he tried to overcome it, about how he saw nothing worthwhile in doing what they were doing there, and how much he valued his own life even if no one else did. . . . And then Carl began crying. She felt that, his tears on her shoulder, his head fallen there; giving in, giving up. Crying and telling her how guilty he felt. Guilty. "Guilty, Missy. For telling him to go. To do it. And now you're going to hate me. You will. You'll blame me. You'll blame me as much as I blame myself. . . ." Hopelessness in the way he hooked his head over her shoulder. Hopeless and dependent—and expectant too. What would she say to this man, the only man she'd ever known in her whole life, who was breaking to pieces in her arms? What? Could she put him back together again . . . and herself too?

She sat there holding him up in the moonlight. Under control again—getting there slowly, anyway. Breathing deeply. Waiting . . . before she said anything at all. Wanting to say something . . . different. So he would know and realize that from now on she would be different. Not like Loretta, different. Nor Evelyn or Corinne, different. Nor like "the rest of them," but like Melissa Geiger, different . . . different from the way she was when they met. She was. She—everyone—had to be. Since Adam's dying she had changed. That had changed her the most. That had rearranged things in her head, like rearranging old familiar furniture in a new strange room—which is what they had been talking about on the beach, about how life had changed around them, about how it was cheating them all, which is what she had wanted to talk to him about when she exploded . . . when he had tried to stop her from talking. But this time the biggest difference was that she hadn't given in to him and his wishes, his needs of the moment. She always had. He always expected her to. And tonight she hadn't, and so the truth had come spilling out of him and out of her too.

"Carl . . . first of all . . . I don't hate you. But I am angry. Deeply angry. . . . Are you listening?"

"Yes."

"Nothing can stay the same, Carl, not even me. I'm fifty-three years old. Not eighteen. Never eighteen anymore. Most of my . . . our . . . life is over with. The Levittown part certainly is. The way we all hoped it would be when we moved out here—that's all over with. And, Carl? Because I believe that, I also want you to know that I'm not going to spend what

319

there is left of my life with you, the duration of it, polishing our furniture, day after day polishing it and that's all. I've got a mind that works as well as my arm. I'm not just the extension of a dust cloth. From now on I want...I want...Dammit, I don't know what I want." She leaned against his chest, listening. For his heartbeat. Strong. Strong. Strong—and then a flutter, a whooshing sound. And then, again. Strong. Regular in its irregularity. "Carl? What did the doctor really tell you?"

"He told me I was getting too old for my age."

"You see? That's what I'm telling you too. Not talking has made you that way. An old man. Before you ever should be or need to be." She listened, leaning on his chest, to the beat of his life. It filled her ear. It filled the room, the whole house, her clean, polished, Godless house. Hers. His. His beat hers. His life hers. Her little life—and outside their lives, outside their home, the dead dark weight of empty space, waiting for her, for him, ever after. Without Jesus. And she had made a home that no one wanted or needed or cared about. Such a lovely house. As pretty as a picture. Lush, healthy green everywhere, and shine and glint and color, her needlepoint, her macramé-ing, her rug hooking, her tatting and crocheting and knitting, her home—and the beat of his life....

She thought of that morning, that time just before she ever knew Carl, and her father sending her off to the World's Fair, 1939. "Not an everyday occurrence, young lady. A world's fair is something you remember all your life." She had. She remembered it, as if it were that proverbial yesterday. So vivid. Perfect clarity. A keen, sharp, stabbing image, light in the darkness of their bedroom, stepping off the school bus at exactly the same moment, both of them—and now her father was settled in senility into that nursing home in Rockville Centre, the beat of his life unheard. No one to cry over him.

Why was life always working itself out in ways no one could ever explain or prepare for or anticipate?

Why did she feel it was always less than one had hoped it would be? She loved Carl. She did, but...all day, at the beach, driving home in Corinne's cramped VW, in the back of that tiny little car, choked by the fumes, she had felt this mood coming on. And before dinner too, while she washed the salad greens and diced the chicken, the ham, the cheese for the salad, and set the jug of hot tea on the counter to cool, stirred the chocolate for the pie, whipped the cream, baked the crust, all that time she had felt the dark wall of her control collapsing, breaking up into little pieces: alone. She felt alone. Misunderstood. Left alone with the sense of loss. She had lost something. Her son. Her life. Her self. Why?

For what good reason?

For Hecuba? As Aaron had always said whenever he was asked a question for which there was no answer, when he was asked to explain an elusive *Why?* about some way of the world: For Hecuba!

She smiled for his chest to see. Her revels now were...no, they weren't ended. Her periods, yes. They were ended, her flushes, finished. Not her revels. Even then, just then, Carl moved in a way that said he wanted her.

And she wanted him.

What if the mood she had felt all day was not a mood but a fact? Of her life. Every day. And hidden under *doing.* What if her loneliness were real? Were true. She put her arms around him. "Carl, you must promise to talk more. You must. To the girls. To Donald. To me. You must try. Because if you don't...if you don't try...then the whole thing has been a waste. Everything will be. Including Adam's dying. Including...me. I don't want to...I don't like...I don't deserve to end up my life feeling that way."

He was nodding, yes, yes, yes. She felt it. He didn't say anything immediately, he just kept smoothing his love and pleasure over her back, in bigger and bigger circles. "You're right. Missy. You are. I apologize. I will. I'll try."

31

Cynthia

[1]   Sandy was having trouble turning the key in the lock.
Aaron was struggling up the drive with a valise, and she
could hear the telephone ringing. Four...five...six. She got
to it by the tenth ring.

Evelyn: relieved; all the ladies would be. She was sure
Cynthia had said on her last card: Home before the end of
August.

"Well, it is before, Ev. It's the last day of. Would we miss
your Labor Day party?...Worried? About me? What more
can happen to me, except dying! Although there was a bomb
scare at the Milan airport, just after we boarded the plane.
We were delayed two hours leaving, but I've got a charmed
life, Ev. You know that. Tomorrow's Labor Day and we're
home in time."

"Tomorrow's party is very important. To me it is, and
Harold, of course, and I didn't want you and Sandy to miss
it. And Aaron. Did Aaron go to his apartment or did he come
out with you? Listen to me going on. It's unlike me. Loretta's
here, by the way. Stop me. I'll bet you have to go to the
bathroom. Go ahead. I'll call back later...no I won't. I won't
bother you. Rest up. Sleep. Welcome home to all of you. We'll
see you at three tomorrow. Welcome home."

As a matter of fact, she did have to go to the bathroom,
and if she didn't go instantly, the telephone would ring again
for sure and it would be Arlene and then she'd never get to
go. Although, come to think of it, Arlene probably was at
Jones. Perfect day. Dark in the house. Musty. The water in
the commode was rusty. A month since the last flush. She
flicked dust from the seat. She sat down—and damned if the
telephone wasn't ringing again, just as she had predicted: it
was Arlene. Sandy handled her: Cynthia was in the bathroom; Cynthia was fine, just fine, but she'll probably want
to rest up, "...so she'll call you later, Arlene, or maybe to-

morrow morning. I've got to help Aaron with the bags. See you tomorrow at Evelyn's."

Sandy had gone about raising the wooden blinds, opening the windows, putting on a recording. What? Vivaldi, she thought, as she went out to the living room. Crisp. All the better to work to. Baroque music to return home to and work to... without even removing his cotton shirt-jacket. And it was hot. Dog-day hot. Nothing crisp in the air coming through the open windows. "Perhaps we need the air conditioner, Sandy. It's stifling in here. It's worse than when we came in."

He nodded. He said nothing. He closed the windows, lowered the wooden blinds, turned on the air conditioner, went to help Aaron with the last of the bags.

The valises had been too much of a strain for Aaron.

The whole trip had been too much for her. The whole trip— but she did not feel relieved to be home.

Sandy made Aaron sit and rest on one of the new Breuer chairs. He came to her to ask her if there was something she wanted, a cold drink? tea? "But what would we have in the house? Nothing. Dumb me. Perhaps I'll just go up to the store and get us something. The two of you can rest." He led her to the sofa. She let him. She was tired. She wished she was still in Italy, on the rattan sofa in the house they'd rented along Lake Como. She wouldn't mind that one bit. She wouldn't have minded never coming back to Levittown. That's what she needed: a whole new change of scenery... and Melanie could drive up from Milan whenever—but Sandy was waiting for an answer. Sandy was staring at her, waiting for a response. Patient Sandy, waiting. Calm. Cool. Collected. Even aging beautifully. No. She didn't want a thing. She might even take a nap, "...in a while, though. I want to sit here for a while and listen to the music with you. I'm having jet lag....I wish we were back in Como."

"So do I," Aaron said. Lugging the valises had turned Aaron paler than usual. Was she as pale as he?

Sandy had gone to the bedroom to turn on the air conditioner there. "For your nap, Cynthia," he called out.

"Oh, how I wish it," Aaron repeated. And then, "How was Evelyn?"

"She asked for you. Loretta's here, you know."

"I didn't. That's good. It'll be good to see her. It's been such a long time. Since before your..." He stopped, he breathed deeply, arching his hand over his forehead, thumb on one temple, index finger on the other, covering his eyes. Ever since his stabbing he had begun covering his eyes that way, shielding himself from something he saw, but saw inside himself, she thought. Curious she thought that. Shielding himself from something he sees inside. The curious Graybeard Loon! Inward-looking! But, of course, what was there to look at outside himself here in Levittown! On Wonder, on Wisp, on Weaving, or even Wisdom or Wishbone lanes? Trees all grown. Hedges grown. Azaleas and impatience and pachysandra and rhododendron. The same. All the same, only older. More mature. Like Aaron looked, in his faded clean dungarees, his clean blue denim shirt, his new Italian boots, all shiny, spruced up—a gift from Sandy—and his gray hair cut short these days, his beard trimmed close to his gaunt face. An orderly face these days, except for the thin pink scar lines. Presentable. No longer really loonlike. Mature. Sensibly sad. Retiring. Shy. Arrogantly shy—and what, apart from his relationship to Sandy, had he to be arrogant about? Curious, his quiet arrogance. His shielding himself. His looking inward. Of what was he wary? She knew she was smiling. Sandy came back, sat down next to her. He smiled too. Of what were the three of them wary? That it deserved smiles and/or laughter—reality?

"What's so funny, Cynthia? Did Aaron say something funny? Did he? Really?"

Aaron's hand fell away from his forehead. "Never fear. Aaron's here to spread the gloom. Never fear. I don't disappoint."

"Actually, what he said, Sandy, was not funny. I was smiling because he stopped saying what he wanted to say, to spare me. Aaron is considerate and compassionate and . . . careful. So are you, Sandy. You've always been. All that and more." Sandy only nodded. He wasn't listening to her. He was listening to Vivaldi. A cello concerto. Had to be Vivaldi. "He was going to say he hadn't seen Loretta since before my operation. And that's been almost seven years. It is seven years. Seven years of good luck."

"Yes," Sandy said. He turned to her. "The best luck." He held her hand.

"I'll go for a nap. I feel very tired."

He lifted her hand to his lips. He kissed it.

"How European. How . . . nice." She was smiling again. She stood up. "I'll sleep for an hour or so. You can leave the music on. It helps me sleep."

324

*   *   *

[2] Timing. Time. Seven years of it which she almost hadn't had. Still, after so long, when she tried to sleep on her right side, there was an aching, a radiating pain around the scar marks. She had always enjoyed sleeping on her right side because then if she woke during the night she could watch Sandy sleep. No more of that. No more of Sandy. Her fault. Not really his. She hated being seen. She hated seeing it herself. Even when she undressed, as she had for her nap, changing from her traveling suit to her robe, a fresh silk robe from her bureau that smelled of Patchouli. Among the many things tried, shared, introduced to Cynthia by Melanie, Patchouli remained her favorite, that fresh, pungent oil scent. When she dropped her blouse, as soon as she undid her padded brassiere, automatically she turned away. A habit. A seven-year-old habit. She embarrassed herself. She shivered, knowing the sight of herself reflected in the mirror. The shiver persisted. The air conditioner. Too high...and too noisy. She couldn't hear the music. She couldn't hear them....

Hear them what? Doing what? Saying what?

She couldn't fall asleep easily. She was overtired. She was letting her mind run away with her. To where? Of what was she wary? And whatever it was, what could she do about it?

Where was her will? Her famous iron will? Her iron-door will? Rusted over. Eroded. Bruised. Scarred...unsexed, in order to stay alive. Stay alive for what? Fifty-three years old and with a clean bill of health. Alive and healthy. For what? To stay alive without...sex. No sex with Sandy anymore...but of course, she must make herself remember, there are—as Missy had reminded her so many times during those first years—so many other things to a life. You read, Missy had said, you love music and concerts and art and going to museums. Maybe you'll even learn how to paint, Missy had suggested. Cynthia had never tried. She had never, in fact, developed a hobby that really ever caught her up. Never. Nothing. Even Corinne was beyond her in that way. Corinne could play the piano beautifully. No one else in their group could do that. And Evelyn, in addition to her causes and her compassion, was a first-class cook, as good a cook as Missy....Maybe Cynthia should try writing. Or maybe she could try real estate. Or work for a travel agency. Maybe she should combine all of those. She could write a book about buying property in northern Italy. She could...she would do nothing at all. She would stay close to Sandy. She would watch after him for as long as she was able. That was her lifelong hobby: watching after Sandy Klein. She would continue to watch after him and never ask him what he was thinking or feeling or wishing for. Never. That way she would never have to know. She could imagine. She could let her imagination run away with her to... where? To what he and Aaron were doing just then in the living room? Sandy's free-flow living room.

Or were they in Melanie's bedroom?

No. The record had just ended. Someone—Sandy; he never even let Aaron touch his hi-fi equipment—was changing it.

Mozart. A voice. An aria. *"Dove sono..."*

Of what was she wary?

Of what was she wary that she could do anything about?

She was alive. She would stay alive for as long as she could. That's what mattered.... She had encouraged Sandy's friendship with Aaron. When she had thought she would die, she had urged Sandy. Take a night off. The ladies will come in. Call Aaron. Go to a concert with him. Go to a play. Go to the opera. He needs a friend, she had said to Sandy. Aaron is alone too. He had been, then. Especially after the mugging. He wasn't anymore. He was with them more of the time than not. The three of them: each a part of each other's lives by now. And she had done it, thinking that she would die, that Melanie would be nowhere near, that Sandy would be alone too, like Aaron had been, then.

She needed to sleep. Oh, how she needed to sleep.

[3] Sandy was sitting on the edge of her bed. He was watching her. It was dark in the bedroom. He had changed his clothes. A white polo shirt. Dungarees. Adidas. Aging... handsomely.

"Hello," he whispered. "Welcome back."

"I had a good sleep. What time is it?"

"Late. Close to eight." He took hold of her hand. "I went shopping. I put some kind of a dinner together. Nothing much. Only the delicatessen was open this afternoon. I tried to make it Italian feeling. Are you hungry at all?"

"Yes. I think I am. I can't remember when I ate last."

"A long time ago. Before we left Milan. With Melanie and Paolo at the airport." Sandy stared down at his hand holding hers. "I miss Melanie already."

"I do too." She raised herself. She touched his cheek. It

326

was smooth. He had shaved. He had showered. He smelled...alive.

She could see herself reflected darkly in the bureau mirror behind him. Her full-cut gray hair in terrible disarray. Her long, worn, sunken face, gray and still. There he sat, in the mirror, in front of her, smiling at her. "Thank you, Sandy."

"For what?"

"For being here when I woke up."

"Where else would I be?

She wouldn't answer that. She didn't have to. "I think I'll shower too. Is there time before dinner? Is Aaron starved?"

"Aaron's sleeping. I'll have to wake him next. Go shower." He leaned toward her. He kissed her forehead. "You looked so satisfied while you slept. I hope you really are."

She held him to her. Her little boy. He always had been. He always would be. "I am. I have had the best of luck...and affection." She moved him back, at arm's length, staring at him, smiling. "Now, go wake Aaron."

[1] "Loretta! Enough. Please? For one second? Because the next exit is us—if this traffic ever starts moving again! Harold, why don't you just drive down Welcome first and I'll be able to see if they're home yet. I'm sure Cynthia said before the end of the month on her card... and then maybe you can drive up to North Jerusalem. Maybe a store's open there. I need some anchovy paste for the rémoulade sauce. I forgot to buy it yesterday. I'd forget my head..."

"You're changing the subject again. You're always changing the subject, Ev. Ever since I got here. Every time I try to talk about what I consider important, you change the subject. What's with you, Ev?"

"Not a thing. Not with me. It's you, Loretta. The only thing you consider important... is you. Every time you open your mouth it's I, I, I. Never an idea. Just I. After all, Harold's here. I'm here. We're stuck in this car in traffic. Don't you want to ask either one of us a question about us? About both of us?"

"Don't have to worry about my feelings." Harold slapped the steering wheel impatiently. "I'm just as happy to be left out, Loretta. I wouldn't say anything anyway. Right, Ev? I'd never admit anything. I'd never reveal anything. I'll never change. Isn't that how you classify me? Your husband who never talks anyway? Who's always tired?"

"If you two are going to have an argument right in the middle of the Southern State Parkway, well, you can stop the car—"

"You haven't noticed, have you, Loretta? We are stopped. For ten minutes already." This time Harold squeezed the steering wheel until his fingers turned white. "You could walk home faster from here. Didn't I tell you? I told you, Ev. Either we leave the beach earlier or later. Never at the time we did. It's Labor Day weekend, for Christ's sake. People are going farther out these days. To Fire Island. As far from us

328

as they can get. Personally, I never wanted us to go to the beach in the first place. But no, we had to—"

"Blame that on me, Harold. That's my fault." Loretta leaned forward, reached across Evelyn to touch Harold's arm. The Chevy Impala was big enough for three up front, and Evelyn had wanted to sit that way, so they could talk without having to raise their voices. It was too hot to waste energy—but they had anyway. Harold had. And now Loretta was calming him. Evelyn joined the effort by patting his bare leg next to hers. He, all of them, were still in their bathing suits. A drive which should have taken no more than fifteen, twenty minutes, was now stretching into forty-five minutes and they were all beginning to feel the salt sweat and itch of the ocean on their skins. Evelyn was. She couldn't wait to get home and shower, so if Harold didn't want to drive down Welcome Lane to check on Cynthia, or for the anchovy paste, she'd understand. "... because I was the one insisted, Harold," Loretta was going on, "I thought this would be a good chance to see all the ladies at once. On the beach, without having to do a special event at your house. I didn't want you to have to do that on my account."

"But we are having a special event, Loretta. We always have a special event on Labor Day weekend. That's what I meant before, everything is I, I, I. From what I read, everyone in California is that way. Narcissists, and that other thing, the thing that Aaron always talks about... what's that word? I can never remember it. I can remember things from thirty years ago perfectly, but something I did last week, or need for the rémoulade sauce, that I can't remember for five minutes."

"Age, Ev. That's all it is. Even you, my darling friend. You're getting old."

"You said it, Loretta, not me. She, Ev. Remember that... when you bring it up later." For the first time since he had gotten up that morning, Harold was smiling, he was almost about to laugh—at her expense. He could be so... so unfair... well, never mind. More importantly, what was that word of Aaron's? And what was old age? "My darling friend," Loretta said. My darling *old* friend. They were. Older. Evelyn took hold of Loretta's pudge of a hand, squeezed it, settled it back on Loretta's lap. Good old Loretta, who looked younger than any of the ladies on the beach that morning. California air....

And then the line of traffic started up again, inching

ahead. A few more yards and they could get off the parkway. Once they were off, it would just be a matter of minutes. Never any traffic on Wantagh Avenue. Never used to be, anyway—but who could tell these days. Anything was possible these days. Evelyn could even remember when the Southern State Parkway was never crowded. The good old days...good old Loretta. Good old Evelyn Selden née Howard. Good old Spring Lane and Levittown when it was young and they were too and the trees and shrubs along the Southern State were striplings and undernourished bushes and when, driving off onto Wantagh Avenue, there was still some farmland visible to the east. No more. Gone. Gone with the wind, as Cynthia was wont to say.... *"Wont,"* another Aaron word, and so what was the other one? And..."Harold? Aren't you going to go down Welcome Lane?"

"That you managed to remember?"

"Please. No sarcasm. Just love and affection today. Please? Is it a deal? You too, Loretta?"

"Okay by me."

"Because Labor Day weekend I always get nostalgic. Always. I always have. Ever since my hotel days."

"I'll admit it. I forgot about your Labor Day parties, Ev. But *you* have to remember, it's been a long time between parties for me. I left for the Coast the summer of 1967. So I missed the one that summer. And this'll be the ninth since then. Labor Day 1975! That's a lot of parties down the old drain. How many years since the first?"

"Nineteen-fifty was the first. Tomorrow's will be the last. The last of them, Loretta. The twenty-sixth."

"I don't believe it. You? You're going to break a tradition? Evelyn Selden's giving up too? Never. Before, you were telling me you're finished with people and causes, and now it's traditions? You're going to give up on *them?* You're going to take on the *I?* I don't believe it."

"Don't. Because it has nothing to do with giving up. It's something else entirely. It's about...us and—"

"Did I ask you not to?" Harold's voice was instantly raised again. "Did I or didn't I? Would you listen to me once in a while?" He was waiting to turn off Wantagh Avenue onto North Jerusalem; he was waiting for Evelyn to look him straight in the eyes. Why should she! Why did she have to!

"What is this *about us* routine? What's going on? Because I know something's bothering both of you. Ever since I stepped off the plane you've both been acting strange. You
330

start talking and it turns into an argument. The two of you never were that way, at least not in front of people. Corinne and Lionel, yes. But you two? Never. And if you're not fighting or about to fight, you're changing the subject.... Harold, you could turn already—"

"I'm going to, goddammit."

"I asked you to drive down Welcome, Harold."

"And I asked you, Ev, to leave me alone. I know where I'm going."

"Well, then, turn already." Loretta's laughter only served to annoy him more.

"Loretta, just knock it off. I mean it. I'm in no mood." And then, finally, he turned.

Evelyn stared out, past Loretta, toward General Mac-Arthur High School and to Jonas E. Salk Junior High School next to it. She'd listen to him, all right! She'd wait to listen to him, even if it took all day for him to say something. She swung her head to the left, to make sure he could see how angry she was, but then, unfortunately, the view past his profile weakened her, saddened her. That ugliness out there: the W section, the last *new* section of Levittown, grown up ugly. Not the trees, not even the plantings. They were lush with color and growth, so grown up they almost hid the houses nestled behind them. Not even the lawns. They were green. They were healthy. It was the adornments. The embellishments. The jockey statuettes. The Christ-Madonna plastic sculptures. The donkeys. And the low little white wicker fences, white plastic filigree work by Rubbermaid. Rubbermaid fences. Ugliness. How she hated doodads and dadoes and gimcrackery and gimmicks and gingerbread and excesses all over the surface of something beautiful. She hated... herself just then, for having given in to Harold's demand. It had been a demand. An order—and unreasonable. Superstitious and silly: that no one of their friends could be told about their decision before Eli heard it from their lips. And how could they even be sure Eli and Aggie Geiger would get home from Toronto in time for the party tomorrow? Because at the party she would tell her friends, no matter what Harold said! Eli wouldn't care one way or the other. And not to tell Loretta just then? Silly. And not to let Loretta go on talking about her loneliness, her lovers, her life in California? Cruel. Harold. Herself. Crueler of her. But not intentional. No. Because she thought she was protecting Harold, protecting Harold from hearing what he didn't want to hear

331

about. Wrong, too. Wrong. Wrong. Wrong. "I'm sorry, Loretta. I apologize. I *was* changing the subject before. Harold—"

"Don't start *Harold*-ing me. Harold has enough on his mind right now as it is. And also, by the way, do you at least see that the stores are closed? I'll go out later and get what you need. I have to get out of this bathing suit already." He turned left into the W section and on down Welcome Lane. Cynthia and Sandy and Aaron? Not home yet. Sandy's Volvo was still locked up inside their garage. Probably their plane arrived later than Evelyn remembered. Farther down the block, Audrey was turning her old Pontiac up to the garage door. They had left the beach later, and they were home earlier: the Widows' Auxiliary—Audrey, Sally, Edna...and now Ina. "Audrey told me at the beach she's seeing someone. She's going to bring him to the party. She asked me...I forgot to tell you, Harold. I told her yes, of course, as long as he's worthy of her. I didn't think you'd mind if he came, Harold. I'm sorry I forgot to mention it. I'm forgetting more and more. I can't remember exactly when Cynthia said their plane would arrive home today. I'm sure it was today—but please remind me, if I should forget that too, to call Cynthia's later. They have to be home later. And I also promise, Loretta"— Evelyn took hold of Loretta's hand in both of hers, squeezed it affectionately—"we'll continue our talk later. I won't change the subject...whether Harold's present or not. I promise....Later. Okay? No hard feelings, Loretta?"

"Never. Not me. I'm made out of cast iron, and anyway, I love you. As they say out in Hollywood, I've always loved you, Ev. No offense intended, Harold. Out in Hollywood I've even learned how to love myself. Others as well, but myself first of all."

"That much even I can tell, Loretta." Suddenly Harold was turning the car around, a U turn, and heading it back toward North Jerusalem. "That I hear plenty of. Yourself. First. Always first. Didn't anyone in Hollywood tell you you're just plain selfish?"

"Harold? Where are you going? What are you doing now?" Evelyn would not let go of Loretta's hand, even when Loretta tried to pull it away, especially then she wouldn't. She held it tighter. Loretta didn't deserve to be hurt that way.

"You wanted anchovy paste, didn't you? So we're going up to the Turnpike to get it now. Not later."

"I thought you wanted to get out of your bathing suit."

332

"And you said you were hungry. So it's a fair trade."

Silence. The three of them absolutely silent, while Harold drove them purposely—it had to be purposely, because he could have taken a more direct route—through the S section, down Spring Lane, past the former Zweig, Massi, Selden mansions. For spite. Spiteful. Cruel. Their old color, gone. Their milky yellow with white trim all pink now, and with a wire-mesh fence all around the house and the lawn overgrown. And the trees needed pruning, the windows needed washing, toys and bicycles everywhere needed collecting. Why was Harold doing this!

And then past the village green—which had failed. The ghost of an idea. Perverse, Harold. Going backwards, Harold. "Harold, why—?"

"Don't *Harold* me. You wanted something. You'll get it."

Hempstead Turnpike was bumper-to-bumper with slow-moving traffic, slowly moving past small gaudy shops and big gaudy shops, past fast-food, fast-deli, no-quality shops, neon nothingness everywhere the eye turned, or turned away. Evelyn hated driving up to the Turnpike. Harold knew it. The Turnpike was a miracle mile of ugliness, Levittown's promised land of profits. Soem village greens! What was the use of anything, if this is what it all came down to in the end.

Harold kept going until he found one deli that was open and had anchovy paste. "Now we can go home."

She would say nothing. There was nothing for her to say just then.

Anyway, Loretta took up the attack. Hurt earlier, now she was angry. "So now that you've showed off your muscle, Harold, maybe now you'll honor us—or at least me—with an explanation. I'm supposed to be your friend, not your enemy—which brings me back to where we were when we left the beach. I was trying to describe how I felt being...alone, separated from a whole lifetime of straight habits, how it felt to take up a whole new way of life at my age, and then first you changed the subject, and then you did too, Ev. You were both afraid to face what I was talking about. Everybody I ever knew in Levittown, except maybe Corinne, was afraid to face that kind of reality. If I can't talk to you, to both of you, why did you let me come here? What's the point of our friendship? What's our history about?"

"Of course you can talk to us, Loretta." Evelyn put her arm around Loretta's shoulder, drew her close. "Of course you can. Only, some things don't need to be talked about. Some things are just understood."

"I love you, Evelyn, but that's plain bullshit. And I think *you* know that. I don't really know what Harold knows. He never wants to say."

"Not now, Loretta," Evelyn pleaded. "Later? We'll talk later. Please?"

[2]   But *later* was a long time coming.

After showers and lunch, Evelyn had calls to make— thank God, Cynthia *was* home—and Loretta, want to or not, was going to have to meet with Joe about some money he still owed her, from years back owed her which she could use, no question about that, so would Harold please lend her the keys to the Chevy, because Joe agreed to meet her half-way, in Hempstead, for a face-off; and then Harold and she had cooking left to do for the party and she had some baking to do—her traditional baking: her mother's apple cake and pinwheels, her grandmother's butter-sugar cookies. She always made them for Labor Day; whether anyone else cared or not, she cared. She remembered. Harold, by way of con-ciliation, said that he cared, he appreciated, he remembered too.

She supposed he did—but she wouldn't say so to him. She wasn't saying anything to him. She was busy. She had things to do. She wasn't ready to talk about what had happened in the car, "...not yet. I'm still too angry with you."

"With me? Not Loretta?"

But she wouldn't answer, because that would have started it up all over again.

He went into the den, stretched out on the sofa there, and napped.

And after that, Loretta came back—unwilling to talk about anything pertaining to the past or men or both. She wanted a Scotch, before dinner, and some wine with it, and afterward, only when they were—all three—outside on chaises, out side by side by side in the darkness, Evelyn in the middle, Evelyn the mediator, only then was *later* able to begin.

Easier to ease out of petty angers in the darkness, to talk rationally and feelingly among friends, especially on so hot a night. Hot. Humid. Heavy. The weather report, earlier, on Channel 2, had predicted a fifty-fifty chance of rain for Labor Day. "Always seems to rain on Labor Day," Evelyn remembered. "Up at the hotel, I remember it always rained on Labor Day."

"Funny, I don't remember that."

"What's funny, Harold, is how you remember only what *you* want to remember, and then that's supposed to become the truth," but that wasn't exactly the best way to begin to ease out of their petty angers of this day—and of the day before, and the day before that, and from before Loretta arrived. It had started...when? Exactly when? Had something happened to begin it? Was there a moment, a still point she could isolate, examine, and then perhaps be able to say—the way Aaron sometimes did with a character in a book—Aha! There. That's it. That's when it started, this anger, this frustration she felt, he felt. There. And then end one circle of their life together, leap across space to the beginning of a new circle. Like Loretta's leap into a new life, that leap Harold called selfish, and which she felt to be courageous. "What's even funnier, Harold, is how even now you won't respond to what I just said."

"What's the point?" Sad. He sounded so sad.

"The point is...there is no point if I have to make it for you."

"Okay. Then I will." Loretta lit up. Then she too was ready to begin to say what she had started to say when they left the beach. "The point is that Evelyn wants to talk to you about what's on her mind. So do I. But you won't. You won't even try. Then you go ahead and call *me* selfish. That hurt. That really hurt. And, as if that weren't enough, I meet Joe and I get it with both barrels. Talk about selfish. Remember, I never asked him for alimony. Christ, that would have been a joke. But he owed me some money from selling furniture. Less than a thousand dollars. I wrote him for it. I wanted to use it to come east. To see the girls. Instead, I have to ask my friends for a handout. Joe doesn't even know the girls are coming here tomorrow. Fortunately, I didn't say anything about it first because today he tells me that if I bother them anymore, he's going to the judge and tell him I'm a lesbian and not fit to see them. That's worse than selfish. That's not human. The bastard...I don't mean that. Not even now. I feel sorry for him. He's alone too. But I swear, with a little bit of effort, I could kill him....What's the use? It's all bullshit anyway. A thousand bucks isn't going to make any difference, as Aaron used to say, in the grand scheme of things. When I get back to California, what's a thousand bucks more or less going to mean? You know, Harold, you might just say something? Who knows when you'll ever have the chance, face to face, again? Not that you care, I suppose, if I never come east again."

But even then, Harold remained silent, so silent, Evelyn couldn't even hear his emphysema wheeze. "Harold? Are you sleeping already?"

"I'm not sleeping. I'm trying to relax. It's the first chance I've had all day. It's too hot to talk—but I'll guarantee it won't rain tomorrow. That's what you started to talk about, wasn't it?"

"That's what *you* want to talk about. Very funny."

"And I asked you a direct question. Well, semidirect." Loretta sat up. She sipped from her wineglass. There was enough dim light coming from the living-room lamp for Evelyn to see tears in Loretta's eyes. A rare sight. Loretta set her glass down on the grass, rubbed her eyes with the heels of her hands. "Well, Harold? Nothing to say? That's the Levittown way, isn't it? Buddy-buddy with the guys. Never talk about anything that matters. Nothing controversial. Nothing honest about each other. Play golf. Play tennis. Play poker. Everything in your heads stopped after the war...except us. We didn't. And that's what you can't stand. The ladies keep trying to spring their traps. But that, of course, you don't want to talk to us about. You just want to feel superior to us, to me especially, because I had the guts to be myself. You can't stand that, can you? And what about your friend Sandy? You ever talk to him about what he feels? Or Lionel? Or Carl? To say nothing about Aaron. Why don't you talk men things to Aaron? He'd tell you some things you might not want to hear."

"Loretta!" Evelyn sat up then, faced Loretta. "Let's not do that. I don't see the point to doing that."

"That's the strangest thing about you, Evelyn. You come to the edge of the great divide and you won't jump across. You read all you read. You learn all you learn. You do all you do—all your life you have—and then you stop. I always think I know you, the way women know each other, I mean, from inside their cages, but then the next minute, I realize I don't. I know Corinne better. I understand why Corinne's...where she is. But you? No. When it gets right down to it, you're the most private person I know. I'll bet not even Harold really knows you. Does he? Do you, Harold? And don't tell me you don't want to talk about it now."

336

"I'll talk. But I'll say what *I* want to say." And then he sat up too. Evelyn moved back against her chaise so that Loretta and Harold faced each other, faced each other in the darkness of the backyard, under the willow. "And only what *I* want to say because, to tell you the truth, I don't understand half of what the hell you're talking about. But I know what *I* know...about myself, about my friends, about my wife. I know all I need to know about them to be happy enough with them and my life...as it is. I worked hard all my life to get where I am. I'm honest. I don't play around. Evelyn's never had to worry on that account, like some others—I won't mention names, but you know as well as I do. I never stopped Evelyn from doing things she wanted to do. I'm proud of her being involved with all she's done. I think the job she's got now, trying to help others who can't help themselves, is the kind of job she was made for. I think...I think I...I don't know what else to want, goddammit. I love my children. I wish it were possible for Danny to be home here, especially now, because if you'd ever stopped to ask us anything, you'd have found out that his girlfriend Deedee is about to have a baby, which may not be important to you, but it is to me...and it is to Evelyn. We're going to be grandparents. Our first grandchild—and our own son can't even come home here. And another son doesn't really want to come out here, and Eli will come and then he'll go...." Harold held his head between his hands, lowered himself, leaning toward Evelyn.

"Which is why, Loretta"—Evelyn reached out for Harold's hand—"which is why we've sold our house. We're going to move into Manhattan. And as far as I'm concerned, that's *my* leap across the great divide, cage and all. No two people do their lives exactly the same way. No two people can, because inside, where the doing starts, everyone is different. Some people can do just so much and—" But before she could say more, Harold stood up, still holding on to her hand, forcing her to stand up too.

"We've got a lot to do tomorrow. Ev and I are going to bed."

Loretta sank back in her chaise, continuing to look up at them. "I'm sorry I...butted in. But you know how it is when you're in transit. You say things you wouldn't ordinarily say, especially if you don't know when you'll have the chance to say them again, if ever." She kept looking up, first smiling, then crying, quietly crying. "Good luck...with everything."

Evelyn leaned down, kissed Loretta, hugged her. Her dar-

337

ling friend was very much alone—for the moment. "If Eli gets here and you're still up, tell him to wake us."

"Will do. Never fear. Loretta's here."

[3] She lay there in the dark, waiting, the air conditioner quietly whirring them on their way into the night—and then Harold's busy breathing, busier these days whenever he labored at anything, at sex just then, the sounds of his effort rushed against her neck, rushed and fell back, rushed, fell back. He was in a hurry. Always in a hurry. Faster and faster. Not out of fear that he would fail. He never had. Not on the battleground of their bed he never had. A battleground. It was, for most married people. A fight. A struggle. A lifetime of lunging, back and forth, back and forth, undercover. They were, under a light cotton quilt. She held on to it and to him. She squeezed him tighter and tighter against her. Her handsome Harold! Her handsome graying, aging, lunging Harold. In a hurry. Faster and faster. Afraid he'll miss the boat, the train, the plane. He had—and the parade—but, all things being unequal—they are, they were, they always will be...there, there, there, Harold, there and there, yes—unequal, people, things, chances, all that considered, "I love you, Harold," she whispered in his ear.

"Why, I wonder?" he whispered back into hers.

"Because that's how it happened to me...once upon a time." She held his head still on her breast, stroking his hair, settling it, settling him, because now he would kiss her—he did—and then he would roll away, back to his side of the bed—he did—turn on his side and move into sleep in a matter of minutes. "And to me too," he whispered, and then his busy breathing resumed its familiar quietly busy rhythm beside her.

Comforting. It. Him. The familiar boundaries, patterns, pieces, of their lives together. No two people do it the same way.

She lay there in the dark, thinking, the air conditioner whirring her on her way further into the night.

[4] From deep inside an old dream, she sprang up: Eli. In the kitchen. Home. His step. Heavy steps. The gallumpher!

Three-thirty, glowing on the dial of the radio alarm clock on Harold's night table. She would go out to greet him. She had fifty questions ready to rat-tat-tat at him.

338

Which he would hate. "Don't district-attorney me, Ma," he'd say right off. So she would stay put and listen.

Backpack, off. A thudding. A jangled clang of metal hooks, louder than the whir of the air conditioner. Then his bedroll, unhooked. Method. Meticulous—but only with those things he used and needed.

The refrigerator. She had at least remembered to buy grapefruit juice. He loved grapefruit juice. And if there was any news about Danny and Deedee, he would wait until morning.

Up the stairs. Gallumph. Gallumph. Gallumph.

He would see Loretta's things. He would understand. She was in Morty's bedroom.

Stepping more carefully then because he had seen her things in the bathroom. Flushing.

And then he was in his own bedroom, where he hadn't been for over a month, and from where, in a few days, he would go away, back to school, forever, because when he came home again, there would be no familiar bedroom to come home to. His boots: the first one loud, the other soundless, remembering them down below. Hello, sweet, thoughtful, good, beautiful Eli. Oh, if ever she said anything like that out loud to him, or to any of her sons, hell to pay....

When she fell back against her pillow, she realized that Harold had awakened too. He touched her hand, patted it. "Okay now? Now you'll be able to sleep?"

"Yes." But she couldn't. Not yet. She couldn't find her way back inside her old dream. She couldn't remember Aaron's word. She couldn't remember anchovy paste. A harum-scarum. Yes—and her mind now in the middle of the tumble cycle. Eli home. Morty in Boston. Danny about to become a father. Harold busy breathing again beside her. In sleep. Wheezing. Phlegmy. Emphysema, the doctor had said, giving him exercises to do, telling him to go on with whatever he was doing in his life, but to do it slower, to breathe slower, to play tennis, if he could, bicycle, if he could, do anything, if he could—but to remember, after all, that he was a man of fifty-seven who had holes in his lungs, and always would, until the day he died, which didn't have to be for a long time, if he was careful, if he was sensible, if he relaxed more, took it easy, didn't rush so, stopped pushing himself so much...how? How to do that if, your whole life, you've been pushed into place and been forced, by circumstances they call it, to stay put? How, if you know you've been made a victim, can you

339

do anything else but fight, every day, fight, inching your way ahead, inching, every day, inch by inch by inch, out of one war and into the other daily war: the way of our world. Yes. That's life. That's living. And now—watch out—here comes dying, ready or not....

So, therefore and howsoever and whence...she keeps running up ahead to see if she can see what's coming up for them, up ahead, before there is dying up there in their future, dying, theirs, one after the other, one before the other, no matter what. Her school, her job, no matter what—dying. Whether they sell their house or not. Whether they cut themselves free from their used-up past, from Levittown, the suburb that never really was. A manmade dot on the map. No history. For aging veterans of an all-but-forgotten war. For Jews. For Catholics. She never did get to know many Protestants. They always lived in the real suburbs, had the real money and the real power...hypocrites. For Evelyn and Harold Selden, Levittown and...dying. So, therefore, why bother? Why bother at all? Because...if they sell their house...if they cut themselves free of a used-up past, they make...they have the chance to make...more of the future.

But Harold fights her. Every time she tries to do what she thinks might change their future for the better, he fights her, fights the idea of change, fights the future, fights, fights, fights, because...because he wants to do some part of it over again, because he feels, coming closer and closer and closer to the end of it, coming closer and closer to...dying...that he's been cheated out of some...thing...some prize...he deserved. He did. He does.

Cheated. A victim. Both of them were—but they were together, for better or worse.

And whenever she thought those thoughts, she thought of her mother's words, her mother saying to Harold, holding Danny on her lap, *her* first grandchild, saying to Harold, "After you've seen so much dying...if you don't give yourself the chance to choose one thing over another, what's the use? It's a sin if you don't take the chance now. It won't come again...this time." As if it were five minutes ago, her mother saying that, those words returning, haunting her, haunting Harold, the dead you loved and lost always haunting you, always there in your head.

Middle-aged memory: a monster with a thousand fingers pulling you back to a past that's gone, done with, dead as a doornail, that chance for Harold.

So . . . go to sleep.

Find your way back inside that old dream about . . . about . . . once upon a time: those years at her grandmother's hotel.

And on Labor Day they would sit on the dining-room porch, her grandmother, her mother, her aunts, herself, and they would wave good-bye to the guests. Year after year after year.

But then there was that one Labor Day when she stood next to Harold and watched her grandmother and mother and aunts waving good-bye, and she imagined they were waving good-bye to her, to herself as a girl, because they all knew she was in love, they all could tell that she and her life had been touched into living by Harold and that she was a woman then, from then on, because Harold touched her arm then, to start her moving off the dining-room porch, away from the others, to the front lawn of the hotel, where they could be alone to talk about what would happen now that the summer was over and they probably couldn't get to see each other until the following summer. What would they do? What could they do, except wait? And as they talked, she kept feeling the spot on her arm where his fingers had touched her, as if it were the point in the center of a whole new circle for her life to spin around. Nineteen-thirty-seven, that Labor Day. Fifteen years old. She turned on her side to watch the rise and fall of his busy breathing. . . . Fifteen years old.

Fifty-three years old, and in between, their life—so far.

And inside her, the memory of that moment, that old dream. Loving him, and sex with him, and the warm way he held her then, the first time, and afterward, the way he had of finding the girl alive in the woman of her, even once in a while now, when, suddenly, for no reason either of them could understand, the young part of each of them surfaced. Once in a while now . . . once in a very long while. But, no matter, because always in their touching of each other was the possibility that they might just touch into life once more the young part of how they had loved each other years before. . . . No one else could ever know that about their beginning, about him, about her, and what they shared in silence.

Not Loretta. Not any of their friends. Not even their children.

At the beginning, alone together, and in the future, together, for as long as they could be . . . and taking a chance, making a change, leaving Levittown, inching ahead, inch by

341

inch by inch, the end of one circle—and then the leap across space to the beginning of a new circle, together. And why?

Because. Because that's life. That's living: changing—as women well know. Month after month, waiting for it to happen. Year after year after year. And then there is the irrevocable change: the pause that doesn't refresh, that seems for a while—it did in her case, anyway—to end everything.

And men? They turn away. They refuse to see the changes all around them. Death thoughts, men's. Not green, growing thoughts about life.

Such a grandiose idea for a lady of Levittown to entertain in the middle of the night before Labor Day 1975. Well, be that as it may, her life might end up being a little life, but her thoughts, at least, should grow grander and grander. That's part of life too. That's living too: growing, proceeding. That's what matters. Whatever prepares you to proceed is all that matters, is the only matter that mattered to her, that, and the memories of who prepared you.

Solipsistic...yes. Aaron's other word. Yes. So now she could sleep.

She turned on her right side. She always fell asleep on her right side. She always looked out through the high bedroom window at the rectangle of sky she could see through it. A few stars out there now. The jet stream was streaming. The Canadian high was dropping lower.

Solipsistic...not her. Never.

The air conditioner was whirring on in its own sweet way.

[5] She stopped her mixing, looked up and out of the kitchen window. Sunlight, falling out on everything, for the first time that morning. Sunlight. Through the tall oak. Through the thick-leafed maples. On the rust, white, and orange mums and last-of-the-summer roses in front of the house directly across the street. The sun coming out had stopped her. It wouldn't rain on the party. "Sun, Harold."

"Didn't I tell you?" He never missed a beat of his chopping: eggs and onions.

She was finishing the rémoulade sauce, finally. Harold had already deveined the shrimp. Hundreds of them, it seemed to her. And, yes, just before the sun had distracted her, Loretta had. Loretta was waiting for a response.

"I'm still waiting, Ev, sun or no sun, to hear why people shouldn't be honest with each other. At least about themselves, they can be honest."

342

"Why, Loretta? Why must everyone *know?*"

"Because sex is behavior. You carry it out of bed with you—if you're honest you do, anyway. If you hide it, you're not you."

"Loretta"—Harold did stop chopping then—"maybe it's time for you to go pick the girls up at the station. Even if it's early, go. Go for a drive. Here's the keys to the Chevy."

"Just what I said yesterday. You're afraid I'll talk this way in front of Eli, aren't you? You hear him moving around upstairs, so you want me out. And you don't want me to say anything to Aaron. You don't want me to rock the boat in front of Sandy and Cynthia and all our so-called friends. Sometimes, Harold, darling, you're so transparent, but sometimes, even I know when to behave. I'm your guest. I know my place." She held him from behind, hugging his shoulders. "Never fear."

"Does everyone in California talk this much?" Evelyn tasted the sauce. Something missing. Something...capers. She had forgotten to put in capers. "You used to listen more."

"That's one of the healthiest ways I've changed. I express myself. Openly. Directly. Today I'm nervous. I admit it. I haven't seen the girls in a year and a half. That was the last time I ever had enough money to bring them out there...but, anyway, I'll take the keys. I'll get the hell out of here, only, before I go, between the three of us—even if you don't like my saying it, Harold—in this fucking world, and in Cynthia's position, if my husband was able to find pleasure somewhere and with someone like Aaron, I'd be damned glad. Let me tell you..."

But there was Eli. Just standing there smiling. Groggy, but smiling. Under the circumstances, that pleased Evelyn, because he was even more receptive to her kisses and hugs and then Harold's, and, lastly, Loretta's, who also said she had better get the hell out, before she was thrown out. She slapped her dungarees, flattened then pulled at her tight gray curls before she rushed out.

Evelyn sat Eli down. She was ready to rat-tat-tat—but first some grapefruit juice.

They stood on either side of his chair. Evelyn smoothed his hair away from his eyes, from around his cheeks. Too long. Unmanageable. And why hide such a face! The best of Harold in it. The best of herself...well, not so much in it as around it: his hair, lustrous black. When he took care of it. When he got it to shine. Too much road grease in it now. And

343

he had her one dimple. And her old hair color. The original color. Hers was gray now, the gray covered over by Corinne's borrowed bottled red rinse.

"I'll make you eggs." Harold was after the skillet even before Eli's close-to-inaudible, "No, Dad. It's too late."

"Never." He was at the fridge for the eggs, the butter, the cream cheese, "...and a toasted bagel. Bet you haven't had one of those for a while."

"In Toronto." But Harold wasn't listening. He was cracking and poking and breathing, fast. In a hurry. So she would have to hurry her questions along.

First, about Aggie. "You took her home last night, I presume?"

Nod. Hair falling back into disarray, covering him up, covering up his dark, sleepy eyes. "Aggie and I did not—I repeat, Ma, did not—at any time, have sex. Make sure you tell Missy so there's no confusion. We're friends."

"You're nineteen. Both of you. That's what you are. You're children. You're in school. You're going back to school."

"Will you cease and desist, Ma? When I wake up, you can do that part of the game. The big thing—literally and figuratively—is Deedee. I was almost going to stay because she's ready to pop any second. But I decided I better be home for the party. Danny thought so too. They're into natural childbirth. I had a good time there, even though I feel as if I hardly know Danny." Harold set the platter down. They stood there, on either side of him, watching him, she, waiting for the best moment to tell him; Harold, uncertain, asking her with his eyes to wait a while longer, at least until after he had finished the eggs.

They sat down.

She would wait. She was so happy to have him home, even for just the few days he'd be home. And when he went back to Buffalo, when he left Levittown this time, he would be leaving for good...but Levittown had never meant very much to him. That much he had said. No web of memories for him to rip apart. No grandparents left for him to enjoy. Poor Eli. Left for his parents alone to love—and they did!

"Coffee?" Harold quickly got him some. Fast. Always in a hurry.

She reached for Eli's chin. She kissed him.

He moved his head free. "Come on, Ma. Don't get sticky now."

"I feel sticky. I feel good about letting you know I love you. Is that a crime?"

"Will you let him eat, Evelyn!"

"Eli, your father and I have some news—"

"Not now, Ev."

"As well now as any other time." No more delays. Eli looked up. "Your father and I have decided to sell the house and move into the city."

No shock. Surprise. Plenty of that. And his dimple. A smile. "How did you ever convince Dad?"

"Why do you say that? I'm all for it. It's time for us to move. I'm all for change...as long as it makes sense."

"I am too, Dad. Congratulations." He took hold of her hand and Harold's. "A great idea. You'll probably be able to walk to work, Ma."

[6] Three-oh-five. The first guests arrived: Arlene and Max. Wouldn't you know it! She was almost finished dressing, and Harold was out in the kitchen, finishing his carving: the turkey, the ham, the brisket. He had no time for the Zweigs.

But Loretta did. From under the willow tree where she was sitting, lotuslike, with Maria and Angela, she rose, without hesitation, and went to Arlene. They embraced. Evelyn watched. They actually seemed glad to see each other. Time invested. Time spent together, even misspent, means something. Yes. Why not? Evelyn turned back to her mirror.

Some lipstick. Dry lips. Summer sun. Eye shadow. Light blue. To lighten the dark circles. Thrusts and parries at her hair—without really touching it. She liked it shorter these days. These summer days. She liked it blonder than redder. Splashes, dabs of Straw Hat: Fabergé Americana for Labor Day.

A printed cotton-silk caftan waited on the bed. Red-or-ange-yellow. Festive. Cool. Gauzy. Not a giant caftan. She had had it taken in a touch here, a touch there. Why go to all the trouble to diet if no one can see the results? And who can serve food from inside an oversized caftan!

She leaned back from the mirror, squinting, pursing her lips, assessing. Another parry. Another trust. Yes, it will do. It will have to do. Diet or not, still overweight. And overaged. Overprepared for the event that awaited her outside. Well, it would be the last of its kind. She heard Eli gallumph across the floor upstairs. He was ready.

She met him at the bottom of the stairs. He wore his best

345

patched-up dungarees. Clean ones, because she had kept them home for him. And his newest creased blue denim work-shirt. His hair had been washed. It hung free from its center part. Buoyant. It bounced. She called out for Harold. He was ready. He joined them. He was smiling, his old Gary Cooper movie-star smile—at least that's what she saw. He wore his new chinos and the forest-green silk-jersey shirt she had bought him for this occasion. Between them, her arms behind their waists, she led them outside onto the patio: a Levittown sampler; the last of the Seldens, Labor Day 1975. Amen!

And, "Welcome, Arlene. Welcome, Max. You have to tell me all about Israel. Missy said you had a great time. That's going to be our next trip....Eli, why don't you go talk to Maria and Angela..."

And there came Rita and Abe and Audrey, with her new friend from Great Neck, Manny. They came from around the side of the house, past the most recently planted stand of Japanese pine—fast growers, too fast, but the new owners could do what they would with them—and she was kissing and helloing and Loretta was taking them from her for more of the same, even though she had seen them at the beach the day before. Warm. Warm. Wonderful friends. Most of them. Then Sally and Edna and Ina, all at once, and Harold and Eli were asking around for drink orders.

[7] A big party. The biggest ever. It spread all over the backyard.

People everywhere she looked. Under trees. Sitting on the grass, lolling back, heads back for the sun. Because there was sun, a whole cleared sky of it. And a fresh breeze, warm, but with September in it, the beginning of autumn in it. And in the farther corners, shade-lovers circled in the shadows there, circling in clusters that came together, broke apart, reshaped. Their friends. Some of whom they'd lose. Some would always be their friends, no matter where they moved: Selden history.

She mixed. She went from cluster to cluster, listening, taking on the words, the bits and pieces of sound and laugh-ter, and asking: Another drink? Some food? Plenty of it. Next to the bar. Help yourselves, please. And searching out the sight of particular people, sipping from her Scotch, wondering what would come next. Where would they be next year at this time?

And was it right?

Was it wrong?

To take a chance? To make such a change?

Back and forth. Back and forth. Time ticking away. Time—and never enough of it to make more of it.

The clusters circled, round and round, breaking apart, reshaping.

She saw, through an opening, Cynthia, seated in a white rattan chair set well back in the shadows of the deepest shade. Blousy printed silk covered her from head to foot. She was talking. She always talked these days, constantly, so no one would ever have the chance to ask her, to tell her, anything. Sandy was behind her. All in white. White flannels. A white silk shirt. From Italy, he had told her. Irresistible, Sandy was still. Blond hair thinning. Aaron and Loretta were next to him, talking between themselves, Evelyn thought, about their world, coming closer and closer. Aaron was denimed and dungareed, frizzled neatly these days, and oh so lean, too lean, almost frail, nodding, nodding, quieter these days, mute since his mugging, since Sandy, as if he had exchanged the cry of his honesty for affection. There are worse things, far worse. And Cynthia's head moved back, even as she spoke, to Missy and Carl and Aggie—about Melanie probably, about Italy probably, because Cynthia felt that what she finally wanted to do, she had said a minute or two after they had arrived, was to move to Italy, move to Lake Como, nearer to Melanie and Paolo. Why not? Her head fell farther back, she was taking in the sky, the sun, looking there for the hope of her life, which was to go on living, longer, longer, with one breast, with Sandy, with Aaron, living...however.

Evelyn made her way over to where Eli was. The young crowd. Maria and Angela were there, chain-smoking, both of them. They had turned pretty enough, hardened enough to get by enough, on their own, because they were going to have to be on their own, separated from Loretta, for the duration, according to Joe's law. She hugged them both. And then Martin Aronowitz and Susan Margolies, both of them off to Cornell Medical School the next day, and Mark Moskowitz, Penny Plotkin, Phil Newman, Sandra Rabinowitz— and there came Aggie. "Aggie, Aggie, Aggie, it's so good to see you." Evelyn was going to cry. She moved away.

To another cluster: acquaintances, from the cancer drives, the Multiple Sclerosis days, Muscular Dystrophy, SANE and the anti-Vietnam-ers, the joiners, the doers. She would miss them.

347

And the theater group-ers. Corinne was there, fluffing, pushing, twisting her hair up in back, Rita Hayworth style. Corinne reached over to chuck her under the chin. Lionel was up at the bar, helping Harold, bulging out of yet another of his horrible Hawaiian shirts. No end to them. Corinne was all slinked out in clinging burgundy Qiana. Corinne! They held each other.

Evelyn moved through and beyond the politicos, her Democratic Party leftovers. Not a hero in the bunch. Not here, not anywhere in the Party. An end to her politics. Useless, that effort. She stepped around the back of the garage, away from the sounds, for a moment, away from the party, for a moment alone...among the vegetables. Harold had cleared a space between the side of the garage and the hedge of the adjoining property. A small rectangle that got western sun. He had planted vegetables there. She leaned against the garage wall. She closed her eyes, facing the sun. It blinded her. She would collect herself. For a moment—among the vegetables. A patch. A clearing. A memento from the past: potato fields, cauliflower, broccoli, and brittle brown corn stalks, that October when they drove out there from Brooklyn to see the model homes up on the Turnpike, Morty and Danny, her mother and father, October 1947...as if it were five minutes ago.

And soon now Levittown would be over for them.

She opened her eyes.

Breeze-blown, she heard her name being called.

Harold was looking for her. And Eli.

Danny! It had to be about Danny.

She hurried around to the front of the house and inside, to the telephone in the kitchen. The receiver was off the hook. "Danny?"

"Ma? You're a grandmother, Ma. A girl. Seven pounds, three ounces. A healthy girl, Ma. Miriam. We're calling her Miriam. Ma? You there?"

"I'm here. I'm here—and I wish I were there, with you...and Deedee. Is she well? Is she okay?"

"Fine. Mother and baby doing fine. You'll come up soon. You'll see her soon."

And then Harold and Eli were there. Harold wanted to talk to Danny again. "Do you need any money? Do you need anything?"

She was crying. She was holding on to Eli and Harold and crying.

Then there were Loretta and Missy and Cynthia and Corinne, all of them crowding around her, crying with her, congratulating her, congratulating Harold, who had hung up, who was being hugged next by Gladys and Audrey, by Sally and Ina and Edna.

Evelyn was being urged along, out of the kitchen, through the living room, past her fireplace wall, her pictures, her past. She waved, and then they were all passing through the den, moving toward the outside, to where the whole party was waiting to wish them well: the first grandparents in the group, "Hurray!" And they would be the first couple to move out of Levittown from their original group. Fitting—she would tell them now.

But not just then. Not just yet.

Rita and Toby and Esther and Ruby and Rose were hurrying across the grass to her, and Arlene was yelling, "Congratulations, Grandma. You're a grandma." Of course, Arlene—but they embraced anyway. And the husbands were grabbing for Harold, Lionel, Carl, patting him on the back. "You old son of a bitch," Carl yelled, "you got there first." Missy moved him back to let Sandy get hold of Harold.

And then Aaron.

Aaron was drunk. Aaron just wanted to say to, "Evelyn...and Cynthia and Corinne and Missy and Loretta ...we've seen each other to the very end. Now it begins all over again, but somewhere else." Loretta had told him. "So good night, ladies, good night, sweet ladies. Good night, and hello, Evelyn. Hello, Grandma." Aaron swayed back. Sandy was there. Sandy took hold of him, led him to Cynthia's side.

Harold held on to Evelyn. Eli was next to them. A Levittown sampler: a picture to hang on a new wall of her memory. "But for now," Evelyn shouted, "let's get on with the party."

A NEW DECADE OF CREST BESTSELLERS

☐	KANE & ABEL *Jeffrey Archer*	24376	$3.75
☐	PRIVATE SECTOR *Jeff Millar*	24368	$2.95
☐	DONAHUE *Phil Donahue & Co.*	24358	$2.95
☐	DOMINO *Phyllis A. Whitney*	24350	$2.75
☐	TO CATCH A KING *Harry Patterson*	24323	$2.95
☐	AUNT ERMA'S COPE BOOK		
	Erma Bombeck	24334	$2.75
☐	THE GLOW *Brooks Stanwood*	24333	$2.75
☐	RESTORING THE AMERICAN DREAM		
	Robert J. Ringer	24314	$2.95
☐	THE LAST ENCHANTMENT		
	Mary Stewart	24207	$2.95
☐	CENTENNIAL *James A. Michener*	23494	$2.95
☐	THE COUP *John Updike*	24259	$2.95
☐	THURSDAY THE RABBI WALKED OUT		
	Harry Kemelman	24070	$2.25
☐	IN MY FATHER'S COURT		
	Isaac Bashevis Singer	24074	$2.50
☐	A WALK ACROSS AMERICA		
	Peter Jenkins	24277	$2.75
☐	WANDERINGS *Chaim Potok*	24270	$3.95
☐	DRESS GRAY *Lucian K. Truscott IV*	24158	$2.75
☐	THE STORRINGTON PAPERS		
	Dorothy Eden	24239	$2.50

Buy them at your local bookstore or use this handy coupon for ordering.

COLUMBIA BOOK SERVICE (a CBS Publications Co.)
32275 Mally Road, P.O. Box FB, Madison Heights, MI 48071

Please send me the books I have checked above. Orders for less than 5 books must include 75¢ for the first book and 25¢ for each additional book to cover postage and handling. Orders for 5 books or more postage is FREE. Send check or money order only.

Cost $_____ Name _____

Sales tax*_____ Address _____

Postage_____ City _____

Total $_____ State _____ Zip _____

* *The government requires us to collect sales tax in all states except AK, DE, MT, NH and OR.*

This offer expires 1 January 82   8158

NEW FROM FAWCETT CREST

NEW FROM POPULAR LIBRARY